PRAISE FOR THE BLADE MAGE...

"The Blade Mage delivers big-muscled magic and high-octane thrills."

— **Gary Phillips**, *Matthew Henson and the Ice Temple of Harlem*

"Phillip Drayer Duncan has done it again. First with the Assassins, Inc. series and now with The Blade Mage. His characters and the situations they get themselves into and out of have me laughing out loud—and I don't often, even on the inside. I read two comic writers, Duncan and Robert Asprin's Myth series."

— **JC Crumpton**, *Silence in the Garden*

"Witty, action-packed, and never one to shy away from the unexpected. Phillip Drayer Duncan is not to be missed."

— **J.H. Fleming**, *The Queen of Moon and Shadow*

"BLADE MAGE is an action-packed series full of humor and heart, with a protagonist who understands that true magic comes from loyalty and friendship."

- **Julie Jones,** *Blood Follows Blood*

"The reclusive Blade Mage is unexpectedly thrust into the role of executioner and ordered to kill his best friend. Written with a keen sense of wit and humor, Phillip Drayer Duncan delivers a thrilling journey in a world filled with magic and mystery."

- **Shayne Easson**, *The Rhythm of a Jaded Heart*

...AND FOR PHILLIP DRAYER DUNCAN'S OTHER NOVELS

"Not since the feud between the Hatfields and Mccoys, has anyone made a bunch of hillbillies interesting, and that's just what Phillip Duncan did with Moonshine Wizard."

- **Jason Fedora**, *The Truth of Betrayal*

"ASSASSINS INCORPORATED boasts the sort of writing that avid readers crave to come across between the covers of a book."

-**Kristofer Upjohn,** *Horror is Art*

THE APPALACHIAN ARGUMENT

By

PHILLIP DRAYER DUNCAN

Sign up for the Phillip Drayer Duncan Newsletter to receive a **FREE** digital copy of *Catalysts,* a collection of 3 stories from the Blade Mage & Moonshine Wizard series. Nearly as much content as a full novel, this collection includes:

The Generic Mage (Blade Mage)
The Last Great Blade Mage (Blade Mage)
The Hunt for the Dark Wizard (Moonshine Wizard)

Sign up for FREE at **<u>PhillipDrayerDuncan.com</u>**

Book Seven Of...

ALSO BY PHILLIP DRAYER DUNCAN

The Blade Mage:

The Blade Mage

Of Song and Shadow

The Memphis Knights

Rebel Medicine

The Southern Circle

Anything But Cozy

The Moonshine Wizard:

Moonshine Wizard

The Distilled Shorts Collection:

First Job

The Ogre & The Primates

A Sword Named Sharp

Hunting one Like Us

The Monster Beneath the Bed

The Hunt for the Dark Wizard

Assassins Incorporated:

Assassins Incorporated

Assassins Incorporated: Rehired

THE APPALACHIAN ARGUMENT

1

Everything was cool until...

"Uh, what's that?" I asked, eyes glued on the glowing rod the scuzzy dipshit had just pulled from the fire.

"What's it look like?" Scuzzy Dipshit replied, a grin plastered on his oily face.

The others were smiling as well, in a 'One of us. One of us,' sort of way.

I didn't like it. I didn't like it one bit.

"It looks like a branding iron," I said, glancing between each of them.

"You've passed the tests," Scuzzy Dipshit said, still grinning. "This is the final step. Then you'll be one of us, Fritz."

The others pulled up their sleeves, showing off their scars while I tried not to cringe at the use of my name.

Fritz.

Worst possible name. Axel's idea, of course.

"Right," I said, studying their scars. "That is...something."

"It's a rite of passage," Scuzzy Dipshit explained. "Your official welcome into our brotherhood."

"And sisterhood," the one female in the group added. I hadn't known she was a lady at the start, rail thin as she was. Too many suckles upon the ole dope pipe, I reckoned. Her face wasn't so oily, but it was covered in old scabs. She licked her cracked lips. "And afterward, we can couple."

Ewww.

No thank you, madam. Nope. There would be no coupling.

I hadn't gotten laid in a while, but I wasn't that desperate. I would never be *that* desperate. If I ever was, I'd feed myself to an abasy or a vaklif instead.

This was dumb.

The objective was to infiltrate their pissy little gang. See if they had ties to any bigger baddies. I'd seen enough to know they'd broken the Solemn Covenant, but nothing that linked them to the real monsters. The ones I really wanted to find.

So, basically...

This was a giant a waste of time.

But I had agreed to see it through. To gain their trust and see what secrets they might reveal.

Problem was...

The trust circle would only be completed once I let them stick me with a branding iron.

"Let's talk about this," I said, putting on my most thoughtful expression. "There's a lot that could go wrong with branding. What if the Cabal learns about our secret symbol? Second, it could get infected. If my arm falls off, I won't be much use to you guys. Third, that looks *really* hot."

I thought my reasoning was perfectly reasonable. My new friends didn't agree. Sourpuss expressions all around. Bunch of babies.

"You don't want to take our mark?" one of them asked. He was a bit slow, this one. Big burly fella. All meat and no brains. I liked to think of him as Man-buck.

"It's not that," I said, keeping my voice even. "Just thinking through the options."

"The brand is the only way," Scuzzy Dipshit said, jamming the rod back into the fire. Apparently, I'd stalled too long, and he wanted to make sure it was flesh-searing hot. Mighty thoughtful of him. "If you wish to join us, you must take the mark."

"Must I?"

"You must," he said, scowling.

"Well, damn."

He pulled the brand back out, ready to stamp my precious flesh.

"Look, there's no easy way to say this," I said, shrugging. "But..."

They stared at me, waiting with baited, stinky breaths.

I puffed out my chest and used my big boy voice. "You're all under arrest. Now! Move in!"

And then...

We all stared at each other.

It was rather awkward. Their greasy, scabbed-up faces mostly held confusion. I suspected mine did as well.

"Uh," I said, biting my lip. "Move in. Time to go. All the things."

And still...

Nothing.

Fuck bubbles.

"What are you talking about?" Scuzzy Dipshit asked.

I finally came to understand why he was the boss. Before that moment, I'd assumed they'd just appointed him leader because he was the one with ties to a dealer. Or because he'd beaten the others at Rock, Paper, Scissors. Turned out he was slightly less dense than the rest.

A look of anger stretched across his features. "Are you Cabal, Fritz?"

"Uh, well, that's actually a great question," I replied with a chuckle. "Sort of wondering that myself at the moment. Based on the amount of nothing happening. Just... Hold on a second."

Scuzzy Dipshit seemed about to speak, but I held up my hand, causing him to pause.

"Let's try this again," I said, glancing up at the ceiling. "NOW!"

And...

Nothing.

Had they gone out for pizza?

"Well, this is awkward," I said, offering my friendliest smile. "So, here's the thing, guys. And gal. It's been a lot of fun getting to know you these past couple of weeks, but... There's no way in hell I'm letting you touch me with that brand."

"You don't want to be one of us?" Man-buck asked.

"No," I said, shaking my head. "I'm afraid not."

"And no coupling?" the lady asked.

"No coupling," I assured her. And myself. *Icky.*

Still, they all seemed very confused. All except for Scuzzy Dipshit. He was pissed.

"Who are you?" he asked. "Who are you really, Fritz?"

"My name isn't Fritz. It's Wyatt Draven, Blade Mage of the Ozark Mountain Cabal. Tada!"

I thought dropping my title might, like, I don't know, inspire some fear. Make them surrender or cower. It did neither of those things. Adding "tada" was for a bit of flourish. I'd never heard anyone use it in a non-corny, unironic way. And I still hadn't. Apparently.

They just stared at me, dumbfounded.

Everyone except Scuzzy Dipshit.

"Cabal dog!"

He charged me with the branding iron.

If I had let him sear my flesh willingly, it would have been on the arm. Now it was aimed at my face. That was not an improvement on the situation.

Fortunately, I had a magic sword.

Dyrnwyn popped from its hiding spot on my back and into my hand. I swiped upward, slicing through the branding rod. Then I kicked Scuzzy Dipshit in the dick.

He crumpled over, holding his man parts.

The rest of the gang fired to life. They might not have understood much, but they'd figured out their boss was in trouble and I was now the bad guy.

"Anytime guys!" I shouted. "Like, now would be fantastic!"

Once more, nothing happened. Well, not nothing. Just not the something I wanted.

The chick who had wanted to "couple" with me raised a wand and started whipping it about. Black smoke rose, filling the room.

I coughed and took a step back.

Dyrnwyn vibrated in my hand, warning me of incoming danger. Which was considerate, but I would've preferred the trick where it cleared the magical smoke. I couldn't see a damned thing, thus rendering the warning completely useless.

Something slammed into me and knocked me through the wall.

Not into the wall. *Through* the wall.

We were in an old abandoned warehouse because... Well, because of course we were. Now, we were outside on the ground.

I landed on my back with Man-buck on top of me.

Looking up into his dimwitted face, I realized... He was crying.

"You betrayed us, Fritz!" he shouted in my face. "We was your friends!"

"Well, in fairness—"

His meaty hands wrapped around my throat and squeezed.

I imagined my head popping like a zit.

Dyrnwyn was still in my hand and had taken the form of a knife so I could stab him. Problem was... I didn't want to kill the big, dumb idiot. He didn't deserve that. Some of the others, maybe. But Man-buck? He was a harmless fool who'd just fallen into the wrong crowd. I wasn't so jaded as to want to end his life.

Fortunately, I didn't have to make that hard choice.

Unfortunately, I was saved by a moron.

"Hey!" a voice called from the darkness. "Get your sweaty mitts off my life partner!"

Then Man-buck got hit with a lightning bolt.

Given my lack of oxygen and being on the verge of passing out, how could I have known it was a lightning bolt?

Because it shocked the shit out of me, too.

The thing about electricity, which the Jell-O-brained caster had forgotten, is that it's conductive. Isn't science fun?

The jolts sent my feet to dancing and butt cheeks to bouncing. I shook like a booty in a bounce house.

Pretty sure I lost a few seconds.

One thought slipped through, though...

I am going to slap the shit out of Axel.

My sense of reality returned, and the big idiot was still on top of me.

He was no longer trying to choke me, which was nice, but he was sobbing woefully, tears and snot raining on me.

To hell with a slap. I am going to kill Axel.

I moved my head to the side, trying to avoid the fluid drain, only to see Scuzzy Dipshit charging toward me with the broken branding rod held high.

A blur cut across my vision.

"Dragon Kick!"

And then Axel dragon kicked Scuzzy Dipshit right in the chest, which sent him tumbling back into the warehouse.

Axel got *really* into his dragon kicks. He launched himself right off the ground, imitating Bruce Lee. I had to admit, he'd gotten pretty good at the move. But he hadn't learned how to stick the landing.

He came down on top of Man-buck, who was still on top of me. What little oxygen I had summoned into my lungs was vacated once more.

Annoyed, I reached for my pocket, where my father's wand was tucked. I slipped it free and pointed the end into Man-buck's ribs. I fired a blob of magical energy right into his chest, which shot the big brute into the air with Axel riding atop him.

I rolled clear, and the two crashed down beside me.

My troubles weren't over.

Another of my new friends raced from the darkness, charging on all fours. That wasn't completely unexpected. I knew a couple of them were were-critters.

I had guessed he was a doggo of some kind. That was the most common.

He was not a dog. Nor a cat.

He was...something else.

His face was covered in fur and his snout had elongated, and that was all the time I had to wonder at his species because he started hurling spikes at me.

My shield came up, stopping the missiles before they pierced my chest. It was good that my reflexes knew when to shield, because the rest of my brain was staring at him, dumbfounded. What the hell were those spikes?

I didn't have time to think about it. More of the rag-tag gang poured out, wands raised.

This wasn't ideal.

If I was out for blood, I liked my odds. I didn't really want to kill these idiots, though. Not if I could help it.

As a rainbow of spells pelted my defenses, I wasn't so sure I would have a choice. Where the hell were the others?

A giant fireball slammed down between my foes, smashing into the dirt like a mini-mushroom cloud. Smaller fireballs sprouted from the top and shot off in every direction, like Mario's flower power. These were heat-seeking, though, and one shot off toward each of the enemies attacking me.

My entire gaggle of foes was forced on the defensive. All except for Man-buck, who was still on the ground crying. Now he was screaming, his ass on fire like that Terrance and Phillip flick.

Finally.

The cavalry had arrived.

My team has joined the fray.

My team.

The same team who'd ignored my earlier call-to-action. I'd feared they'd abandoned me. All except Axel, of course. I knew better than that.

One of our new recruits, Jamie, appeared first, coming to stand alongside me. She raised her wand and cast some kind of goofy fireworks spell. Reminded me of Jubilee from the old X-Men cartoon. It was about as useful, too. It distracted our foes, but sure as hell didn't convince them to surrender.

Oh, right.

This was the point where I needed to remind them they should do that. The surrendering thing. Guess I was too used to fighting to the death. Usually, my enemies weren't keen on giving up.

"Hey, uh, you guys should give up," I said, super professional like. "So, uh, simmer down now!"

Oddly, that did not have the desired effect.

The were-critter, who I thought was part porcupine, leaped at Jamie.

She didn't see the attack coming, so I shoved her out of the way. She could thank me later. Just then, she was busy hitting the ground and yelping.

I force-punted porcupine man back toward his buddies. I still wasn't super used to my father's wand. Despite loads of practice, occasionally I misjudged how much power to cast with. Porcupine man flew backward, end over end.

In fairness, it had been a reasonable response, one built into my reflexes.

What I hadn't expected, nor could have known, was that the impact would cause him to pre-maturely ejaculate the rest of the spines off his back. It was like someone had sat down on the red button at the missile factory.

Oops.

Also, to my credit, most of the spines pricked his friends. Most of them.

But...

Jamie had to cover her head to avoid taking two in the face. They buried in her forearm instead.

Double oops.

Another member of my team came running around the side of the building and caught a spine in the shoulder.

Triple oops.

And Axel... Poor Axel.

He had just found his feet, but had his back to the porcupine man when the spike parade went marching. He caught three, right in the butt.

Axel screamed bloody murder and hopped around, holding his cheeks.

Quadruple oops.

So, basically... I nailed it.

Clearly, I was doing a smashing job at this whole leadership thing.

Seeing his gang pelted in porcupine spines, Scuzzy Dipshit roared and charged at me again. He'd given up the broken branding rod and had traded it for a black wand and a buck knife.

But I had a sword, so...

A big burst of white energy slammed down between us, blinding me. I also felt a sense of... Like I was flying.

A moment later, I crashed down on my ass, blinking.

"Enough!" a voice called.

Looking up, I realized everyone on the field had been knocked down. Everyone except Axel, who was still doing his Peter Rabbit impression.

Parker Grimm strolled out of the darkness, his platinum wand raised.

"That is enough," he said, voice cold. "You're all under arrest."

"Yeah," I said, clambering to my feet. "What he said!"

Parker turned and scowled at me, shaking his head. " 'Tada,' Wyatt? Really? 'Tada?' "

I shrugged.

The sauced-up sorcerers got the hint. They finally simmered down. Scuzzy Dipshit continued scowling at me, but didn't attack.

The remaining members of my team moved in and began collecting their weapons.

"Hey, Wyatt," Jamie said.

I turned and saw she was still on the ground, holding her arm where the spikes had lodged.

She gave me a sheepish smile and said, "Listen, uh... I don't think this is going to work out."

I sighed. I'd expected as much. She, along with the other three, were not full members of my team. They were with us on a trial basis. It appeared that trial was over. Which meant it was back to just Axel, Parker, and me. Yet again.

Forcing a smile, I offered her a hand up. "I understand. Let's see about getting your arm fixed."

2

"It wasn't *that* bad."

Parker glared at me. Master Serrano gave me a pitying smile. Axel stared off into space, humming the Adam West *Batman* theme. We were back at the Castle, doing our after action debrief.

"Don't glare at me, Grimm," I said, matching his ire. "If the team had shown up when I called, we could have gotten the jump on them. Probably wouldn't have been a fight at all."

Parker rolled his eyes. "You didn't give us enough warning. Nor did you follow the plan."

"They wanted to brand me!"

"Still..."

"Still, what? Are you telling me you would have let them brand you?"

"We would have gotten you healed," he said, not quite answering the question. "A healer could've cleared the scar, no problem."

"You can't be serious," I said, struggling with my patience.

"Gentlemen," Master Serrano said, putting up his hands. "Fighting among ourselves isn't getting us anywhere."

"Neither is getting half the team spiked," Parker said, rolling his eyes. " 'Tada.' "

"My butt hurts," Axel said, his first contribution to the conversation. "Like, a lot."

"There was no way I could have known that would happen," I said, crossing my arms. "And where were you anyway, Parker? What took you so long to jump in?"

"I was assessing the new recruits. Wanted to see what they could do."

"Oh," I said. "Didn't realize that was your job. Thanks for letting me know, boss."

Parker opened his mouth to speak, but Serrano held up his hands again. "Wyatt has a point, Parker. He is the leader of this team. Not you."

Parker put on his pouty face. "He's not ready to lead a team, clearly. That was our seventh mission. Seventh debacle. And we're back down to just the three of us again. No one wants to be on the Blade Mage's team. We've just about scared off every possible recruit."

To that...I couldn't really argue. It was true. Our leadership kept finding fresh recruits, but so far, none had lasted longer than a mission or two. It wasn't like a regular task force. No one, aside from Grimmy, was being forced to stay on. They reluctantly volunteered to join, then quickly volunteered to get the futz out.

"I could probably find some people," Axel said, nodding along.

"No," both Parker and I said at the same time.

Serrano sighed. "The Archmage mentioned he had some suggestions for new additions, if these last didn't work out."

"Who?" I asked.

Serrano gave me a long look. "You think he told me?"

"Right," I said, sighing. "Maybe this whole idea was a mistake."

"Now that's something we can agree on," Parker said.

"What are you whiners moping about?" Axel said. "Squirrel Nuts Squad is the best."

"Stop calling us that," I said, glaring at him. "I don't want it to catch on."

"Then come up with a better name," Axel said. "Oh, wait. You can't. Because Squirrel Nuts Squad is the best name in the galaxy. Also, the strike teams have claimed, like, every other cool animal's name."

Again, Serrano put up his hands. "Guys, listen. I hate to say it, but Wyatt, Parker, you could both learn something from Axel. He's got the right attitude. Or, at least, a positive one. You two need to do the same. And you need to figure out how to work together."

"Oh, we work together just fine," I said, casting a sideways glance at Parker. "Until Grimm randomly decides he's in charge."

"Somebody has to step up," he said.

Master Serrano dropped his face into his hands. That silenced both of us. Me, out of respect for Serrano. Parker, because Serrano was a master, and he was typically a good little choirboy.

Truth was, I felt bad. The Master Librarian had not asked to oversee my team. In fact, the only reason Archie had assigned us to him was because he knew I respected Serrano and wouldn't want to let him down.

And here I was, letting him down.

"Master Serrano is right," I said, sitting up straight. I turned my gaze on Parker. "Look, Parker, I know we rarely see eye-to-eye, but I *am* trying. And I know you don't want to be here. Going from super shamus to being a member of my team wasn't exactly..."

"A promotion?" he asked.

"Right," I said.

He shrugged. "I did get a pay bump."

"Really?" I asked.

"Guess the Archmage figured I deserved it for putting up with you."

"Or it was hazard pay," Axel offered.

"Or that," Parker agreed.

"The point is..." I said, trying to get the icky taste out of my mouth. "I *do* respect your experience. You've led teams. I haven't. But I also need you to communicate with me. I'm the one held accountable."

He snorted. "Do you even know what that word means?"

"Oh, fuck..." I caught myself, reigning in my temper. I turned back to Master Serrano. "We done? I'm late for lunch."

"Who are you having lunch with?" Axel asked, glaring at me.

"Alyita. And yes, you can tag along. Then I have a session with Master Washington. No, you can't tag along for that."

"Yes," Master Serrano said, cutting Axel off at the pass. "I think we're done for now. In fact, I think you should hold off on taking any new assignments for a few days. I think we all need some time to settle down and come at this thing fresh. Maybe take the rest of the week off?"

My initial reaction was to refuse. I didn't want it getting back to Archie that my new team was taking extra time off. But Serrano was probably right. I needed some time away from Parker, and he probably needed the same. Plus, there wouldn't be much point in taking another case until we found some new recruits and somehow convinced them to join.

I nodded reluctantly. "Yeah. I could use a few days. I need to get back to Treat, anyway."

"That settles it, then," Serrano said.

Before he could say more, Axel jumped in. "Squirrel Nuts Squad meeting adjourned!"

3

"Relax, Wyatt. Let the energy flow."

I tried to do just that. Who knew making a wizard staff required so much damned focus? Well, probably anyone who'd gone through the trouble. At least beyond the hand-holding version we got in wizard school. Not that Wren Weevel wasn't holding my hand. He very much was. Metaphorically speaking.

"Concentrate," he said, keeping his voice soft. Soothing, even.

I am concentrating, damn it!

Just, not on the right things...

"It's slipping," he warned. "Careful."

Not helping.

Concentrate, stupid brain.

"And..."

Come on...

"Gone," he said, sighing.

I opened my eyes, seeing him standing over me, holding what would someday be my very own magical stick. If I could ever hold my focus long enough. Made me wonder how Axel had managed the patience. And he'd done multiple wands.

"Sorry," I said, hanging my head.

"Rome was not built in a day, my friend," Weevel said, patting me on the shoulder. "It took at least two or three days."

I snorted.

"You seem to be struggling with your attention today," he observed.

"Focus isn't my strong suit."

"Yes, but more so than usual." He set my future staff back on the workbench and took a seat across from me. We were in the back of his shop. When I'd first visited, I'd only seen the front, which held his magnificent collection. I hadn't realized he made his exquisite wands and staves right there on site.

Weevel gave me a long look and said, "What's on your mind, Wyatt?"

"Lots," I replied, shrugging. Then, realizing his concern was genuine, I added, "It's the team thing."

"Not going well?"

"You could say that." I shrugged. "I may not be cut out to be a leader."

"Perhaps. I fear I'm not one to give advice on such things. I've worked alone ever since I finished my apprenticeship, and that was ages ago. Before you were even born, I'd guess."

"Yeah, maybe that's the problem. I was out of the game for a long time. Since I've been back in it, most the time it's just been Axel and me. We've had allies along the way for some of our...more exciting incidents. But I've never led a team. Not in any official capacity. Haven't even been on one in a long time."

"Well, perhaps it is simply a matter of finding the right teammates."

"So far, I have managed to keep two. Fire and Ice. Parker Grimm is the quintessential cardboard cutout corporate cat. He does *not* want to work for me. Like, at all. And then there's Axel. You know what he's like. Between the three of us, we haven't been able to hold on to anyone that our dear leadership has sent over."

"Hmm," Weevel said, rubbing his chin. "Well, I imagine becoming a good leader is much like honing any craft. Years of practice and an open mind."

"I'm keeping an open mind. It's the years of practice I'm lacking."

"Sure, but have you sought guidance?"

"Well, I've got Master Serrano, but..."

"But he is one man and a rather busy one, I would guess. Can't imagine being a Cabal master leaves one much in the way of free time. Still, if I put my business hat on, I see a path forward. If you would indulge me for a bit of unsolicited advice."

"Consider it solicited."

"Were I to find myself in your position, I would seek the wisdom of those already performing as I desire. And those falling short. Study them. Ask for their advice. When I sought to become a wandmaker, I took up an apprenticeship. I had a master craftsman teach me. But when I sought to become a master myself, I branched out further, studying the work of others. I shared notes with my peers and studied their work, too. And I paid attention to artisans I thought overrated. I did the same again when I sought to grow my business."

"I would think those are two very different things."

Weevel shook his head, then adjusted his glasses. "It would seem so, but most pursuits can be broken down as simply. When I sought to grow my business, it wasn't the greatest craftsmen I studied. It was those wandmakers whose businesses thrived. I stepped outside of my industry as well. Business, at its core, is similar across all fields. One is either selling a good or providing a service. You can learn from those who've done well at either. And you can learn even more from those who've done poorly."

"I hear you, but that seems terribly simplified."

"Which is the best way to solve a problem, is it not? Take yourself, for example. I bet you haven't thought about it this way, Wyatt, but you're selling a service. You're selling your leadership to the Cabal. You have concerns about your ability to deliver that service. I would pursue knowledge from others selling a similar service. Likely you'll struggle to find anyone with time to mentor you, but you can seek them and observe. The masters and the Arcane Guardians. Or even the Archmage. Some of the strike team leaders. See what they do, assess why, and whether you agree with it. That's how you learn."

I nodded. He was right.

"Remember, these things take time," he said. He must have noticed that my gaze had shifted to the unfinished hunk of wood on his work-bench. "As do great magical instruments."

I sighed again. "Sorry. I feel like I've wasted your time being an idiot."

"Not at all, my boy. It's always a delight to see you. And I am not so backed up on orders. We have the time we need to craft you the perfect staff. This bit of work requires no stress on your part. Save your worries for other things."

"Thank you," I said, meeting his gaze. "I really appreciate it."

"And I appreciate the Archmage's money," he said, winking. "And, you know, how you saved our little town, of course."

I met his grin with one of my own. "I'm ready to try again, if you'd like."

"I think we should call it a day," he said. "You need time to clear your head. Best not to rush such important work. Besides, Myrna will be delighted when you get to her place. Knowing that woman, she probably already knows you're in town."

I chuckled. "You're probably right. Glad you guys gave me a house so I can still stay at Myrna's."

He shrugged. "Sounds like you have some work to do before your place is livable anyway."

"That's the truth," I said, shaking my head. "The ride is pretty sweet, though."

"That it is," he said, a twinkle in his eye. "Did you bring the python with you? I'm sure Myrna will be happy to see her as well."

I nodded. "Weekend at Burmese is with Axel. They're both probably scaring the hell out of everyone at the candy shop."

Weevel snorted.

"Say, do you know much about familiars?" I asked. "Since we started up the team thing, I haven't had time to dig into it. Mostly, I just have a big-ass python roaming around my house at her leisure. But I don't really know what I'm supposed to do with her."

"Sorry, Wyatt. I don't think I can help you with that one."

"Fair enough," I said, rising to my feet. "Thanks, Weevel. Really. You've given me a lot to think about."

"It was my pleasure."

"Oh, and tell Poppy I said hello."

4

"But think about how awesome it would be," Axel said.

"We have been through this before," Paeter said, crossing his arms. "The answer is no."

"Come on, Paeter," Axel said, grinning. "Don't be an ass."

The onocentaur glared at him. "You will *never* ride me into battle."

Axel threw his hands up, frustrated. "But it would be so epic! At least let me ride you around the yard."

"No."

"Why not?"

"Because I'm grilling," Paeter replied, clacking his tongs.

It was a valid point. One my hungry tummy agreed with.

"Let it go, Axel," I said.

"Thank you," Paeter said, nodding at me.

"At least until the burgers are done," I added, grinning.

The onocentaur glared at me, then returned his focus to the work at hand.

Mary Beth chuckled from beside me. "I don't think Axel will ever give it up."

"He won't," I assured her. "But if Paeter relents, Axel will want to ride him all the time. So, make sure he holds his ground. You guys should have never saved us at the church."

"Oh, I don't know about that. We do enjoy our dinners together. By the way, Axel has been bugging me about helping him enchant more stones. After the last time..."

"His fart rocks," I said, rolling my eyes. "The smoke bombs came in handy, though."

"I will help him make some more, if you think it's a good idea."

"Sure," I said, shrugging. "I don't think it'll hurt anything. And they *did* get us out of some trouble."

"Fair enough," she said, studying me. "You seem to have a lot on your mind."

"I do," I admitted, casting a glance at Axel and Paeter. They weren't paying attention. *Good.* "Been thinking a lot about this whole team thing. Don't really know what I'm doing. Wren Weevel gave me some ideas on how to, well, come up with some ideas, but I'm not sure... I'm not sure I want to lead a team."

"Oh?" she raised an eyebrow.

I shrugged and again made sure Axel wasn't paying attention. "When the Archmage offered, I saw it as a chance to get involved. To improve my relationship with the Cabal. But I never aspired to be a leader. Not really. When someone gets hurt... On that last job, none of my crew were seriously injured, but a few got hurt. Axel, included. And I felt..."

"Like it was your fault. That you were to blame."

"Exactly," I said, nodding. "What if someone had gotten killed? Their life would have been on my hands."

She nodded.

"Maybe I should step down," I said, sighing. "Maybe I should just go back to the way things were."

"That wasn't working so well, though, was it?"

"No."

I stared off at the trees, my mind wandering. She was right. There wasn't a good solution.

"Do you know what I think?" she asked.

I turned my attention back to her.

"I think you have the makings of a fine leader, Wyatt. Wait..." she said, putting up her hands. "Before you argue, remember, Paeter and I weren't always hermits. I *am* royalty. I have been both a leader and a follower. Through years of both, one thing stood out to me."

"What's that?"

"Good leaders rarely want to lead."

I stared at her, unsure what to say. I mean, I'd heard people say that before, but never really thought it was true. "Most of the leaders I've known, the ones who were good at their jobs, whether I want to admit it or not, have always seemed..."

"Sure? Confident?"

"Yeah."

"That is developed over time," she said, shaking her head. "But I assure you, the best leaders carry those same fears. It's like this, Wyatt: leadership requires sacrifice. A good leader seeks to take care of their people, and worries deeply about their wellbeing. And weighs those needs against the needs of the mission. They seek to serve those who follow them, often putting their own desires aside. Those who seek fame, renown, and status are ill-prepared to make such sacrifices, though they will pretend otherwise. The best leaders are those who step up when no one else is willing. Who take charge when it's needed. Who are willing to make a decision on their own, good or bad. But most importantly, they are willing to listen and follow, just never blindly. I have seen you display these qualities."

"Thank you," I said, nodding at her. "That means a lot."

"I do not say it lightly, nor seek to hand you false praise. You have what it takes. It will take time to learn all you need. But you are not alone. My advice would be simple: stop beating yourself up and focus on making the right decisions. Keep your humility, Wyatt. It will serve you well."

"Hey, what are you guys talking about?" Axel asked, wandering toward us. "Did you ask her about making more magic stones?"

Mary Beth and I shared a glance, then I turned back to Axel. "They will help you make more magic stones, but no fart rocks."

"Aw," he said, scowling. "But I want them!"

"And," I said while I had his attention, "no more harassing Paeter about riding him."

Axel huffed. "You people were invented before fun."

"And there," Mary Beth said, winking at me, "was a small, but perfect, example of what I meant."

5

"Any idea what this is about?" I asked Parker as we strolled toward the Castle proper.

"No," he said, shaking his head.

"Think we're in trouble?" I asked, glancing over at him.

"I know I'm not," Axel said. "I've been on my best behavior."

Parker and I both stopped to glower at him.

"What?" he asked. "I have."

We kept our faces deadpan.

"Well, shit," he said, sighing. "I'm sure if it was something I did, he wouldn't have invited both of you."

"That's true," Parker said, glancing over at me.

"It must be about Squirrel Nuts Squad," Axel said, nodding happily. "Yup. Can't be about anything I've done."

We started walking again.

"Oh, shit," Axel said, stopping. He stared from me to Parker and back again. "You don't think he's going to disband us, do you?"

I was glad to see he'd finally caught up. He seemed genuinely worried about it. Which sort of made me feel bad, because though I didn't want my team disbanded in disgrace, there was a part of me that would have been relieved. Certainly the look on Parker's face told me he hoped that would be the case.

"Oh, toot," Axel said, eyes widening. "You don't really think that's it, do you?"

Parker and I shared a look, and again, I didn't miss the hope in his eyes.

"Come on," I said, starting forward. "There's only one way to find out."

"This is...eerie," Parker said, eyes roaming Archie's office.

"What is?" Axel asked, kicking his feet up on the Archmage's desk. There had been three empty chairs waiting for us when we were escorted in, right in front of Archie's desk. In the past, there'd always just been two. Guess he kept spares and had them set out to account for all his guests. How thoughtful.

I knocked Axel's feet down and glared at him.

"Being in here, waiting," Parker said, looking around. "I've never been in the Archmage's office without him present."

"Oh, don't sweat it," Axel said, kicking his feet up again. "He just does this to us to make us sweat. Right, Wyatt?"

I knocked his legs off the desk again, but didn't reply.

"He's just trying to get us off our game," Axel said, again putting his dirty shoes on Archie's desk. There were bits of dried mud that had already chipped off, creating a dusty mess. "Last time, he pulled a fast one on me. Had me admitting all sorts of stuff. Not this time. I'm ready for him."

"That remains to be seen," Archie said from behind us. He strolled forward and sat down across from us, smiling. "And, Mr. Gunner, if you wish to keep those feet, you'll remove them from my desk immediately."

"Yes, sir," Axel said, dropping them to the floor.

Archie stared at the dusty spot, then back up at Axel. It didn't help that Axel was wearing a shirt which read, "Growing old is mandatory, growing up is optional." The Archmage's face remained impassive, but a slight twitch of his eye told Axel all he needed to know.

"I'll, uh..." Axel popped up from his seat. "I'll be right back."

"Do return quickly, Mr. Gunner," Archie said. "We have much to discuss."

"Back in a flash," Axel called, halfway to the door.

Once it shut behind him, Archie turned his gaze on me. "Do you think he will return?"

"If he doesn't, you can turn him into a toad."

Archie nodded. Apparently, he liked that idea.

Then we sat in awkward silence, staring at one another. That was fun.

Finally, Axel returned with some wet paper towels to clean up his mess.

Once that was done, he plopped down in his seat and...tossed the dirty paper towels over his shoulder.

The Archmage blinked a few times, then turned to me. "And you live with him?"

"He's much better at home."

"Truly?"

"No."

"Okay, let's calm down, gentlemen," Axel said, glaring. "I am a blessing to all of you and you know it. So, let's just—"

I didn't miss the casual flick of Archie's wand.

And once again, Axel had been muted. His mouth was moving, but no words came out.

"There," Archie said, grinning. "Just the way I prefer him."

Axel fell back in his seat and sulked.

"So, down to business, then," the Archmage said, folding his hands and placing them on his desk. "How are things going with the team, Wyatt?"

"Uh, well, they are, uh, going," I said, glancing at Parker for help. The former shamus was no help at all. I should've known better. He wanted my team dissolved. Wanted to be free of me. I turned back to Archie and shrugged. "We've had a few hiccups."

"Hiccups?" he asked.

"Yeah. Hiccups."

"That's an interesting way to put it," he said, still smiling. Usually his friendly grandfather routine was welcome. Just then, I didn't like it. Didn't like it all. "Would you use the word 'hiccup,' Mr. Grimm?"

"Train wreck," Parker said without hesitation. "That's what I would call it."

"How disappointing," Archie said.

My heart sank.

Which was weird, because a few moments earlier, I'd been convinced that having my team disbanded was probably the best thing. Now that I was staring down the barrel... Well, I wasn't so sure.

"Very disappointing indeed," the Archmage continued.

I hung my head, not meeting his gaze.

"I expected better of you, Parker."

"Huh?" I said, looking up.

Parker fidgeted in his seat. "Sir?"

Archie kept his gaze on Parker, ignoring me. "You've had a remarkably successful track record. Quite the success story, in fact. Every team you've been a part of, including the ones you've led, have all been quite successful. Here we have partnered you with the Cabal's own Blade Mage, and you say it is a train wreck? Well, what have you done to correct the course?"

"Sir..." Parker said, visibly shaken. He swallowed a lump in his throat. "I am not in charge of this operation."

"No, you are not," Archie agreed. "Yet you've challenged Wyatt the whole way. I expected that, with your experience, you'd be a perfect guide to help him along. Someone who could lead by following. Help set an example. But it seems you're more interested in seeing him fail. Here I have given you a challenge, one worthy of your previous success, and you've, what? Given up? I feel as though you've thrown this opportunity back in my face."

Parker blinked rapidly, unsure what to say.

"It's, uh... It's my fault," I heard myself say. Kind of surprised me, because I didn't really want to stick up for Parker. But I felt compelled to.

Archie's gaze met mine for only a moment. "We'll come to you, Wyatt." Then he was back on Parker. "Speak up, Parker."

"I, uh," Parker looked away. "I could have done better."

"Yes, you could have," Archie agreed. Then he turned to me. "Do I need to point out your mistakes, Wyatt? Or do you have the self-awareness to identify them yourself?"

"Uh, well," I said, considering my words. "I don't have much leadership experience, but I think, perhaps, I could have made a few better decisions."

"A few indeed," Archie said. "I never thought I would say the following words, and am disturbed to find myself compelled to do so. Axel has been the best performer on this team."

It was my turn for rapid blinking. Then I turned and looked at Parker, who met my gaze with equal surprise. We both turned and looked at Axel, who was grinning like an idiot.

Then he put up his hand.

Archie stared at him for a moment. "Axel, do you have something you would like to say?"

He nodded.

"If I unmute you, am I going to regret it?"

Axel started to shake his head, then shrugged and nodded.

"Well, now I'm curious," Archie said, waving his wand again.

Axel beamed. "All I wanted to say is that I appreciate the compliment."

"You're welcome, Mr. Gunner."

"And..." Axel said, nodding with far too much enthusiasm. "I've worked really hard to keep these two in line, but they're both degenerates, so it's been a real challenge."

"I'm sure," Archie replied.

"And...though, I don't relish the responsibility, I will take over as Lord General Commander of this team, since clearly that's what you're hinting at. Just be sure, though, because once you put me in charge, things are going to be a lot different. But don't worry. I'll make you proud, sir, Archie, sir."

"And..." Archie waved his wand again. "That's enough of that."

Axel resumed sulking.

The Archmage turned back to me. "I didn't actually summon you here to berate you, though we were clearly overdue for a catch up. And no, gentlemen, I did not call you here to disband the team. Against the wishes of the council, and perhaps my better judgment, I've decided..."

He paused. For like, a long time.

"To invite Squirrel Nuts Squad along on a diplomatic mission."

"Uh..." I said, holding up my hand.

"Not a classroom, Wyatt," he said, annoyed.

"Right." I shook my head. "Did you just call us Squirrel Nuts Squad?"

"I did."

"That is...not the team's name."

"Odd," he said, "because that's what everyone has been calling you."

Again, both Parker and I turned to glare at Axel. He held up two thumbs, grinning from ear-to-ear.

Freaking Axel.

"Anyway," Archie said, "this trip will be similar to when you joined us in New Orleans."

"Oh..." I sat up straight.

"But with less murder and death. Hopefully. The Appalachian Argument is putting together a little conference. They wish us to attend. I am, again, against my better judgment, inviting your team to participate. What do you say?"

I opened my mouth to speak, then shut it again. Something told me I needed to be careful about how I answered. The Archmage said he hadn't called us there to disband the team, but that didn't mean he wouldn't. He obviously wasn't pleased with us. I had a suspicion this was a test. If we refused or hesitated, that might just be it.

Seeing the twinkle in his eye, I knew I was right.

"We would be honored," I said, nodding.

"Good," he replied. "Should be a nice, quiet trip. A good team-building opportunity. A chance for you and Parker to figure out how to work together. And for you to get to know your new teammates."

"New teammates?" I asked, glancing at Parker, who only shrugged.

"Ah, yes," the Archmage said. "Since you've had trouble keeping volunteers, I've taken the liberty of assigning some folks. Not on a trial basis, mind you. Consider them full-fledged members. I think you'll be delighted by my additions."

There was something about the way he said that...

"Can I ask who?" I said.

His reply came in the form of a smile.

Oh, crap.

6

"Oh, hell no."

I agreed with the sentiment.

I agreed with it very much.

Unfortunately, it had come from the mouth of one of my new recruits. There were three of them. And I couldn't believe a single one of them stood before me, assigned to *my* team. This was a worst-case scenario. It would have been better if Archie had disbanded us after all.

He had to be having himself a good laugh. A big, fat, wet, smacking laugh.

I stood there, blank-faced, staring, while two of my three newbies vocalized their displeasure.

Parker and Axel were every bit as stunned as I was.

"Fuck this," Anthony Burns said, crossing his arms.

"Right?" Security Supervisor Fred said, while using his fingers to comb his stupid handlebar mustache. "I'd rather be a nomad than deal with this."

"Ha," Anthony scoffed. "I'd rather try to convince the Colonial Coven I'm a lesbian witch and see if they'd let me join up."

"Wait, are they *all* lesbians?" Security Supervisor Fred asked, eyes widening. "Can you even imagine?"

"Oh, I can imagine," Anthony said. "Of course they are. They're all women, right? Don't allow in any swinging dicks. Gotta be lesbos. You ever heard of one hooking up with a dude?"

"Come to think of it, I haven't," Fred replied.

I had...nothing to say to that. Nothing at all. I was rendered speechless. The amount of stupid...

And they were...on my team.

Anthony Burns and Security Supervisor Fred.

This was a nightmare.

I turned to Parker, who only shook his head. Some help he was.

I dared not look at Axel. He was ready to burst. Any moment he'd lose his composure and fall over, chortling until snot bubbles burst from his snout.

The third addition remained silent, but I wasn't sure I felt any better about him than I did the other two. In another time and place, sure. But now...

"It's not happening," Anthony Burns said again, this time with a dismissive motion. "No fucking way."

"Shut up, Burns," Parker said, the first of our original trio to speak up. "Unless you're ready to tender your resignation, this *is* happening. Quit moping." His gaze shifted to Security Supervisor Fred. "And you... You've been crying about getting on a strike team for years. You finally get a chance to get out of security and immediately start whining?"

"I..." Fred started.

"You what?" Parker asked, tone icy. "You're grateful the Archmage saw fit to give you this opportunity?"

"The Archmage?" Fred said, eyes widening. "The Archmage assigned me?"

"Assigned you?" Parker repeated, shaking his head. "Promoted you, more like."

"But he was involved?" Fred asked, licking his lips. "The Archmage knows who I am?"

And that was the moment.

Axel lost his shit.

He fell over, barrel-laughing all the way to the ground. Howling like a hyena and curled up in the fetal position. Crying, face as red as a cherry. And yes, snot bubbles burst from his snout.

The rest of us just waited.

Finally, he got himself under control long enough to look up at me. "Archie really hates you."

I glared at him. Beside me, Parker crossed his arms.

"Oh, don't get me wrong," Axel said, putting up his hands. "It's not just Wyatt. Clearly, he hates *all* of you."

"What about you, shithead?" Anthony asked. "You think you're here because you're his best buddy?"

"Anthony," Axel said, shaking his head. "I'll have you know, the Archmage said I'm the most responsible. Or respectable. Something like that. He certainly made it clear I'm the one person he can rely on. Said as much. Wyatt and Parker could tell you."

"That's not what he said," Parker replied, shaking his head.

"Pretty sure it was," Axel said, a thoughtful look on his face. "That's how I'm choosing to remember it."

"He muted you," Parker said. "With magic."

"For real?" Anthony asked, grinning. "Wish he'd teach me how to do that."

"You and me both," I replied, joining the conversation. "Listen, guys... I, uh... Well, frankly, I don't know what to say."

I shrugged.

They stared back at me, deadpanned.

I shifted my gaze back to the third addition, wondering what he thought. Whatever the case, he didn't just remain quiet. He didn't move. Like a statue. I couldn't have done it. Too fidgety. But then, he'd had a lot of practice. He'd spent ages staring at a blank wall.

Barrett.

My former teammate was the third addition to my team.

I hadn't even known he'd been cleared for duty. Last I'd known, he was still sitting in his room, staring at that wall.

And that... That scared the shit out of me.

The former Barrett... I would have killed to have him. He was a big, hulking brute. Looked like an NFL edge rusher. His very appearance could de-escalate a tense situation. And when it came to a scrap, he was every bit as nasty as advertised. An expert at close-quarters magical combat. Someone you didn't want to tangle with in a tight space.

But it wasn't even all of that.

Barrett had been cool, calm, and collected even in the worst circumstances. He was also a big teddy bear. An empath who tried to do right by everyone. Someone who fought to make sure everyone got along. Just the sort of person I needed.

Now, though...

I wasn't so sure. Was he ready for field work? Would he tear off in a mad rage at the first sign of trouble? Or would he just stand there and watch the rest of us get ripped apart? I didn't know. And *that* was what scared the shit out of me.

"So, who's the big guy?" Fred asked, rubbing his mustache. He reached out a hand to Barrett. "I'm Security Supervisor... Err... I'm, uh, just Fred now, I guess."

Barrett's eyes were locked on mine, I realized. Studying me. He ignored the offered hand and continued staring, making me uneasy.

"Huh," Fred said, pulling his hand back. "I think he might be even less happy to be here."

"Can't be less happy than me," Anthony said, crossing his arms again. "Looks like he wants to tear you apart, Wyatt."

"You sucker punch him, too?" Fred asked.

"Probably nearly got him killed," Anthony replied. "Just like he did to me."

"That it, Wyatt?" Fred asked, grinning. "You nearly get this big guy killed?"

"Enough," I heard myself say.

There must have been something in my tone, or maybe the look on my face. Whatever the case, both Anthony and Fred saw something that erased the smirks from their stupid faces. *Good.*

I hadn't planned it that way, but they were digging awfully close to old wounds better left alone. Not just my own, but Barrett's, too. No, I hadn't nearly gotten Barrett killed. But I'd been there when our former teammates had betrayed him. When they'd killed Malik, our old team leader. When they'd stabbed Barrett in the back and left him for dead.

I'd been there for that. I'd seen the aftermath. Seen what my old friend had become. What he was now.

That wasn't something we were going to joke about. Ever.

I felt the rumble in my chest simmer, the tremors of rage fading. The red fury subsided, and I realized that while I had my bluff in, I should make the most of it.

Ha, make the most of it!

My team couldn't have been a worse assortment if the Archmage had called in some of my old enemies. Hell, I might have been better off with the obayifo, some demons from Memphis, and the Devil Baby of Bourbon Street.

Enough.

That one was for me.

No point feeling sorry for myself.

I'd been in the shit with everyone present, except for Fred. That meant more than just liking each other. We'd fought together.

Anthony Burns was an asshole, but he was handy in a scrap. He had a toxic personality, but in the swamps, when it had come down to brass tacks, he'd been ready to sacrifice himself for the greater good.

I knew the man Barrett could be. If he came back around to his old self, he'd be invaluable. Even if he didn't, just having his bulk would scare a lot of idiots.

Parker was by the books and had the personality of a cardboard box, but he, too, had stood beside me through countless nasty situations. Often showing up at the end with the cavalry. And whether I liked it or not, his experience was irreplaceable.

And Axel was...Axel. As sure as a mountain and as shifty as the wind. Always one to ride the lightning, he was with me no matter what.

Fred was just an asshole. Every team needed one, I supposed. We had two. Well, actually, we had five, maybe six, depending on Barrett. Point was... Just because I didn't see a redeeming quality in Fred didn't necessarily mean he didn't have one. I mean... Surely, he had one.

"Listen, guys," I said, letting my gaze drift from face to face. "We all have history. Some of it better than others. None of us are thrilled with this... What, Axel?"

"I just wanted to say," he said, glancing from person to person, "I'm delighted to have everyone on board."

I glared at him, as did the others.

"What?" he asked. "You guys, all trying to work together? This is gonna be a hoot."

"Anyway," I said, getting back on track, "the Archmage selected every member of this team himself. Do you think he's a fool? Axel, put your damned hand down."

Axel scowled but lowered his hand.

"Our Archmage is anything but a fool." I turned my gaze on Fred. "Yes, he knows who you are. And he knows our...history, rest assured. He knows more about each of us than we'd probably be comfortable with. Right, Grimm?"

Parker nodded, though I could tell he was uncomfortable, not knowing where I was going with this.

I continued, "It might seem like a mismatch. Certainly does to me. As Axel put it, it feels like he's having a laugh at our expense. But if there's one thing I've learned about the Archmage, it's to never underestimate him. Never assume he's made a mistake. He wasn't chosen by the Archstaff by accident. He's crafty. And he's always ten steps—no—a hundred steps ahead of the rest of us. He chose each of you for a reason."

I paused, letting my words sink in.

"He either thinks you're the right fit for this team, or he's testing you. I would assume both. And if the Archmage *is* testing you, do you really want to fail that test? Especially at the launch?"

Anthony and Fred both sighed. Barrett maintained his silence.

"Exactly," I said, nodding. "We have to work together. Have to prove we're up to the challenge. I'm not asking for your undying loyalty. Hell, I'm not even asking for your respect. Let's start simple. I'll try to be cool so long as you do. Deal?"

Parker was the first to nod. No hesitation. A big leap from where we'd stood a few days ago. Apparently, Archie's ire had shaken him. *Good.*

Fred was next, though he sighed. "Guess this really is the only way I'll ever get off the security team. I'm in."

Anthony's nose scrunched up like he smelled something foul. "Whatever. You're going to get us all killed either way. Might as well make the most of it while I can."

"That's the spirit," Axel said.

Anthony scowled.

All eyes turned toward Barrett. He gave only the briefest nod.

That was that.

My new team.

"Everyone get in here," Axel said, sticking his hand out. "Squirrel Nuts Squad on three!"

Anthony responded for the rest of us.

"Fuck off, Axel."

7

I stood in the doorway, staring into the darkness of the old house.

I wasn't sure I was ready for this.

Wasn't sure I was prepared to...

"Stop being dramatic," Axel said from behind me. "Let's go."

"Axel..."

"It's just a house, you big baby."

"It is... Was... My dad's house."

"And now it's yours," he said, pushing me from behind. "Let's go."

I moved my feet forward, into my father's old place, hand searching for a light switch.

When I was a kid, my father had several places around the Cabal territories. But I supposed I'd grown up here as much as anywhere. It was a simple suburban house, right on the Castle Grounds. It wasn't one of the mansions near the golf course, like most of the bigwigs had. No, my father had had simple tastes. Never one for flare.

I hadn't been there since his funeral.

Afterward, I'd wondered what had happened to it. Who had ended up with it? No one would say. Archie and Marius's doing. Shain Stone, too, though he'd at least been reluctant. I'd spent years scraping by while they had held onto my father's wealth and estates, waiting until *they* felt I was ready.

I was still pissed about that.

But that was a problem for another day.

I hadn't been in any hurry to visit the old place. Or his others. I wasn't even sure which still existed. I needed to catch up with Stone about that. Also a problem for another day. As were my finances. Apparently, I had some amount of money to my name, but I'd been so damned busy dealing with the team thing, I hadn't taken the time to look into it. I was neglecting my fortunes and my familiar. Hopefully things would settle into a rhythm soon, though. It would be good to understand how much wealth I actually had. And to learn more about my snake.

Just then, my immediate concern was one of a more practical nature. The next morning, we were due to head east for the Appalachian Argument's conference. And since Cabal leadership despised sleep, we had to meet before the sun came up. Last time we'd played this game, I'd had to get on the road before the dawn had showed us its butt crack. My cabin was a little over an hour from the Castle, and I didn't enjoy getting up super early.

So...

I'd decided to get over myself and stay here so we could sleep for an extra hour.

Still, imagining the old ghosts walking through that quiet place unsettled me. Made me uneasy. Maybe Axel was right. Maybe I was just being a baby. But it didn't feel like mine. It felt like it belonged to my father, and being there, in his old place... It made me sad.

I missed him.

Even more now, it seemed. I'd been thinking about him a lot lately. Wishing he was around to guide me. He'd have known how to get me on course. How to advise me. When Weevel had suggested I find leaders to study, it was my father I'd thought of first. He'd always seemed so confident.

Axel found the light switch before me.

It was exactly how I remembered it. No dust or cobwebs, either. Clearly Archie or Marius had ensured it was well kept. I appreciated that, despite my frustrations with them. At least they'd taken care of my dad's old place.

Behind me, Axel asked, "Do you think Weekend at Burmese will be all right?"

I turned, glancing at him. "Why wouldn't she be?"

"She might get lonely," he said, shrugging. "You should have brought her."

"I'm not bringing a big weird-ass python on our field trip."

"That weird-ass python is your familiar."

"I still don't even know what that means. Or what I'm supposed to do with her. Look, Paeter and Mary Beth are going to go check on her. And it's not like she relies on us for food."

"Maybe not you, but I feed her," he said, and rather indignantly.

"You do?" I asked, raising an eyebrow.

"Oh, yeah. Well, I try. I gave her some Cheetos the other day. She must not have been hungry, though, because she didn't seem the least bit interested."

"Axel..."

"Wyatt..."

"She's a snake, dumbass," I said, shaking my head.

"So?"

"So, she doesn't like Cheetos."

"Don't be ridiculous. Everyone likes Cheetos."

"Snakes don't eat Cheetos. They eat mice and shit."

"I know that! I went and got her a mouse from the pet store. But..."

"But?"

"I couldn't bring myself to feed it to her." He sighed. "When I looked into those tiny little eyes, I just...couldn't."

"Wait... So, what did you do with the mouse?"

"So," Axel said, completely ignoring my question, "now that we've made it through the threshold, let's get past the next awkward question."

"Is there a mouse roaming freely in my house right now?"

"Do you want your old room? Or your dad's? Asking for a friend."

"Axel, did you let a mouse loose in my house? And if you did, you do know Weekend and Burmese will probably eat it, right?"

"Your room? Or your dad's?"

I turned and met his gaze. I hadn't even considered. My father's room was the master, which was the biggest in the house. And it had its own bathroom. My room was smaller. It did not have its own bathroom.

It might have seemed a simple decision, but it wasn't.

This wasn't just about a single night. Now that we'd broken the seal, we'd likely be staying there often. So long as I had a team, I needed to be at the Castle more than I had in the past. Axel had been groaning about the drive for weeks. We both had.

No, whatever decision I made, that would be our living situation for the foreseeable future.

Did I take my dad's old room? Claim it for myself? Try to put my ghosts behind me? Or did I embrace the specters of my childhood and reclaim my old room? More importantly, which would I rather Axel claim? Whichever the case, he would make it his own. Star Wars posters on the walls, bean bags on the floors, and random odds and ends scattered about.

I glanced over at him. "You get the guest room."

"What?" he asked, crossing his arms. "I refuse! This is an atrocity and it will not stand!"

"You can always go stay at your dad's."

"Right. So, guest bedroom. Great choice. Love it."

He sauntered off down the hall, his bag over his shoulder.

I stood alone, turning in a slow circle, taking in the old place. Finally, I sighed and moved off toward my old room. Maybe someday I would take my dad's. But just then, it still belonged to his memory. I was fine with that.

8

"Squirrel Nuts Squad?" the wizard asked, then glanced down to check his clipboard.

Yeah, buddy, I can't believe it either.

After confirming that was, in fact, the name he was looking for, his head popped up again, eyes scanning. "Squirrel Nuts Squad?"

"Here," I said, waving. I tried to ignore the many strange looks. And the smirks.

"You're here," he said, trying to hide his own smile. He pointed toward a big black Escalade. It matched the others in the convoy. "Keys are in the ignition."

"Fucking Squirrel Nuts Squad," Anthony said, shaking his head. "Whose dumbass idea was that?"

Both Parker and I turned and stared at him, neither replying.

"Right," he said, shaking his head. "Of course."

"Who?" Fred asked. "I don't get it."

No one bothered to reply. And Axel was off chit-chatting with another team.

Just like before, it was too early for this shit.

I hadn't dressed the part, either. Screw it. Jeans and a t-shirt. The rest of the assholes could wear their suits, prim and proper wizards they were. I was done worrying about all that. Barrett didn't seem to care, either. He was dressed in sweats. Parker and Anthony wore the same damned suits they'd worn as shamuses. Fred had a suit, too, though it was clear he'd just bought it, and it didn't fit quite right. He looked like an idiot. Especially with that stupid mustache.

"Fred, you've got the wheel," Parker said. Then he turned and gave me a sheepish look. "I mean, that's, uh, what Wyatt said."

That wasn't true. I had said no such thing. Parker just felt bad that he'd stepped in, playing boss again. I guess it was hard for him to turn off. I wasn't bothered about it, though. Not this time. Though I was curious why he'd chosen Fred.

"That's right," I said, allowing him to save face. "Unless someone else wants to drive?"

Barrett slung his duffel bag off his shoulder and dropped it at our feet. Without a word, he moved around to the driver's door and got in.

"Guess Barrett wants to drive," I said, shrugging.

"Well," Parker replied, "I was worried about fitting him in the back, anyway."

The thought hadn't even occurred to me. Again, Parker was thinking like a leader and I wasn't. I might've tried to tell myself it was just because it was early, but that would have been a lie.

"You, uh, want the front passenger seat?" Parker asked.

I met his gaze. "You can have it, Grimm."

He nodded and glanced at Anthony and Fred. "What are you two doing? Waiting for Wyatt to sign your permission slips? Start loading stuff."

Anthony and Fred grumbled, then started loading the back.

That I definitely approved of.

"Parker, can I talk with you real quick?" I asked.

"Yeah," he said, nodding.

We moved out of earshot.

"Listen, Wyatt," Parker said. "My bad. I didn't mean to... You know."

I put up my hands. "That isn't what I wanted to talk about. Well, it sort of is. Look, you've been doing this shit for a long time. I didn't even think about the seating arrangements. I've got no problem with you stepping in for things like that. It's other times, where..."

"I know," he said, nodding. "I'll try to do better."

"Thanks. That wasn't it, though. I was thinking... You should officially be my second-in-command. Normal strike teams do that. So should we. I mean, I'm sure everyone views it that way, anyway."

"Even Axel?"

"No, he thinks I'm *his* second-in-command. Which is kind of my point. Axel will never listen to you. On the flip side, Anthony and Fred both hate my guts. So, what if we tried to split the team in half, at least when we're out in the field? Like, we agree on the plan. I make the calls with you as my second, but Axel and Barrett stick with me. Anthony and Fred stick with you. I have a better chance of wrangling Axel, and you've managed Anthony before."

Parker nodded along. "Makes sense. I don't know a lot about Fred or Barrett. Just what I've heard."

"Right," I said. "That's why we each get one. You get the one that hates me. I think he'll be more inclined to listen to you than me."

"You think Barrett will follow your orders?"

"I'm not sure," I admitted. "I think the old Barrett would have been a perfect addition."

"But now?"

"I don't know."

"Do you think he's stable?" Parker asked, lowering his voice. "Do you think he's safe?"

I opened my mouth to reply, then shut it again, considering my words. I might have said that I was worried about his mental state. Also could have said I was worried about his physical state. The last time I'd gone to visit him, his mom had told me that his lung might not fully recover. That he may never be cleared for field work. Instead of any of that, I said, "I think Archie put him with us for a reason. Might be more about him than us, though."

"I don't follow."

"Barrett and I used to be pretty close. Maybe Archie thought putting him with me would help him recover some of his former self. Bring him out of that shell he's built. Or he thought he would be useful to us. Or both. I wasn't kissing ass before when I said no one was placed here by accident. For the rest of us, it might well be a test to see if we can work together. For Barrett, though, I can't help but wonder if this is the Archmage's way of easing him back."

Parker nodded. "Seems like something the Archmage would come up with. We need to keep an eye on him, though."

"I know," I replied, turning my gaze back toward the SUV and statue in the driver's seat. "He was a good guy, Parker. Back when we were both on the Kingsnakes. I'd love to have *that* guy on our team."

"Let's hope we can find him." Parker rubbed the back of his neck. "All right, Wyatt, I think it's a reasonable plan. I'll take Big Balls Burns and Handlebar Mustache. You get Yankee Doodle Dandy and the Incredibly Silent Hulk."

I gave him my best Dwayne Johnson eyebrow. "Was that a joke, Grimmy?"

"Hey, I *do* have a sense of humor, you know? Just usually, when I'm around you and Axel, there isn't anything funny going on."

"Well, maybe we'll get to see it on this trip. Should be pretty laid back."

"You say that, but I haven't forgotten what happened in New Orleans."

"Nor have I. As long as no one invites us fishing, we should be fine. But this time, if I get kidnapped, try not to lose me."

"No promises." Parker glanced over my shoulder and motioned behind me. "I think someone wants your attention. I'll fetch Yankee Doodle and get everyone loaded up."

"Thanks," I replied, and turned to see who it was.

I blinked, wondering if my tired eyes deceived me.

Alyita.

Seeing my expression, she waved.

Like most of the people slowly loading up, she had a bag over her shoulder.

"Are you...coming with us?" I asked.

She nodded. "Heck yeah! You didn't know?"

"I don't know anything," I said, shrugging.

"I'm sure I must have mentioned it," a voice said from behind me.

I recognized the voice, of course. Even if I somehow hadn't, Alyita's visceral reaction would have told me who it was. Her eyes widened like the singer from her favorite band had just stepped out. It wasn't, of course. It could have only been one person.

"Archmage," I said, turning.

He offered me his standard-issue smile and motioned toward Alyita. "Your young friend is going to be meeting with the Appalachian Argument leadership and representatives of the Eastern Cherokee. It seems they've had some disputes, not unlike our own with the Oklahoma Cherokee. They're quite interested in how we built a better relationship. They are particularly interested in getting Alyita's feedback, as a student coming in from the Cherokee to learn our ways of magic."

"That's...amazing," I said, glancing back at Alyita. She still seemed too shell-shocked to say much.

"I'm glad you agree," the Archmage said, "because you'll also be asked to participate in many of those conversations."

"I will?"

"Of course. You are the one who brokered our new deal with the Oklahoma Cherokee. Our friends in the east are quite interested in getting your perspective." He fixed me with a coy smile. "I'm quite sure I told you all of this."

"I'm quite sure you didn't." I scowled back.

No, Archie wasn't senile. He was just a dick. Sometimes.

"Master Serrano has the details," Archie said, then glanced at Alyita. "My dear, you might ought to figure out which ride you're in. We'll be leaving shortly."

"Right," she said, blinking. "Of course. Um, thank you, Archmage. See you at the festival, Wyatt."

With that, she sped off, looking for her ride.

"Festival?" I asked, turning back to Archie.

Of course, he had disappeared.

What was she talking about? What festival?

9

Mothman Festival.

That's what the sign said.

I glanced over at Parker. "Did you know about this?"

He shook his head. "Now that I'm a distinguished member of Squirrel Nuts Squad, no one tells me anything."

"We prefer to fly by the seat of our nuts," Axel said, chortling to himself.

"Come on." I noticed the rest of our caravan was headed into the small hotel. "Let's see what the room situation is."

The Cabal had booked out all the rooms. That was about all I knew. The hotel was privately owned. A quaint little spot. Not rundown, though. A short way from Point Pleasant, West Virginia. Apparently, we were stopping there for the night.

"They've already been reserved," Parker said. "Two to a room."

"We bunking together, boss man?" Anthony Burns asked, eyes fixed on Parker. "Just like old times?"

"No," Parker replied. "I'm with Barrett."

"What?" Anthony asked, annoyed. "Then who I am with?"

"You're with Fred," he said. "Unless you want to swap Wyatt and share with Axel."

"No, uh, I'm good bunking with Fred."

Parker and I shared a look and I held back a laugh. Quick thinking on his part. We hadn't laid out any room assignments. Parker had just seen an opportunity to secure a quiet roommate. Or maybe I wasn't giving the former shamus enough credit. Maybe he wanted a chance to learn more about our silent addition. But, come on... Who wanted to bunk with Anthony Burns?

On the other hand, putting Anthony and Fred in the same room might produce enough bro juice to be hazardous. I'd take the risk. I certainly wasn't bunking with Fred.

Parker took off to find our keys and I stood out on the street, studying the sign.

Mothman Festival.

I'd heard of the folk legend before, but knew little about it. Certainly hadn't known they had a festival. Apparently, the Appalachian Argument's leadership had suggested our convoy stop in and enjoy the festival before driving the rest of the way to their compound. Much like our own Castle, their base was tucked away in the hills somewhere, hidden from the civilized world.

In the meantime...

Point Pleasant, West Virginia. Home of the Mothman Festival.

A chance to take in the scenery and enjoy ourselves.

If this was how the Appalachian Argument rolled, I might have been on the wrong team. I couldn't imagine the Cabal encouraging guests to do anything fun. No, they were all blah, blah, blah, boring business stuff.

I thought it was cool, and I was looking forward to checking it out.

I was also curious what lie the Cabal had told the hotel staff. We certainly would not pass as a sports ball team or a traveling orchestra. Not my problem, though.

Unfortunately, I quickly discovered something that was. It was just after Parker returned with our keys and I headed off to find my room. Axel had already wandered off, having spied a bird or something.

I was just about to unlock my door when I heard raised voices from a few doors down.

The first was a man's voice. Rather upset. Whoever was on the other end of his fury was receiving quite the scolding. Could've been anyone.

It wasn't, though, I realized, as soon as I heard the indignant reply.

"Give it back," Alyita's voice said. "Now."

Well, damn.

"Listen here, little lady," the man said. "First, you will speak to me with respect. I am a senior member of the Cabal's education department. I do not tolerate barbarism or foolishness. Especially from youngsters. You have no business with a weapon. You're lucky I don't turn you in and have you expelled. I don't know how the Cherokee do things, but in the Cabal, students don't carry weapons, especially when they've been presented the honor of attending such an important event. You are representing both the Cabal and the Cherokee, though I can't imagine why anyone thought that was a good idea based on your behavior up to this point."

The man tracked Alyita's gaze, which had looked up at me as I leaned against the door-frame. He turned to face me.

He stared at me, eyes wide, confused. "Can I help you?"

I nodded, noticing the tomahawk in his hand. "She bring that?"

He nodded and fidgeted with his glasses. He was a short balding man who clearly held himself with a distinguished sense of self importance. Reminded me of Elementalist Locklyn. "I am ashamed to admit it, but yes. She brought a weapon, if you can believe it. Who are you?"

"You responsible for her?" I asked, ignoring his question.

"I am indeed," he said, again adjusting his glasses. I would say he looked down his nose at me, but that wasn't quite right, since he was shorter. So, I guess he looked up his nose at me. "I am a member of the Cabal's education board. I was asked to come along to share notes with my peers in the Appalachian Argument. Sadly, I've been asked to monitor this riff-raff throughout the trip."

"Not anymore," I said.

Reaching over, I swiped the tomahawk out of his grip.

"What's the meaning of this?" he asked, glaring at me. "Who do you think you are?"

"Who do you think I am?" I asked, shrugging.

"By the looks of it, some ruffian," he said, crossing his arms. "Cabal muscle, no doubt. Probably along for training or some such. Give me back that weapon and leave me to discipline my charge."

"Where'd you find it?" I asked, ignoring his outstretched hand.

"In her bag," he said. "I must insist you return it at once."

My humor drained, along with my sunny disposition. "You went through her bag?"

"That's right," he said. Perhaps he felt stupid with his hands outstretched, so he moved them to his hips in a Superman pose, though it wasn't super imposing. "I thought it best to ensure she didn't have any contraband. Imagine my surprise when I found that ax."

"You," I said, speaking slowly. "a grown-ass man, took it upon yourself to go through a teenage girl's bag?"

"Uh, yes, that's right," he said, not backing down. "I am responsible for her. It's up to me to ensure she behaves and represents us appropriately."

"Yeah, about that... You won't be dealing out any discipline with this one. And since I didn't make myself clear, let me try again... I'm relieving you of your duty. You'll still need to make sure she has her schedule, handle the administrative bullshit, but you aren't in charge of her any longer. I am."

The man turned from me to Alyita, who was now grinning like a little asshole.

"Wipe that smirk off your face," I said, glaring at her. When the man turned back to sneer at her, I gave her a wink.

"This is highly irregular," he said, re-focusing on me. "I cannot simply hand over the responsibility of my charge."

"I wasn't asking. Which brings me to my next point: you're never going to speak to her like that again, or we'll have a problem."

He started to protest, but I held up my hand.

"And..." I waited until I was sure I had his attention. Didn't want him to miss this part. "If you go through her belongings again, I'll break your fucking jaw. Cool?"

He took a step back.

"I'm guessing you don't work with youngsters often," I said, fixing him with my meanest glare. "Grown-ass men aren't supposed to dig through young ladies' things. You're lucky her grandfather isn't here, or you might've gone home in a bag. I'm half-tempted to dish out some discipline myself, and it won't be aimed at her, if you take my meaning."

"But, but..."

"And seeing as how her grandfather will hold me accountable for her well-being anyway, I'll go ahead and take that responsibility on in an official capacity. Alyita is now under the watch of Squirrel Nuts Squad. Got it?"

"Squirrel Nuts Squad?" he asked, fidgeting with his glasses. "Just who the heck do you think you are?"

"Oh, right," I said, chuckling. "Wyatt Draven. Blade Mage."

And that... That did the trick. *Tada!*

His pomp deflated, replaced by fear. It wasn't the title. It was my reputation, no doubt. Rumors about me being trouble. Stories about me punching security supervisors. Tales of the things I'd done and the monsters I'd slain. Not everyone in the Cabal knew my face, but they damned sure knew my name.

And he was afraid.

Good.

"I, uh, I see," he said, not meeting my gaze. "I will, uh, inform my superiors. And, uh, trust you to handle the situation as you see fit."

"Thank you," I said, stepping out of the door-frame. "You may leave."

He shuffled out in a hurry, disappearing around the corner like he had diarrhea.

I glanced up at Alyita. When I knew I had her attention, I tossed her back her tomahawk. "Maybe keep that hidden."

She caught it with a deft hand. "I will. Didn't think the creep would go through my bag."

"Yeah, that's uh... I'll mention it to Archie."

"Archie?" she asked, raising an eyebrow.

Oops.

"Yeah, uh, Archie is someone I know pretty high up. Don't worry about it. I'll make sure the guy gets looked into. Creeper."

"Thanks," she said, looking away. "I guess, uh, maybe I shouldn't have brought my hawk."

"You've been in the shit," I said, shrugging. "Can't blame you for wanting to protect yourself. I doubt everyone else will be so understanding, though. And that guy's superiors may try to overrule me. So, let me know if he gives you any more trouble. Otherwise, you're with us."

"I get to go with you?" she asked, looking up. "And Axel? To the festival?"

"Yeah, of course. Who else are you going to roll with? Not that boring creep."

She smiled. "Thanks, Wyatt."

"Wait," I said, glancing around. "Did you get a room to yourself?"

She shrugged. "I think there's a lady from the Cabal who's supposed to be bunking with me."

"Ah," I said, nodding. "I was about to be super jealous. I've got to share with Axel. Anyway, get settled in. We're two doors down if you need anything. We'll see about finding dinner soon. Then we've got the festival tomorrow."

With that, I shut her door and headed to my room.

10

"Took you long enough," said the woman glaring at me.

I fought the urge to glance over my shoulder, in case she was speaking to someone else. I knew better.

Master Battle Mage Zephyrine Castillo was no fan of mine. I knew that. I hadn't known she'd come along on the trip. Nor had I known she'd be standing outside the room I was planning to enter. Lucky me.

"Master Battle Mage," I said, dipping my head. "Good to see you."

She harrumphed. Guess she had expected me to acknowledge her insult.

"The big guy in there?" I asked, motioning behind her.

A runner had come knocking on my door, informing me the Archmage wanted me to meet him in the conference room. That was weird since he could've just used mind-speak. And then the runner had bolted off, which left me to figure out where the hell the conference room was. Turned out, our tiny little hotel had one. Singular. I couldn't imagine it got much use.

"You know," she said, crossing her arms, "when the Archmage summons you, it's best to hurry."

I considered pointing out that I had hurried. Considered pointing out that the minion hadn't bothered telling me where the conference room was. In fairness, I hadn't thought to ask. Point was, I wanted to rebuke her incriminations.

But there was no point.

When I'd first returned to the Cabal, I'd thought all the masters hated me. Abhorred me, even. Serrano was the first I'd won over. Many of the others had softened their skepticism, if only just a little. The Master Battle Mage, though?

She had nothing but ire for me.

Did not like me one bit.

And I didn't know why.

I mean, other than my reputation for blowing shit up.

Maybe she was just a hard-ass.

Maybe she didn't think I deserved Dyrnwyn.

Maybe she thought I was an idiot.

I saw little use in crossing verbal swords with her. So, instead, I offered her a friendly smile and said, "I'll keep that in mind."

Her eyes narrowed further.

Apparently, that wasn't the right thing to say, either. *Futz it.*

"Are you looking forward to the Mothman Festival?" I asked. "Axel thinks there will be funnel cake."

Without replying, she stepped away from the door, allowing me to pass.

Message received. We were done.

I opened the door and stepped into the tiny conference area. It turned out there was more than one room after all. I found myself in a more casual setting, with a couple of couches and lounge chairs. There was a table as well, with water and coffee. There was a door that led into a corporate-style conference room, but the lights were off and it wasn't in use. Instead, Archie and the others were seated in the waiting area, making use of the more comfortable furniture.

Naturally, I recognized Master Serrano immediately, as well as Master Shamus Abigail Yazzie and Master Spiritualist Mateo Gray. It was the other face I didn't recognize.

The stranger looked like a plumper version of Diamond Dallas Page. Even had the eighties rock band hair. His face was gruff, aged by the sun. Jeans, work boots, and a flannel shirt. I didn't get the impression his outfit was a facade. He wasn't some new age social media hipster dressing that way to be ironic. It was who he was. And he wore a big grin on his ruddy cheeks.

When he turned and looked at me, I found his gaze cool and calculating, but not unfriendly.

"Ah, Wyatt," Archie said, offering me a smile. He motioned toward the stranger. "I wanted you to meet my old friend, Supreme Enchanter Tate, of the Appalachian Argument."

The man stood and reached for my hand. "Wyatt Draven, a pleasure to make your acquaintance."

"Thank you," I said, grasping his hand. His grip was firm, but not crushing. He understood his strength. "Nice to meet you."

"Supreme Enchanter Tate leads the Appalachian Argument," Archie said, winking at Tate. "With a little help from Supreme Curator Whitaker and Supreme Shaman Sams, of course."

"More than a little," Tate replied with a snort. "I'd have run the Argument into the ground if not for those two. Tried to convince one of them to take the job, but they'd not have it. So, here we are. Me in charge, with two Arcane Guardians to nag me senseless."

Noticing the look on my face, or perhaps reading my mind as often seemed the case, Archie explained. "The Appalachian Argument does not hold an Arch-staff."

I nodded, figuring as much. None of the United States guilds had all eight of the Arcane Artifacts.

"Right," Tate said, nodding. "We have but four, sadly."

"Sad, indeed," Archie agreed with a nod. His voice remained neutral. Political. Wise. He didn't brag that we had five. "Still, four is respectable. And they are held in worthy hands."

"That they are," Tate agreed, then glanced my way. "You might have guessed it from their titles, but Supreme Curator Whitaker holds a role similar to your own Grand Curator Begay. And Supreme Shaman Sams is like your own Grand Shaman Nguyen. Where we differ is we have two Arcane Paladins instead of one." He glanced between Archie and me. "Uh, do you guys use that same terminology?"

"Yes." Archie nodded. "We use the same monikers. Arcane Seers and Arcane Paladins. And you, my friend, though having one less than us, are fortunate to have an even split. I'm sure Wyatt would appreciate it if we had more than one Paladin."

"The way I hear it, your Blade Mage is doing just fine on his own." Tate winked at me. "We have a Defender and a War Mage. Both look forward to meeting you."

I blinked, struggling to find my voice. The only other Arcane Paladin I'd met was Byron Walker of the Southern Circle. Another Blade Mage. To meet a Shield? Or a Hammer?

In the before times, in the long, long ago, when there were few enough guilds that each still retained all eight Arcane Artifacts, the Blade Mage had led the other Arcane Paladins. The Hammer—or the Ax, or as they were more commonly known—the War Mage served as the Blade Mage's right hand. The Defender, or Shield Mage, served as their left. And the Hunter protected their rear. At least, that was how I understood it.

Point was, those four positions went together, just as the Arcane Wand, Scepter, and Ankh went along with the Arch-staff. I'd tripped up in New Orleans when I'd learned the Southern Circle used different titles for their positions. It appeared the Appalachian Argument did the same. So it was that Grand Enchanter Gunner, Grand Curator Begay, and Grand Shaman Nguyen were under the Archmage and his Archie Staff. In the Appalachian Argument's case, they had both a curator and a shaman, but no archmage. I would have thought one of those two would have led. But assumptions make an asshole out of you and everyone but me. Think that's how that saying goes. Anyway...

The Ozark Mountain Cabal had all four of the Arcane Seers, but only the one Arcane Paladin. Me.

During my father's time as Blade Mage, he'd never had the other Arcane Paladins at his side. Nor did I. Nor would I. It wasn't like any other guild would give up their precious Arcane Weapons, nor the people who held them.

Still, to have a chance to meet a couple of them...

I realized I had drifted and re-focused on the conversation.

Tate was saying, "Though some argue we only have three Guardians."

Archie offered him a sympathetic smile. "Hopefully our efforts here will help to ease some of that burden."

I didn't know what the hell they were talking about, and I didn't think it would be wise to butt in. Although I felt rather odd, standing there like a jackass. Everyone else was seated. But the Cabal masters remained silent as well, listening. So, at least I was on par with them.

Tate's gaze turned my way. "Yes, I'm hoping your Blade Mage can help us make some strides in that direction."

"Uh...what?" I asked, blinking. Maybe I should have been paying closer attention.

Tate chuckled at my discomfort. Archie was no help, nor were the masters. I thought about using mind-speak to ask Serrano, but Tate went ahead and explained.

"Supreme Shaman Sams," Tate said. "He came to us from the Cherokee. The, uh, Eastern Cherokee, you might call them. Course, we refer to your Oklahoman Cherokee as the Oklahoma Cherokee. So, all's fair. Point is, Sams came to the Argument years ago, in a time when our relations with the tribe were better. No one made a fuss back then. Sams has been one hell of a leader. There's just been a bit of fuss here lately. "

I raised an eyebrow, but refrained from rudely asking.

Tate chuckled. "Sams is, uh, how I do I put this? Well, he's ancient. He was our Supreme Shaman before I was in diapers."

"Which sort of leads to the problem you have today," Archie said.

"Right," Tate said, nodding. "Sams is old. His health is failing. At the same time, our relationship with the Cherokee has...hit a few snags. And, of course, there are those among our order who don't want the Cherokee present when a new shaman is chosen. And there are those among the Cherokee who argue the Arcane Ankh should go to them when he passes, so it will be forced to choose from among the Cherokee. It's all a mess."

"A mess we're hoping to help with," Archie said, giving me a knowing look. Although I didn't know what the hell it meant.

"That's where you come in," Tate said, beaming.

"It is?" I asked, glancing between the two.

"Of course," Tate continued, nodding along. "Don't be modest, Wyatt. When it comes to guild and tribe relations, no one in a hundred years has been as successful in establishing mutually beneficial terms as you. Our folks hope to learn something from you."

"Oh," I said, because I couldn't think of anything clever to say. I had known the Cherokee were happy with the terms I'd agreed on. That was sort of the point. But the council... They had never seemed too hip about what I'd done.

I could practically feel Archie's amusement.

I could also sense discomfort wafting over from the masters. Except for Serrano, who probably felt some measure of pity for me.

Taking a steadying breath, I looked Supreme Enchanter Tate in the eyes and told the truth. "I don't know about all of that. I just did what I thought was right, what I thought would work best for both sides. I have a ton of respect for the Cherokee."

"Well said," Tate replied, nodding at me. "That's what we need. I'm not asking you to teach a seminar on multi-cultural negotiations. No, sir. What I need is for both sides to cut the bullshit. Just like you did. Hopefully, they'll follow your example."

There was a brief snort from somewhere in the room. Which was pretty shitty, considering the only other people in the room were high-ranking members of the Cabal.

The only reaction was a twitch in Archie's eye, but he didn't look at whoever had made the sound. Doubtless, he knew. They'd hear from him soon.

Tate, for his part, only chuckled. "I like someone who can cut through the noise. Get shit done. I look forward to having you at our compound. Before that, though, enjoy the festival tomorrow. Take in some of our cultural. Then enjoy the drive into the hills to get to our compound. Couple more hours down the road."

"Sure," I replied. "Looking forward to it."

11

"Funnel cakes, here I come!" Axel declared, skipping ahead of us.

"He is way too excited," Parker said, shaking his head.

"He's just trying to make up for your lack of enthusiasm," I replied.

It was true.

Both things.

Axel was through the moon. Of course he was. We were approaching downtown Point Pleasant, where the festival was being held. It didn't take much to get Axel jazzed. He would've been eager to attend a knitting festival. This, though? A cryptid-themed festival? Yeah, he was through the roof.

Thing was... We'd met our fair share of cryptids. Out in the shit, we'd both fought and befriended creatures that were otherwise believed to be fiction. Axel had taken to Googling them, which often provided erroneous results. Still, he was infatuated. This festival would only fuel his fire. Plus, funnel cakes.

And Parker... He took himself too seriously.

I turned and studied the other faces walking along with me. Anthony and Fred took themselves too seriously, too. And Barrett... Poor Barrett.

At least there was one other smiling face in the mix.

Alyita took off, skipping along behind Axel. Glancing over her shoulder, she said, "Come on, you uptight grown-ups! Let's have fun!"

"She's right," I said, glancing over at Parker. "Might as well make the most of it."

"Celebrating the things we hunt is not my idea of fun," Parker said.

"Yeah, and it's not like we're going to find any fine ladies here," Anthony said. "Right, Fred?"

"That's right," Fred replied. "Probably just weird middle-aged dudes."

I paused and turned to face him. I didn't say anything. Didn't think I needed to. I thought my glare would help the irony blossom. Nope. Wilted and died on the stem.

"What?" Fred asked.

I shook my head and turned to Parker. "You're looking at this all wrong, Grimm. First, you should be grateful so many people find this stuff fascinating."

"Oh, should I?" Parker asked.

"Look," I said, motioning ahead. We hadn't even made it into the main event area yet, and already we were surrounded by people in costumes or cryptid t-shirts. "Some of these folks are just out to have a good time. Good for them. Others, though, they have at least some interest in the spookier side of life. They're intrigued when our world bleeds over into theirs. Fascinated by the things they don't understand."

"Your point?" Parker replied.

I sighed and stopped walking, turning again to face all of them. "If they knew what you were, you'd be a celebrity."

Parker crossed his arms. "But they can't find out."

"Exactly," I said. "That's what makes it fun. We're hiding in plain sight, among thousands of Normans. Normans who are celebrating our world."

"You really think it's going to be thousands?" Fred asked. "The town population sign only showed, like, five thousand people."

I shrugged. "Axel Googled it. Said the festival brings twelve to fifteen thousand."

"Damn," Anthony said, then nodded. "Definitely going to be some ladies, then. Have to be."

I rolled my eyes and started off again. "Come on. Let's try to have a good time."

We caught up with Axel and Alyita, both of whom had stopped.

They stood to the side of a massive line. It only took me a moment to realize what it was for. Down the street was a man-sized metal statue of a creature which, I could only assume, was Mothman. Hundreds of people were in line, waiting for their chance to take a selfie in front of the statue.

Axel wore a scowl on his face as we caught up.

"What's wrong?" I asked.

"I want a picture with the statue," he said, pouting.

"So, get in line," I said, motioning toward the waiting people.

"And waste precious time?" Axel said, putting his hands on his hips. "I think not. Say, do you think we would get in trouble if I, you know..."

"No," I said.

"Just a little..."

"No," I repeated.

"What's he hinting at?" Parker asked.

"Lightning," I replied. "Or something else."

"No one would ever know," Axel insisted. "I'll be super sneaky about it. Just something to clear the crowd out."

"Absolutely not," I said, glaring at him. "Don't even think about it. Archie will mute you permanently."

His eyes widened. I didn't think he'd considered that possibility.

"Fine, *Mom*," he said, rolling his eyes. "I want funnel cake. And tacos. And a t-shirt. Oh, and I want to do the museum. And there're supposed to be cryptid talks. Won't that be fun? What does everyone else want to do?"

"I want to get my picture with that," Alyita said, pointing down the street where a ginormous, life-sized, blown-up Stay Puff Marshmallow Man swayed in the breeze.

"Wrong sport," Axel said, scowling. "That's Ghostbusters. This is supposed to be about Macho Mothman."

"Tell that to the cosplayers," Alyita replied, motioning around.

She wasn't wrong.

There were people in all sorts of costumes. Many were in what I assumed were Mothman cosplays. Each looked a bit different. Some were in all black while others were more gray. Most had big red eyes. Made sense that they were different, though. It wasn't like there were any photos of the cryptid. For my part, I doubted Mothman was even real.

Sure, I'd thought the same thing about sasquatches before we'd met Scotty, but with Mothman it seemed like there was too much info out in the public. The Appalachian Argument would have shut it down if there really was a human-sized moth creature with big red eyes. That's what I would have expected the Cabal to do, at least. Sweep it all under a rug. There certainly wouldn't be any festivals. Maybe we could ask someone in the Argument about it when we made it to their compound.

There were loads of people clad in other cryptid costumes as well. Several Bigfoots were strolling about. I had a feeling they'd regret their costumes as soon as the late summer sun took hold. It'd be damned hot in all that fur.

But there were other cosplays, too. A few Jedi went strolling by, as well as a Deadpool. Someone else was dressed as the headless horseman. I wasn't sure how they could see. Must have had eye holes in the chest. That was the only thing that made sense.

One particularly creepy fella in a blue jacket glanced over at me. Noticing my eyes on him, he fixed me with a big ole grin. No idea what he was cosplaying. Not sure I wanted to know.

And there were witches and wizards, of course. More witches, naturally.

As a particularly attractive group of witches rolled by, Anthony all but salivated. It didn't help that the lead witch wore a sash which identified her as "The Bride." Doing his best Matthew McConaughey impression, Anthony said, "All right, all right, all right."

"For fuck's sake, Burns," I said, shaking my head. "Go chase some tail already. And take Fred with you. His mustache will make a magnificent wing-man."

Anthony glanced at Fred, seeming unsure. But eventually, he shrugged and set off.

I turned to Parker. "What about you?"

Parker sighed. "I'm just along for the ride."

"Great," I said, turning my focus on Barrett.

I didn't need to ask him. He didn't even make eye contact.

"Okay, then," I said, nodding at Axel. "Let's go find a funnel cake."

Axel found his funnel cake, all right.

We all did. Even Grumpy Grimmy, though he mostly just stared at his, terrified of getting powdered sugar on his fancy suit.

"And it's shaped like him," Axel said for the thousandth time. "So cool!"

"We know," both Alyita and I said at the same time.

Axel scowled.

It *was* pretty cool, to be fair. Our funnel cakes were shaped like Mothman. Everything at the festival seemed to be shaped like Mothman, or at least bore his likeness. Mothman-shaped cookies. Mothman-shaped pancakes. The works.

I glanced over at Parker, who looked miserable staring at his dessert. "Dude. You know you don't actually *have* to wear suits everywhere? Sometimes it's okay to wear normal clothes."

Parker's eyes came up to meet mine, gave me a once over, and then drifted over our group. What he saw were jeans and t-shirts. His gaze drifted back to his own suit.

"Wait..." Axel said, studying him. "Did you not realize you were dressed differently?"

"I choose to look the part," Parker said, tilting his nose up.

Uh oh. Being snooty was not an FDA-recommended method of dealing with Axel.

"The part of what?" Axel asked. "An uptight corporate clown? Look, Grimmy, just because you popped out of your momma wearing a two-piece doesn't mean you have to wear one out in the heat."

"I don't want to hear any mention of my mother ever come out of your mouth again."

"That's funny, because I sure came—"

"Axel!" Time for me to jump in. That's why I got paid the big bucks. "No."

"He started it." Axel huffed, but then something else caught the attention of his squirrel brain. "Oh, what's this?"

I followed his gaze and noticed a young man in a letterman jacket had sparked up a conversation with Alyita. He was a handsome lad, too. I wanted to hit him.

Surely that said something awful about me. He had done nothing wrong. He'd simply approached and started speaking to the teenager in my care. Certainly Alyita, formerly Pathkiller, did not need my protection. Still...

Apparently, I wasn't the only one who felt that way.

The young lad's swagger drained away when he looked up into the face of Barrett, who'd taken up a position just behind Alyita, arms crossed. Barrett had once played defensive tackle for the University of Oklahoma. The thing about defensive tackles was, they weren't small. But they *were* scary. They earned their job murdering quarterbacks.

Just then, that poor kid looked an awful lot like a high school quarterback. And Barrett looked like he should've continued his career into the NFL.

The kid froze, like a squirrel who's just realized he's within reach of a Rottweiler.

He decided he had other places to be.

Alyita turned, glaring up at the big man, unimpressed. "What the hell? We were just talking."

Barrett didn't flinch. Didn't turn away. Just held her glare.

"Yeah," I said, moving their direction. "So, that's going to be a rule, I think. No boys."

"Seriously?" she asked, fixing her glare on me. "What's wrong with talking to boys?"

"They're wild animals with bad intentions," I said, shrugging.

"So I can't even talk to them?" she asked.

"Not so long as I have to worry about your grandfather holding me responsible," I said.

She looked to Axel for help. He shrugged. "Look, as much as I hate taking Wyatt's side, I think he's right. I didn't like it either. Made me feel yucky."

"Yucky?" she replied, narrowing her eyes. "You guys are so immature. Grow up."

She turned, at last, to the one grown-up on the squad. But much to my surprise, Parker took our side. "Eh, they might be right, Alyita. Teenage boys only think about one thing."

Alyita glared at each of us. "You guys are *all* against me? Misogynist much?"

"Maybe." I shrugged again. "Call it what you want, but we're dudes. We remember what it was like being young dudes. And young dudes are...the worst. Look, the point is... I don't know what the point is. But I'm responsible for your safety, so unless you want to end up back under the watchful eye of the education board guy..."

"No boys." She rolled her eyes. "I know lots of teenage boys, guys."

"Eh, no you don't," Axel said, shrugging. "I mean, you think you do, but, and I'm putting this nicely: they're monsters. Every goddamned one of them."

"Just because you were immature and gross doesn't mean they *all* are."

"No," I said, scratching the back of my head. "It's like this: humans are... Eh, people are... Well, it's not just people. It's other things, too. Look, I'd lump every sentient being into three categories. The first are animals. Beasts who live by their baser nature. Like a suck-face who's just turned. They can't control their urge to feed. The second group are those who can refute their baser nature. Us humans, for example, and some other sentient species. Point is... Our ability to control our urges is what makes us unique. Special, even. It's our ability to determine right from wrong. Like a vampire who's learned to control their hunger and no longer feeds on people. Does that make sense?"

"Sure," she said, but the look on her face told me I was doing a poor job of explaining...whatever the hell it was I was explaining. "So, what's the third group, Professor?"

"Sentient beings, like us, who could control their animal urges but choose not to. Or those who understand right from wrong, but choose wrong anyway. The vampire who has other options, but chooses to feed on people."

"Okay, so where do teenage boys fit into this?" she asked, clearly still annoyed.

"Group one," I said.

She studied me. "Surely not all—"

"Group one," Axel repeated. "Just like Anthony and Fred."

She glanced at Parker, who shrugged. "Mostly group one. With a few exceptions. I'd like to think some fall into group two. Many fall into group three."

"Point is..." I said, trying to bring it home, "intelligent young ladies, such as yourself, are clearly developing members of group two. Therefore..."

"Therefore, I need a group of man-apes to protect me from dudes my own age?"

"Uh, yeah," I said, nodding slowly. "I think that's what I meant. Maybe."

She looked around at the others. Axel and Parker nodded along with me. Even Barrett gave a slight nod.

"And you don't think that's a little fucked up?" she asked, hands on her hip.

"Might be," I replied. "Might be very fucked up. Doesn't change our instincts to look out for you, though. So, get over it."

"Whatever," she said, rolling her eyes again.

"Hey, Wyatt," Axel said, changing the subject. "You should check out those witches."

"I've seen enough fake witches today," I replied. Mostly because after I'd just ranted about keeping Alyita from boys, the last thing I wanted to do was ogle a bunch of slutty costumed witches. That would have been weird. And hypocritical.

"I didn't say they were fake," Axel said. "And you *really* should have a look."

I turned, following his gaze. Sure enough, there was a group of witches. They were even dressed the part. Except...

"Wyatt?" one of the witches said, staring at me.

I sucked in a sharp breath, trying to find my voice. It was lost for the moment. Stuck somewhere in my throat. What wasn't lost was the irony of the rant I'd just given Alyita.

Finally, I managed to find my voice.

"Eilidh?"

12

We stared at each other, neither speaking.

Which made it weird for both my group and the witches surrounding her.

There were six of them, all dressed like witches. And why not? They could get away with it here.

My friends seemed rather amused. Well, Axel and Parker, anyway. Barrett didn't seem like anything. Alyita just seemed confused.

The witches, though, they *all* were amused.

"What are you doing here?" Eilidh said, taking a step toward me.

My breath hung in my throat again. It was her. It was *really* her.

I hadn't seen her since...

And she was still as beautiful as I remembered. Stunning, even. She had the hood of her cloak pulled up over her head, but the various shades she'd dyed her hair poked through. She had the fox charm necklace around her neck, too. Just how I remembered her.

"I, uh..."

"What's this?" the witch beside Eilidh asked. She was older, and had an enormous nose and a sharp chin line. Like she was made for being a witch. "Is this one of our hillbilly cousins?"

"He's from the Ozark Mountain Cabal," Eilidh said, not taking her eyes off mine.

"Ah, so one of our *other* hillbilly cousins," the big-nosed witch tittered. "Come along, dear. Better to not cavort with those beneath our station."

"Beneath your station?" I heard myself say. The insult reeled me back to my senses. "I can only assume you're here for the same reason we are. To join the Argument's conference?"

"But of course," the witch said, her enormous nose pointed skyward. "But that doesn't mean we should sully ourselves by loitering among mouth-breathers."

"Mouth..." I repeated back. "Who the fu—"

"Come, dear," the witch repeated, ignoring me. "Perhaps we can find someone worth conversing with. Not likely in this hole, but surely we can do better than this."

With that, the snooty witch turned away, the others cackling along after her.

Eilidh held her ground for just a moment, eyes still locked with me. It looked like she might have something to say, but in the end, she broke eye contact and followed the others.

I stared after her, watching her leave, heart pounding in my chest.

"Well, that was... Uh..." Parker said, but didn't finish.

"Hilarious?" Axel offered while chomping on his funnel cake.

"Sure," Parker said. "That's what I was going to say. Hilarious."

I was too shell-shocked to respond.

Eilidh.

She was here.

She would be at the conference.

This entire trip... She would be around.

"What the hell?" Alyita said, voice dripping with scorn.

I turned slowly to face her and found she had both hands on her hips.

"What was all of that?"

I didn't have an answer. Couldn't think of anything to say.

Fortunately, that was never a problem for Axel. "That was Wyatt's last lady friend. This should make things interesting."

"Oh, great," Alyita said, rolling her eyes. "So, I'm not allowed to talk to boys, but Wyatt can talk to his lady friend?"

"Clearly not," Parker said. "It would seem they're too good for the likes of us."

I watched Eilidh disappear into the crowd, hoping she might look back. She didn't.

I turned to the others. "Come on. Let's go check out more of the festival."

* * *

"Well, that's peculiar," I said, motioning toward the base of the statue.

The line was still too long in front of the statue, but Axel was happy to go behind and take a picture with Mothman's butt. He knelt so his face would be in line with the statue's buttocks and gave a big thumbs up. Alyita snapped the picture.

That wasn't what I found peculiar. It was what I noticed around the base of the statue. Beans and Sprite. Lots of both. As I watched, the next person in line moved up to the statue to take their pic. Only first, they set down a can of pork 'n' beans and a bottle of Sprite.

"What the hell?" I said to no one in particular.

Which was convenient, because a no one in particular answered.

A random dude wearing combat boots, camo pants, and an ill-fitting Mothman t-shirt offered a reply. He had long hair, mutton chops, thick-rimmed glasses, and wore a fedora. I was pretty sure he was fresh off of Bigfoot's trail.

"An offering," he said.

"An offering," I repeated. "Like..."

"Like an offering," the guy repeated, shrugging. "Not sure why. Lots of people bring beans and Sprite."

"That's...something," I said.

"Personally, I believe the Mothman would prefer flesh," he said, giving me a serious look. "Human flesh most likely, but I'm sure he's eaten plenty of deer when he can't find a person to pluck away."

"Uh huh," I replied, unsure what else to say.

"He has also been known to eat dogs," the man assured me. "A creature like that, though, you can be sure lives off wild game, mostly. Too risky eating people. It's kept itself hidden for a long time."

"Or it never existed," another man said. I glanced over and saw this was an older dude. He had the look of a guy who wasn't comfortable in his summer clothes. Like he would have preferred a suit and tie. Probably how Parker would've looked if he tried to dress casually. I pegged him for a doctor, or a lawyer, or maybe even a professor. "I'll never understand people's fascination with urban legends."

"And yet you're here," Cryptid Bro replied, giving the older man a condescending look.

"Amusing my grandchildren," the older dude, who I decided to refer to as Professor Nope, said. "They thought it would be fun."

"It *is* fun," Cryptid Bro said. "And educational."

"Hardly," Professor Nope said with a sneer. "What are you? Some kind of cryptid chaser?"

"I'm a researcher. And I'll have you know, witness accounts concerning Mothman are among the best documented of any cryptid."

"Nonsense. Just because a few people back in the sixties reported seeing the creature doesn't make it real."

As the argument heated up, Axel, Alyita, and Parker moved in closer. I guessed they were just as intrigued as I was. It was, I hoped, to be a battle for the ages. Also, it helped get my mind off...other things.

Cryptid Bro was ready to sling facts. "There were three unrelated accounts within a short time span, all before it was made public. Multiple eyewitnesses during two of those accounts. So, unless you believe all those people got together and planned the whole thing, then you must admit something strange was going on."

Professor Nope returned fire, slinging a festive eye-roll. "Of course there was something strange going on. We know what it was: a bird off of its migratory pattern. A full-grown, six-foot tall sandhill crane. Something folks in West Virginia wouldn't have seen often. That was before the internet."

"Come on, man," Cryptid Bro said, hands on his hips and that condescending smile plastered on his ruddy cheeks. "You can't really think a crane would have scared folks like that. That all of them would've mistaken it?"

"Have you seen a sandhill crane? If not for television and the internet, if you ran into something like that, you'd probably think it was a monster, too."

Axel couldn't help himself. He had to jump in. "Cranes don't have glowing red eyes, though."

Professor Nope rolled his own eyes again. If he kept that up, they'd end up facing the back of his skull and he'd be blind. "That's hardly proof of anything."

Axel shrugged. "You have to admit, though, it was weird that the gravediggers, the kids on the road, and the dude at his house all said the creature had glowing red eyes."

"The sandhill crane has a red patch on its head, around the eyes." Professor Nope said. "So, it was most likely light refraction, which made them think it was glowing eyes."

"Light refraction?" Cryptid Bro said before firing more missiles.

I ignored the argument for a moment to glance over at Axel. "You read up on Mothman?"

"Of course," he said. "Didn't you?"

"Uh, no." I shrugged. "Didn't occur to me. Also, you know how I am with phones."

"Right," he said. "I'm basically an expert on the subject, so if you have any questions..."

"I don't." I returned my attention to the debate.

Cryptid Bro was mid-rant. "All those eyewitnesses at the bridge—they all saw the same thing. A winged, man-like creature soaring around, just before the bridge fell."

"That doesn't mean anything," Professor Nope said. "It was a terrible tragedy, no doubt. It's human nature to turn to the extraordinary during such times. I suppose you're one of those who believe your Mothman tore down the bridge? A bit of wickedness, rather than failed engineering?"

"I wouldn't presume the creature's intent," Cryptid Bro replied. "But many believe he appeared as an omen. That he appears when bad things are at hand. Others suspect he intended to save those people, arriving too late."

"Of course," Professor Nope said, shaking his head. Guess he was tired of rolling his eyes.

"You must admit," Cryptid Bro said with a tone that indicated he thought he really had something. "It's very strange how reports of Mothman dropped off after the bridge incident."

"No, it isn't strange, you dolt," Professor Nope said. "A horrible tragedy occurred. Only the most unscrupulous sort would continue making up stories about him after that. Look, there's just no evidence to support Mothman, or Bigfoot, or the Loch Ness Monster. They are children's tales. Next thing you're going to tell me is Harry Potter is real and there are wizards running amuck, living in secret societies, casting spells at one another."

Well... That one struck a little close to home.

My group and I all shared a look.

Also, the debate was drawing a crowd. We didn't like crowds.

Ironically, in most public spaces, Professor Nope would have easily had the mob on his side. But this was Mothman Festival, and he found no allies. Cryptid Bro was the one fighting the good fight, at least as far as the attendees were concerned.

I motioned to the others and we moved on.

We wandered through the museum next, then found our way to the local retirement home, where guest speakers were regaling folks with tales of the supernatural. I wasn't sure I wanted to spend my afternoon listening to conspiracy theories about the world I lived in, but...they had air conditioning.

As the day dragged on, the heat in Point Pleasant wasn't any more friendly than it was back home. So, if that meant hanging out in a retirement home listening to dudes like Cryptid Bro talking about chasing Bigfoot, or some of the locals retelling their accounts of Mothman, it was worth it.

There was a twisted part of me that wished we could've brought along Scotty the Sasquatch. I bet people would've been stoked at how good his "costume" was. They'd have wanted to take pictures with him. Guess I always had a soft spot for irony.

I tried to pay attention.

But my mind kept drifting elsewhere.

Eilidh was there, somewhere at the festival.

I thought about her often. Sure, after the incident in Memphis, we'd only shared a single weekend together, but it had been a damned good weekend.

And now...she was somewhere nearby.

Had she been happy to see me?

I couldn't say. She'd just sort of stared at me, at least as surprised as I was. But was she happy to see me? That part wasn't clear.

She certainly hadn't stuck around to chat. But then, her big-nosed witch sister had insisted they move on. Back when we'd first met, she'd also been along with some of her fellow witches from the Colonial Coven. They'd bossed her around. Maybe this was the same.

I could but hope.

But why hope? What was the point of that hope?

We might as well have been from different worlds. There was little use pining for her. Eilidh's place was back east, mine in the Midwest.

Still... We had been friends, if nothing else. She was someone I trusted.

At least...she was someone I *had* trusted.

Now, though?

I sighed and tried to pay attention to the UFO talk.

13

I couldn't take it anymore.

I couldn't handle another moment of supposed experts lecturing about the supernatural world.

Yeah, that was what it was. Definitely wasn't anything else.

That was why I braved the heat and wandered off on my own.

Because I didn't want to listen to any more sessions.

It had nothing to do with Axel sharing personal details about... Well, whatever it was I'd had with Eilidh.

Each time a lecturer finished, as soon as the applause died down, he'd jump back into it. Explaining to Alyita, Parker, and Barrett how I'd completely swooned over her and was a big ole idiot anytime she was around. Usually, his attention span was short-lived. But for some reason, each time a speaker finished, he'd pick up right where he'd left off. It didn't help that Alyita had lots of questions. She had a lot of sympathy, too. I didn't want her pity any more than I desired Parker's amused looks. Just then, Barrett was my favorite. I wasn't sure he was even listening.

Everything Axel said was true, in his own little twisted mind. Per usual, he did not paint me in a particularly good light, though he seemed to think he did.

So, I left.

I wasn't worried about leaving Alyita with the others. I knew Axel would watch out for her. And if he did anything stupid, I knew Parker would watch out for him. I was reasonably confident Barrett would watch out for everyone. Especially Alyita.

So, I bailed on the retirement center and walked around on my own for a while.

There was lots to see. Plenty of vendors to peruse and costumes to gawk at. I saw a killer Batman cosplay, which was second only to a really solid Darth Maul.

A part of me hoped to see Eilidh again, but the wiser part of me knew it would go like before. We weren't likely to get a chance to speak. Not with her homie witches around.

That was an accurate assessment. I did see her again. Twice. And twice, she ignored me, not even looking my direction.

I also spotted Anthony and Fred. They were hanging out with a bachelorette party, though not the same one as before. They'd found another. Who'd have known that doing your bachelorette party at a cryptid festival was a thing?

There were other members of the Cabal around as well, of course. So far as I knew, pretty much the whole caravan was supposed to come to the festival. I didn't spot Archie or any of the masters, though. Maybe they were still hanging out with Supreme Enchanter Tate. He seemed like a decent guy. Way more laid back than Archmagus Melacon of the Southern Circle. Maybe it had to do with not having an arch-staff. Then again, Archie seemed laid back at times, too. Other times... Not so much.

As the sun gave way to nightfall, I grabbed another Mothman funnel cake and made my way down by the river. The Ohio River, that is. Point Pleasant sat alongside its banks. The town had a beautiful set of stones steps that led to the river's edge, not far from the Mothman Museum. During normal times, I reckoned it was just for people to sit beside. A way to get near the water's edge. During the festival, though, they'd used barges to build a stage out on the water, where live musicians were putting on a show. An amphitheater, with the stone steps serving as seats. A pretty rad setup.

Umm... Did people still say rad? Whatever. I'd long ago given up any hopes of being cool. Brooding wizard, I could pull off. I'd be even better at it if I grew a long wispy beard.

Anyway, I figured we still had a few hours to burn.

I thought about using mind-speak to let the others know where I was, but figured Axel would have guessed. Where there was live music, there was often a Wyatt to be found.

There was a steady flow of traffic to and from the amphitheater, but not like on the street. That was a boon. Since they'd put the amphitheater on the river, it required moving away from the bulk of the festival. *Darn.*

I had a pleasant stroll, appreciating the thinning crowd.

There were plenty of people around the stage, but there were a few free steps.

Being a grown-ass man, and wandering alone, typically no one appreciated you sitting by them. So, it was a bonus when I found a few vacant seats to occupy. The first band was rocking some bluegrass tunes. I dug it.

The temperature was slowly dropping, and I had good tunes, beautiful scenery, and a greasy cake covered in powdered sugar. Not bad.

I sat through several bands, impressed by each. I'd never heard any of them before, but they were all good. Local groups, most playing for tips. They had talent. And style. I was lost in it for a time.

Then I felt the itch.

Like someone was watching me.

My sword, ever present on my back, let off a little tingle.

A warning.

Someone *was* watching me.

I glanced at those around me. A few families on vacation. A couple of harmless cryptid chasers. A few folks in cosplay. As a rule, I figured folks in cosplay were harmless. It wasn't like Darth Maul was going to whip out a double-bladed light saber and fry my guts like Qui Gon. What? Too soon?

Casually, I let my gaze travel out a little further, taking in the crowd. Everyone seemed focused on the music, or focused on their companions. No one in front of me was turned around, eyeballing me. That would have been too obvious.

I might have passed it off as garden variety paranoia, if not for Dyrnwyn's warning. The sword had never let me down before.

That meant the itchy feeling on the back of my neck was likely coming from behind me.

I turned casually, as though stretching. Nothing stood out, but for some reason, I felt my eyes drawn back toward town. Toward the taller of the buildings. I couldn't see atop them through the dark. Yet...

I felt my eyes drawn to one in particular. An old brick building, just behind us. I stared up at the tall roof, wondering what darkness might be loitering up there.

I saw nothing.

Still acting as though I were stretching, I turned slowly around and...

There.

A concrete path down to the river's edge, away from the park. I wasn't sure how far it went, and I could only see a short distance because there was a retaining wall blocking my view. Inconvenient for me just then, but probably pretty handy when the river flooded.

Anyway...

I caught a glimpse of a familiar face.

Or at least I thought I did.

Just for a moment.

But it still remained on my peripherals. And I could feel their eyes on me. Which made me think my focus on the rooftop was a false flag. A red herring. The real source of the itch stood by the water's edge, watching me.

I considered how to look without making it obvious I was looking. I'd already done the stretching routine.

Oh, to hell with it.

I turned.

There she was.

Sophie.

My former teammate. Or someone who looked an awful lot like her.

I couldn't say for sure, because she stood some distance away, just at the edge of the park's light. But...

She was staring right at me.

I blinked. Yup. Still there.

She turned then, disappearing into the darkness.

I slid my hand into my pocket, touched my wand, and used mind-speak. *"Axel. Water's edge, near the amphitheater. I'm about to head down the trail leading south. Find me. Hurry. Trouble."*

He tried to reply, but I ignored him.

I rose from my seat. I'd have to hurry if I didn't want her to get away.

14

I am not a clever man.

That's what crossed my mind as I eased through the crowd. More than likely, that same mind was playing tricks on me. All I would end up doing was following a stranger in the dark. And a woman, at that. Probably wouldn't go over well.

Also, if it was Sophie, then following her alone was stupid.

Not that I couldn't handle Sophie. The last time I'd seen her, she was trying to kill me. That was after she'd been bumping uglies with a pretend loa. She'd certainly upgraded her tool chest, at least where her attack spells were concerned. Back in the day, she'd never engaged in violence. She'd always been our intel. Still, even with a few attack spells, I felt confident I could handle her.

It was who else might be with her that concerned me.

I didn't know whether Gabby had survived the cottonmouth kiss. Wouldn't have surprised me. She was one tough cookie, and had become a very mean b-word. I didn't relish facing her.

And there were the other members of my former team.

Not to mention all the other nasty shit Sophie had aligned with.

So, if that was really Sophie, following her into the dark and away from civilian eyes was stupid. Really stupid.

I eased my way through the crowd, determined to follow her anyway.

I smiled at people as I passed, being polite and trying not to bump them with my invisible sword. That was one benefit of not having my staff anymore. Made it easier to move through a crowd.

I excused myself past Darth Maul, offering him a friendly smile, which he did not return. Didn't bother me. No reason for him to break character.

Stepping around him, I went to excuse myself past the next person, and...

Eilidh.

I'd been so focused on the direction the Sophie mirage had gone, I hadn't been paying attention to the people right around me. I mean, I'd realized there was a gaggle of witches, but I hadn't realized they were Eilidh's witches. I'd assumed they were just cosplayers. Not witches cosplaying witches.

Eilidh's eyes widened, just as I'm sure my own did.

"Wyatt," she said.

"Eilidh," I replied.

Well, this was awkward.

"Excuse me," I said, trying to keep my focus on the task at hand. "Just, uh, trying to get past... Sorry to, uh, bother you."

"Oh," she said, stepping aside. "It's no problem. You, uh, seem..."

"Huh?" I said, pausing.

"Is something wrong?" she asked, narrowing her eyes.

Before I could answer, her big-nosed friend noticed me. "Oh, it's that man-boy again, the one who struggles to speak. My, isn't he adorable? Oh, and he seems to have a fascination with Eilidh. How cute."

Ignoring the insults, I glanced back at Eilidh and gave her a nod. Then I stepped past, hurrying to make up lost time. Sophie's mirage had disappeared.

At least it gave me an excuse to get away from that awkward situation. And to try not to think about it. Eilidh had occupied too many of my thoughts that day. I needed this distraction, even if it was just a false alarm.

But Dyrnwyn had barked at me, hadn't it?

There was, I had to admit, a genuine possibility I'd totally missed what the sword had tried to tell me. My silly mind could have simply overlaid an image of Sophie over someone who looked somewhat similar. After all, what the hell would she have been doing there? If that was the case, then I might have been walking away from whatever Dyrnwyn had wanted me to see.

As I moved away from the crowd, I mumbled, "All right, sword, am I headed in the right direction?"

It pulsed.

Okay, so maybe Dyrnwyn thought it saw Sophie, too.

Ahead on the path, there were a few stragglers about. Not many, though, as the trail led further from the festival.

It was a beautiful spot. The glow of the little town over the Ohio River. The dull roar of the festival and the fading bluegrass. The nice little walking path.

Ahead, I saw no sign of Sophie.

I used mind-speak to give Axel an update. They were headed in my direction, but he couldn't tell me how far away they were. I cut the connection and kept scanning. I was going to feel like an ass when my team showed up for my wild goose chase and I had no goose to show them.

Ahead, the path wrapped around and joined another walking path. I paused at the intersection, looking both ways. There were still a few people milling about. Nearby, one person was dressed in a Fallout vault suit and a gas mask. Their friend was dressed as a New California Republic Ranger. Yeah, I knew a few video game things. I mean, my stupid wizard magic made short work of every console I'd ever owned, but Axel was pretty good at warding them to nullify my sad mishaps. I'd been slowly catching up on years of missing out.

I nearly complimented the two, but instead offered a nod and followed the trail leading further away from the festival. The way I figured it, if that was Sophie, she probably wouldn't have headed back toward the crowd to lose me. Well, actually, she might have. But if she did, the chances of finding her were null. If she'd gone the other way, then I'd have at least a chance.

Starting forward, I kept my eyes scanning. The retaining wall was on one side, a patch of trees on the other. It wasn't a great place to plan an ambush, which gave me hope this wasn't all some elaborate trap.

A little further on and I spotted another silver statue, not unlike the Mothman statue. Only this one didn't feature the visage of a monster. Instead, it was a woman. Her kit was fresh out of the 1700s: a wool coat and a wide-brimmed hat. She also held a musket. At the base of the statue were the words, "Mad Anne Bailey."

Who the hell was Mad Anne Bailey?

I didn't have time to wonder because, as I stood staring at the statue like a moron, Dyrnwyn vibrated again, this time much more violently. I knew that setting and it wasn't for pleasure.

I dove to the side as a pink blur shot right over my head.

Hoping it hadn't hit the beautiful statue, I rolled to my feet, reached for my wand, and summoned Dyrnwyn to my hand.

Darth Maul stood back down the trail, holding up a wand.

And that really pissed me off.

Not because I'd been ambushed. I was used to that. It was because the asshole was wielding a wand instead of a double-bladed lightsaber. Jerk could've at least had a staff. If Axel had been there, he'd have been outraged.

The two Fallout cosplayers also stepped from the shadows, wielding wands.

Uh oh.

I glanced back in the other direction and saw a Batman coming toward me with a Ninja Turtle on his heel. It was Michelangelo. That also felt really wrong.

Great. I was about to be killed by my favorite things.

Also, and again...

I am not a clever man.

15

"You were supposed to wait," a familiar voice said.

Two more figures appeared from the shadows. Actually, several more assholes appeared, approaching from either direction. But it was those two particular assholes who held my attention.

Sophie was one.

Yup. Hadn't just imagined her.

But Sophie wasn't the one who'd spoken.

That voice belonged to my old pal Gabby.

Her face was hidden beneath a hood, but there was no mistaking her voice.

Just as I'd feared. She was still alive. Lucky me. Surely she wouldn't bear me any grudge. Right?

The Darth Maul cosplayer fidgeted for a moment, then summoned some confidence. "I had a clean shot."

"Did you?" Gabby replied, hood tilting in my direction. I clearly stood unharmed.

Cosplay Maul went ahead and fidgeted some more.

"Hi, Gabby," I said, offering my most friendly smile. Then I nodded at Sophie. "Sophie. Nice to see you both again. Listen, you might cut buddy boy some slack. He obviously isn't too bright. Dressed up as

Darth Maul wielding a wand? No staff? Lame. Besides, you know I'm very elusive."

"That's why he was supposed to wait," Gabby said, stomping toward the guy. "Tanya was supposed to take the shot."

"Tanya?" I replied, surprised by the mention of my ex. Apparently it was a day for awkward Blade Mage love life encounters. Boo for that. "Tanya is here, too?"

Gabby didn't reply. She was busy.

She made a casual flick with her wand and Cosplay Maul's arm jerked upward and straight out, seemingly of its own volition. If the move surprised me, he was even more stunned. He stood there, staring at his rogue arm and the wand held uselessly in his possessed hand. Which was why he didn't notice when an even bigger surprise came.

Gabby rammed a knife into his throat. Not a little knife, either. A big ole Rambo knife.

He gasped, gurgled, and fell to the ground, clutching at the handle.

I thought about telling him he should just relax. Nothing else to do. It'd be over soon enough.

Instead, I focused on my old buddy Gabriella. "Obi Wan did it better. He cut him in half."

She ignored me and knelt for her knife, ripping it clear, along with a bunch of important throat junk. It was brutal, but also an act of mercy. It let the poor guy get to dying more quickly.

Finally, she rose and turned to face me. Slowly, she pulled back her hood, which was pretty anticlimactic in the dark. She was polite enough to raise her wand up by her face and flip on the flashlight mode, like a kid telling scary stories around a campfire. Gabby didn't need to tell any stories. Her face was scary enough.

"Eek," I said, cringing despite myself.

Her face was... Uh... How do I put it?

Fugly.

FUBAR.

A fucking mess.

The snake bite had done more than a little damage. She was damned lucky to be alive. Damned lucky.

Which made me unlucky, since I was the one who'd thrown the big ole biter at her.

In fairness, she had totally deserved it.

Well, actually... I wasn't sure anyone deserved that. One half of her face was puffy and scarred, like the skin had melted away. It hadn't grown back right. She kind of looked like Two-Face, but without the fun colors. Still, she had missed an opportunity to dress up. Would've paired nicely with the Batman cosplayer goon. Part of her hair was missing, too, like it had just dripped from her scalp.

"So, uh," I said, trying not to stare. "How'd you know I'd be here?"

"Who said we did?" she replied.

That was...something. I mean, they'd gone to all this trouble to set up the trap. Sure seemed planned.

"As you have no doubt guessed, Tanya has you in her crosshairs. I wouldn't make any sudden moves."

"Yeah, I haven't forgotten." I glanced over at the two Fallout cosplayers. "Hot tip. Never date a sniper. Especially a sorceress sniper. They can take out their anger from further than you can see. Guessing she has something particularly nasty planned for me."

"Count on it," Gabby said.

"Kind of surprised she hasn't blasted me already," I said, glancing toward the taller buildings a few blocks over. Maybe my sense that someone was watching me from the rooftop wasn't so off base after all.

Gabby nudged Dead Maul with her boot. "If this idiot had waited another second or two, I'm sure she would have. Her plan was to take the shot when you were looking at the statue. She knew you couldn't resist something shiny."

"That is...totally fair, actually." I shrugged. "Do you know who she is? Mad Anne Bailey, I mean? Never heard of her. Cool statue, though."

Ignoring my comment, Gabby said, "I'm also kind of surprised she hasn't killed you yet."

"Maybe she wanted to give us time to catch up? Tanya was always very thoughtful and considerate."

"Really?" Gabby asked with a chuckle. "That's what you remember?"

"No. I remember her being a back-stabbing bitch, mostly. Still surprised she hasn't taken a shot. Unless, perhaps, she wants to take me alive?" I let a little hope slither into my voice at that last part.

"We're not taking you alive," Gabby assured me. Then she glanced over at Sophie. "Reach out to Tanya and see what the holdup is. I'm running out of patience, and I'd really like to kill Wyatt myself."

I guessed she was concerned I would pull a stunt, so she wanted to keep her attention on me. That was fair because I would have totally pulled something... If I had thought of anything worth trying.

Sophie closed her eyes, brow furrowing in concentration. Mindspeak. But Sophie had known Tanya for a long-ass time. They would've had a solid connection. Which meant Tanya was a good distance away. Almost certainly on one of those rooftops.

Sophie's eyes popped open, a look of concern on her face. "She isn't answering."

Gabby scowled and shrugged out of her cloak. Beneath it, she wore combat gear. She'd said they weren't there for me, but clearly she'd come dressed to party.

To the others, she said, "Here's the deal. Wyatt is mine. I've kicked his ass a thousand times, but he's a slippery little prick. He sucks at dying."

"Aw, you say the sweetest things," I replied.

She ignored me. "He can't leave here alive. So, if he somehow gets the best of me, hit him with everything you've got. Don't hold back. Don't get cocky. I'm telling you, he's like a cockroach. Just won't die and he fucks up everything."

"Hmm." I nodded. "Might put that on my business cards. Also, funny that you mention how I fuck everything up."

I hurled Dyrnerang and dove behind the statue.

If Tanya had had me in her sights, I would've been toast. Clearly, she hadn't. Instead, I just had a loaf of cosplaying sorcerers to worry about. How many? Too damned many!

I ran for it.

Past the statue, through the grass, and toward a nearby copse of trees. My father's wand was in my hand and I cranked my shield up to eleven. I couldn't pause to assess what carnage Dyrnerang had caused, but judging by the screams, shouts, and shortage of attack spells, it had certainly gotten their attention. I summoned it back to my other hand.

"Don't let him escape!" Gabby ordered, which was a bummer because it meant Dyrnwyn hadn't taken her out.

Don't get me wrong, I would have loved to sit down with her to figure out why the hell she'd turned to the dark side. That wasn't going to happen, though. Every time I saw her, she was just all, kill, kill, kill. Blah, blah, blah. Exterminate, exterminate, exterminate. Maybe she should have been a Dalek.

It sucked, though, because I really wanted to know. We'd been friends once. Or...

Maybe we'd never been close, actually.

Maybe I had just thought so. I had certainly looked up to her.

The last time we'd duked it out, she'd been well-prepared for my sword-chucking ways. I'd kind of hoped my new Dyrnerang upgrade would have caught her off guard. I wasn't out of surprises, though. I hadn't had my father's wand last time, either. That gave me hope.

The number of goons she had... Eh, not so much.

A rainbow of spells whizzed past my head, hammered my shield, and scorched the earth around me.

I glanced back. Couldn't help myself, just to make sure they hadn't wrecked the statue when I'd dived behind it. I still didn't know who Mad Anne Bailey was, but I didn't want to see her damaged. I would've felt bad.

Plus, it might have made her mad.

Get it? Mad?

Right. No time for jokes.

It didn't seem like the statue had been harmed. My shield, on the other hand, was getting rocked and rolled. With my old staff, it would've been toast already. With my father's wand, it held long enough for me to hit the tree-line. Then I dove for cover, and prepared to bolt again if I needed. Last time, Gabby and her friends had tried to drop a forest on my head.

Catching my breath, I considered what a risky game they were playing. There were Normans just a brick's throw away. If any of them saw us, they would think they were missing out on the most epic LARP of all time. But if I could somehow slip away from these clowns and make it back to the festival, I might disappear into the crowd. Surely they'd be less inclined to hurl magic at me with so many people around.

Which reminded me of another problem.

Using mind-speak, I called out to Axel. *"Abort! Abort! Don't come over here! I'm surrounded! Way too damned many!"*

"Uh, that's going to be a problem."

"Why?"

From somewhere back the way I'd come, I heard Axel's voice. "Dragon kick!"

Damn!

It was no wonder my pursuers weren't pursuing. They'd been attacked.

"Uh, we need help," Axel's voice said into my mind. *"We're surrounded! Way too damned many!"*

Double donkey damn!

I ran out from behind my tree of protection and raced back toward pain and an early grave.

Axel was on the ground wrestling with the two Fallout cosplayers.

Parker was trading spells with five enemy wizards.

There was no sign of Alyita. That was a relief.

But Barrett...

Donkey dunking dragon damn!

The big dude had his eyes on Gabby. She seemed every bit as surprised to see him as he was to see her. If she hadn't known Barrett was with me, then maybe she'd been telling the truth. Maybe they hadn't come here for me...

It didn't matter.

I could figure that out later. *If* we survived.

It was time to fight.

16

Barrett charged at Gabby like a freight train.

A magically enhanced freight train.

I still didn't know what sort of shape his lungs were in. If it was a problem, he wasn't acting like it. I didn't know much about the spell, but blueish waves of energy trailed behind him as he ran. He held his wand like he was a holding a football.

Gabby stared at him, dumbfounded, not realizing she was about to be flattened.

Barrett barreled into her and...

Gabby shimmered and disappeared.

A fake.

An illusion.

The real Gabby appeared behind him, raising her Rambo knife.

Barrett had already been stabbed in the back by one of our former teammates. Last time, it had been Zeke. Guess Gabby didn't want to be left out.

The big guy turned, though, swinging his wand like a baseball bat. Interestingly enough, a blueish bat appeared at the end. It barely missed Gabby's nose, and she staggered back a few steps.

Then I had my own problems to worry about.

Sophie, who'd been standing off to the side being useless, turned her attention my way. That wasn't an immediate concern. The fact she ordered the rest of the goon squad to attack me was. I was the belle of the ball, after all. Didn't I feel special?

An asshole wearing a Scream mask pointed his staff at me like Babe Ruth announcing a homer. Guess he wanted to show me his was bigger. But it's not all about the size. My little wand could pack a punch.

I hit him with the ole double pumpkin trick.

It worked. Poor schmuck ended up on his bum and hopefully re-thinking his life choices.

And then even more of them turned their focus on me.

I threw Dyrnerang just to keep them on the defensive. As I'd feared, any jerks who were rolling with Gabby knew to watch out for flying swords.

Then something horrible happened.

I'd just thrown my sword when another of them leaped out at me from the shadows. I hadn't seen or heard him. I just caught movement from my peripherals and noticed a sword coming from my face.

Not fair! That was my game!

I aimed my wand center mass and summoned a pumpkin blast.

His wand was in his other hand, and he easily deflected, still coming on.

I staggered back, narrowly avoiding a chop to the face. It was some kind of modernized, broad-bladed machete. Not like the cheap kind found at the local sporting goods store for whacking bushes. This thing was meant for killing people. And I was people.

Summoning Dyrnwyn back to my hand, I parried the next attack and finally caught a look at my attacker.

That... That was the worst part.

The bastard was cosplaying Blade.

Trench coat. Sunglasses. All of it.

As he kept on coming, the other mages circled around me. Five of them, at least. Could've been more. By that point, the shadows were breeding sorcerers.

Sure enough, another leaped out at me, this one swinging a chain. Who brought a chain to a magic fight?

I dodged to the side and came up, defending magical attacks with my shield while cosplayer Blade charged me with his sword again.

Come on, Dyrnwyn, I thought. *Do the thing where you make his sword go away.*

Ask and you shall receive.

His next attack came down and Dyrnwyn cut his stupid machete sword right in half.

I dodged another chain strike and threw Dyrnerang at the Blade wannabe. It took him right through the chest.

That's right.

I killed cosplay Blade, just the way Blade would have. I was sure Wesley Snipes would approve.

I felt pretty good about myself until a nasty spell rocked my shield from behind. I didn't even see what it was, but the impact caused me to tumble forward, face-planting. I rolled to my hip just in time to see the chap with the chain raising it once more.

That was going to hurt...

Except his body jerked sharply and he stood upright, on his tippy toes. Of note, there was a shard of ice sticking through the front of his throat. I was pretty sure I hadn't put that there.

He fell as limp as his chain.

And there was Eilidh, in all her witchy glory. She had summoned her ice-scythe, a blade made of ice protruding from the end of her staff. Blood dripped from its melting end.

She spun and flung the ice blade off, hurling it toward the next of my attackers.

I rolled to my side and raised my wand. That was definitely a benefit of having a shorter casting device. Using my staff from the ground had always been awkward.

I hurled pumpkins while Eilidh cast ice shards.

We were outnumbered, but our attackers backed off anyway.

I took a moment to assess the battlefield.

Looking Parker's way, I saw him summon some kind of radial blast that knocked back the mages surrounding him. Even their shields didn't stave off his attack. I hated to admit it, but Parker Grimm was a badass. He wasn't in need of immediate help.

Axel, though... Last I'd seen, he'd been rolling around with two of the baddies. Now he had four, but somehow wasn't dead, which really said a lot about what a pain in the ass he could be.

Two more jerks were headed his way, but they were our jerks. Anthony and Fred. I realized Parker must have called for them. More proof he was cut out to be a leader. It hadn't even occurred to me that two more members of my team were out there to be called upon.

To their credit, Anthony and Fred raced right in to help Axel.

There was only one problem.

Axel didn't see them coming. He probably assumed they were more bad guys. Somehow, he'd gotten a hand on one of his drumsticks. Axel being Axel—and surrounded by assholes—did what any reasonable Axel would have done. He summoned a lightning bolt right on top of himself.

Everyone in the immediate vicinity was knocked from their feet and set to thrashing. That included Anthony and Fred, as well as Axel himself.

I turned my attention to Barrett.

He was doubled-over, gasping for breath.

Shit. His damaged lung!

Gabby stalked toward him, wand raised.

I charged, knowing I couldn't cover the gap in time.

Someone else got there before me.

It was Alyita's turn to slip from the shadows. She raced toward Gabby, tomahawk in one hand and her wand in the other. She was sneaky, too. I certainly wouldn't have known she was coming. But sneaky was Gabby's game. That had been her role back in the day. Our infiltrator.

Gabby spun, firing a spell at Alyita.

Alyita dropped into a slide and came up swinging.

Gabby back-stepped, easily avoiding the attack. She still had her knife in one hand and her wand in the other.

Shit.

Alyita was pretty nasty with that tomahawk. Something I knew well. But she was playing to Gabby's strength, and my former teammate had years more experience.

They moved in a blur, only coming to a stop when Gabby backhanded Alyita across the face. Focused on the weapons, Alyita hadn't expected a backhand. She reeled backward. Gabby moved in for the kill.

And then I was there.

I hurled a series of pumpkin blasts at Gabby, forcing her on the retreat. She was grinning, having found the target she really wanted.

Eilidh covered my rear, staving off the other assholes who'd found their courage again.

Gabby rolled to the side and came up firing green blobs of some kind. Each drilled my shield, threatening to snap it. I replied with more pumpkin blasts. To that point, I didn't have much of a strategy. It had been all about getting her away from Alyita.

Strangely, it turned out her strategy was the same.

Behind me, Eilidh said, "Wyatt!"

I risked a glance over my shoulder and saw Sophie had a hold of Alyita. One hand was wrapped around the young woman's hair. Her other held a wand to Alyita's throat. She was backing away, dragging her. Several of the goons followed.

"Who's the little lady?" Gabby asked, sneering. "Someone you care about?"

I growled and charged toward her. She might have been better at close-range fighting, but I had a magical sword, didn't I?

I swung down, swiping Dyrnwyn right through her laughing face.

And...

Her image flickered, still laughing, and disappeared.

Another illusion.

I glanced behind me.

Gabby stood beside Sophie, shaking her head at me. Then they fled, running toward the same trees I'd hid in moments earlier, dragging Alyita with them.

Her tomahawk lay near my feet.

I scooped it up, stuck it in my belt, and glanced back at the others. Parker was fine. Barrett was still down, struggling not to pass out. Axel,

Anthony, and Fred were still recovering from their shock, as were the bad guys around them. They weren't all winning, but they were all alive.

I couldn't let Gabby slip off with Alyita. No way in hell.

Eilidh met my gaze and nodded.

We started after them.

17

"Who is she?" Eilidh asked, racing alongside me.

"Which?" I replied, because running and talking was hard.

"She's a witch?" Eilidh asked, glancing over at me. "What does that mean?"

"Huh?"

"You said..." She paused, catching her breath. "She's a witch."

"No. Which. Like, which one?"

"Oh," Eilidh replied. She might have rolled her eyes. "I know the other two. From your former team. Met them in Memphis. Remember?"

Of course. *Duh. Doh. Derp.*

"Alyita. Long story. Tried to kill me. A bunch. Now friends. Responsible for. Her safety."

"Sounds about right," she replied, flashing me a grin.

I smiled back, feeling feelings I hadn't felt since... Well, like, five minutes earlier.

We were racing through a small park. Our enemies had just entered the trees on the far side. A great place to lay a trap, if they weren't keen on escape.

"Can't let them..." I sucked in a breath. "Take her. All costs."

"Understood."

We entered the tree-line.

And that was when they sprang their next trap. Or tried to.

Sophie was just ahead, still dragging Alyita.

Gabby had slunk out of sight. That meant she had a plan for me.

Two sorcerers stepped out of the trees, wands raised.

I threw Dyrnwyn at the one on the right. Eilidh hurled an ice shard at the one on the left.

They both dipped back into cover. Two more took their place, forcing us on the defensive. Still, shoulder to shoulder, they were going to have a hard time breaking both our defenses.

"That a wand?" Eilidh asked, twirling her staff about. "Never figured you for the sort."

"Long story." I was still trying to catch my breath, and a little embarrassed. Not because of the wand comment, but because I was breathing raggedly, and she seemed fine. I'd been working on my cardio for ages. "Magic-nullifying monster. Scary bastard. Snapped my staff."

"Once again." She deflected a magical attack, replied with an attack of her own, then grinned at me. "Sounds about right. Good to know you haven't changed, Wyatt."

The way she said it... I wasn't sure if it was a compliment or insult. The words were friendly, but her tone seemed so...formal. Like I was an old buddy from high school she'd just run into at the grocery store.

I didn't have time for such reflection. People were trying to kill me.

We were outnumbered, but holding our own.

Gabby was still mysteriously missing. I expected she would leap out, yell surprise, and stab me in the back at any moment. This was her game, and I had little choice but to play it. So long as they had Alyita.

They could lure me anywhere. I was predictable that way. And they damned sure knew it.

What they couldn't count on was Alyita.

She'd once gone by Pathkiller. That name better suited her just then.

Alyita was Cherokee, not just by blood and birth, but by upbringing. She's been raised in an older way, by hardened people. She was scrappy as shit.

Sophie... Not so much. My former intel enchantress might have been beefing up her battle magic, but she clearly had taken no lessons in grappling.

Alyita saw her chance and took it.

One second, Sophie still had her. A moment later, when my gaze passed over them again, both were on the ground. I didn't know what happened, but grinned when I saw Alyita's foot crash into Sophie's jaw.

Then she was up and moving.

Another of the sorcerers tried to tag her with a spell, but Alyita was too quick. She darted between the trees, zigging and zagging, until she made her way to us.

Meanwhile, Sophie was spitting and cussing. I knew what the cussing was for, but in the dark, I could only assume the spitting had to do with a busted lip or broken teeth. At least I hoped. Sophie deserved that and more.

Alyita slipped in behind Eilidh and me.

"You all right?" I called over my shoulder.

"Lost my wand and my tomahawk. Clocked that bitch, though."

"Your hawk is on my belt," I said. "Right hip. Grab it."

"Hell yeah!" she said, and I felt her grab it. "I'm going to put this right in the center of that blonde bitch's—"

"No," I said. "Now you're going to get the hell out of here. Eilidh will cover you."

"Oh?" Eilidh said. "And what, leave you behind?"

"That's a shit plan, Wyatt," Alyita said.

"I'll be right behind you," I said, glancing at Eilidh. "I need you to get her out of here."

The witch scowled at me.

"I'm not a fucking child, Wyatt," Alyita said. "I can hold my own. You know that."

"I do." I paused to focus on my shield. The attacks were still coming. "There aren't many people I'd rather have my back, but..."

"But what?" she asked. "Don't start about my grandfather."

I *was* thinking about Elder Morgan. I was thinking about how devastated he'd be if something happened to her. How I couldn't live with myself if I failed to protect her.

Instead, I said, "You don't have a wand and this is a magic fight."

She huffed but didn't argue, which meant I was right. The end.

I risked a glance at Eilidh. "Please. Protect her for me."

"You can't take them all alone," she said, not looking at me. "I know what you're capable of."

"I've upgraded since the last time we danced," I said, leaning closer. "I need to know she's safe."

"I can hear you, asshole," Alyita said. "I'm not running off with your girlfriend and leaving you with these assholes."

"Girlfriend?" Eilidh asked.

I tried to ignore the disdain with which she said it.

"I'm sure the others are on the way," I said. "I just have to survive for, like, two minutes. I'll be right behind you. Now, go."

"Fine," Eilidh said. She looked back at Alyita. "Let's move."

Alyita growled, but made no more protest.

The two of them backed away, Eilidh shielding.

Now I just had to make sure my own shield held up long enough for the cavalry to arrive. Surely my team was coming, right? I mean, they had had a lot to deal with, but...

Parker Grimm was better at... Well, not leading. I wouldn't say that. In fact, I didn't know what kind of leader he was. Probably a boring-ass, stale bread, by-the-books kind of boss. A perfect middle manager.

Parker Grimm was better at running Cabal operations.

And while this was no proper Cabal operation, there were other members of the Cabal at the festival. He would have been smart enough to call on them. Surely. Not to mention Eilidh would call on her fellow witches. There had to be Appalachian Argument folks around, too, I assumed. So, there had to be more help on the way.

Surely.

I hoped.

And what were these idiots doing, attacking out in public like this, anyway? I mean, sure, they'd lured me away, but...

What the hell were they doing here?

This whole thing made no sense.

Again, I was getting lost in my thoughts when I should have been focused on not dying.

Once Eilidh and Alyita were a fair distance away, I started forward, toward the assholes who wanted to kill me. No one had broken off to pursue them. I was the target. Gabby wanted me dead something fierce. Tanya, too, though she'd apparently stopped answering her mind phone. What was that about? What did it mean? Had our people, or the Argument's, spotted her?

If only the poor Normans knew how much magical mischief was going on around them.

I ducked behind a tree and summoned more magical energy to reinvigorate my shield.

On my own again, it was time for a new game plan. Sure, I was still worried about how my team and friends were faring, but I had to trust they could handle themselves. Right then, I just needed to worry about my own damned self. Mostly because...

I wanted to go on the attack. Just to give back. A little community service.

I stepped out from behind the tree and let Dyrnerang fly. The assholes might've been prepared to play "Dodge the Flying Sword," but had they ever played "Oh, Shit, That's a Tree"?

We were about to find out.

The little copse was dense, and like me, the asshole brigade was also using trees for cover. Dyrnwyn might've been a logger in a previous life, because it had no problem dropping them.

My sword cut a horseshoe path through the air, trying to take out mages and shrubbery alike. Trees fell. Sorcerers screamed. A good time was had by all.

While my sword was doing its thing, I summoned pumpkin blasts, aiming at anything that was moving. I hoped that, in the chaos, a few of them would've lost focus on their shields. I was right. I caught at least one asshole off-guard, slamming him against a tree with a thud.

What fun! In fact, I was having so much fun, I went ahead and did it all again.

That was when Gabby almost got me.

Without my sword in hand, it couldn't warn me. I reckoned she knew that.

So, as soon as I threw it the second time, I turned and punched the air. If I was mistaken, I would've looked ridiculous. Instead, my fist slammed right into her already fugly face.

It wasn't a perfect shot. More of a glancing blow. It wasn't like I knew precisely where she'd appear.

She still caught me with her dagger.

A practical personality, Gabby didn't care about making me suffer. She didn't want to gloat. Just wanted me dead. That was payback enough for her. So, she'd appeared just behind me, planning to slam her dagger in the back of my neck. Instead, when I turned, the blade ran across my cheek, slicing the soft tissue open and then glancing off my ear. White hot pain lanced through both.

I jammed my wand upward toward her abdomen in a stabbing motion. I intended to pumpkin blast her the hell away from me. She was near the top of the list of people I didn't want to tangle with up close.

Gabby was quicker, though, and, also using her wand like a knife, she parried my attack. My spell shot off into the dark.

Then her knife leaped at my face again.

I darted back, nearly tripping.

She stayed on me, charging in.

The only thing that saved me was the fact her minion mages were morons. Or they hadn't seen her appear behind me. Either way, one of them launched a purple blast of energy at me. Staggering back, it missed me entirely, but drilled Gabby's shield. Her knife, which would have been planted in my neck, raked down my chest instead.

Still hurt like hell. Ripped right through my shirt, bounced off my ribs, and took a bit of belly fat with it.

Not pleasant.

Dyrnwyn returned to my hand just then, and I thought I might return the favor. I charged, swinging.

A puff of smoke appeared where Gabby had just been and I stumbled through it, coughing.

Something slammed into the back of my knee and I fell forward, smacking my face against the side of a tree. The bark grated my face like cheddar. The impact was worse.

There was that old saying about seeing stars when folks whacked their nuggets. Just then, all I saw was bark, and it was moving, the patterns slithering like snakes.

That wasn't good.

I tried to rise but staggered again, a little disoriented.

Somewhere in the back of my mind, I was sure Gabby was creeping up behind me.

I whipped around, swinging my sword at her throat. Only, apparently I'd dropped Dyrnwyn and my brain hadn't caught up. I was right about Gabby charging in, though. My sword-less arm slapped her right across the face. It was an awkward slap and probably hurt my hand as much as her face. Her knife glanced off my shoulder again.

It was hard to think, what with still seeing bark. One thought stood out, though. I was laughing at myself. Not for the slap. No, I'd chortle about that later. It was the deeper, meaner part of my mind which heckled me. I'd arrogantly thought I'd just needed to hold off for a couple of minutes. No problem. What an idiot. Gabby was carving me up like a fat Christmas ham.

I had to get away. Had to put some distance between us.

Staggering still, I stumbled into a tree, bounced, and aimed for the next one. Rudely, Gabby pursued.

Guess she thought she had me.

Little did she know what an idiot I truly was. I mean, I'm sure she remembered. But my dumbassery had only increased in the years since we'd worked together. Guess she hadn't picked up on it back in the swamp.

I pointed my wand at the ground and fired a force spell at my own feet.

I believed I could fly.

It worked. Sort of.

In my brain-addled state, I once again forgot how much more powerful my spells were with my father's wand.

Launch control, this is Wyatt. Prepare for lift off.

I sailed upward, back snapping through tree limbs. Luckily, I avoided any spine snappers. And I *did* successfully put some distance between Gabby and me.

But what goes up must come down.

I slammed down on my ass, fearing I'd broken my butt.

Then I continued to tumble. Downward. Apparently, I'd landed on a slope. *Oops.*

My roll ended in a splash, my head sinking beneath water.

That was...unexpected.

I sat up, sucking in a breath as my head broke the surface.

Pain shot from end to end.

I was bleeding all over, sure I'd broken something this time. Only one thing was certain...

I was about to pass out.

Blinking, I realized I was sitting in the water. Having my head beneath it a moment earlier hadn't been a strong enough clue.

The river.

I'd landed in the Ohio River. Looking up, I saw car lights passing by on a bridge. Heard the dull roar of the festival still ongoing.

Looking down, I still had my wand squeezed firmly in my grasp. That was a surprise, though I doubted I had the strength to use it. My sword, though. I'd have to summon it. I'd dropped it somewhere...

Gabby stepped through the trees, Sophie and the others just behind her.

Uh oh.

I was in no condition to continue the bout. They had me. I was done for.

Gabby knew it, too. She raised her wand. So did the others.

At least she wouldn't make a show of it. She'd just kill me and be done with it.

If I called for my sword, maybe it would stab her through the back on its way to me.

A black shadow fell over them, blocking my view. For a moment I thought it was just my throbbing head conjuring fever dreams.

It wasn't.

A black mass crashed down on my attackers and they spread, screaming and hurling magic.

My dumb brain chortled. The idiots. *All those cars on the bridge will have surely seen the light show. You're all in big trouble now.*

Yeah, I definitely wasn't in my right mind.

And then the black mass turned and twisted into the air, gliding toward me. I stared up at it, thinking I must have really lost it. Banged my head too hard. I had to be imagining...

The black mass descended on me, embracing me. I felt arms around me. A sense of weightlessness, as if I were airborne once again.

I had to be imagining it...

A fever dream indeed. Either way, just then, passing out seemed like a perfectly reasonable thing to do.

As I drifted into the darkness, one thing stood out to me, one image burning into my mind.

Bright red eyes.

18

"Should have let him die," a strange, whispy voice said.

"No, no," another replied in a similar pitch. "We can't risk the wrath of the dark one."

"Bah, the dark one," a third voice said. "What concern is he?"

"You know," said another.

There were too many. They blended together. Also, I was pretty sure I was dreaming. Their voices not only held that strange pitch, but seemed to echo, as though we were in a cave.

"We grow stronger. Soon we won't have to fear anyone."

"Bah, we should have gone to Bipple. Met with our real friends. Now, we have to go to the Argument? Waste of time."

"We have to take this thing to them."

"Not unless he wakes up."

"If. *If* he wakes up."

"Enough," a sterner voice said. "We go to the Argument either way. We have business there. Our friends at Bipple will wait."

"Business? With the Cherokee lovers? What business?"

"Whatever business I say," snapped that sterner voice. "We wait for him to wake. Or die. If he dies, we leave him. If he wakes, we take him. I'll have no further discussion on the matter."

That quieted them down.

All the voices, they had that strange pitch. Raspy and a little whiny. And they all seemed rather grumpy. Unhappy about someone in their care. *Oh. Wait.* Was that someone me? Anyway, they all seemed annoyed about the whole situation, frustrated and full of malice. All except for one.

"Not if," said a kinder voice. "When. His injuries are not so bad. Surely the dark one will be pleased."

This was met with several snorts.

"Still think we should've let him die," another said.

"His wounds were not so grave," the kinder voice said again. "Might have made it without us."

"Could have slit his throat."

"Enough," the commanding voice boomed. "It's done. So shut up. Tuthid, check him."

"Yes, Feogh."

I heard a shuffling and became acutely aware of another presence hovering over me.

Hmm. Maybe I wasn't dreaming.

I forced open my eyes and caught a blurry image of a...garden gnome.

That couldn't be right.

I blinked and tried again.

Still looked like a garden gnome. Didn't have the pointy hat, but it certainly had the small round face. A man's face with a long wispy beard and bushy eyebrows. Reminded me of the Gnomes cartoon I watched as a kid. His eyes, though... They were crescent-shaped, and had a soft glow, like... Well, like the moon.

"He's awake," the face said, bushy eyebrows raised. This was the kinder voice.

"Are you sure?" There were several heavy footfalls and another gnome face peered over me, this one not so kindly.

"See?" said the kindly one. What had they called him? Tuthid? "See, Feogh? He's awake."

The other, Feogh, who I took to be the leader, grunted in reply. "You awake, man-thing?"

"Uh..." I replied. That was the closest I could get to finding my words just then.

Where the hell was I? And why was I surrounded by glowing-eyed garden gnomes?

Above their faces, all I saw was darkness. A stone roof, perhaps? There was too little light to tell.

My mind jumped backward, trying to load its latest data entry. Apparently, the timestamps were wonky because it was really struggling. Funnel cakes. Eilidh. Bachelorette party. Darth Maul. Eilidh. Gabby. Mad Anne Bailey. Eilidh. Glowing red eyes... *Oh. Shit.*

Maybe kissing that tree had done more damage than I'd thought. How hard had I hit my head? Here I was, imagining that garden gnomes were leering over me.

I felt a sharp pain on my arm. A pinch.

"Ouch," I said.

"Hmm," Feogh said, nodding. "Guess he is awake then."

With that, the grumpy one turned and stomped away.

"Don't mind him," Tuthid said quietly. "Take your time. Get rest. We still have a while before we need move."

"Where? Where the hell am I?" I asked, trying to sit up.

"Easy," Tuthid said, holding up his hands. "Don't pull the mud apart."

"Mud?" I asked, shaking my head. I was so confused. Glancing down, I saw I was, in fact, covered in mud. Parts of me, anyway.

I was shirtless and down to my boxers, lying on a bed made of... I don't know... Weeds of some kind. It was no wonder I felt a little chilled, half-naked, wearing nothing but boxers and mud. Judging from its placement, I guessed there was mud over each of my wounds. *Wonderful.* Also explained why it felt like something was glued all over my face. That was probably mud, too.

As if to answer, Tuthid said, "Best get more goop. Keep mud moist. Don't want it to crack. Then the magic spills out."

The little guy was dressed in what appeared to be discarded toddler clothes. In the dim light and through the grime, I could just make out a faded Mickey Mouse on his baggy t-shirt.

I didn't know what to say or do, so I merely watched as he stuck his hand in a wooden bowl full of...mud.

He scooped out a fat dollop and flung it on my chest. Then he used his wee little hand to rub it around.

Wait...

I studied him, my brain firing back to life. Tuthid wasn't a garden gnome. He didn't have the hat, which I was sure was a legal requirement. Nor was he only a foot tall. He was, however, by my estimate, only about three feet tall.

Turning my head toward the sound of the grumpy voices, I confirmed I was, in fact, inside a cave. I also confirmed, or so I thought, that I was suffering from a serious brain injury, because there were more three-foot tall men, all with long wispy beards, dressed in discarded toddler clothes, and all had those strange, glowing eyes. A couple of them were even wearing dirty onesies. It was like I'd fallen into the care of a bunch of kindergarteners who had the heads of old men. And the beards. It was... It was flipping weird.

I'd seen a lot of weird shit. I'd woken up in a few strange places, too. Never in the care of...whatever the hell these things were.

"Who are you?" I asked, turning back to my caretaker.

"Tuthid," he said, grinning. "Tuthid Pugh."

"Right. I am, uh, Wyatt."

"Nice to meet you, Wyatt," Tuthid said, nodding.

"I meant to say... Uh, what are you?"

"What?" Tuthid replied, pausing from mud smearing. He seemed confused. Then the realization hit him. "Ah, we are the moon-eyed people."

As if that was answer enough.

That part could wait, though.

"And, uh, how did I end up here?"

"Dark one brought you."

"Dark one. Right." I shook my head. Every answer only brought more questions. I went for something a little simpler. "Why are you putting mud on me?"

"Heal wounds." He raised an eyebrow. "Why else? Humans do not use mud on wounds?"

"Uh, not usually, no."

"Odd," he said, shaking his head. "Why not?"

"Tuthid!" the one called Feogh said from where he sat among the others. "Stop the chatter! The human is not a pet!"

The others found this mighty amusing. They all chuckled, sounding like an orchestra of poorly tuned violins.

"Yes, Feogh," Tuthid said, cheeks reddening. He wouldn't meet my gaze then.

"And you, man-thing," Feogh said. "You be quiet. Just be grateful we healed you."

"I am grateful," I said, glancing between Tuthid and Feogh. "Just curious, is all."

He glared back. "Don't be. Just rest your stupid head. In a few hours, we go. If you're not ready, we'll leave you. The Argument can come find you."

"The Argument," I said. "You plan to take me to the Appalachian Argument?"

"Where else?" he replied, then turned back to his friends.

He said something too low for me to hear. His pals all laughed, though, cutting their eyes at me. That was fine. They could laugh at my expense. Hopefully, it would improve their pissy little moods. They certainly needed it.

I had other things to worry about. Like, for starters, how had things turned out for my friends? What of Gabby and Sophie? Had they escaped? And what about...

Opening my senses, I reached out for Dyrnwyn.

It was gone. My connection severed. A sickly feeling tightened my guts. My sword was too far for me to reach. I felt...icky. Like something was desperately missing.

But there wasn't a damned thing I could do about it. Not yet.

I laid my head back and tried to relax.

19

"It's time," Feogh announced.

I wasn't sure what had led him to that conclusion. So far as I could tell, the little chap didn't have a watch, nor could we see any daylight from within the cave.

That said, I also didn't know what it was time for, exactly. He could have been announcing his next bowel movement for all I knew.

Tuthid started toward me, appearing through the shadows. The only light was a small fire set near my makeshift bed. I assumed it had to do with the healing mud. I'd gotten the impression their strange-looking eyes allowed them to see in the dark. Just a hunch.

I didn't know how long I'd been there. Didn't know how long I'd slept. I'd drifted in and out. Often, when I'd awoken, I could hear snores throughout the cave, which led me to believe most of my short-statured friends had also been sleeping. So, night, perhaps? Was it still the same night? I didn't think so. I suspected more time had passed, though I had little frame of reference.

Tuthid Pugh made his way over, motioning. "Come, man-thing. Heard Feogh. It's time."

"Time for what?" I asked, hoping it wasn't time for a Wyatt-sized snack.

"Time to go." He said it like I should have known. Like I had any idea what the hell was going on. "Come. Your clothes are here."

He had my clothes piled in a corner. Seemed a fair place for them, dirtied, bloodied, and torn as they were. My jeans, socks, and Vans were more or less all right. My t-shirt... Not so much. It had been shredded in multiple places. I pulled it on anyway while Tuthid nagged me about not disrupting the mud.

What was it with this little guy and his mud?

I mean, I couldn't complain. Despite the injuries I'd taken, I didn't feel terrible. None of my wounds hurt too bad. Whether that was the mud or their magic, I could not say. Probably both.

I was sore and stiff, though. And hungry. I couldn't remember the last time I'd eaten. The moon-eyed people hadn't offered me anything. Guessed they hadn't figured on keeping me long enough to make it worth feeding me.

By all accounts, they were to lead me to the Appalachian Argument. This could've also just been a guise to get me outside just so they could feed me to their pet brontosaurus. Who knew? But if what they'd said was true, then I was sure the Argument could hook me up with a shower and a meal, if not a new t-shirt as well.

I was pleased that my wallet was still in my pants. It was damp from my dip into the Ohio River, but that was nothing new. More importantly, my father's wand was in my pocket and my revolver was still holstered to the belt. That was no small relief. Losing the revolver would have sucked. Losing my father's wand would have been devastating.

As it was, the rounds in my gun might have been ruined. I had spares in my duffel bag, if I ever made it back to it. I would need some oil and cleaning supplies, too. For the moment, I was just happy I hadn't lost my handy dandy backup *'Oh, hell everything has gone to shit'* vaklif-slaying 9mm.

When I was ready, Tuthid led me further up the cave to where the others waited.

Feogh wasn't happy. What a surprise.

"Took too long," he said, shaking his head at Tuthid. "Ole timely Tuthid, always costing us time. Your pet ready?"

"Yes, Feogh," Tuthid said, hanging his head. "The man-thing is ready."

"Pet?" I replied, scowling at the troop leader. I was a little offended he hadn't addressed me directly. Guessed I was beneath him.

"It speaks," he replied, still focused on Tuthid. "Looks alive, after all. Nursemaid Tuthid, we'll call you now. At least you're good for something."

The others chuckled, but Tuthid only lowered his eyes.

I felt the stupid part of my brain heating up. The one that led me to say dumb shit when I probably shouldn't. I knew nothing about these people. Didn't know what they were capable of. They may have been small, but for all I knew, they could have magic to rival Archie. And I was also short one magical sword, which meant I wasn't much better than a hedge mage.

Talking shit would have been the height of foolishness.

But when had that ever stopped me?

"You guys are kind of assholes," I said, grinning at Feogh.

The little dude let out a growl. I didn't think he enjoyed being spoken to like that.

"How dare you?" he said, glaring up at me. "We cared for you. Saw to your wounds. This is your thanks?"

"From your own lips, it was Tuthid who cared for me. The rest of you wanted to leave me to die, no?"

Feogh didn't miss a beat. "The effort of one is the effort of all."

"And that's why you're such a jerk to him?"

"Typical man-thing," he said, shaking his head. "Sticks his nose where it doesn't belong. No better than a Cherokee."

"I'll take that as a compliment," I said, grinning at the little turd. "I rather like the Cherokee."

That was...not the right thing to say.

Gasps went up all around. Even Tuthid stared at me, wide-eyed.

Uh oh.

Feogh, for his part, had murder in his eyes.

Now I'd done it.

Had they saved me just to turn around and kill me?

My hand eased toward my wand.

"Dark one..." Tuthid said, licking his lips. His eyes remained glued to the cave floor.

"What about him?" Feogh hissed.

"Dark one will not be pleased if..."

"Enough," Feogh said, turning away. "Long journey. We go. Let's be done with this man-thing and return him to other animals. Tuthid, you're responsible for him. If he falls behind, we aren't looking for him. We won't look for you either. Understand?"

"Yes, Feogh," Tuthid said, still not meeting his gaze.

Feogh disappeared down into darkness.

A few seconds passed and the next of the moon-eye headed off. A few more seconds and then the next went. It continued like this until Tuthid and I were the last.

Then he led me out of the cave.

We stepped out into a dark forest, the last rays of sun just visible over the horizon.

I paused, staring at it.

Tuthid waved me on. "Come on, man-thing. You heard. We can't fall behind."

"Right," I said, moving alongside him.

He walked at a clip, nearly a jog. Fortunately, with his tiny legs, I just had to walk at a brisk pace to keep up. At least until he led me onto the trail.

His small people used game trails to move about. I say game trails because that's what they looked like. They may well have been trails the moon-eyed people created themselves.

Clearly they hid from the human world, which explained why the crew had split up to traverse the forest. Tuthid moved quickly, and nearly without sound, passing under low branches. I could not do the same and often fell behind. He would wave for me to hurry along, afraid his leader would indeed abandon him. So far as I had seen, the little guy might've been better for it.

Not long after we started, our trail led us through a small clearing and I could walk alongside him again.

"Tuthid," I asked, "how long have I been in your care?"

"Since yesternight," he said. "When the dark one brought you."

That made me feel better. I'd only lost a day. I wondered what my friends thought. Or my team. Did they think I was dead? Had they reported to Master Serrano and Archie that I had been murdered? They certainly hadn't been looking for me, it seemed. This wasn't like in Louisiana. So far as I knew, no dark sorcery was hiding my presence. Then again...maybe the moon-eyed people had such magic.

"Who is the dark one?" I asked.

Tuthid paused, shrugging at me. "You know. He brought you."

"I don't know," I replied. "All I remember was a shadow falling over me before I passed out. I remember red eyes, though."

"Yes," Tuthid replied, nodding along. "Dark one."

So, I hadn't imagined those bright red eyes. That was...something.

"You can call me Wyatt, you know?"

"Thank you, Wyatt Man-thing."

"That isn't, uh..."

"We shouldn't talk," Tuthid said, bright eyes glancing over at me. "Feogh will not be pleased."

"Screw that guy," I said, nearly tripping over a stick. "Damn it."

Tuthid chuckled. "Wyatt Man-thing's eyes are not so good in the dark."

"No, Wyatt Man-thing's eyes aren't. Guessing yours are?"

"Oh, yes," he said, nodding happily. "Better in the dark. We are opposites. In the daylight, we struggle to see."

"Fascinating," I said, and meant it. "Where did your people come from?"

"What do you mean?"

"I mean...where did the moon-eyed people come from? Did you migrate here from somewhere?"

He stopped again, looking at me, confused. "Moon-eyed people are from here, Wyatt Man-thing. This is our home."

"Oh," I said. "I didn't know."

"No," he said, letting out a little growl. "Dirty, stinky, wicked Cherokee. They drove moon-eyes away. Many many turns ago. More moon cycles than you can count. Before Tuthid was born even, in the long, long ago. Now we've returned to make this our home again."

"Wait..." I said, trying to piece together what he'd told me. "So... Are there more of you?"

"Oh, yes, many." He nodded happily. "Tuthid is honored to join the special council. Though, Feogh and the others...not so pleased."

"Special council?"

"First to return," Tuthid said. "To reclaim our place in the homeland."

"And how's that going?"

"Cherokee are still here," he said, voice grave. "Not as powerful as they once were, though. Tuthid thinks they are not such a threat. They haven't attacked us. Feogh disagrees. Feogh says we should make war. Tuthid is not so sure."

I stopped walking, considering.

Tuthid turned back, waving me on. "Come."

I started walking again. "What of the Appalachian Argument?"

"Ah, the Magic man-things. Yes. We were invited to a special meeting. Tuthid thinks it an honor. Feogh thinks it's trick."

"What of your women, Tuthid?"

"What do you mean?"

"I mean, why are there no women with your troop?"

"Women-things? For important troop business?" It was his turn to pause. "Feogh says women-things don't belong in serious business. Tuthid is not so sure. Tuthid's mother used to be invited for serious business. Tuthid's father trusted her council. And Tuthid's friend Mirin, very smart. Wise. Tuthid trusts her council."

I raised an eyebrow. "Friend, huh? Sounds like Tuthid maybe likes Mirin."

Tuthid's big, glowing eyes blinked at me. "Yes... Tuthid likes Mirin very much. That's why she's my friend."

"I meant...maybe more than a friend."

That didn't seem to translate.

"Mate?" I asked.

"Oh," Tuthid said. I couldn't tell in the dark, but I suspected he was blushing. "Mirin... Mirin will take a mighty warrior for her mate. Most likely. Maybe Feogh."

"Tuthid is not a mighty warrior?"

"Tuthid... Tuthid can fight plenty. But the Others... Feogh. They say Tuthid is weak. Stupid. No use in a fight."

"If that's the case, then why were you invited for the council?"

"Tuthid's father was a great chieftain. He is no longer chieftain but still respected. Feogh is now our chief. He said I was invited because of my father. No other reason."

"Fuck Feogh," I said, shaking my head. "Don't listen to him. I think you're plenty worthy."

Tuthid remained silent for a long while. Finally, he said, "Come. Let us talk no more."

With that, he set off ahead of me, and I did my best to keep up.

20

We walked long into the evening.

Or night. I sort of lost track of time, constantly fighting to not trip over my own feet or get lost. Tuthid's bright eyes were like a lantern in the dark. I locked onto them and just kept plodding toward them. My face ran through many branches. And more than once, I walked straight into a tree.

But finally, we reached our destination...

Rivendell.

Okay, maybe not Rivendell. More like...

Hillbilly Rivendell.

I'd always thought the Castle was pretty badass. Beautiful, too, tucked away in the Boston Mountains. It was like a hidden fortress, large and expansive.

The Appalachian Argument's stronghold was more beautiful still.

Built onto the side of a mountain were a series of towers and pathways leading into the hillside. Soft lights gave it form. It really did look like some hidden elven city. At least on the outside. I suspected there was more of it within the mountain, so maybe the guts looked more like a dwarven city. I looked forward to finding out.

What surprised me most, however, was the group waiting for us by the entrance. I had to assume there were multiple entrances since the tiny trail didn't have any parking. Surely the Appalachian Argument wizards used vehicles like the rest of us. But where were they?

Our path led us toward a short tunnel lit by candlelight. A little way in was a set of large, intricately carved double doors. I wondered if we would have to speak friend to enter. *Right.* Enough with *The Lord of the Rings* references.

Anyway, back to what surprised me...

Several people were waiting for us. There was no sign of Feogh, nor the other moon-eyed people. As advertised, they'd left us behind. Fortunately, Tuthid had known the way, or had somehow picked up their trail. Most of the door greeters were strangers to me. Likely members of the Argument. But there were a few I recognized.

Squirrel Nuts Squad.

Or at least a few of them. Axel, Parker, Anthony, and Fred. No sign of Barrett. That concerned me.

"About time!" Axel said, racing toward me. He held something out in his hands. "Here. Take this damned thing. I can't handle the responsibility."

I knew what it was before he held it out to me. I had sensed it as we'd gotten nearer. Felt its presence beckoning to me.

Dyrnwyn.

I sighed with relief, taking it from him. Feeling whole again.

"How'd you find it?" I asked.

"It found me," he said, shrugging. "Came floating right to me. Spooked the shit out of me, too. I tried to get away from it, but it just followed me around until I grabbed it. At first, I thought... Well, it doesn't matter."

I raised an eyebrow.

"He thought you were dead," Parker said, giving Axel an amused chuckle. "He was convinced you had died, and the sword had chosen him as your successor."

"I most certainly did not," Axel said, huffing.

"Bullshit," Anthony Burns said, rolling his eyes. "He ran around proclaiming himself the Blade Mage. Said there was a new sheriff in town. Told us we needed to bow. All that shit. Sure you can imagine."

"Really?" I asked, raising an eyebrow.

As if in answer, the sword pulsed in my hand.

"Well, what was I supposed to think?" Axel said. "And your sword was none too happy with me about it. Moody thing. Started vibrating all angry like. That was when I figured you were probably still alive and it had just chosen me as the most responsible person to hold on to it for you."

This was...new.

If what they were saying was true—and I had no reason to doubt them—it meant Dyrnwyn had sought Axel. Did the sword understand he would hunt me down? That he was the most likely person to return it to me? Just how sentient was my damned moody sword?

"Besides," Axel said, scowling at me, "it's your own fault for tricking us into thinking you were dead. I knew better, though. Told everyone. Said Wyatt was too big of an asshole to die."

"Bullshit," Anthony repeated.

"He was crying," Fred said, smirking. "Like...a lot."

"I was not!" Axel said. "And even if I had, there is nothing wrong with crying over a lost friend, you man-buck meathead. Also, if I *was* crying, it was only because I'm sad for your upper lip, having to carry that terrible mustache around where people can see it."

"My mustache is beautiful," Fred said, stroking it all gross-like. "You're just jealous."

I turned my attention to Parker, the only adult in my immediate vicinity. "Wait. So, how did you guys know I was alive? And how'd you know I'd be here now?"

"The Argument told us," he replied, shrugging. "Or rather, they told the Archmage, who informed Master Serrano, who then informed us. Didn't say where you were or what happened, exactly. Just said you were alive and on your way. Master Serrano came and told us you'd be arriving soon."

"Yeah, I kind of figured they were just saying that," Anthony said, shrugging. "Kind of thought you were dead."

"You sound disappointed," I replied.

He shrugged.

"Right," I said, then realized Tuthid had disappeared. The little guy had slipped away without so much as a goodbye. Probably had to catch back up with Feogh. "Is Alyita all right? What about Barrett?"

"Barrett has been...quiet," Parker said. Seeing the look on my face, he said, "More so than usual. After the fight, he seemed to have some trouble breathing. Seems all right since, but, uh..."

"He's upset," Axel assured me.

"How could you even tell?" Anthony asked. "Big weirdo seems the same to me."

"Yeah," Fred said.

I focused on Axel, who again assured me, "You should probably talk to him."

"And Alyita?" I asked.

"Oh, she's fine," Axel said, chuckling. "A little grumpy. You'll see."

I didn't know what that meant, and he wasn't keen on elaborating.

"So, did anyone grab my stuff from the hotel before you guys left? And when did you get here?"

"We grabbed your stuff," Parker said. "We got in around noon. We're only a couple of hours from Point Pleasant. Don't know how you covered so much distance."

I considered. We certainly hadn't walked that sort of distance. How far had I been carried? Didn't matter. There were more important things to worry about. "Do they have a shower in this fortress?"

"Come on," Parker said, waving me forward. "We'll show you to your room."

"Awesome," I said. "Don't suppose you can show me to a cheeseburger, too?"

Behind me, I heard Fred whisper to Anthony, "Well, I'm glad he's alive. Otherwise, I would've been sent back to security."

Anthony snorted.

It was good to know how much my team had missed me.

21

I was wrong.

It wasn't Rivendell.

That was, indeed, only from the outside. But I was also sort of right about my next guess.

The interior of the Appalachian Argument's stronghold was everything I'd hoped it would be: like a dwarven city from a fantasy video game. Or at least as close as I'd ever get to visiting one.

My team led me into a massive open cavern with walkways and bridges leading every which way. Doorways and building fronts were carved right into the rock walls. Soft lights kept everything visible, just like outside. Kind of reminded me of a swanky hotel, with mood lights all around the lobby. That was, if a really fancy hotel was built inside a cave. Or a grotto, maybe? I had no real frame of reference. Dwarven city. That was what it was. Simple enough. There just weren't many dwarves running about. Mostly wizards, but there were certainly some other supernatural types.

We crossed several walkways, revealing just how vast the complex truly was. It stretched further into the earth than I would have thought feasible.

Eventually we entered a long hallway, not unlike a hotel hall—

minus the rock walls, of course. There were rows of doors, but instead of numbers, they had symbols I didn't recognize. Likely numbers in some forgotten script. That was how wizards liked to roll.

"Rooms?" I asked.

"We each got one!" Axel said. "Most of the Cabal is in this hall. At least, that was the impression I got from going door to door."

"You didn't?" I said.

"Oh, he surely did," Anthony said. "Knocked on every damned one. When they answered, he asked if they're heard the good news."

"And then?" I asked, not really wanting to know.

"And then he proceeded to ask if they'd heard about their lord and savior," Parker said.

"To which he replied?" I asked, noting the wicked grin on Axel's cheeks.

"Axel the Awesome," he said, grinning from ear to ear.

"That's not so bad," I said, sighing with relief. Probably wouldn't get me in too much trouble.

"He did it at two in the morning," Fred said.

That... Yeah, that was probably going to get me in some trouble.

Before I could delve into it further, I noticed Barrett standing outside one of the doors. He stood, quiet, like a statue, just standing there. It was...creepy.

I paused, glancing at the others. "Um... What's he doing?"

"Standing guard," Axel said.

"Over what?" I asked.

"That's Alyita's room," Parker said.

"Yeah," Axel said. "Since you disappeared, both Eilidh and Barrett have been watching over her like mother hens. Barrett wouldn't let her out of his sight. Eilidh comes by to check on her damn nearly hourly. It's adorable."

Barrett's head turned toward us. His eyes met mine. He didn't so much as blink. Just looked at me for a moment, then turned his face forward again.

We all stood there for several seconds, bathing in the awkwardness. Weird as hell.

What did it mean? What did it tell me that both Eilidh and Barrett had declared themselves Alyita's personal guards? As far as Eilidh went... I wasn't quite ready to think about what that meant. Barrett, though. Was this some kind of sign of respect for me?

"Your room is right over here," Parker said, motioning.

"You have my room key?" I asked, moving in the direction he'd pointed.

"Of course," he replied, pulling an old-school skeleton key out of his suit jacket. As he began to work the lock, he said, "Axel wanted it. For some reason Master Serrano thought it would be safer with me."

"They were worried I'd misplace it," Axel said in a huff. "As if."

Parker glanced back at me and I nodded. They'd made the right call.

He opened the door and swung it open. "This is your spot. It's like a king suite at a hotel. You've got a little living room, a bedroom, and your own bathroom. We brought your stuff from the hotel."

"Thanks," I said as he handed me the key.

He offered me a sympathetic smile. "I'm sure you're tired, but I think Master Serrano intends to come by. Said he wanted to check on you."

"Great," I replied. "And there I'd hoped to take a shower and go straight to bed."

Parker shrugged. "You've probably got time for a shower, at least. I'll let him know you're getting settled. Axel will see if he can find you some food."

"I will?" Axel asked.

"Yeah," Parker said, glaring at him. "You will."

Axel grumbled, sighed, and then shrugged. "Meh, I could eat. I'll find something. They have wicked good barbecue."

"Thanks, guys," I said, nodding at each of them. "I appreciate you looking after my stuff, and... I don't know... Meeting me at the door."

Parker nodded, then turned and disappeared down the hall. Anthony and Fred followed.

"Right," Axel said, nodding at me. "Guess I'll go find us some grub."

"All right," I said, still holding the door.

It seemed like he had something more to say.

"What?" I asked. It was better to just pull the Band-Aid off.

"Glad you're alive," he said. "I mean... I'm a little disappointed I don't get to be Blade Mage. But... Well, I'm glad you're alive. Asshole."

With that, he turned and disappeared down the hall.

The next surprise was in my bedroom.

Tired, exhausted, and desperately in need of that shower, I stumbled into the bedroom, searching for a light. There wasn't a switch like a normal hotel, so I raised my wand and called up a little light. There, near the door, was a chain hanging. Had to be the light.

As my hand reached for it, though, I caught movement out of the corner of my eye.

Something on or near the bed.

Oh, god, I thought. *Has the team pulled a prank on me? Did they lead me into someone else's room?*

Staring through the glow, I couldn't see anything. The bed, still hidden in the shadows, seemed empty. I didn't detect any further movement.

My imagination, then?

I stood frozen, scared to tug on the chain, sure I'd seen movement. I was also scared to push more power into my wand. I was equally scared to drop the light and move back out of the room. If this was someone else's room... If someone else was over there sleeping...

Whose room would they have led me to? My first fear was Archie's. But I knew Parker wouldn't go for that. He wouldn't have gone for Serrano, either. In fact... Parker Grimm wouldn't have partaken in pranking me.

Which meant...

Surely it was my imagination.

I yanked on the chain.

A soft light filled the room.

The bed was...

Not empty.

Nor was there a person in it.

A yellow head stared up at me, tongue flicking.

"Weekend at Burmese?"

I blinked, sure that couldn't be right. We'd left the python back in Arkansas. Paeter and Mary Beth were keeping an eye on her.

Yet...

How many other big-ass banana pythons did I know?

"Is that you?" I asked, refusing to move from the door.

She just stared at me. But I was sure it was her.

"Holy shit," I said, moving closer. "How'd you get here? Did Axel bring you?"

No answer came.

That was the only thing that made sense. Had to be Axel. The little jerk must have hidden her in a suitcase or something.

I shook my head and glanced around the room. My duffel bag was on the floor, as promised. The shower still called my name.

"Well, I guess you're here," I said, shaking my head at the snake.

She flicked her tongue in reply.

"Right. I'm going to take a shower. You... You stay out here."

Still, the snake did not reply.

The shower was heavenly.

Once my medicinal mud was washed away, I studied my injuries. I'd feared a few of the lacerations were deep, but from what I could see, all were sealed and halfway healed. Moon-eyed magic mud was the shit.

When I returned to the living room, I found Axel waiting with two styrofoam takeout boxes. He was seated on one of the couches, already working on his.

I glared at him.

He looked up, pulled pork hanging from his lips. With a mouthful of food, he said, "That's no way to greet someone who brought you dinner."

"Axel..."

"Wyatt..."

"Why is there a big-ass python in my room?"

"What?" His eyes widened and his gaze darted toward the bedroom door. "Is there really?"

"There is."

"Damn. Should've brought Weekend at Burmese. She could've had a play date."

"Pretty sure the big-ass python *is* Weekend at Burmese."

"Huh?" he said, seemingly genuinely confused. I studied his face, looking for his tell. I could usually see through him, at least when he was trying to sell a lie. He seemed legit confused. "That can't be possible. We left her back home."

I crossed my arms, refusing to let down my glare.

He popped up and moved past me, watching me with suspicion. As if I were the one pulling some nonsense right now.

Still cautiously watching me over his shoulder, he opened the door and peeked inside.

A big smile cracked his lips. "Weekend at Burmese! How did you get here?"

"You telling me you didn't bring her?" I asked.

"Hell no," he said. "Where would I put her? I barely had room for my clothes with all the beef jerky, Oreos, and action figures I packed."

"You brought action figures?"

"In case of an emergency." He shrugged and started back toward the couch.

I sat down opposite him and scooped up the container he wasn't in the process of devouring.

The barbecue was as advertised: magical.

I'd just finished woofing it down when there was a knock at the door. Axel jumped up to answer it while I wiped the barbecue sauce off my cheeks. I assumed it was Master Serrano. It wasn't.

Alyita stormed in. Her face lit up as soon as she saw me and she raced over to give me a hug.

"Uh, hello there," I said, feeling awkward about the embrace. "Good to see you, too."

Then she punched me in the chest. Right in the chest wound. The same spot where Gabby had slashed me. Still, it wasn't too bad. Just stung a little, thanks to the magic mud.

"What's that for?" I asked.

She put her hands on her hips. "You said you'd be right behind us. You said it would be fine. Instead, you tried to take on all those assholes by yourself."

"Yeah!" Axel said, stepping up beside her with his arms crossed. "We're both very disappointed in you, young man."

"I, uh..." I glanced between the two of them, unsure what to say. "It wasn't like that. I *did* try to escape. But Gabby came out of nowhere. I couldn't get away."

"Then you shouldn't have sent me away with that witch!" Alyita said, scowling. "Freaking Mary Poppins."

"Eilidh?" I asked, nearly laughing. "Mary Poppins?"

"Well, that's how she treated me! How she's *still* been treating me." Alyita rolled her eyes. "Won't hardly let me out of her sight. Keeps checking on me, like we're best gal pals or something. It's annoying."

"Huh," I said for lack of anything better to say. I was surprised. I mean, Axel had told me as much, but I had assumed he was exaggerating. That didn't seem like Eilidh's style. Unless...

Was she doing that for me?

"The big burly brute, too," Alyita said. "He's still standing outside. Waiting to escort me back across the hall."

"Huh," I repeated.

"And don't change the subject," Alyita said. "We were berating you for leaving us!"

"Yeah!" Axel said.

I couldn't tell whether he was actually annoyed with me, or just echoing Alyita for the fun of it. Almost certainly the second one.

"I don't like being treated like a child, Wyatt," Alyita said.

"Yeah!" Axel replied. "Me neither."

"Then stop acting like one," I said, glaring at him. I turned to Alyita, softening my expression. "Look, I know how it seems. I'm sorry. Wasn't my best move. And I'm sorry if you felt like I was treating you like a kid, but I do trust you have to my back. Honestly."

"But you're more worried about what my grandfather would think," she said.

That was...true.

Elder Morgan was someone I looked up to. And Alyita... She was a teenager. Granted, she was a teenager who'd nearly killed me several times. But...she was sort of right. I had treated her like a kid. Maybe I shouldn't have.

"You're right, Alyita," I said, sighing. "I'm sorry."

An awkward silence passed between us.

"And?" Axel asked.

"And what?" I said.

"Are you going to apologize to me?"

"No. In fact, I'm kicking you both out of my room. Now. It's been a long night."

Alyita sighed. "That's probably smart. We do have a meeting in the morning."

"We do?" I asked, raising an eyebrow.

"Of course," she said. "Don't you know your schedule?"

I shook my head.

"Real mature, Wyatt," Axel said, shaking his head.

"You know what?" I pointed at the door. "I'll figure it out tomorrow. Now, go."

Reluctantly, they both marched out. And that was precisely when Master Serrano came a-knocking.

Damn it. I'd all but forgotten he was coming. I was beginning to miss my weed bed. And the mud.

22

Master Serrano didn't keep me long.

Mostly, it seemed like he just wanted to make sure I was all right. No surprise from the Master Librarian. He was good people.

He didn't have answers to any of my questions, though. Or he wasn't open to discussing them if he did. He couldn't, or wouldn't, tell me how I'd ended up with the moon-eyed people. Or how the Argument knew I was safe and sound with the mean-spirited little folk.

I mean... I was smart enough to piece together that Feogh's crew would've let the Argument know they were on the way, and that I was with them. That seemed a simple enough explanation. But I really wanted to know how I'd ended up with them in the first place. Who had saved me? All I could remember were those glowing red eyes... Which of course made me think of... No, couldn't have been. That would've too much. Too on the nose. He wasn't real.

He did bring me a printed copy of my schedule for the "conference," which was due to begin in the morning. It seemed my leadership had signed me up for a variety of meetings and chats with the various other attendees. And a few presentations, too. Boy was I excited for all of that.

He also left me with a bit of advice. Something I'd already been planning to do, but I'd intended to leave it for the next morning. He thought I needed to speak with Barrett, and sooner rather than later.

So, once the master took off, I fought off the urge to go to bed and made my way to Barrett's room. I'd half-expected to find him still standing in front of Alyita's door, but that wasn't the case. I guessed since I was back, he didn't feel like he had to. But I didn't know which room was his. I used mind-speak to ask Parker. I'd considered asking Axel, but knew he'd likely show up and/or ask a million questions. Guess that was one benefit of having Parker around. He just gave me an answer. No questions.

I knocked lightly on the door.

I was about to knock again when he finally opened it.

Barrett towered over me, a blank expression on his face. He was dressed in pajama bottoms and a t-shirt, but it didn't look like he'd been asleep.

He didn't invite me in, just stared at me.

"Can we talk?" I asked.

That might have been a stupid question, since the big man didn't really do the whole talking thing anymore. But it sounded better than asking if he wanted to hear a monologue.

For a few moments, I didn't think he was going to move. I half-expected him to slam the door in my face. Instead, he turned and started into his room, leaving me to catch the door before it shut and locked me out. If that happened, I was pretty sure he wouldn't open it again.

I followed him into his suite. It looked like mine had when I'd first walked in. Unused. Like no one was staying there.

Barrett sat down in one of the living room chairs.

I sat down across from him.

And then we stared at each other in an awkward, miserable silence.

I wasn't sure what to say. Well, maybe there was one thing...

"I wanted to tell you thanks."

He raised an eyebrow. I'd take it. That was as close as he'd come to communicating with me since he'd joined the team.

"For watching out for Alyita. I appreciate it. She's mean as hell. Definitely can take care of herself, but... She's just a teen still, right? And after the things she's been through..."

Maybe talking about the things people had been through wasn't the best idea. Or maybe it was. How the hell was I supposed to know?

"I feel responsible for her," I said, shrugging. "She can probably kick my ass, but still, if something happened to her, I would feel responsible. So, thank you for looking out for her. I appreciate that."

He replied with the hint of a nod.

"Also..." Again, I wasn't sure how to start. "I wanted to make sure you're all right."

Nothing.

"Look, I'm pretty new to this whole leadership thing. And frankly, I'm a moron. I should already know the medical status of everyone on the team. And I don't. I don't know how your recovery has gone. When I first came to visit your house after... Your mom told me they weren't sure your lung would fully recover. She said she wasn't sure you'd work again."

Nothing.

"And I probably should have made sure I knew your status before we went out in the field. Not that I knew we were going into a battle. It was supposed to be a peaceful trip. Point is...obviously, you have a limitation."

"I can fight."

The words came out as a rasp. Barely audible. A whisper of a whisper. But there was some fire behind them. His eyes bore into mine. Maybe he was afraid I intended to sideline him.

"I saw you out there. You looked like the Barrett I remember. At least at the start. But I also saw you struggle. Something we need to keep in mind. Something I should have known."

He didn't reply.

"It's my fault." I held his gaze. "I should have known. Should have made sure I knew. And I should've acted accordingly, backing you up quicker."

"I..." he started, then looked away.

I waited.

When he still didn't speak, I asked, "You lost your shit when you saw Gabby?"

Another of those brief nods. Then, to my surprise, he spoke. "Lost my cool. Shouldn't have. Overdid it. Won't happen again."

"I'm not worried about that. In fact, I made the same mistake. I thought I saw Sophie and followed her. Alone. That was stupid. Walked right into their trap. Look... I trust you, Barrett. And I'd damned sure rather have you with me than not, I promise you that. Especially if our old team is here in Appalachia. Even more so, since they're gunning for me."

We stared at one another.

"I have no intention of putting you on the sideline, if that's what you're worried about. But... If we run into any more bullshit, you've got to stay calm and cool. You can't run at them like a freight train."

His eyes narrowed.

I put up my hands. "I know, I know. Your specialty is close-ranged magic. You're an absolute beast. But you also haven't been in the shit for a while. You're out of practice. And you have a lung injury. Your stamina isn't what it was. We'll have to build back to it. That is...if you still want to be on the team?"

His eyes narrowed further.

"I'm going to take that angry expression to mean you do."

"It's not that," he said, teeth gritted.

"It's that you're no use if you can't get in close and bring the pain?"

He looked away.

"Listen, man. You've always been a beast. You're used to being a beast. Not me, though. I've been working with limitations for a long time. I'm not half the wizard you are. Not half the wizard anyone else on our team is. Except maybe Fred. Don't know about him. Point is, I've been fighting scary a-holes who should've been able to kill me no problem. I've had to learn to work with my limitations. It's the same with your breathing. That's all. Don't overthink it."

His eyes drifted back to me. A good sign.

I continued, "Not long ago, my staff was snapped in half by a big-ass beak-faced monster who could nullify magic. It was the pet of a dark wizard, and he had a legion of assholes behind him. I gave my sword to Axel and knowingly walked into their trap with nothing but a wand I'd never used before and a revolver tucked in my waistband. That was it. Somehow, I made it out of there."

I rubbed my chin, considering.

"In Louisiana, we were up against all sorts of nasty shit. Just running around the swamp fighting to survive. Our enemies were breeding like rabbits, and most of them were considerably more powerful than me. You know how I survived both? Or any of the bull- shit that came before? Oklahoma? Memphis? All of it? Wits, grit, and good friendships."

He snorted. "Sounds like something for a greeting card."

"Good, though, right? I just made it up. Point is... You've got to accept your limitations and figure out how to work around them. And you have to count on your team, even if it's not the team you want. It's all we can do."

Again, he said nothing.

"All right." I rose to my feet. "You don't need me to preach at you. Hell, I'd probably be dead a hundred times over if not for the shit you taught me back in the day. And really, I just wanted to thank you. For what it's worth... I'm really glad you're here, Barrett. Really glad to have you with us."

I started for the door.

"Wyatt," he said.

I turned back to meet his stony gaze.

"Yes?"

"Did you know?"

I raised an eyebrow, surprised by the question. "Did I know what?"

"Did you know our former teammates would be there?"

"Don't you think I would have told you if I did?"

He didn't reply.

"No, Barrett. I didn't know. It was as much a surprise to me as it was to you."

When he didn't respond, I turned and started toward the door again.

"Awful coincidence," he said at my back.

I turned back once again.

"I was asked to join your team," he said, eyes boring through me. "And on our first mission..."

"Wasn't even supposed to be a mission," I said, realizing what he'd meant. So much had happened, I hadn't stopped to think about it. But now that he mentioned it... "Our old team shows up."

"Seems awfully convenient."

"It does."

"Makes you wonder."

"It does," I repeated.

I exited his room with a lot on my mind.

23

The Argument had a special cafe for its guests.

A cave cafe.

Honest.

That was what the sign said.

Coffee Cave Cafe.

Just big enough for all the Argument's guests to pile in for breakfast. Most, anyway. I didn't see the moon-eyed people, but there were several other strangers about. Wizards from some of the other guilds, I reckoned. Members from other supernatural organizations, gangs, or whatever. All there for the Argument's conference. Or rather, at that moment, all there for free coffee and pancakes.

I also recognized many members from our own Cabal, ones who'd traveled with us.

I was on the lookout for one particular face, one that wasn't from the Cabal. One that I owed a big thank you. Just a thank you. No other reason. I wasn't like, desperately hoping for a chance to talk to her or anything.

Right.

Anyway... The Coffee Cave Cafe had a buffet with all the works.

And a walk-up bar for custom omelet orders. Another for fancy coffees, if one required something better than the help-yourself drip coffee.

I was proud to say Squirrel Nuts Squad went to breakfast as a team. Plus Alyita. It took some work to get Barrett moving, but I had planned for that. I pounded on his door until he opened it and then demanded he join us for breakfast. He had stared at me, blank-faced. I think his plan was to do that until I went away. Little did he know how much practice I'd had dealing with stubborn ass-hats. I lived with Axel, after all. I went straight for the big guns. Told him it was an order. From his boss. Who was me. His glare had hardened, but he'd reluctantly joined us.

There was something odd about community breakfasts, especially when there were a bunch of people around you knew, but didn't know particularly well. It was...invasive. Sort of. Not necessarily in a bad way. It was just like... Well, you didn't get to see how people went about their breakfast at home. It was almost like breakfast was a private act. But when you were traveling, it was all out in the open. Which was...weird. Maybe it was just me, but I realized something interesting.

Our breakfast plates said something about our personalities.

For example, Parker's plate was perfectly arranged. Mostly fruit, with a small pile of eggs, and one piece of bacon. Obviously, the man liked to party.

Both Anthony and Fred packed meat on their plates in unceremonious piles, just like the protein bros they were.

Barrett's plate looked much the same, but organized neatly. And he had some pineapples.

Alyita had very little on hers.

And Axel... His was packed to the moon, ready to tumble. Then he grabbed a second plate and did the same. A third plate was just for pancakes.

I stacked mine high with eggs, bacon, and biscuits and gravy. Then I grabbed another plate for fresh fruit and tried not to stare at the delicious-looking baked goods. I convinced myself I wouldn't return for a blueberry scone or a blueberry muffin, knowing it was a damned lie. I would come back for both.

More than anything, though, I was excited about coffee. I wanted *all* the coffee.

Especially after Master Serrano had informed me I would be in silly meetings all day. I was a wizard with a magical sword and a reputation as a wrecking ball. What business did I have sitting through talks and presentations? That was for, like, smart people.

Speaking of which, I was kind of regretting not bringing a dress shirt. Not that I owned one.

We ate in companionable silence, a dull roar of conversations around us.

"So, how'd yesterday go?" I asked, glancing around the table.

"Pretty boring," Axel replied with a mouthful of pancakes.

Parker sighed. "You're only saying that because the Archmage came around and threatened to mute you permanently if you weren't on your best behavior."

"I just wanted to explore," Axel said, a sour expression on his face. He glanced at me. "Archie made me stay in my room, for like, days."

Parker rolled his eyes. "We got here in the early afternoon. He only had to stay in his room for a few hours."

"But I wanted to explore!"

Again, Parker rolled his eyes. So did Anthony and Fred. I was on Axel's side this time. I also wanted to explore the dwarven city. Bunch of boring-ass grownups.

"We'll find time to explore today," I assured him. "Assuming you actually stayed on good behavior and Archie, er, the, uh, Archmage didn't ground you."

"Should be fine," Parker said. "The Archmage was mostly worried about him while you were missing. He was...a lot to handle."

"I was not," Axel replied, shoveling in another forkful of pancakes.

Alyita snickered. "Axel was ranting and raving about putting together a war party to come find you."

Parker gave me a sidelong glance. "Even after we were informed you were safe. So, what we're saying is, don't go missing again. Your weird little sidekick can't handle it."

"More like weird little butt buddy," Fred said, elbowing Anthony. "Am I right?"

Much to my surprise, Anthony scowled at Fred in a "why are you touching me" sort of way and said, "Stuff it, Fred."

The former security supervisor seemed rather taken aback. He'd thought he'd found a budding friendship with the meathead who didn't like us. But the thing Fred didn't know was...

"Hey, Anthony, remember how sad you were that time you thought I died?" Axel asked.

That brought a look of surprise from everyone at the table. Even Barrett raised an eyebrow.

Anthony scowled, looking away. "Wasn't like that."

"Sure was," Axel said, beaming. "So, there Anthony was, captured by two voodoo loa, an overgrown rabid raccoon, Frankenstein's monster with an ax, some angry little people, the Devil Baby and his nutsack lizards, some swampbillies with pitchforks, and a bunch of ninjas. Things weren't going well for the shamus. Not going well at all."

"Is that how you remember it?" Anthony asked, eyebrow raised. "Ninjas?"

"The vampires," I said, trying not to laugh.

"Oh, right," he said, shaking his head. "Rabid raccoon?"

"The Rougarou," I offered.

"Right," he said.

"Anyway..." Axel scowled at both of us for interrupting his story. "So, there Anthony was, all captured and caught—"

"I don't think everyone wants to hear this," Anthony said.

"Hush," Axel replied. "Stop interrupting."

Anthony grumbled to himself, but didn't interrupt.

"It looked like it was all over for super shamus Anthony Burns," Axel said. He was really sliding into storyteller mode. "And the big baddies, they looked over at Wyatt, and they were all like, 'Sup, bruh.' And Wyatt was all, 'Sup, bruhs.' And they were all, 'If you want this super shamus back, you must surrender.' But Wyatt, he gave them some serious stink-eye. Made them really re-think things. And then...Anthony asked where I was."

He paused, pretending to wipe a tear from his eye.

"Wyatt told him I was dead. And Anthony..."

"For fuck's sake," Anthony said, shaking his head again.

The others were enraptured, though. The story train had left the station. There was no stopping it now.

"Anthony was brave as hell," Axel said.

"Wait, what?" Anthony asked, perking up.

"He looked Wyatt in the eye and said, 'Screw it, Blade Mage. I don't want to live in a world without Axel. It would be too lonely and cold. Kill these mofos!' And that's when I set off the bombs."

He sat back, pleased he'd ended on the right note.

Everyone else stared at each other, then looked to Anthony or me for some kind of confirmation. Other than Parker, of course. He hadn't been there, but he'd certainly been read the after action report.

"We've been close friends ever since." Axel's expression was serious, his tone solemn. "Not as close as Wyatt and me. Or even as close as Scotty and me. Or Paeter and Mary Beth. And there's Shain Stone, of course. He's like a big brother to me. And Uriah, and, well, all the Knights. August Bones of course still ranks higher. And the entire populace of Treat. And the voodooists, come to think of it. Oh, and I can't forget my homegirl Eilidh, of course. Anyway, after all those other people, Anthony is number one in my heart." He made a heart symbol with his hands and held it over his chest.

"Uh...thanks," Anthony said. "I think."

"Oh, hey, there's my homegirl Eilidh right there!" Axel said.

My head jerked up and I felt a tinge of embarrassment. I hoped no one noticed. The others turned and looked as well.

"Now, there's a story I want to hear," Alyita said. "I want to know how you two met her."

"Involved a bunch of demons and bikers," Alex replied, waving.

Eilidh's head turned toward us, but only for a second. For the briefest moment, her eyes met mine, and then she looked away. Of course, she was with her gaggle of witch sisters, so that was probably why. Hopefully I'd get a chance to talk to her at some point. Preferably away from big-nose.

Axel seemed to think now was the time.

"Eilidh!" he yelled. "Hey, Eilidh! Over here! Eilidh!"

She tried to ignore him, but finally remembered who it was she was trying to ignore.

An annoyed look on her face, she turned and waved back at Axel.

"Hi!" he said, still shouting across the room. "You should come sit with us!"

She turned away without reply. A couple of her witch friends snickered, finding the entire scene rather funny.

Axel looked crestfallen. "That was...unexpected."

"She's with her coven, Axel," I said. "You remember how they were."

"I remember when they got their heads chopped off."

"Before that."

"Oh," he said, eyes widening. "They were kind of bitchy. Witchy bitchy. Bitchy witchies."

"Exactly. Might be this group is the same."

"Plus, they're here on business," Parker said. "Like us. Might be good to remember that. We're here representing the Cabal. Try to make a good impression."

"I am." Axel threw up his hands. "I haven't done anything fun in, like...days. What more do you people want from me?"

"If you could refrain from yelling across the room, that would be nice." Parker added an eye-roll for dramatic effect.

Axel looked at him like he was a potato. Then he glanced over at Eilidh again, then back to me. His eyes narrowed. "What did you do?"

"Huh?"

"I've given it careful consideration," he said. "Eilidh wouldn't ignore us, no matter how bitchy her friends are. Eilidh is the coolest. So, that only leaves one logical conclusion."

"That I did something?"

"That's right," Axel said, crossing his arms. "I went to all the trouble to get you guys together and then you ruined it. So, what did you do this time?"

That garnered me some awkward looks.

Anthony glanced over at Eilidh again and then back at me. "You hooked up with that?"

I didn't reply.

Apparently, that was answer enough because he gave me an approving nod and said, "Nice."

"Huh," Fred said. "I really thought you and Axel were like... together."

"A common misconception," Axel said. "Wyatt's fault, really. Always referring to me as his life partner. Idiot. Sadly, no, Wyatt is not my type. Nor are, well, any dudes, actually. I like ladies. I like them an awful lot."

"This conversation is getting weird," Alyita said, then glanced at me. "So, you and the witch were a thing?"

"Yeah, boss," Parker said, giving me a wicked smile. "Spill the beans."

I glared at both of them. They already knew. Axel had given them plenty of details while we were at the festival. They were just egging me on for their own amusement.

I used my empty coffee cop as an excuse to get up.

Also, Eilidh had drifted toward the drink station. Her fellow witches hadn't joined her.

It might be my only chance.

She had just finished filling her cup when I approached. Reaching for the sugar and creamer, she glanced up at me, seeming surprised.

"Refill," I said, holding up my empty cup, mostly so she wouldn't think I'd walked up there just to talk to her. Which was weird, considering we *had* been friends. And we'd left things amicably. We'd agreed on our short time together. And we'd parted well. It shouldn't have been weird.

It was, though. Weird as hell.

She said nothing. Didn't even look at me.

"I, uh, did want to say thanks," I said. "For, uh, looking after Alyita. I really appreciate it."

"Yeah, sure." She still wouldn't look at me. "It was no problem."

And with that, she sauntered away.

I refilled my cup, not sure what to think.

Maybe I'd had it right before. Maybe I'd over inflated our friendship. Maybe everything we'd gone through in Memphis and our brief tryst didn't mean anything to her. Not like it did to me.

I sighed and rejoined my team.

24

"Ah, Wyatt, I trust you are well."

The Archmage. Standing outside my door along with Supreme Enchanter Tate. *Wonderful.*

"I've been worse," I said, not quite returning his smile. This was the first I'd heard from the big man since my little...incident. Also, I was pretty sure I was due for a meeting of some sort shortly. Point was, why the hell was he by my room?

"Are you going to invite us in?" he asked.

"Yes, of course," I said, moving to the side.

He strolled past me, but Tate stopped to give me a slap on the shoulder. "Glad to see you on your feet."

"Thanks," I said, following the both of them into my little living room area. "It was...an interesting experience."

"I don't doubt it," Tate said, shaking his head. "Listen, sorry about that. Should've never happened."

"What *did* happen?" I asked, glancing between the two of them. "The last thing I remembered was I was about to die and a shadow fell over me. Then I woke up among the moon-eyed people."

"The moon-eyed people," Tate repeated, grinning. "They're a trip, aren't they?"

"Not sure that's what I'd call them," I replied. "They seem to have a real chip on their shoulders. Not too friendly. Except for Tuthid. That little guy was all right."

"You didn't get on with the others?" Archie asked.

I shook my head. "They seemed annoyed they couldn't leave me for dead. They weren't the easiest to understand, but from what I could piece together, they only helped me because someone they referred to as 'the dark one' told them to. You guys know what that means?"

Neither showed their cards. They just stared at me, Archie with his grandfatherly smile and Tate seeming mighty amused. That told me they knew something.

"A question for another time, perhaps," the Archmage said. "Supreme Enchanter Tate and I just wanted to check on you."

"And to apologize," Tate said, meeting my gaze. "Again, that should have never happened in our territory. I'm embarrassed."

"I'm not," I replied. "I'm pissed off."

"That, too," Tate said, nodding. "You have every right to be."

"Not at you," I said to clarify. "Not at the Appalachian Argument. At my attackers. I want to find them."

He glanced over at Archie, then back at me. "Yeah. Magnus mentioned that. Former teammates of yours. I can understand why you'd want some payback."

I turned my gaze on Archie. "Is this where you guys tell me to behave?"

Tate responded instead. "Hell no. We've got feelers out. We're looking. And when we find them, you're welcome to join in the fun."

That...surprised me.

The Archmage nodded as well.

"And as for the dark one?" I asked. "The shadow thing that scooped me up? I'm assuming they're one and the same. Do I get to meet my savior?"

Tate grinned again. "Let that question lie a bit longer. You'll get an answer before long."

"Sure," I said, turning my attention to Archie. "There's something I'd like to ask you about...privately."

"I can step out," Tate said, starting for the door.

"That won't be necessary," Archie said. "Wyatt can hold his question for another time, I think."

That... I almost lost my cool. Almost. I was already annoyed by their game about the dark one. But not knowing whether Archie knew about my former teammates... He was probably testing me. Same as always. So, instead of being an ass, I smiled at Tate and said, "I enjoyed the rest of the festival. Pretty sure my team did as well."

"Good," Tate said.

"Listen, Wyatt," Archie said. "We wanted to ask you about the moon-eyed people. We were rather hopeful you'd...made friends with them."

"Why would you think that?" I asked. "Have you met those little turds? Mean-spirited pricks, most of them. Not Tuthid. He's cool."

Archie gave me one of those smiles which suggested I should shut up and listen.

"Given your history of..." He paused, as if he couldn't find the word. Of course, this was the Archmage, so it was probably all just part of the performance. "...history of befriending some of the more obscure and—dare I say, *reserved* species of the supernatural world—we had hoped you might have made some progress with the moon-eyed people."

"Why?" I asked, glancing between the two of them.

"What do you know about them?" Tate asked.

I shook my head. "Nothing. Well, I know they don't like the Cherokee."

"That's the problem," he said. "The moon-eyed people were originally from these parts. A long, long time ago, practically ancient history, they had a conflict with the tribe of old. The Cherokee gave them the boot and they disappeared from the Appalachians. More recently, they've returned. They want to reclaim their former home."

"And that's a problem?" I asked. "The Appalachians are mighty big. Plenty of space."

"I agree," Tate said. "As do most among the Argument and Cherokee. Problem is the old grudges. Before Feogh took over, we were making some headway with the previous chief. The Cherokee don't bear any grudges. Ancient history, as far as they're concerned. They don't care whether the moon-eyed folks are around or not. But Feogh and his supporters, they want old feuds addressed. They don't want to play nice unless the Argument takes their side. But even then... I think they have a taste for blood."

"And this while you're negotiating better terms with the Cherokee," I said, nodding along. "That can't help."

"You've got the measure of it," he said.

I turned to Archie. "So, you were hoping I would have made some headway with them because..."

"Because your voice has been requested in the dealings between the Cherokee and the Argument," he said. "In fact, you're due for a meeting shortly, as is Alyita."

"That's right," Tate said. "Elder Morgan out of Oklahoma, he recommended we bring you in on the discussions."

"He did?" I said, genuinely surprised. That meant a lot to me, coming from him. I hadn't even known he had a relationship with the Eastern Cherokee. Made sense, of course, in hindsight.

Seeing the look on my face, Tate said, "We're not asking you to get involved in the negotiations or anything like that. But we thought it might be good for both folks from the Argument and the Cherokee to hear your side of the story. How you worked things out between the Oklahoma Cherokee and the Cabal. You'll be meeting with our Grand Shaman and a few members of the tribe, if that's all right?"

"Of course," I replied. "No problem."

"And," Archie said, "as I mentioned, that's why Alyita is here, too. Both sides are intrigued to learn firsthand what her experience has been like, coming from the tribe to train with the Cabal."

"Okay," I said, sighing. "So, you were hoping I had made good with the moon-eyed people so they would also be more inclined to come to the table?"

"Precisely," Archie said.

"Well, I'm afraid I laid an egg. Feogh doesn't like me. Same with the rest. Tuthid was the only one who gave me the time of day, and that poor little guy has a hard enough time with the others."

"Don't give up hope," Archie said, meeting my gaze. "Tuthid may yet prove a beneficial ally. Time will tell. I would encourage you to continue building that relationship, if you can."

"Sure," I said, then glanced at Tate. "But wouldn't it be better if one of your own people took that initiative?"

"It would," he agreed. "But Feogh is distrustful of the Argument. Any attempt to engage with his people would be met with suspicion and possible hostility."

"I think I understand," I said, shrugging. "But don't expect much."

Archie only smiled. "We shall see."

25

Tate led Alyita and me through the underground fortress, giving us something of a tour. We were on our way to our meeting. I wasn't looking forward to it. Diplomacy wasn't really my jam.

The tour was cool, though.

At least until Tate needed to make a stop and left us in the hall waiting. That wouldn't have been bad except Eilidh and the Traveling Sisterhood of the Bitchy Witchies passed by.

Noticing them, I offered a slight nod. A polite nod. Just to acknowledge their existence.

Eilidh's eyes flicked to mine, but for only a moment. About what I expected.

Alyita, though, on seeing her, raised a hand to wave. Then she smiled at the rest. "Witches."

Big-nose paused, studying Alyita like a cut of meat. She didn't look my way at all. I might as well have not existed.

"It's a shame," Big-nose said.

"What's that?" Alyita asked, confused.

"That you've found yourself tied to those dullards in the Ozark Mountain Cabal. Eilidh tells me you have quite the spirit." She paused intentionally, allowing Alyita's gaze to move toward Eilidh, who made a point of looking away. "If you seek an upgrade, the Colonial Coven would be honored to host you."

"I'm not Cabal," Alyita said. "I'm Cherokee."

"Still." Big-nose shrugged. "It's of little consequence. We always have room for another sister. The Coven welcomes women of power. Something to keep in mind."

Big-nose glanced at me, as if recognizing me for the first time. She made a sniffing sound, like she'd caught a whiff of something foul, then moved on, the others following.

Eilidh didn't make eye contact with either of us.

Guess that answered that question. Eilidh hadn't hung around Alyita for my benefit. She'd been trying to recruit her.

I felt like such an idiot.

"Well, that was awkward," Alyita said, watching the witches disappear down the hall.

"Careful with them," I said, then re-thought my warning. "Unless you want to become a witch. Then that's probably the place to go."

"Something tells me they'd want me to give up my ties to my tribe. And my grandfather."

"Maybe. I don't know enough about them to speculate. Eilidh is the only one who ever gave me the time of day. Well...used to, anyway."

Alyita stared at me, an amused expression on her face.

"What?"

"You know that's what I meant, right? With the awkward comment? I wasn't referring to that other witch's statement. I was talking about Eilidh. Acting like we don't exist."

"Oh."

"I mean... I get her ignoring you. No offense. You have history. And you're a dude. Clearly her fellow she-woman man-haters don't approve. But giving me the cold-shoulder? Couldn't get her to leave me alone yesterday. Now, I'm chopped liver. Wonder what's changed?"

I stared at her, keeping my thoughts to myself.

Tate appeared just then, saving me from an awkward conversation. Well, almost.

As we started down the hall again, Alyita leaned in and whispered, "It's her loss, you know?"

I didn't reply.

The supreme enchanter led us to a chamber lit in soft amber lights. There was a large table of stone in the center, with chairs seated around it.

Several people waited for us, including Master Serrano. That was a relief. I preferred having an adult in the room. He gave us a little wave.

Tate motioned to the others, getting their attention, then turned back to me. "Wyatt, Alyita, allow me to make some introductions. I trust you already know Master Serrano. Would be kind of awkward if you didn't."

I met his smile with one of my own. "It would be, especially considering he's sort of my boss."

Tate chuckled and pointed toward a middle-aged man who had long black hair and dressed much like Elder Morgan and some of the other elders from the Oklahoma Cherokee. "This is Tsali, a medicine man of the Cherokee."

I reached out and shook his hand. Alyita did the same. He gave us both a quick study, saying nothing. He wore an amiable smile, but his eyes were shrewd. Piercing.

Tate turned to the next. A man near my age, he was handsome, well-kempt, and was wearing a dark suit. He, too, had the look of a warrior about him. "This is Christian, our Defender."

My eyebrows rose. "An Arcane Guardian."

The man nodded and stuck out his hand to me. "A pleasure to meet you, Blade Mage."

I could hardly think of what else to say. Another Arcane Paladin, and this one, the Defender. The Shield-Bearer. I was sure he had it with him, but it was hidden, just as Dyrnwyn was veiled on my back.

After he and Alyita shook hands, Tate turned to the final man. He was ancient. Tall and thin, he reminded of a wispy old tree who'd weathered the storms of time. His eyes, too, were shrewd, but there was a kindness there. Not soft, but the sort of kindness earned through years of conflict. A kindness based on wisdom and experience. "And this is Supreme Shaman Sams."

He offered me a slight bow and reached out his hand to take mine. Despite his age, his grip, though trembling, was firm. "Wyatt Draven. An honor to meet you."

"You as well, Supreme Shaman Sams," I said, dipping my head.

"You remind me of your father," he said, a twinkle in his eye, "during his younger days. In those early years, after the sword chose him."

That... I hadn't expected that. Didn't even know how to respond. I stood, staring at him, dumbfounded.

He turned to Alyita. "And you, already I can see your grandfather's mark upon you."

"You know my grandfather?" Alyita asked. I was glad she seemed as surprised as me.

"Of course," he said. "I count Elder Morgan among my most trusted friends. I mentored him once, long ago. Over the years, I've come to trust his council. I hope you do as well."

Alyita seemed stumped. Speechless.

"Though," Sams said with a mischievous grin, "at your age, I'm sure you find us old folk to be a bore. I certainly had a rebellious streak in my teens, though that was very long ago. Before the dinosaurs, even. Your grandfather, too, as I recall, had something of a rebellious nature."

"I, uh, think I've gotten over mine," Alyita said.

"So," Tate said, taking over the conversation. "I thought this would be a good group to start the conversation with. Shall we take our seats?"

We did. Alyita sat on one side of me and Master Serrano took the other.

When everyone was seated, Tate said, "So, Wyatt and Alyita, the Archmage invited you here so we might learn about the relationship between the Ozark Mountain Cabal and the Oklahoma Cherokee. There'll be plenty more discussions as we go along. But I wanted to start with something a little less formal. I thought, perhaps, Tsali, Shaman Sams, and I might just ask you some questions. Would that be all right?"

I kept my sigh internal. Outside, I grinned. "Sure. Sounds great."

26

When the first meeting ended, we had time to pee, grab a coffee, and then make our way to the next.

Rinse and repeat. All damned day.

It was like being back in school.

Or how I imagined a business conference might go. If, you know, I'd ever been mature enough to attend something like that.

The many meetings were held in a centralized location, like the mountain fortress had a convention center. And they all ended simultaneously to keep schedules streamlined. Made sense, but it also meant we were fighting through a herd of somewhat familiar faces each time a session ended.

I wasn't sure how many times I could answer the same awkward questions about my role in negotiating new terms between the Oklahoma Cherokee and the Cabal. And there were some parts of that story I didn't feel inclined to share. Like the parts concerning Alyita trying to murder me. That wasn't anyone else's business. The problem was, I wasn't sure how much my audience knew, or didn't know, about those events. Fortunately, most of their repetitive questions centered on why I'd made certain concessions and what goals I'd hoped to achieve with them. I wanted to throw up my hands and admit that I'd had the master watcher sneaking in suggestions in one ear while I'd listened and agreed to whatever Elder Morgan had wanted with the other. It wasn't complicated. And I didn't deserve whatever accolades they thought I'd earned. But...

Archie would have known that.

As would Master Serrano.

Both men knew the truth, as did Elder Morgan, who it seemed Tsali had chatted with at length before we got here. I suspected the same of Shaman Sams.

So, why was I here?

Perhaps I deserved more credit than I was giving myself.

Maybe Archie and Master Serrano thought I'd handled the situation well. Maybe it just didn't seem like it from where I sat. But maybe that was how things went sometimes. Maybe no one cared that Master Jackson and Elder Morgan had guided me through that process. I was the one who'd stamped my name on it. Maybe that was enough.

Whatever the case, answering the same questions was getting boring.

It was a relief when I found out I had a session, along with Parker and Axel, to discuss supernatural crime fighting. That wasn't what it was titled, but that was what I heard. It was meant for special investigation teams to swap notes on best practices. Since Squirrel Nuts Squad —which was how they introduced us—was a team, we'd been invited.

There were several members of the Appalachian Argument there, including Christian, the Defender. I hoped to get another opportunity to speak with him, but I was at the mercy of the schedule.

To meet another Arcane Paladin. That was...

I mean, I'd met Byron Walker, who was another Blade Mage, which is also an Arcane Paladin. And of course, the Cabal had four Arcane Sages. But...aside from Byron, I'd never met another Paladin, and certainly not one who wasn't a Blade Mage. I'd never met an Arcane Hunter, Defender, or War Mage.

There were also members of the Colonial Coven around, though I didn't run into Eilidh or Big-nose.

And representatives from the Southern Circle, though I didn't recognize any of them. Nor had I known they were going to be in attendance. But then, I also hadn't known members from the Great Lakes

Coterie or the Rocky Mountain Chantry would be there, either. There were several other groups represented as well. Most I'd never heard of. A group of vampires who policed a town somewhere in the northeast. A crew of were-critters out of Minnesota. All sorts of supernatural players. Smaller organizations, like...

What? No way! Hell yeah!

A familiar face stepped into the room, scanning the crowd, colors on display.

His wardrobe better matched my own. This newcomer wasn't dressed for success. Well, if you counted dressing fancy as dressing for success. In our line of work, steel-toed boots and bullet-proof vests made more sense. In his case, riding boots, jeans, and a leather vest.

One bearing a logo I held dear to my heart.

I blinked, ensuring it was really him. There was no mistaking the patch, nor his stone-faced glare.

Brother Barajas, Turcopolier and Sergeant at Arms of the Memphis Knights.

Two other knights followed him, but I didn't know their names. I hadn't spoken to Uriah and had been unaware the knights were going to have a presence here. Of course, they probably hadn't known I was going to be here, either. It occurred to me I should probably start calling my friends before attending supernatural conferences. Well, except for Paeter and Mary Beth. Those two wouldn't be caught dead in a place like this. And Shain Stone, well... The very idea.

Barajas's eyes scanned the room and landed on me. The quiet, knife-wielding, motorcycle-riding, demon- stomping biker gave me the slightest hint of a nod and made his way over. Without a word, he took a seat beside us. The other knights followed suit. He didn't say shit. Didn't need to. Brother Barajas and I would never be in the same bowling league. But there was a quiet respect between us. We had bled together. More than once. And so the day went on. Meeting after meeting. Strange face after strange face. Some became more familiar as time went on, and it wasn't lost on me that a lot of people used the opportunity to mingle and network. I probably should've been doing the same.

It was weird, though.

After years in the Cabal, where I had a less than stellar reputation, it was strange being around a bunch of people who didn't know futz all about me, but knew what my title meant. Well, that wasn't entirely true. Apparently my name had gotten around. I was famous, in a way. Lucky me. Exaggerated tales of my exploits had made the rounds. Some people gave me sidelong glances, like I was a psycho murderer on the brink of madness. Others all but asked for my autograph. Every stranger I met had a different reaction, but mostly all asked the same question...

Were the stories true?

And that... That was a question I didn't know how to answer.

Fortunately, the breaks between sessions didn't allow much time for chit-chatting, so it was easy enough to make an escape. But...I heard there was to be a ball that evening.

27

A flipping tuxedo.

It had been waiting in my room.

I certainly hadn't brought it. I didn't own one. Then again, I hadn't brought my snake either, and there she was, lying right beside the tux. I wondered whether she'd given the delivery person a fright. Axel was still adamant he hadn't brought her. How the hell had she gotten there?

Whatever.

I hadn't been sized for the tux, either. Yet when I put it on, I found it fit perfectly. And much to my surprise, it had a special pocket for my wand. And the belt had a hardened indention, right where I kept my concealed revolver. When I clipped the holster to it, it held snug. Perfect. It was like someone had custom designed this tux for me. Creepy.

Even weirder, I realized there was a slit cut in the back of the jacket, just in the right spot where I could strap Dyrnwyn over the dress shirt and put the jacket on over it. The handle slid right through the slit, leaving me access without having to wear it over the top.

Who the hell had put this thing together?

It was...disturbing.

And I was super grateful a few minutes later when I met my team in the hall.

Squirrel Nuts Squad was dressed to the nines. Everyone was in tuxes.

Parker looked the same as always, a tux only being a minor step up from his usual dark suit. Same for Anthony. Security Supervisor Fred might have oiled his handlebar mustache. I didn't ask. Didn't want to know.

And Axel...

Futzing Axel.

He was dressed in his orange Dumb and Dumber tux with the top hat and cane.

I was pretty sure that thing had been ruined during our fight at Mr. Love's house, which meant he'd bought another. Of course he had.

"Good," I said. "Everyone remembered their tuxes. Great."

Parker gave me an amused expression. "Of course. It was on the memo."

"Right," I said, nodding along. What fucking memo?

"There was a boring one like yours on my bed," Axel said, poking me in the chest with his cane. "But I brought my own. What loser thought I was going to dress like the rest of you penguins?"

What loser, indeed?

I felt like someone was playing a cruel joke on me. Like, seriously, there'd been a memo? I hadn't gotten a memo.

Like a hardcore team of well-dressed, badass sorcerer dudes, we waited in the hall for our adopted crew member. Alyita wasn't a proper member of the team, but for the trip, she might as well have been.

And like all dudes who've ever had to wear a tux, we waited. And waited.

Until she finally appeared from her room, wearing a black dress with her hair done up and looking every bit the part of a pissed-off teenager.

She glared at us, seeming very upset.

"What's wrong?" I asked, studying her.

She shook her head. "Doesn't matter. Let's go."

She started down the hall, but Axel stuck out his cane, blocking her. He looked like he was about to ask a question, but paused, a thoughtful look on his face. Then he nodded, seeming to pick up on something the rest of us had missed.

I glanced at Parker, who only shrugged. I didn't know why I kept looking at him. Like Shamus Extraordinaire had any better chance of understanding Axel than I had. Guess it was just nice to have someone else to glance at when he was being all...Axel.

"I got this," Axel said, nodding at Alyita. "Come on."

He turned and started back toward her room.

Alyita bit her lip, staring at him, unsure.

I still didn't have a damned clue.

Alyita moved past him and opened her door. Axel followed her in.

"Is that, uh..." Anthony said, glancing between Parker and me. "Something we should be concerned about? You know, the weirdo going into the teenage girl's room?"

"No," I said, voice firm. "Axel is the last person I would worry about. Or have you forgotten about Branson?"

Much to my surprise, Parker nodded his agreement. "Curious what this is about, though."

"Same," I said. "Anyone have an idea?"

Barrett, of course, said nothing. Fred and Anthony both shrugged.

I used mind-speak.

"Axel, what the hell is going on?"

"Isn't it obvious?"

"No," I replied.

"You're such an uncultured swine, Wyatt."

"Whatever. Is Alyita all right?"

"Of course she's all right. She just needs a little help with something."

"What?"

"Wyatt, you know her mom died when she was young..."

"So?"

"So, she was raised by her grandfather. Around medicine folk."

"What are you trying to tell me, Axel?"

He sighed. Which was really annoying for just being a voice in my head. *"Never mind. We'll be out in a few minutes."*

With that, there was nothing left but to wait.

It was more than a few minutes. Like, ten whole minutes. But who was counting?

Me. I was counting.

But when they reappeared, I noticed an immediate difference. Alyita was wearing makeup. Not a lot, but a little. And she was smiling.

"Ready," she said, nodding at me.

"All right," I said, motioning the others along. "Let's go to the ball."

As the others started down the hall, I glanced at Axel. He only shrugged.

And it all made sense. Alyita had wanted to dress the part. She'd wanted to wear makeup, but that was something... Something a young lady who'd lost her mother and had been raised by her grandfather didn't know how to do. And Axel...

The world got weirder by the day.

I slapped him on the back and we headed off.

To the ball.

28

I froze, taking in the ballroom.

When I broke from my trance, I was glad to see it wasn't just me. The others were every bit as stunned as I was.

We were in a large rotunda, dimly lit. Intricate carvings lined each wall. Wizards of old, I assumed. Previous members of the Appalachian Argument, their likenesses cut into the stone. My gaze drifted upward to see the images continued up the rounded ceiling high above us. There, depictions of ancient battles showed, a dim light circling around them and seeming to tell a tale.

Near the center was a large opening, showing a tunnel cut up through the mountain. It opened to the sky and the stars above. By some trick of light, the tunnel seemed to capture the starlight, brightening and feeding it into the ballroom. That was the only source of light. Somehow, deep down in the mountain, an opening to the sky, so far above, fed in starlight. Enough for a ball.

It was...stunning.

Around us, other folks were dressed the same: tuxedos and beautiful gowns. Few were dressed down.

I noticed the moon-eyed people straight away. Huddled together, their eyes glowed brightly in the dim light, matching the stars above.

They stood by the wall, seeming uncomfortable and out of place. Sadly, they were not dressed in toddler tuxes. They still wore their terrible twos garb, stains and all. They couldn't have seemed less interested in the whole affair.

Tuthid glanced over at me. I offered him a smile and a wave, which he returned with enthusiasm, at least until Feogh noticed. Then he dropped his hand and looked away.

The three Memphis Knights were also there, leaning against a wall and keeping their own company. They still wore their jeans and leathers, but Brother Barajas had added a bow-tie. Perhaps his idea of a joke.

He offered me a nod and tipped his beer toward me.

I led the crew to a table near the wall where a pair of servers were taking drink orders.

I went for an old fashioned, then stopped Alyita when she asked for a glass of wine. She ended up with a soda and a scowl. I'd had plenty of awkward conversations with Archie, and was sure to have more still. Being to blame for underage drinking, especially at a different organization's party, was not one we were *ever* going to have.

Once drinks were sorted, my initial thought was to claim a spot along the wall as well. Maybe even join Barajas to see if he'd share his. But then I remembered why we were there. We had a job to do. Needed to mingle.

I spotted Master Serrano standing alongside Master Castillo. The master librarian looked right at home in his tux. He was used to this sort of thing. The master battle mage had also favored a suit of sorts, though not exactly a tux. She looked like an early 1900s mobster, minus the hat. She did have a chain hanging from her pocket, though. Her pinstripes were a deep crimson that shimmered beneath the starlight. Her soft blonde hair was fixed for comfort and action. The look suited our master battle mage.

I did not suit her.

Her scowl spread the moment she saw us starting toward them. And there I thought I'd been fortunate to spot a couple of friendly faces.

"Draven," she said with a curt nod. "Good to see you didn't get lost on the way."

"Or kidnapped," I said, matching her scowl with a grin. "Good evening, Master Battle Mage." I nodded toward Serrano. "Master Librarian."

"Evening, Wyatt," Serrano said. "You clean up nice."

Master Castillo snorted. That wasn't very master-like.

I motioned to my team. "I trust you both know everyone."

Parker made a quick nod, as did Anthony. Axel had already wandered off. Barrett was silent. Alyita seemed ill at ease. And Fred, poor Fred, was a nervous wreck. His voice trembled as he spoke. "Master Battle Mage. It is an honor."

Master Castillo forced a smile. She was no doubt used to people being nervous around her. Not only was she a master, but she was the bloody master battle mage. Which meant she was over most of our combat crews. In an alternate universe, a team like mine would have reported to her rather than the master librarian.

Wait... Was that why she was so sore at me? Nah. She just didn't like me. Never had.

At any rate, she amused herself by speaking to Fred, who looked like his bowels were about to fall out of the bottom of his pants.

Amused, I turned to say something to...

I froze.

At some point, I'd have to shovel my jaw off the floor, but for the moment, I was a block of ice, incapable of moving. Incapable of intelligent thought.

Eilidh.

She wore a sleek black dress, which hugged her curves, yet maintained her modesty. She was stunning. Absolutely beautiful.

Her gaze met mine.

It was like traveling back in time.

We'd been here before.

Memphis. It was now, as it was then. My breath hung in my throat at the sight of her.

This time, she looked away, tearing her gaze from mine. My heart might've gone with it.

We wouldn't dance this time; I was sure of it. She and her witches wanted nothing to do with us.

"She's really pretty," Alyita said, yanking me back to reality.

I hadn't even realized she'd moved alongside me. Over my shoulder, I saw the others were still being entertained by the two masters. They weren't paying attention to us.

I smiled at Alyita. "Yeah."

"You really like her, don't you?"

"Nah," I said, shrugging. "Just a passing fling. No big deal."

"Sure," Alyita said, rolling her eyes. "That's why you're staring at her with your tongue hanging out of your mouth."

"I was not."

"Were too."

"Whatever, Alyita," I said, knocking back a drink from my glass. "Not having this conversation with you. And it's really not a big deal."

"I call bullshit," she said. "You should go talk to her."

"I don't think that's a good idea."

"Why?"

"In case you forgot, her witch sisters aren't big fans. And even when they aren't around, she doesn't seem inclined to talk with me. Best to just let it lie. It's not like I can just walk up and start talking to her."

Even as the words left my mouth, I noticed a jackass in a mandarin-colored tuxedo walk right up to Eilidh and begin speaking to her. The witches wore their sneers and a few might have even flung their insults. Unbeknownst to their bitchy asses, Axel was immune. And he wasn't the one they wanted to spar with.

Much to my surprise, though, Eilidh excused herself from the witches and walked off to the side with Axel so they could have a private conversation.

"Huh," Alyita said. "Would you look at that? Looks like you *can* just walk up and start talking to her."

I glared at her, then took another sip of my drink.

"Do you think they're talking about you?" she asked.

Both Axel and Eilidh turned, looking our way. Only... It wasn't me they were looking at.

"I think they're talking about you," I said.

Alyita's eyebrows rose. "Me? But...why?"

"Ah, there you are," said the voice of the Archmage from right behind me.

Alyita and I both turned to find him standing just behind us. He gave Alyita his grandfatherly smile and said, "I do trust that is just a soda you're drinking my dear?"

She nodded, staring up at him nervously.

He turned his gaze on me. "Come with me, Wyatt. I have someone I would like you to meet."

I shrugged at Alyita and followed Archie.

Barrett's eyes met mine as we moved away, and he moved to stand alongside Alyita. Her silent guardian.

The Archmage led me through the crowd.

This wasn't the Cabal. He wasn't the Archmage here. I wasn't even sure everyone knew he was. Despite that, people split apart, moving out of his way. We didn't have to work around a single group but walked in a straight line toward our destination. Perhaps they could sense the power radiating off of him. Or maybe it was just the way he held himself. Whatever the case, he was a bit like Moses parting the Red Sea. No one stood in Archie's way.

I recognized Supreme Enchanter Tate ahead. He was also dressed in a tux, though he didn't seem any happier about it than me.

Supreme Shaman Sams stood beside him, the only person in the vicinity who wasn't dressed to kill. He was garbed the same as before and looked tired.

They were surrounded by a handful of others.

Archie made the introductions.

The first person was a pump elderly woman in a black dress. She had hard eyes but a kindly smile.

"Supreme Curator Whitaker," Archie said, offering a slight bow. "I present you Wyatt Draven, Blade Mage of the Ozark Mountain Cabal."

She held out her hand to me. "A pleasure to make your acquaintance."

"It's an honor," I said, taking her hand in mine.

"The honor is all mine," she said. "On behalf of the Appalachian Argument, please do except our apologies for the...circumstances you found yourself in on the way here."

"It's no problem," I said. "I've made it here in one piece."

"No thanks to us, though." She still held my hand in her grip. Then she patted mine with her other hand. "We should find a way to make it up to you. And Sams is right. You *do* remind me of your father in his younger days."

"Thank you. I take that as the highest compliment."

"As well you should." There was a twinkle in her eyes. "Though Connor had a tendency for mischief. I hear you have similar tendencies."

"Mostly exaggerated." I wasn't sure what else to say. It wasn't like Archie had briefed me on what I should or shouldn't share. It was the Southern Circle all over again. He wasn't trying to hide me in a cupboard, but he damned sure wasn't showing me off, either. No, this was his way of throwing me to the wolves. Forcing me to fend for myself.

Curator Whitaker gave me a knowing smile. "Someone must carry that rebellious banner. The rest of us are getting too old." She leaned in. "But I'll tell you, young man, back in the day, I got into an awful lot of messes alongside your old man."

"Come on, Whitaker," Tate said, grinning. "You've always been an angel. I'm sure of it."

She gave her peer a friendly snort before turning back to me. "Don't listen to Tate. He was right there in the mix. Or lagging behind, as it were."

"As I recall," Sams said, his voice nearly inaudible over the surrounding fervor. "You were all troublemakers, and it was me who often had to pull you *all* out of the fire." His gaze turned toward me. "That includes your own Archmage, Wyatt. Don't let him fool you. He wasn't always so calm and calculated."

I glanced over at Archie, who made no reply. He didn't shrug or nod, only wore that same Morgan Freeman smile.

There were a few things that stood out to me about the Appalachian Argument leadership. First, they were more laid-back than the Cabal's big bosses. Or at least it seemed that way. Second, Supreme Curator Whitaker had a lot more charisma than our own Grand Curator, Noah Begay.

Grand Curator Begay seemed like a robot. Most everyone assumed it had to do with his role. Like his head was so full of knowledge, it left him little room for social norms. This wasn't the case with Supreme Curator Whitaker. She seemed like a friendly grandma. Like she might bake me some cookies and give me twenty bucks for my birthday.

Two other people started toward us. One was Christian, the Defender. The other was a rather tall and broad-shouldered woman, who I'd yet to meet.

"Ah, there they are," Whitaker said, patting me on the arm. "And at the perfect time."

I turned to face the newcomers and offered a friendly smile. They studied me like I was a cut of meat. Neither smiled.

"This is the Blade Mage?" the female asked. There was only a hint of disappointment in her tone. "I thought he'd be bigger."

Christian cast her a sidelong look, then turned to me. "Don't mind Daisy."

"No problem," I said, holding my hand out to Daisy, who stared at it for a moment before finally grasping it. Then she tried to crush my knuckles. "Daisy. War Mage."

"Nice to meet you," I replied.

"Likewise," she replied, though her tone said otherwise.

Daisy certainly wasn't impressed with me, and she did little to hide it. She was tall, broad, and seemed to wear a permanent scowl. She kept her blonde hair pulled back in a ponytail, despite the occasion. And she was dressed for battle. No fancy dress for her. Kind of reminded me of Master Castillo.

"Hopefully the three of you will have time to get to know each other," Supreme Curator Whitaker said. "Just now, though, I believe our special guest is about to arrive."

"Special guest?" I asked. I hadn't heard anything about a special guest.

Even as the words left my mouth, I noticed that the room darkened slightly. Everyone else seemed to pick up on it as well. It was like someone was dimming the lights.

All eyes drifted upward toward that opening in the ceiling, which let in and intensified the starlight.

It was nearly blacked out, as though a cloud were passing over. Only this darkness seemed to writhe and move, descending through the hole toward us.

A nervous tension built around the room. Every conversation died. Now there was just a nervous whisper here and there. And a gasp or two as it became clear something was coming down to join us. Something dark.

I glanced over at Archie, who seemed not at all concerned. Not that he would have, anyway. I doubted there was much that could shake him. And even if something did bother him, his mask would never slip. I knew that much. Still, seeing that he wasn't going for his wand told me I had nothing to fear.

My gaze drifted back up, trying to make out any details.

The problem was, whatever reflective trick they used to bathe the room in starlight depended on the light coming from the hole. With the dark shape blocking the tunnel, we were bathed in darkness instead, which made it harder to see what was coming. Pretty sure it wasn't Santa Claus.

And then I saw them.

Red glowing eyes.

The same eyes I'd seen before I passed out.

As it descended into the room, the starlight came through once more, spilling over its shoulders like a spotlight.

It hovered above us, a man-shaped entity, black wings beating softly to keep it airborne. Its body was muscular, masculine in design.

A man's body. But not.

Its skin was an ashen black. Very human-looking feet reached up to rather human-looking legs. There appeared to be no genitalia, despite it wearing no clothes. Where those parts should have been was just...nothing. Like an action-figure. Past the waist was a very human abdomen rippling with muscles. Pecs that would have made any body-builder jealous. Long human arms.

But that was where the human likeness ended.

It had massive bat-like wings, which held it airborne. And the head...

I'd never seen anything like it.

Its head was anything but human. Round and nearly featureless, it bore the face of an insect rather than a man.

And those eyes...

Huge, glowing red eyes.

Bug eyes.

They were staring down at me. Or at least, it felt that way. Hard to say, big as they were.

The ballroom was dead silent.

No sound could be heard beyond ragged gasps and heavy breathing.

The creature descended, gliding toward where we stood.

I cast another glance at Archie, who was still at ease. If he didn't seem bothered, then I wasn't going to, either. Obviously the Argument leadership knew what was going on.

Turning my gaze back to the creature, I realized its trajectory was bringing it right toward me.

Others moved clear, allowing it space.

It landed right in front of me, staring down with those big red eyes.

And then it spoke.

"Wyatt Draven. I am quite pleased to find you in good health."

29

"Uh...hello there."

Not my best line.

But I damned sure couldn't think of anything clever to say.

I was used to weird shit, but this was new, even for me. It wasn't every day a man-bat-insectoid floated down and commented on my health.

"I trust the moon-eyed people treated you well?" the creature asked. Its voice sounded like it was coming through a barrel. Echoing and baritone. Like it was summoning the words from somewhere deep inside. It may well have been. I didn't see its mouth move.

"Yeah, they were, uh..." I took a moment to consider my words. "They treated my wounds and got me here."

"Good," the creature said, turning its head. "Supreme Enchanter Tate. I hope I am not late."

"Not at all, my friend," Tate said. Then, stepping alongside the creature, he glanced around, ensuring he had everyone's attention. An unnecessary gesture. Of course he did.

"It is my honor," the Supreme Enchanter said, "to introduce you all to the Appalachian Argument's dearest ally and a member of our own council. The one and only—"

"Please," the creature said in a low voice.

Ignoring its plea, Tate continued.

"*The* Mothman."

Members of the Appalachian Argument started up the applause. The rest of us were still too stunned. Me, especially. Too on the nose, indeed. I hadn't thought it possible that *the* Mothman had saved me from the Mothman Festival. That just seemed like... *Whatever.*

In short order, we pulled ourselves together and joined in, clapping along.

Mothman made a slight bow, turning in a slow circle.

I had the impression he didn't appreciate the attention. But he probably should have thought about that before he dropped in all super dramatic like.

Once the applause died down, Tate spoke again. "Thank you all for joining us this evening. I know many of you have traveled from afar. We are grateful to each of you. And we've had many great conversations already. Over the next few days, many more important discussions will occur. Tonight, however, kick back and relax. This is meant to be fun, even if Supreme Curator Whitaker insists we all wear fancy dress."

Several in the crowd laughed. I assumed they were from the Argument.

Whitaker rolled her eyes, but smiled.

"Seriously, everyone," Tate said. "Please, make yourselves at home and have a good time. There are drinks and refreshments!"

There was another round of applause and then everyone began mingling again.

I turned to Mothman, who still stood beside me. "Hey, uh, thanks for saving me."

"Oh, of course," he replied. "I only regret I did not get there sooner. I first noticed there was trouble brewing when I spotted unfamiliar mages atop the roofs. At first I mistook them for Argument wizards. Perhaps a security detail. Imagine my surprise when they fired upon me. After that, I saw your battle and found you alone and in trouble."

"How'd you know who I was?"

"You're the Blade Mage," he said, as if that were answer enough. "And I apologize for hauling you away from the others. At first sight, I thought your injuries were more severe, and I couldn't wait around and risk being seen. I knew where the moon-eyed folk camped. A bit of a haul, but they are excellent healers."

"Well, I appreciate it," I said.

"You have made some dedicated enemies for them to have gone to such trouble."

"I suppose so," I said. "Though I don't think they all walked away."

"Indeed not."

"And I sure would like to find them."

"Speaking of which." Mothman turned his attention to Tate. "Supreme Enchanter. We should speak. I believe I've located the one you seek."

"Oh?" Tate asked, raising an eyebrow. "Already?"

"Yes," Mothman said. "Perhaps..."

"Maybe it's best if we speak in private," Tate said, glancing at Whitaker and then Archie.

Mothman's gaze turned my way, then flicked toward Christian and Daisy. "Would you not include your Arcane Paladins? Should they not hear what I have to say?"

"Wait," I said, "you know where Gabby and Tanya are?"

He shrugged his massive shoulders. "These names are unknown to me. I presume they were your attackers. No, I fear I was unable to track them. Some...strange magics shielded them from me."

"Us too," Christian said, brow furrowed.

"Indeed," Mothman said. He turned his attention back to me. "No, it was another target I sought. This one, I found."

"Where?" Tate asked. "Where is Cowan hiding?"

"That is the thing, Supreme Enchanter," Mothman said. "He is not hiding. He is in the open. Or at least, he was a short time ago. At the hoedown."

"Hoedown?" I asked, noticing the eye-roll from Daisy and the sour expression on Christian's face. It occurred to me I probably shouldn't have been butting in, but I couldn't help myself.

Christian answered my question. "The Hillfolk Hoedown. It's a—"

"Disgusting place," Daisy said, finishing for him.

Christian shook his head. "It's a supernatural gathering, of sorts.

Takes place weekly, tucked away in the hills. They have music, booze, and vendors. Sort of a big weirdo free-for-all."

"And Cowan is there," Tate said, rubbing his chin. "That's brazen, even for him."

"I don't like it," Whitaker said. "It's as if he's inviting us."

"And I'm not inclined to turn down the invitation," Tate said. "But that bastard knows most of our operators. He'd run at the sight of them. Can't have him scurry off again."

"A shame you don't have a resource available he wouldn't recognize," the Archmage said.

All eyes turned toward him.

He met them with one of his famous smiles. The friendly grandfather one with just a hint of "I know more than you do."

And then all eyes turned toward me.

"What do you say, Wyatt?" Tate asked. "Feel like getting your hands dirty?"

"Sure," I replied.

Tate nodded. "Look, it's not the target you want, but Cowan, he runs in all the right circles. There's a damned good chance he'll know about your friends. Might even tell us where to find them, if we squeeze hard enough."

"I'll squeeze hard enough to pop his head off his shoulders," Daisy said, scowling.

"Answers first, War Mage," Christian said with a hint of a smile.

Only Supreme Curator Whitaker protested. "Let us not get ahead of ourselves. We should plan accordingly and build contingencies. I don't like that Cowan is out in the open. Gives me a bad feeling. Best we approach with caution."

"Sure, Grandma," Tate said, giving the Supreme Curator a wink. I didn't think she appreciated it.

"The Supreme Curator is wise, as always," Mothman said.

Tate turned toward the Defender. "Christian."

"Sir?"

"You get the details from Mothman and start putting together a plan."

"Yes, sir," Christian replied with a curt nod.

"Excuse me," said a voice from behind.

I turned and saw it was Big-nose. Her arms were crossed, despite having a half-empty wineglass in her hand. When she knew she had our attention, she said, "The Argument and the Cabal aren't planning an op and not including the Coven, surely?"

"You want in?" Tate asked.

"Yet bet your supreme ass," she said.

Whitaker, Christian, and Daisy all seemed a little offended. Tate only laughed. "Then gather your gal pals. No time to waste."

"Tate," Whitaker said in a reproachful tone.

Tate grinned at her. "As soon as we have a plan, that is."

"Very well," Big-nose said, moving away.

Everyone went into motion while I stood there, unsure what I was supposed to do, or whether I was supposed to be following someone in particular.

Then the Archmage glanced over at me. "Wyatt, are you still here?"

"Uh, yes?"

"Perhaps you should go fetch your team."

30

"All right, we don't have any time to waste, so we'll get right to it."

The speaker was Christian. His audience included several members of the Argument, the Colonial Coven witches, and Squirrel Nuts Squad. We were all still dressed fancy, having left the ball to find a conference room.

My crew came together faster than I might've expected. Parker was a good boy scout, so I knew it wouldn't take any effort to call him in. Same with Barrett. I knew where to find him, and that was shadowing Alyita. It was the other three I was worried about. Axel was doing Axel things, and Anthony and Fred were, as they so politely referred to it, "trying to get some bitches."

But when I summoned each through mind-speak, they came and met me near the center of the ballroom. Alyita had also come over, of course, but she wouldn't be going along. Fortunately, Master Serrano offered to entertain her. Most times, a teenage girl would have balked at having yet another chaperone. In this case, she was still a little shell-shocked at interacting with Cabal big dogs, so she was pretty excited to get to hang with a master. Plus, Santiago Serrano was like a big, happy Santa Claus. Everyone loved him.

"Our target is a nomad mage called Cowan," Christian explained.

He spoke confidently and made sure everyone was paying attention. The Defender was used to this sort of thing.

Tate and Whitaker sat off to the side, letting Christian run the show. There was no way in hell Archie would have let me lead a discussion like this.

Christian nodded and a screen lit up behind him, displaying an image of the target. Cowan looked like a railroad baron from a shoddy western film. Like he should have been dealing cards in a saloon. In the picture, he wore a red vest over a white shirt, sleeves rolled up. He had a series of rings on his fingers, possibly magical. Balding up top, but that didn't stop the rest of his greasy black hair from hanging past his shoulders. He even had the mustache with the little upward curls.

"He's always been a lowlife," Christian said. "A lowlife with delusions of grandeur. In the past, it was always petty crime. Drug deals, illicit artifacts, smuggling, that sort of thing. Liked to rub shoulders against the Solemn Covenant, but never outright broke the rules. For the past couple of years, he's pushed closer and closer. When there's trouble in our territory, you can count on Cowan to somehow be involved. Six months back, he was involved in an operation that left many people dead, including several of our own. He's been on the run ever since."

Big-nose shot up a hand.

"Yes?" Christian asked, nodding at her.

"And he's just now appeared out in the open? Seems a little convenient."

Christian glanced over at Supreme Curator Whitaker. "We agree. It's odd. But I don't know if Cowan bears us a direct grudge. He fancies himself a businessman. A player. Maybe he thinks he's hidden long enough for things to have washed over. Or maybe he believes he'll be safe at the hoedown. We, uh... The Hillbilly Hoedown doesn't like for us to maintain a presence there. Having wizards around, especially Argument wizards, makes some folk uneasy. I'm sure you all understand."

Pretty much everyone nodded. I was reminded of the Broken Guitar in Branson. So far as I knew, no one had told the Cabal they couldn't be there, but they limited their presence because it was a place for those who had nowhere else. A lot of supernatural folk, especially the ones who didn't appear human, didn't have a lot of places they could let their hair down. The last thing they wanted was a bunch of wizard cops around.

Parker raised his hand, and when Christian acknowledged him, he asked, "Is Cowan considered dangerous?"

Christian nodded. "He's not the most powerful wizard by any means, but like I said, he's slippery. And if you're in his way, he can be a tough customer. So far as we know, he hasn't taken to any of the darker arts. Mostly he favors illusionary magic. Tricks and the like. Backed into a corner, he can be pretty nasty. Have no doubt, if it's you or him, he'll try to make sure it's him."

When no other hands were raised, Christian went on.

"The plan is pretty simple. We're going to get people into the party, get the area surrounded, and then bring the hammer down. But we want to keep our people back, since Cowan is more likely to recognize us. He won't recognize folks from the Cabal or Coven, though. So we'll split you into smaller groups to join the party. Don't worry. The hoedown is used to having newcomers. People travel from all over to participate. The regulars won't think anything is up unless you act funny."

He paused, waiting to see if any hands went up, then looked my way.

"I'll be running the op, but the Blade Mage is going to be our point man. We'll get a few of you others on the grounds first and posted up, then we'll send Wyatt in. His goal will be to locate Cowan, assuming one of you others hasn't spotted him already. Wyatt will try to get close to him—as close as he can without giving himself away. Once he's in range, we'll have other infiltrators move in closer and surround. Then we'll get our own people ready to move in. That's when we bring down the hammer. The Argument will charge in from all sides and attempt to surround and detain Cowan. If he tries to slip away before we can tighten the noose, Wyatt will stop him."

Big-nose balked. "You're planning on putting the Blade Mage on that assignment alone?"

"I figured he would choose a person or two from his team to join him," Christian said, shrugging. "Less conspicuous. A few buddies checking out the scene. Do you have a better suggestion?"

"I do indeed," Big-nose said, sneering at me. "In case you're unaware, Wyatt has a...reputation. Not the most subtle of individuals."

"We're well aware of the stories surrounding the Blade Mage," Christian said, crossing his arms. "Do you have another idea or just petty insults?"

"I do," she said. "Attending the party with his buddies? Please. They'll see right through that. Better to have a couple on a night out, seeking adventure in the underworld."

Christian managed to not roll his eyes. "And I'm guessing you would like one of your witches to accompany him and pretend to be his partner?"

She shrugged. "This... What were you called again? Squirrel Nut something or other? They're unproven. Better to send someone reliable with him."

"And you have someone in mind?" Christian asked.

"Of course," she said, smiling. "I have just the lady."

I was going to protest. Had every intention. No way in hell was I going to take one of her random snobby witches in as my backup. I didn't trust them. And I didn't fancy pretending I was smitten with a bitchy witchy, either.

To hell with that.

I wouldn't do it.

Not a chance.

Big-nosed fixed me with a wicked grin. "I think Eilidh should accompany him."

31

The Hillfolk Hoedown.

Everything I could have hoped for and more.

Eilidh and I were dumped off on a gravel road near a path we were told would lead us straight to the festivities. We trekked along in silence. Even on an assignment together, she didn't want to talk to me. It was weird.

We passed a few strange folk on the way, some leaving the hoedown, others loitering around the trail. The first group we passed had their faces hidden behind hoods. The next two were a middle-aged couple, both wearing overalls and straw hats. I guessed they were trying to get into the theme.

We also passed what I could only describe as a rabbit-faced man, also in overalls. Sounded cute. Adorable, even. He wasn't. Bugs Bunny smelled like a barnyard's butthole. And he was peddling dope. When we turned him down, he informed us he was available for...other things.

Politely declining, we continued on the trail.

Ahead, the glowing orange hue of a bonfire, the sounds of a banjo, and the mumbling roar of a crowd told us we were headed in the right direction.

The trees gave way to a clearing and we caught our first sight of the Hillfolk Hoedown.

We paused, both stunned.

There were at least a couple hundred people, err...people-ish things. Most appeared human, sure, but there were plenty of other varieties. Beings I'd never even seen before.

At the center of the field was a massive bonfire, flames roaring twenty feet into the sky. A giant ring of people danced a circle around it while the band hammered out some hill country ballad. Fast-paced rock, maybe even metal, but with a hillbilly vibe.

A wooden stage was set off to one side with a big-ass crowd milling around in front of it.

The band... How do I even describe them?

The banjo player was a grown-ass man-squirrel. A. Man. Squirrel. Wearing overalls with his bushy tail flopping out the back. A big ole squirrel head. I wasn't sure what his banjo had done to him, but he beat the strings like they owed him money. Every so often, he'd jump, and just like a squirrel, he'd shoot up in the air, still ripping nasty banjo licks. And he'd land again, staying in time with his bandmates.

A humanoid shape in full firefighter garb was on the drums, faced hidden behind a gas mask. I figured he, or she, had to be burning alive in the garb. And I wasn't sure how they could see a damned thing. Maybe they couldn't. Maybe they didn't need to. They had no problem keeping the beat going.

The fiddler was a satyr, hooves stomping as she sawed strings. She wore a deer head for a hat. Not like a hat with a deer on it, no. A deer's severed head sat atop her nugget. The neck of the slain creature was fitted to her skull like a cap. Its mighty antlers swayed back and forth as she moved, and each time she stomped, the deer's tongue popped right out of its mouth.

A frog-person was on the standing base. Might have been a vodyanoy, but I wasn't sure. Didn't look too similar to my Battle Toad buddies. It was wearing Daisy Dukes and cowboy boots. Every once in a while, at just the right moment, it would stick its ass around the side of its instrument. There was a giant heart painted on the back of the denim. The crowd went nuts every time.

An old man was on the guitar. Just a regular old dude in jeans and flannel. Boring.

As they continued ripping and roaring, I heard a car horn and turned to see an old farm truck with a tanker backing toward the fire. People were clearing out of the way. The dancing circle, broken by the interruption, scooted further away from the bonfire and re-formed. Before I could wonder why, another figure in full firefighter regalia climbed on the back of the truck. They held up a hose with a spray nozzle attached to the end.

The crowd went bonkers.

It didn't take a genius to deduce what was about to happen. And what was in the tanker.

The firefighter sprayed diesel over the bonfire.

Flames roared for the heavens. The heathens screamed.

This was... This was my kind of party.

Eilidh... Not so much.

She gave me a nudge. "Come on."

Those were the first words she'd spoken to me since we'd arrived.

I nodded and followed her through the crowd.

We passed Anthony Burns and Barrett, but didn't make eye contact. A pair of Eilidh's coven sisters posed as their dates. They'd been sent in before us.

The two coven sisters had not been happy about their assignment. I figured whichever one had ended up with Barrett was less annoyed than the one attached to Anthony. They were both playing their part, though, scowling like unhappy girlfriends.

I wasn't sure what instructions they'd been given. Barrett, I'd given no instructions. He was big and quiet. If anyone suspected anything of him, it would be that he was hired muscle. Someone's leg-breaker. Anthony, though...

I'd told Anthony to just be himself.

To act like he was on a date with an unwilling participant and to make a point of checking out all the others ladies in sight. He had assured me he could handle that. I'd assured him I had no doubt.

More of Eilidh's sisters were elsewhere, roaming about the crowd, but we hadn't spotted them yet.

Axel, Parker, and Fred would not be joining us. They were hanging back with the Argument's people. Parker was too clean cut for a hoedown. Fred was a douchebag. And he had a handlebar mustache. Also, he looked like a cop. And Axel... He would've had too much fun. No way he wouldn't have drawn attention.

He was not happy.

How'd I know he wasn't happy? Well, for one, the temper tantrum he'd thrown was a pretty solid clue. If that wasn't enough, every few seconds he would reach out through mind-speak to let me know how unhappy he was. I started ignoring him.

That, it turned out, might have been a mistake.

Parker contacted me through mind-speak next. *"Wyatt, we have a problem."*

I paused, motioning for Eilidh to stop. *"What sort of problem?"*

"The Axel kind."

"Damn," I said aloud, rolling my eyes at Eilidh. Then I got back to Parker. *"He slipped away, didn't he?"*

"Yup."

"I'll keep an eye out for him."

"Figured you'd want to know," Parker said. *"Also, Christian is... displeased by this development. And the War Mage, Daisy, she's...rather contrite. Can't imagine Master Serrano or the Archmage will be happy either, when they hear."*

"Wonderful. Did you explain how Axel operates?"

"I tried. Not sure they understood. But they've heard of him. Everyone has heard of Axel."

"Oh. Right. Well, then they shouldn't be surprised."

He snorted. *"That's what I said."*

"All right, well, make sure the others know to keep an eye out for him. We should have known better than to think we could keep him on the sidelines, especially for a party like this... Wait... Damn. He was still wearing his orange tux, wasn't he?"

"Yup," Parker replied and ended the connection.

Given the variety of costumes, maybe Axel wouldn't stick out too much. He'd certainly be easy to spot.

I tried to get his attention over mind-speak.

His response...

"Thank you for calling. Unfortunately, Axel isn't available at the moment. I guess you shouldn't have ignored him. Please go fuck yourself after the beep. BEEEEEEEP."

He would say no more.

I gave Eilidh the rundown, and she used mind-speak to notify her fellow witches to keep an eye out for the idiot in the orange tux. Then we continued moseying through the crowd.

As we walked, Eilidh took my hand. I raised my eyebrow, surprised.

"We're supposed to be a couple on a night out," she said, scowling. "Look the part."

"Right," I said. "Well, your scowl certainly makes us look like an old married couple."

"At least I don't look like I want to take out a magical sword and start culling."

"Is that how I look?"

"It is. You seem uncomfortable and on edge."

"Can't imagine why."

She shook her head and led us toward a long row of vendor tents. The nearest was hawking pulled pork sandwiches and libations. Others were selling wares. One old crone, playing the part of a witch, was trying to sell potions. She made straight for Eilidh, but turned back when she saw the look on the real witch's face. Of course, she didn't know Eilidh was a witch, but the scowl on her face got the point across.

I paused beside an old man selling mason jars full of clear liquid. No markings. No labels. No price sheets. I guessed he didn't take credit cards, either. Nor did he have any other wares. No love potions or supposed magic baubles. No, this old father dealt in a different kind of magic. White lightning. I was sorely tempted to pick up a jar, but Eilidh waved me on.

Leaning in close, like a couple in love, she said, "Stay focused. We're supposed to be doing a job."

"Yeah," I replied. "And part of that job requires blending in, remember?"

She scowled and turned away.

I was keeping an eye out for our guy. I hadn't seen him yet.

Glancing at Eilidh, I said, "You seem annoyed about getting stuck with me."

She didn't reply.

We walked past the next booth. This one was a weapons dealer. He had a few old handguns on the table in front of him. Some old knives as well. Even a few wands. I doubted they had any magical qualities about them. Behind him, he had a few old long guns on display, as well as some swords he'd almost certainly gotten from a local pawnshop.

Eilidh had still never answered my question, so I went with a different tactic. "What did Axel want?"

"He didn't tell you?" she asked, seeming surprised.

"We haven't had time to catch up since the ball. It's been a bit of a rush."

"Right," she said, shrugging. "He wanted to know if I could help Alyita with something, should we have to attend another formal event."

"Her makeup?"

Eilidh nodded. "Axel did a half-decent job. I don't know why that surprises me. But yeah, if the need arises again, I'll help her."

I almost thanked her, but a new thought occurred to me. Was she only agreeing to get close? To recruit Alyita?

She must have seen something on my face. "What?"

"Nothing," I said, moving on toward the next tent.

"Wyatt," she said.

I paused, turning back toward her. "Yeah?"

She bit her lip. And after a moment, she shook her head. "Nothing. Let's go."

I turned and moved along through the next row of vendors. Still no sign of the target.

Ahead, I noticed there was a whole other area of festivities.

Games and gambling.

If our sleazebag wizard was about, this was where I expected to find him.

There were all sorts of games on hand. All sorts of action to get in on.

To our right was a roped fighting pit. A lizard-looking man was trading blows with a monkey-looking chap. The lizard had the power, but the monkey was quicker. Neither seemed to have the upper hand. Folks stood around them, cheering and shouting. The crowd was divided on who they were rooting for, and money was still changing hands.

To our left was a turtle race. Yup. I said it. A futzing turtle race. And it had drawn in just as big of a crowd as the fighting pit, including two of Eilidh's witch sisters. At least, I was pretty sure they were. There were eight turtles racing, each with their shells painted in different designs. A pale man in a circus maestro's costume waved his cane about, imploring folks to get in on the action before it was too late.

We ignored his pleas, just as we ignored the kid shouting for us to get in on betting on the fight.

And then I saw Axel.

He was emceeing a beer pong tournament. How he'd become a host for festivities, I did not know. Wasn't sure I wanted to know. Whatever the case, he was dancing about, waving his cane like the maestro at the turtle race. So, I guessed he fit in.

We were supposed to be incognito, a couple out for a weird adventure. Both of us were stunned at the sight of him. He, of course, was having the time of his life. And the crowd loved him.

He didn't notice us. Or if he did, he didn't react.

"I will, uh, let my sisters know," Eilidh said, snapping me back to reality. "We just passed a couple of them."

"I thought so. I noticed the nice one."

"Nice one?" she asked.

"The only one who didn't join in the sneers every time Big-nose talked shit."

Eilidh chuckled despite herself. "Yeah. That's Mareen."

"Big-nose? Or the nice one?"

"The nice one. Big-nose is—"

I held up my hand. "Don't care. Don't even want to know her name."

"She isn't all that bad, Wyatt. You just have to get to know her."

"Right," I said, rolling my eyes. "She seemed super interested in establishing a budding friendship. Come on. Let's go."

Next up, we passed a cock-fighting ring and a corn hole tournament.

Then ax throwing, archery, mud wrestling, and other shit I'd never even heard of.

And there was our guy.

I spotted him straight away. He was hard to miss, dressed like a snobby banker from a western flick. He stood off to the side of the arm wrestling contest, visiting with a person who wore a burlap sack over their face. Anywhere else, and the two would've stood out. As it was, their costumes were some of the tamer ones.

Just behind them was another stage, this one with a stripper pole. They'd set out lawn chairs for spectators. Right up front, though, there were church pews for pervert's row. They had it all! Including women. And men. And things that looked like women...sort of. And things that may or may not have been men. The dancer on stage had a duckbill where her lips should have been. She popped her top, revealing feathered mammaries. It was...disturbing. The crowd ate it up, though.

"What are we doing?" Eilidh whispered in my ear.

"Trying not to throw up," I replied.

"We can't stand here like this," she said, leaning into me. "What sort of couple would watch the strip show?"

"A weird one," I replied.

"Come on," she said, giving my arm a tug.

It didn't take much to get me away from whatever the hell that was. I mean, other than nightmare fuel. By that point in my wizarding career, I sort of felt like I'd seen it all.

Nope. I definitely hadn't.

We joined the crowd hovering around the arm wrestling, and I made a point of not staring at our guy. Instead, I tried to pretend I was super interested in watching the man with the pig head try to slam the arm of the bodybuilder woman in the neon bikini.

I leaned in, like I was whispering into Eilidh's ear, which was convenient because that was precisely what I was doing. "You letting them know?"

"Of course," she replied, sounding annoyed.

It wasn't my fault she was a more powerful magic user than me. Or maybe it was. Point was... It made more sense for her to use mind-speak than me. We had all set up mind-speak connections before we'd taken off, but I had a suspicion if I tried to reach Christian from this distance, I would have had to close my eyes and really concentrate. Anyone who knew anything about magic would've likely known what I was doing.

So, despite Eilidh's irritation, it made more sense for her to do it.

"Perfect," I said. And since I felt like being an ass, I pecked her on the cheek.

Her eyes widened, staring at me.

I gave her my best boyish smile.

Then I felt eyes on me. And from my peripherals, I knew it was Cowan. He and his sack-headed friend. They were both looking right at me.

This time I used mind-speak. *"Eilidh, they're looking at me."*

"I see that."

"What do you think we should do?"

"Let's move away."

She punched my arm and, using her real voice, said, "Come on. I'm hungry."

"All right," I replied, rolling my eyes. "Didn't I feed you yesterday?"

She took my hand in hers and pulled me back toward the vendors. I won't lie. It felt pretty good having her hand in mine again. I was reminded of our trek into the River Witch's den. The first time she'd held my hand. We'd taken comfort in each other. Not this time, though. This was all business. She didn't want to hold my stupid hand. Which was, like, junior high stuff anyway. How immature could I be?

Immature enough to get myself killed.

Because that was precisely when everything went to hell.

32

A woman stepped out in front of us.

Sort of...

She definitely stepped out in front of us. It was the "woman" part I was a little shaky on.

The creature blocking our path looked more like a cat than a woman. Also, she kind of reminded me of Goro from *Mortal Kombat*.

A slutty cat Goro.

Where a woman had arms and legs and a cat had four legs, she had six appendages, all ending in paws. And her torso seemed abnormally tall and stretched, built so she could move on all fours like a cat while still having a very humanoid torso with two arm-like paws for doing... arm stuff. Just then, she stood upright like a human, but with four arms.

She was covered in tan fur, reminiscent of a mountain lion, but also wore clothes. Sort of. She wore tights around her bottom half and a black vest for her upper half, which had holes for her extra arms and plenty of furry cleavage to show off. Her features were more feline than woman, but she had makeup, earrings, a nose ring, and even a golden necklace.

She had a drink in one hand and one of those old-school long cigarette things in the other.

When she spoke, she sounded exactly how I expected a talking cat to sound.

"What have we here?" she purred. "My, my, what an adorable little couple."

"Uh, thanks," I said, sharing a look with Eilidh.

I started to move on, but Dyrnwyn pulsed on my back. A warning.

Uh oh.

I took another look at the cat woman, suspecting this wasn't a chance encounter.

"I think we're in trouble," I told Eilidh through mind-speak.

"No shit, Sherlock," she replied.

The cat woman flashed us her dazzling smile, showing off rows of sharp teeth. "Now, now. Let's not be rude. No secret conversations."

Uh oh.

If the cat lady knew we'd used mind-speak, that meant she knew magic. And she had to have been quite talented to have picked up on it.

I risked a glance over my shoulder and saw Cowan and his sack-headed friend easing their way toward us. We were about to be surrounded.

But we weren't alone. Axel was also easing his way over, sticking out like a parking cone. I guessed he had seen us after all. Eilidh's witch sisters were also headed our way, having stuck close to Axel. That gave us the numbers if things went sideways. I still had a bad feeling.

How had Cowan known who we were? And why had the cat lady stopped us? Who was she?

"What's the matter?" our feline friend asked. "Cat got your tongue?"

She cackled at her own joke. It sounded like Fran Drescher, at least until she coughed on what I could only assume was a furball.

"Can we help you with something?" I asked.

"Oh, darling, I do believe you can," she said, purring once more. She ran a claw down her cleavage, staring at Eilidh. "My dear, you have such a cute boy toy. This little pussy might have to steal him away."

"I'm allergic," I heard myself say. "To cats, that is."

Of all the things I could have said... And that was what came out of my mouth?

Eilidh turned and stared at me like I was a potato.

The cat lady only laughed.

Then a booming voice called out from behind me, all baritone and southern. "I'd recognize that record-scratching cackle anywhere."

We turned and saw a man walking toward us.

Sort of.

Like before, he was definitely walking toward us. It was the "man" part I was a little shaky on.

Fella was tall. Very tall. Broad, too. And his face…

The face of a man, but mixed with the features of a gorilla. He had long stringy hair and a gray beard to match, but his features belonged to Donkey Kong. Except for the eyes. Those were glowing red and piercing, much like Mothman's.

He was dressed in a faded gray duster, jeans, and rugged boots. A wide-brimmed had sat atop his head. It had seen better days, as had most of his garb. And him. He was like Curious George in the later years. You know, after the Man in the Yellow Hat passed away, and George turned to drugs to cope, which inevitably led to his fall from grace and spiraling fame, then he had to live on the streets for several years, but has now finally sobered up and become a health nut who spends every day in the local gym, trying not to be bothered when youngsters ask for a selfie.

Anyway…

The giant ape-man sauntered toward us with a purpose and a scowl.

The cat lady's eyes widened, but only for a moment. "If it isn't my old pal, the Tennessee Wildman, live and in the flesh. I figured you'd be back in some freak show act by now."

"And I figured you'd be some hunter's rug by now, Wampus." He snorted. "A shame, really. I like the thought of a human wiping their feet on your carcass."

"Oh, please. As if," she said, batting one of her many paws at him. "And shouldn't you be chasing some poor woman through the forest? Or have you really given up that game?" She flashed her teeth at him. "You know what I say: once a predator, always a predator."

"Maybe for you," he replied, crossing his arms. "What are you doing here?"

"Minding my own business, dear. Which is...none of yours. Run along now. You know I can't stand your stench. Nor can anyone else. You'll ruin the hoedown."

Was that what that smell was? I'd only noticed it a few moments earlier. Something strong and pungent. Like sour apples and mildew.

"Trying to run me off already?" the Tennessee Wildman asked. Then he turned his attention to us. "I don't know who you folks are, or what your business with Wampus Cat is, but she ain't as friendly as she lets on."

"We don't have any business with her," Eilidh said.

"Oh, I don't know about that," Wampus said, purring again. She looked me up and down. "This little puss has never had herself a Blade Mage before."

Well, that answered that question.

This wasn't a chance encounter.

From my peripherals, I saw Axel's orange suit moving closer. The witches had to be close, too. As did Cowan, our target. Unless he'd bolted. Obviously, Wampus Cat knew who I was, but did that mean Cowan did? Were they were working together?

The Tennessee Wildman raised a thick eyebrow, studying both Eilidh and me. "A Blade Mage, huh? I'm curious what one of those would be doing here." His gaze turned back to the cat lady. "But not nearly so curious as to what you're doing here, Wampus. I told you last time I seen you: next time we met, I'd kill you."

She purred. "Best get your head checked, Wildman. You're forgetting things in your old age."

"That so?"

"Yes. Two things: first, I'm out of your weight class, hon. Second, I never travel alone."

A whole lot happened in a wee bit of time.

A dark figure appeared out of nowhere, slamming into Wildman. This newcomer was shorter but stockier, and looked even more like a gorilla. In fact, the fur-covered newcomer looked a hell of a lot like Scotty the Sasquatch.

Axel thought so, too.

"Scotty?" Axel called, voice filled with hope. "Scotty, is that you?"

I turned to see Axel racing toward the two. The sasquatch creature was on top of Wildman, trying to bludgeon his head. As Axel closed in, the creature turned and backhanded Axel across the chest. He flew backward, slamming into several people.

It was not Scotty.

I took a single step toward Axel and heard a shout behind me.

I turned again.

It felt as if time froze.

Eilidh was still beside me, but one of her sisters stood just in front of me. It was the nice one. Mareen. She stood with her wand raised, prepared to defend us from Wampus.

Only the attack didn't come from her.

It came out of nowhere, a bright red bolt, fired from a distance. A sniper spell.

And it had been aimed at me.

Tanya.

It didn't hit the target.

Instead, it struck Mareen. The spell disintegrated her shield and charged on through, striking her body.

She screamed.

Eilidh screamed.

I screamed.

As the witch tumbled, both Eilidh and I moved in to catch her. There was a basketball-sized hole in her chest, charred black from the magical attack. She didn't bleed. Tanya's spell burned hot, cauterizing as it seared through flesh.

Mareen stared up at us, wide-eyed, trembling in our arms. She moved her mouth, trying to speak, and...died.

Just like that.

That was how Tanya's spells worked. She struck from afar, her spells multi-layered, much like a steel-cored rifle round. The tip of the spell shattered a mage's shield. The rest passed on through, causing massive damage.

It had been meant for me.

Instead...Eilidh's sister had died in my place.

Eilidh screamed again, hugging her dead sister to her chest.

I grabbed her arm and jerked her away. "Move!"

The next bolt slammed down where we'd just stood.

I had no time to ponder the situation, but one thing stood out...

This was a trap.

Tanya's trap.

A trap for me.

If I'd had any doubt, it melted when Gabby appeared right in front of my face.

She'd intended to stab me in the back, but Dyrnwyn warned me with a pulse. I whipped around just as her invisibility spell shimmered away in front of me. The knife was already moving.

Eilidh's other witch sister was just beside her, saw the attack coming, and reacted more quickly than me. She slammed into Gabby, tackling her to the ground. The knife swiped the air in front of my face as they fell. Both ended up in a pile at our feet.

The timer in my head sounded and I yanked on Eilidh's arm again as another red burst zipped through the real estate we'd just vacated.

That was roughly when the crowd fell into a panic. People screamed. Bodies scattered. I hoped that might've made Tanya hesitate. It didn't. She had no qualms about taking out innocent bystanders. Some poor hipster-looking frog-man ran past just as Tanya fired again. The unlucky bastard went down, just as Eilidh's sister had.

We couldn't stay out in the open. We also couldn't abandon Eilidh's comrade. And I needed to check on Axel.

The witch first.

Eilidh was already ahead of me. She ripped her arm from my hand and started for her friend.

A black shadow flew overhead. I glanced up and saw glowing red eyes.

Mothman.

No sooner had the thought popped in my head than a black cloud began swirling a few feet above our heads.

What the hell?

The red pulse of Tanya's sniper spell shot through the cloud, but it didn't dissipate. In fact, it only grew wider.

It didn't take a rocket surgeon to figure it out. Mothman had summoned some sort of cloud spell, which was blocking Tanya's view of us from wherever she was perched. Probably in a tree somewhere.

I focused back on the problems at hand.

Gabby had freed herself from the other witch, knocking her aside. She might have finished her then, but Eilidh charged in with her ice scythe. Gabby's dagger came up and blocked the attack, shattering the ice. At the same time, she raised her wand, but Eilidh was ready. Twirling her staff, she summoned her shield, blocking whatever Gabby had cast.

Then Gabby kicked her legs out from under her. Eilidh was one mean witch, but getting up close and personal with Gabby was never a good idea.

I charged in then, sword and wand at the ready. Gabby turned her wand on me and summoned the black cloud, like before. I was blinded for a moment, but held Dyrnwyn out in front of me, hoping my sword could cut through the unnatural cloud. It could.

But not before I tripped over Eilidh's leg.

I ate dirt.

I was just grateful it was the ground rather than concrete. I was also grateful Dyrnwyn always made sure I didn't accidentally skewer myself. That would have given our foes a good laugh. All the work they put in to kill me, and I go and off myself? *Hilarious.*

Rising back to my feet, I found myself face-to-face with Wampus Cat.

Uh oh.

Before I could react, she opened her mouth and let out an ear-splitting shriek.

The impact was instant, stunning me. So loud I couldn't think. An all-encompassing sound, drowning out everything else.

It wasn't just me, either. At some level, I retained just enough sense to realize everyone had been impacted.

I also had enough faculty to understand I was in a lot of trouble.

She took a step toward me, still shrieking, and raised a single paw, holding up one claw. She poked me in the chest with it. The razor-sharp talon cut right through my shirt and into the flesh, stopping only when it scraped bone.

The pain was a distant thing, inconsequential to the ringing in my head. Still, it served the purpose she desired. I stumbled backward and fell right on my ass.

She could have killed me. Could have ripped out my throat while I'd stood there, discombobulated and staring at her like an idiot. Instead, she'd pushed me over. She was a cat, though, and they liked to torment their prey.

Dumb move on her part.

Dyrnwyn did its thing.

I became aware of a pulsing sensation in my hand. My sword. And the more it pulsed, the clearer my mind became. I had the impression my sword was sending out waves of energy, pushing back the magical ferocity of her scream. It was still obnoxious, but not overwhelming. An annoyance, but not incapacitating.

I did my best not to react. To not show her I was free.

Around me, everyone from random strangers to my allies and her own buddies were all stunned by the endless scream. Even Gabby was down, clutching at the sides of her head.

Wampus Cat dropped to all six legs, leering over me. A mountain lion stalking its prey. She thought she had me.

She was wrong.

I lunged forward, swinging Dyrnwyn at her face.

She was too quick. Way too quick.

She leaped back, a stunned look on her feline face.

I didn't get her, but I did break her spell.

The Tennessee Wildman charged in then, slamming into her. I hadn't even realized he'd broken off from his fight with the half-squatch. She went down rolling, clawing at him with all six of her paws. He was pretty damned quick himself, though, and leaped clear.

The stocky sasquatch raced by then, still after him.

Wildman was outnumbered, and I wanted to help him, but I had to help my own allies first.

Parker's voice spoke into my mind, *"Wyatt, what's going on out there? What's—"*

Another voice cut him off. Mothman's voice.

"Wyatt, there are more enemies encircling you. You are being surrounded. I suggest you flee."

I disregarded his warning. I would flee as soon as I gathered my allies. I wasn't about to leave Axel, Eilidh, or the other witch behind. No way.

Eilidh and her witch sister were engaged with Gabby again.

What about Axel?

I turned to where he'd crash-landed, but he wasn't there.

Where had he gone? Did that mean he was all right?

I got an answer a moment later when I heard him cry, "Cowabunga!"

That was followed by a lightning bolt slamming down right on top of the stocky sasquatch creature.

"And that's what you get for pretending to be Scotty!" Axel called.

I finally caught sight of his orange suit. He was tucked down behind the turtle race enclosure, lost in the crowd. Everyone near us had been impacted by the cat call. Now, they were in a panic once more, trying to flee.

I figured we ought to join them.

First, though, the half-squatch didn't seem the least bit bothered by Axel's attack. Well, physically, anyway. He seemed awfully interested in Axel. I didn't think they were going to be best mates like Scotty.

Using mind-speak, I said, *"Axel, we've got to get out of here."*

"Just when it's starting to get fun? What, are things not going well on your date?"

"It's not a real date. Remember?"

"I remember that it's important to make the most of the opportunities we have, Wyatt."

I would have told him what I thought about his Zen wisdom, but just then, Cowan and the sack-headed man stepped out before me. Cowan was grinning. I didn't like that grin. I had a mind to remove it from his face.

Axel was going to have to deal with his half-squatch problem on his own.

33

"Easy now, Blade Mage," Cowan said, flashing me a smile. I guessed he thought it was dazzling. A charmer's grin. "No reason for all this fuss. You're surrounded and outnumbered. Best surrender before anyone else gets hurt."

I chucked my sword at him.

I had been hesitant with so many civilians around, but most had fled. The rest were working on it. What few remained, Dyrnwyn would avoid.

The outlaw mage dove to the side. Sack-head did the same.

As soon as my sword left my hand, I charged Cowan, firing pumpkin blasts. I didn't really care about catching him, compared to everything else going on. Not to mention the much juicer targets on the field. But he had been the Argument's target.

My main priority was to survive, and with my allies, of course. Either way, I had to deal with these dicks first, so it made sense to focus my efforts on Cowan.

He blocked my pumpkin blasts with a bit of dramatic flare and returned fire.

A yellow bolt shot toward me like a bottle rocket. Only, instead of striking my shield, it exploded a few feet in front of my face. Instead of a bottle rocket, it was more like an artillery shell. Little explosions blocked my view. Not an attack. A distraction.

Sack-head was less tricksy. He wanted to charbroil my face. His plan involved a sustained fire spell. Basically, he used his wand as a flamethrower. A clever strategy. The magical flames hammered my shield, trying to disintegrate it. Once it succeeded, he could char me to a crisp. I guessed he preferred his steaks well done.

I called Dyrnwyn back to my hand and threw it at him again, hoping it would force him to lose concentration on the fire spell. It worked and I had a momentary reprieve.

Mothman's voice spoke into my mind again. *"I implore you, Wyatt, run."*

It was weird that he could use mind-speak with me, considering we'd never established that connection. Of course, the Archmage had once done the same, and I'd never established a connection with him, either. But Archie wasn't a mythical cryptid, so while it was equally as invasive, it was not so disconcerting. But... What the hell? I decided to roll with it.

I thought my thoughts back at him. *"Appreciate the concern, but we're already outnumbered. Can't abandon the others. Anything else you can do to help?"*

The flamethrower spell slammed against my defenses again just as Dyrnwyn returned to my hand. I threw it again, earning another brief reprieve.

There was no sign of Cowan. The slippery prick might have headed for the hills, or he might've been trying to sneak up behind me.

Axel was zigzagging back and forth, in full flight from the half-squatch.

The Tennessee Wildman was playing cat and monkey with Wampus Cat.

I didn't have time to to turn around and check on Eilidh because the flamethrower hammered my shield again. It was getting tough keeping my defenses together.

"I'm quite busy up here myself," Mothman said. *"Maintaining this cloud is no small feat, my friend. But it does protect you from the sniper's*

spells, though now she's taking shots at me. Easy to evade, but still rather irritating."

"Yeah, she's a real bitch."

"You know her?"

"Yup. She's my ex."

I threw my sword at Sack-head again, earning myself another quick breather.

"Wyatt," Mothman said, *"I find myself questioning your judgment in regards to choosing mates."*

"You and me both, buddy."

Dyrnwyn had just made it back to my hand when it pulsed a warning.

I dove forward.

A red blast of energy sailed over my head.

Glancing back, I saw Cowan stood just behind where I'd been, a surprised look on his face. Apparently, that sneaky trick usually worked out better.

I also got a chance to see what Mothman had been so concerned about. By that point, any civilian with a lick of sense was out of the way. The hoedown was over. Yet there were several people running toward us, most wielding wands and staves.

Uh oh.

There was an awful lot of assholes converging on us. No doubt Christian had backup coming, but they wouldn't get to us before the army of wizards. This was not good.

And then the stupid flamethrower lit up in front of my face again. That was getting old.

"Hmm," Mothman said. *"Perhaps there is one thing I can do. One moment, please."*

"Take all the time you need," I replied. *"I'm not going anywhere."*

He responded with a good-natured chuckle, which was extra weird inside my head.

I didn't bother asking him what he planned. Didn't have time. I had the flames to deal with and Cowan hurling random magic at me. Chucking my sword would get one of them off my back for a few moments, but that was it. My shield was taking a beating. With my old staff, I'd have been cooked already. As it was, my father's wand was keeping me alive, but only just.

I threw my sword for the millionth time.

And then the sky fell on me.

At least, that was how it seemed.

It got really dark.

Even the flames couldn't cut through the darkness.

I feared Gabby had hit me with another of her black cloud spells, which made me really worried about Eilidh and her witch friend.

"*There,*" Mothman's voice said. "*I've lowered my cloud all the way to the ground.*"

Of course.

"*I suspect your sword can dissipate it,*" he continued. "*At least in the area immediately around you. Please confirm.*"

I called Dyrnwyn back to me and found it could indeed cut through the cloud. That was no real surprise. I *was* surprised Mothman had known that.

Interestingly, the clouds regathered where Dyrnwyn melted them away. So, it would only cut a hole through the black in my immediate vicinity. In fact, with the sword in my hand, I could see about two feet in front of me. That was it.

"*Confirmed,*" I said, then took a few steps to the left.

As I expected, a stream of flame shot where I'd just stood. My enemies were blinded, too. *Good.*

"*Wonderful,*" Mothman replied. "*Your foes, without any ancient arcane weapons of their own, should remain blinded. Your allies as well. It's doubtful any posses the means to break my shroud. But I can only maintain it for a short time. Hopefully long enough for you to collect our allies.*"

"*Great idea,*" I replied, studying the darkness before me. "*Not to seem ungrateful, because I really am. My defenses certainly appreciate the break, but even with Dyrnwyn, I can't see well enough to find my friends. Also, can Wampus Cat or that other thing smell me?*"

"*No. My shroud blocks scents as well.*"

"*Nice. But how am I going to find the others?*"

"*I'm going to guide you.*"

"Oh."

That wasn't what I had expected.

"Take a few steps to your right," he instructed.

I did as he suggested. It was eerie, walking through the cloud. Not only could I not see anyone, but things had grown quiet, with all the combatants blinded and lost in the harmless smoke.

"Stop."

I did. And then waited. It felt like I was waiting for hours.

"Continue."

"Wait. What was that about?"

"Please keep moving, Wyatt. This is rather taxing."

"Sorry." I started my feet forward again. *"Just curious."*

"Of course. You were about to walk into the Apple Devil's path."

"Apple Devil?"

"The creature pursuing your friend."

"The half-squatch?"

Mothman chuckled. *"Yes, I suppose that's one way to describe him. A tough species, Apple Devils. Many underestimate them for their short stature. I assure you, though, you'd rather wrestle a gorilla. You're well out of his reach now. He's meandering through the shroud, looking for something to smash. Best to avoid."*

"I do have a magic sword, you know."

"Of course. I considered having you poke him in the back with it, but he's quite evasive, and time is not on our side. Best we waste none of it."

"Makes sense."

"Continue on your current path. Wait..." He sighed. *"Would you tell your friend to hold still? He keeps bouncing about. Looks like he's pretending to be a...ninja."*

I didn't have to ask which friend.

Using mind-speak, I called out to Axel. *"Hold still, jackass. I'm coming to get you."*

He didn't reply.

"Axel?"

"Axel isn't here right now, Wyatt. You're still an asshole and can once again go fuck yourself after the beep. BEEEEP."

"You're still upset?"

"*Upset about my best friend ignoring me? Yes, I am still upset about that.*"

"*You were supposed to be waiting with the others.*"

"*And you are supposed to answer me when I mind-speak you.*"

"*Axel, we don't have time for this. Just stop moving. I'll find you in a moment.*"

"*I already stopped moving, dong-a-tron. You know, I had this whole plan about how to get you an Eilidh together, but now... Now, I'm not going to be your wingman.*"

That wasn't worthy of a reply. I wasn't sure I wanted him to be a wingman. I mean... For futz sake! This wasn't something we should have even been talking about right then.

"*Wait,*" he said. "*How are you going to find me? Can you see in the dark?*"

I considered telling him about Mothman, but then I knew he'd have more questions. Just then, I needed him to shut up so I could focus if Mothman had instructions for me. So, instead, I said, "*Yes, Axel. I can see in the dark.*"

"*No way! Since when? Have you always had this? Did it start just now? Did the sword teach you? Did you read a book that taught you? Was it ninjas? Just the air in West Virginia? Can you see me waving? I just waved. Did you see it? Can you teach me how? That would make me so much sneakier. Do you think...?*"

On and on he went.

Fortunately, Mothman's voice cut right over the top of him. "*Move a little more to your left. No, too much. Yeah, about like that. Walk forward. You're almost to him.*"

I continued on.

"*Wait, move further left,*" Mothman said, exasperated. "*He moved again.*"

"*He does that. Hold on.*"

"*Axel, hold still!*" I mind-shouted at him.

"*Oh, shit,*" he replied. "*You really can see in the dark... I thought you were just messing with me.*"

"*Wyatt!*" Mothman said. "*Hold position.*"

I waited while trying to ignore Axel. It was like having two different radio stations fighting for signal inside my skull. Fortunately, neither had static racket. It was still annoying, though.

"*Several more enemies have entered the cloud,*" Mothman said. "*There are three just ahead of you.*"

"*Should I just attack them?*"

"*No. Just wait. They're moving.*"

"*How are they moving together in this darkness?*"

"*Well, this is something I never thought I'd say before, but the dark wizards are...holding hands.*"

"*That is... I wish I could see it.*"

"*It is...quite the sight.*"

"*Can you see Christian and the others yet? Surely they're on the way.*"

"*They are. Okay, move. Your friend is just a few more steps ahead.*"

As promised, Axel's head appeared through the darkness. First, his eyes focused on Dyrnwyn's glowing blade, then he looked up at me.

"Oh, hey," he said. "Just so you know, I'm still not talking to you."

"Great," I replied. "Let's go."

"*Back the way you came,*" Mothman said.

I turned into the darkness and started back the way I'd come. Axel grabbed a hold of the back of my belt to follow. Apparently, the outline of my head wasn't good enough.

He continued blabbing behind me.

"Axel, shut up," I said quietly. "We're surrounded by enemies."

"Are we?" he asked. "How can you tell? Oh, right, you can see in the dark now. You know, I'm not quite sure I believe you. I feel like there's something else going on."

Mothman spoke into my mind. "*I would advise you to get your friend to be quiet. You're nearing more enemies. In particular, Wampus Cat has sharp ears.*"

"Axel," I said over my shoulder. "I thought you weren't talking to me?"

"Oh, yeah, right," he said, and was quiet again for a moment.

"*And continue,*" Mothman said.

I started forward again, dragging Axel along with me.

Naturally, he didn't stay quiet for long. Fortunately, no enemies found us.

The sounds of battle, however, grew. Mothman confirmed my suspicions. Some of our reinforcements had arrived and were engaged with our foes outside of the black mass he'd created for us. Everyone was scattered into smaller pitched battles, and our folks were outnumbered in most of them. Wasn't anything I could do about that yet.

With Mothman's guidance, we made our way to Eilidh a short time later. Her witch sister was still with her.

Much like Axel, her eyes widened at the sight of my burning sword. Then she looked up into my grinning face.

"Hello," I whispered. "Ready to get out of here?"

"This darkness your doing?" she asked. "We feared it was your former teammate."

"Mothman," I replied. "He made the darkness. And guided me to you."

"I knew it!" Axel said from behind me. "You shithead!"

"Come on." I waved them behind me. "We're forming a conga line."

Eilidh put a hand on my shoulder and the other witch put her hand on Eilidh's shoulder.

Mothman said, *"Let's head to your right now."*

I didn't argue.

I started to the right, the others tagging along with me.

Axel was still out of sorts, but since I wasn't paying attention to his nonsense, he focused on the only other friendly face.

"You know, Eilidh," he said, "I totally get why you don't have the hots for Wyatt anymore. He's kind of a jerk."

"Are you really doing this right now?" she asked.

"Doing what? I'm just saying...I get it."

She didn't reply.

That didn't bother him. "You know, I was going to play wingman for him again, since I was super successful last time."

"Oh, that was you, was it?" she asked.

"Obvs," he replied. "I mean, you two did—"

"Enough," she said. "Stop. I'm not having this conversation with you."

"Good. Because that's not the conversation I wanted to have. I wanted to have this conversation. I was going to try to butter you up and brag on him, but I'm not anymore. Like, I intended to point out how he's really rich now."

"And you think I care?"

"No, I don't think you're that superficial, but it can't hurt to know. I was also going to tell you he has a super sweet ride."

"I don't care."

"And I was going to tell you he has a badass familiar, too. But I'm not going to tell you that now, either."

"Axel, stop—"

"And I was going to point out how much more powerful he's been growing."

"I know, Axel."

"And I guess you also know he has a really big wizard—"

"Axel!" I said, stopping in my tracks. "No!"

"What?" he asked, all innocence. "I was just going to mention you had a new staff being made by a world-renowned wandmaker. And it's really big. I don't see... Oh, you thought I meant... No, Wyatt, Eilidh already knows how big your—"

"Axel, I swear to god," Eilidh said. "Finish that sentence and I'll freeze yours off. Now shut your mouth before you get us killed."

"Hmm," Axel mumbled to himself. "Maybe I *should* tell her all those things. These two are, like, perfect for each other."

"Axel," both Eilidh and I said at the same time.

"Point proven," he said, still talking to himself.

But finally...he shut up.

"*Thank the stars,*" Mothman said. "*I thought for sure they were going to hear you.. Take a few more steps to the right.*"

A few more steps and the Tennessee Wildman's face came into view.

He scowled at me. "Blade Mage."

"Yup," I replied. "Care to join our daring escape?"

"This darkness is you?"

"Nope. Mothman."

He rolled his eyes. "Should've known. Damned goody-two-shoes interloper."

"*Interloper?*" Mothman said into my mind. "*The nerve! He was the one who invaded our op! How dare he! And to think I led you to help him.*"

I ignored Mothman and focused on the Tennessee Wildman. "Look, man, I don't know shit about you, but we're surrounded by assholes who want to murder us. You coming or not?"

He grunted. "Fine."

"Great. Join the conga line. Grab on to Axel behind me."

"Dreamsicle man?" he asked.

"That's what the ladies call me," Axel replied.

We started off into the darkness once more, Mothman directing me. The sounds of battle were louder still. Sounded like a real fun time was underfoot.

"*Move right approximately five steps,*" Mothman said. "*And be prepared to act.*"

"*Why?*"

No sooner had I mentally replied than another head came into view. Cowan's head.

With four people hanging off the back of me, I couldn't really leap into action. I could raise my arm, though. Right as the slippery target turned to face me, looking as surprised as my friends had, I slammed the butt of Dyrnwyn into his forehead.

He dropped like a stone.

"*Because,*" Mothman said, "*I thought you might still wish to catch the target. Awful lot of trouble not to get him.*"

"*Hmm. Fair enough. I'd really like to get Gabby, too. She's the one Eilidh and the other witch were fighting before you turned the lights off.*"

"*Ah. Sadly, she's already slipped from my shroud. Most of them have. Cowan was hiding, however.*"

I turned and glanced at the Wildman. "You mind carrying this dude?"

"Why me?" he asked.

"Because you're the strongest."

He grunted, then scooped Cowan off the ground and tossed him over his shoulder. "Why do you want this piece of wizard garbage, anyway?"

"I don't," I replied. "The Argument does."

He grunted yet again. "Of course you're working with those good-for-nothing assholes. Should've known."

"Good for nothing or not, I'm hoping there's an army of them out there."

"Why's that?" he asked.

It was Eilidh who replied. "Because there's definitely an army of wizards here to kill us."

"Seems like they wanted to kill him," the Wildman replied. I assumed he meant me, but couldn't see because he was behind me.

"Yeah," Axel said, "but when people want to kill Wyatt, they tend to try to kill the rest of us, too."

The Tennessee Wildman grunted once again.

34

We exited the shroud at a run.

A wizard stood just ahead of us. How'd I know he was a wizard?

Mostly because he raised his wand.

Dyrnerang sailed right through his neck. His head toppled as we raced on by.

Behind me, Wildman chuckled. "Nice."

Ahead were the vendor tents. A decent place to get lost.

Mothman had said he was guiding us toward the side of his shroud with the least amount of assholes. Well, actually, he'd used the term "enemies." I preferred to think of them as "assholes."

The rows of tents offered plenty of cover and a chance to slip away. That was precisely what we needed. I didn't love fleeing while our other allies were outnumbered and fighting for their lives, but we had secured the target. Best I could tell, this was like a big game of Capture the Flag. Except, instead of flags, my team was after Cowan. And the other team, well, apparently I was their flag. My former teammates really wanted to kill me. I, on the other hand, really wanted to survive. Selfish, I know.

If we could reconnect with our reinforcements, maybe we'd have a chance to take the fight back to them.

Ahead, two dark wizards stood shoulder to shoulder, slinging spells at our very own Anthony Burns. I picked up the pace and raised my sword, planning to hurl it at their backs.

Before I could, Barrett appeared between two of the tents. Using his magically-enhanced abilities, he slammed into the two like a race car with the pedal down. One of the poor schmucks shanked off into one of the tents, smashing through tables and bringing the entire thing down. The other went airborne, shooting off like a rocket.

"Lift off!" Axel said, laughing. "Look at that fucker fly!"

Barrett whirled on us, wand at the ready.

Then he fell in step as we continued toward Anthony.

"You good?" I asked Barrett, forgetting he was still doing the silent game thing. "If you're good, don't say anything."

Much to my surprise, he actually responded. "Is it them? Are they here?"

I glanced over at him, unsure how to respond. I didn't want to lie, but I also didn't want him flying off the handle again.

Unfortunately, that was precisely when Sophie decided to pop out from behind a tent behind Anthony, wand raised.

Axel reacted first.

He summoned a lightning bolt right on top of her head.

It smacked her shield and dissipated, but got Anthony's attention. He spun and cast his own spell at her. She staggered at the impact, her shield taking a beating.

Sophie glanced back at us, then turned and fled between the tents.

And I wasn't sure what to do.

It might've seemed like an obvious choice. It would've been easy to assume she'd gotten separated from her fellow assholes. We had the numbers to take her. It was a chance to capture one of my former teammates. And that...

That seemed too good to be true.

My Spidey Sense was tingling.

It felt like a trap.

Unfortunately, I didn't get to decide. Barrett did.

Roaring, he took off after her, propelled by magic and moving inhumanly fast.

"*Barrett! No!*" I screamed through mind-speak.

He either didn't hear me or ignored me.

The big guy disappeared around the tent a moment later.

We caught up with Anthony and kept moving. No time to stop for tea. He was smart enough to follow.

Our group rounded the corner and started up the lane. Sophie was way ahead of us, but Barrett was about to run her down.

Until he hit an invisible wall.

One second he was powering forward like a freight train. The next, he was on his ass.

Sophie turned and grinned at him.

Zeke stepped out between the tents. He didn't gloat, though. He wore a sorrowful expression on his face.

We slowed down, coming to a stop behind Barrett.

Zeke looked down at his former best friend and sighed. "You should've just died, big guy." Then his gaze flicked up to me. "Hello, Wyatt."

I never got a chance to reply.

Behind me, a scream sounded.

I whirled around.

Eilidh and her witch friend were bringing up the rear of our little group. I turned just in time to see Gabby appear, knife aimed at Eilidh's back.

There was no time to react.

Eilidh didn't see it coming.

Her witch sister did and threw herself in the way.

The knife came down, burying to the hilt in the witch's chest.

Surprise showed on Gabby's face.

Eilidh screamed and turned to catch her falling sister.

Gabby took a step back and black smoke formed around her. She gave us a wink and disappeared within.

Eilidh held yet another of her sisters, watching her die at the hands of my former teammates.

Turning back around, Zeke and Sophie had started hurling magic. Zeke focused on Barrett, who was doing his best to shield himself from where he lay on the ground in front of us. Sophie cast at the rest of us, serving no purpose other than annoying me.

And "annoyed" didn't begin to touch my feelings.

I was pissed.

Furious.

And still hurt by their betrayal.

I wanted to...

Tanya stepped into the lane.

She looked the same as the last time I'd seen her, just as Zeke did. I hadn't seen either since that day in Memphis, when they'd betrayed my old team and revealed themselves as the back-stabbing asshats they truly were.

More dark wizards stepped out from among the rows of tents, surrounding us.

Tanya didn't twirl her metaphorical mustache. She didn't say anything. Just went on the attack, as did the others.

Spells pounded us from every direction, and all we could do was defend. Well, not me. I threw Dyrnerang, which ripped through tents and made a lot of assholes dive for cover.

Still, the odds weren't in our favor.

Behind me, Eilidh had set her sister down. Her chest was no longer rising and her eyes were closed. Dead. Another down. I didn't know how close Eilidh was with her. Didn't know if they were friends or just business associates. There were certainly thousands of members of the Cabal I didn't know on a personal level. But that didn't mean I wanted to see them die. It didn't mean I wouldn't have felt guilty if they took a knife for me. I couldn't imagine what was going through Eilidh's head just then, but I couldn't worry about it. Not until we got out of this mess. *If* we got out of this mess.

"Everyone," I said, "we need to get to Barrett. March forward at my word."

"You sure have a lot of enemies," the Tennessee Wildman said, Cowan still draped over his shoulder. "Maybe I was better off on my own."

"Nonsense," Axel said. "Sticking with us is where all the fun is."

"Shut up, Axel," Eilidh said, voice cold as she rose to her feet, staff at the ready. "Say when, Wyatt."

"Now," I said.

Together, we all started forward, moving toward Barrett, who was still being pelted with a bazillion spells. Our enemies saw him as the softest target, and while the big man's lung issue had certainly slowed him down, he was still pretty decent at defense spells. Not as good as Zeke, of course.

We made it to Barrett, stepping around and encircling him within our own magical defenses.

Over my shoulder, I said, "Anthony."

To his credit, the former shamus needed no further instruction. He moved to help Barrett up. The Tennessee Wildman beat him to the punch, though, and yanked Barrett right up to his feet.

Tanya held up a hand, then, and her gaggle of dark wizard asshats held their fire.

She locked eyes with me. "Surrender, Wyatt. Give up now and no one else has to get hurt. We'll let your friends go. I don't care about them. You have my word."

I stared at her.

"Hell no," Axel whispered from beside me. "Don't you even think about it."

"Hate to say it, boss, but I agree with Gunner on this one," Anthony said.

"No," Barrett added.

"Yup," the Wildman said. "Was definitely better off on my own."

Even Dyrnwyn pulsed its opinion.

Only Eilidh didn't comment.

"Come on, Wyatt," Tanya said, offering me a sad smile. "Trust me one last time. Like you used to."

"You'll really let them go?" I asked.

Behind me, the others started to protest, but I held up a hand to silence them.

"I will," Tanya said. "It's you we want."

"Huh," I said, winking. "Nice to know you still want me."

She scowled. "Don't be an idiot. We've got you surrounded. Are you really willing to throw Axel's life away? Or Barrett's? Or that witch you seem so infatuated with?"

"Jealous much?" I asked.

"Hey, wait," Anthony said. "What am I? Chopped liver?"

"You and me both, kid," the Tennessee Wildman said.

Tanya ignored them, shaking her head at me. "This isn't a game. Please. For once in your miserable life, do the smart thing."

I sighed. She was right.

It was high time for me to do the "smart" thing. I was supposed to be a leader now. Supposed to set a good example. And it wasn't just my team. That was part of what being the Blade Mage was all about. Being able to make the tough decisions. Being able to make sacrifices for the greater good. I thought about my father and Byron Walker. Considered what either of them would do.

"You're right, Tanya," I said, as much as it pained me to admit it. "It's time for me to make smart decisions."

So...

I threw my sword at her stupid face.

She leaped back, tripping over her own feet.

I called Dyrnwyn back so I could do it again. "You think I'd trust a treacherous bitch who banged my boss behind my back? Then blew his brains out? I don't know what sort of dark wizard paint chips you've been chewing on, but you're out of your damned mind! Get bent, you fucking psycho!"

"Hells yeah!" Axel shouted, and summoned lightning.

"Fuck yeah!" Anthony added.

The Tennessee Wildman snorted.

"So, now what?" Anthony asked.

The sorcerers were pelting our defenses again.

Tanya picked herself up off the ground, looking none too happy. Bummer for her.

"We fight until the cavalry shows up," I said.

"And what if they don't show up?" Anthony asked.

"We fight until we die," I replied.

"Great."

"Don't worry, Burns," Axel said in far too cheery a tone. "We usually survive these things."

"Usually, huh?" Anthony asked.

"Would you guys focus?" Eilidh asked.

"I am focused," Axel said. "And we need to talk about your attitude, missy."

"Axel," Eilidh said, venom dripping from the words. "If you ever call me 'missy' again, I'll kill you myself."

"See, that's exactly what I'm talking about," he said. "You clearly have been spending too much time around uptight witches. Lost your sense of humor. You've been mean and rude. Avoiding us except when people are dying. That hurts my heart. Being away from us, especially from Wyatt, has not been good for you. What you need—"

"Don't finish that sentence," Eilidh said. "Swear to god, Axel, I will plunge an ice pick in the back of your neck. I am not in the mood."

"I'm just saying, if a doctor were here, they's prescribe you a ride on Wyatt's wizard sta—"

"Axel!" I screamed over my shoulder. "No!"

"And clearly," Axel continued, "you can see that a doctor would prescribe Wyatt a ride on your witch's broom."

Anthony snorted. "Nice."

"Thank you, Burns," Axel said. "Glad someone appreciates me."

And that was when the cavalry showed up.

For the wrong team.

Wampus Cat leaped over a tent and came flying down toward us, intending to land right in the middle of our desperate little party. My only warning was a vibration from my sword and I whirled around, spying her in my peripherals. On instinct, I raised my wand and summoned a pumpkin blast.

Much to my surprise, it did the trick. I'd have figured she'd have a magical shield of her own. Maybe she did. But if so, she didn't block my attack.

She let out a very feline yelp as she soared. She came down on four of her six paws. Stupid cats always landing on their feet.

There was another commotion from the other side as Apple Devil tore through a merch tent, batting it out of his way to get to us.

"Well, looky. A couple more problems," Wildman said as he dumped Cowan off his shoulder. The sleeping man hit the ground with a thud, but didn't stir. "I'll try to keep them off of us."

I couldn't argue with that.

"I'll help if they both get close," I said. I had the magical sword, after all.

But I also had a magical shield, which wasn't doing so hot. It was teetering on the verge of defeat, and I could only pump so much energy into it. And I doubted my allies were doing much better. In fact, I was sure of it.

Neither Axel, Anthony, Barrett, or Eilidh had cast any attack spells for several seconds. We were all on the defensive. It reminded me of my duels against Chambers. Our opponents could sit back and rain hell, patiently waiting for us to run out of steam.

I needed to come up with a clever idea.

One of those hare-brained schemes that almost worked the way I intended.

But...

I had nothing.

Our foes were well-attuned to my sword-flinging tricks. They were even prepared for my upgraded Dyrnerang move. Blade would have been ashamed of me.

I felt...helpless.

I didn't like that feeling much. But I also couldn't come up with a damned thing to do about it.

"Get ready," Wildman said over his shoulder. "She's about to pounce."

I had to take his word for it.

I turned my gaze on the half-squatch. He was pounding his chest like King Kong and scraping the ground with his foot like a bull.

"Apple Devil, too," I said. "I'll take care of him. Tennessee, you focus on Cat Woman. Everyone else focus on shields."

"Sure," Anthony said, glancing at Apple Devil. "But what the hell are you going to do?"

It was a fair question.

One I didn't have an answer to.

One I needed to have an answer to in, like, three seconds, because the big bastard charged.

Instead of coming up with something clever, I realized I'd made a mistake. Sure, I had the magical sword, but Barrett was the close quarters specialist. If any of us could stop a charging gorilla in its tracks, it was him.

But it was too late.

I pointed my wand at the creature and summoned a pumpkin blast, hoping it would knock him back like it had Wampus Cat. No dice. Bastard didn't even blink.

Half-squatch charged right toward me.

I leaped out to meet him, jabbing forward with my sword. Dyrnwyn took on the form of a long claymore.

Apple Devil charged right onto the end of my sword, skewering himself. He didn't seem bothered, though, and kept on coming, hammering into me like a city bus. I flew backward, slamming into Anthony, who, in turn, slammed into Barrett. Two of the three of us went down.

It was Barrett who stayed standing. No surprise there.

He took over my fight, slamming his weight against the half-squatch and putting his wand and knife to work. I wasn't sure if he could go toe-to-toe with such a monster at full health, much less with a damaged lung, but I'd already given it my best shot.

Wampus Cat must have timed her attack with Apple Devil, because she was in our midst as well, but the Tennessee Wildman was keeping her busy.

Never one to miss an opportunity to be a backstabbing asshole, Gabby had appeared as well, looking for an easy target. Eilidh was ready for her, though, and went on the attack.

And all that chaos meant only Axel was left shielding us.

The good news was that the gathering of evil asshats had stopped slinging spells when their buddies had pounced us.

There was one I feared wouldn't be so hesitant.

I glanced up and saw Tanya had dropped to one knee. She held her staff up to her shoulder like it was a hunting rifle. She was about to summon one of her sniper spells. Her target was Axel.

Rolling to my feet, I called Dyrnwyn back to my hand. It transformed into a knife, popped out of half-squatch's chest, zipped right between Barrett's legs and landed in my hand.

I hurled it without aim, trusting it to find my target.

Tanya dove to the side to avoid it.

Whew.

That had been close. Too close.

We couldn't keep this up.

Someone was bound to fall. And when they did, the rest of us would tumble down like dominoes. Game over.

And then...

The cavalry arrived.

Our cavalry.

Although they weren't on horses. Or tanks.

A purple lightning bolt shot down from the heavens, hammering down in the center of the dark wizards, sending them scattering. The air shimmered and Christian appeared.

He no longer looked like a pretty boy jock.

Instead, he looked like what he was.

A defender. Captain freaking America.

His eyes glowed with purple light, matching the glowing sigils on the arcane shield in his hand. He held a wand in the other.

His battle gear was one part modern tactical, and one part medieval knight, with chain-mail. He even wore a chain-mail hood over his head.

Dark wizards fled in terror. And well they should have, because he killed two of them in the time it took me to blink.

He seemed to have that situation in hand, so I glanced down the other side of the lane.

A tornado had touched down there, sweeping dark wizards off the ground and hurling them in every direction.

Literally.

It was a spinning blur with a yellow glowing center, unlike any tornado I'd ever seen.

Then it slowed to a stop.

It was Daisy, the War Mage. And it hadn't been the wind that had been batting bozos away, but her mighty hammer. An arcane hammer.

The head glowed bright yellow, matching her eyes. Her garb was less modern than Christian's, and much more medieval. She looked like Thor, with her blonde hair, medieval armor, and the big-ass hammer.

And just like on Christian's end of the lane, the dark wizards fled.

They wanted nothing to do with either of the arcane warriors.

Parker Grimm burst out from between two nearby tents, Fred on his heels. Behind them, more Argument wizards followed. In fact, they were pouring out into the lane from seemingly every direction, along with Big-nose and more of Eilidh's witch sisters as well.

Above us, Mothman soared, red eyes glowing in the moonlight.

I'd like to say that was when we all got to work, kicking dark wizard ass.

But...

Well, we didn't. Not my group, at least.

The battle was over in moments.

The appearance of the other Arcane Guardians had sent our enemies fleeing.

Tanya, Zeke, Gabby, Sophie, and all the rest. They bolted right out. Poof. Gone.

Didn't even say goodbye.

Wampus Cat at least offered me a wink before she went invisible and also slipped away.

Apple Devil didn't make it. The half-squatch finally realized he'd been stabbed through the chest and succumbed. He lay at our feet, struggling out his final breaths.

Christian barked orders and roughly half the wizards set off, chasing after the assholes.

The Defender stalked toward me, looking very annoyed.

I glanced down at Cowan and gave him a gentle kick in the ribs. He didn't react. Then I met Christian's fierce gaze. "Hey there, Christian. Got your target for you."

35

"It was a fucking disaster."

That was Daisy, the War Mage. I wondered how she really felt. If there was any question, she went ahead and continued. "An absolute shitshow."

We were back at the Appalachian Argument headquarters in a conference room. Archie sat on one side of me, Master Battle Mage Castillo sat on his other side. Master Serrano sat on my other side. Across from us were Supreme Enchanter Tate, Supreme Curator Whitaker, Supreme Shaman Sams, Daisy the War Mage, and Christian the Defender. Big-nose, Eilidh, and another witch were also at the table.

It was the after-action debrief and it was going... *Oh, so* well.

Sarcasm. That was sarcasm.

Everyone was pissed. Most presented with more professionalism than Daisy, but it was clear there was plenty of frustration to go around. We'd secured the target, sure, but at what cost? The Argument had lost a few people in the fray, and, of course, the Colonial Coven had lost two witches. Not to mention damage to the Argument's reputation for turning the Hillfolk Hoedown into a supernatural showdown.

The icing on top of the shit sandwich was most everyone seemed to think it was somehow my fault. At least they had something to agree about. And a target for their ire. Not that most of them said it outright.

Scratch that. Daisy glared right at me and said, "And it was his damned fault."

So much for buddying up with the Argument's War Mage.

"Easy, Daisy," Tate said with a sigh. The Supreme Enchanter looked worn out. Exhausted, even though he hadn't been in the field with us. "We're not going to sit here and point fingers."

"Perhaps we should," Big-nose said, sneering at me. I still wasn't sure what her rank was within the coven. If she had an official title, I'd not heard it. "This is the second time Mr. Draven has interacted with the Colonial Coven, and he's two for two. Both times we've lost witches."

I opened my mouth to speak and shut it again. I wasn't about to take the blame for the witches who'd died in Memphis. That was crazy talk. As was this. I understood their frustration. I really did. But I felt guilty enough about the witches dying without taking the full brunt of the blame. That was bullshit.

Archie didn't step in for me. He just sat there, doing his quiet grandfather routine.

Master Serrano did, though. "The frustration around this table is reasonable. Warranted, even. Certainly the losses were tragic. It seems a stretch, however, to place all the blame on Wyatt. None of us expected so many antagonists to be gathered around the target."

"I agree," Supreme Curator Whitaker said, giving everyone a good ole grandmotherly scowl. "We all share in this blame. Perhaps we should not have rushed to move on the target."

I doubted anyone had forgotten that she'd cautioned against the op before we left.

Daisy seemed ready to fly off the handle again, but Christian put up his hand, silencing her. Instead, he spoke. "You're right, of course, Supreme Curator. The Argument bears responsibility for initiating the op without full intel. However, if we're to go through the events as they unfolded, it is not unfair to question certain...decisions."

Ouch.

No doubt that was pointed squarely at my forehead. If I doubted it, the way he glanced up at me was a dead giveaway.

I felt enough guilt without this bullshit.

Futz it.

I spoke up. "Was I supposed to know there was going to be an army of dark wizards? Did you guys know and just not tell me? Or was I supposed to surmise that on my own?"

"No," Christian said, meeting my gaze. "But a certain member of your team didn't follow instructions. Axel wasn't supposed to be at the hoedown."

"Well, it was a damned good thing he was," I said. "Otherwise, Eilidh and I probably wouldn't be sitting here."

He ignored my rebuttal and continued, "Furthermore, your communications were...lacking."

"You didn't even inform your team what was happening," Master Battle Mage Castillo said, taking her turn to pounce. She glared at me. "You easily could have informed Parker Grimm and had reinforcements en route sooner. You even had two on site nearby. You didn't give them a heads-up, either. They had to go looking for you."

Daisy jumped in again. I guessed she couldn't contain herself. "And you could've told us where you were going when you broke free of the cloud so we didn't have to hunt your ass down. Have you never run an op before? I would have expected more of a Blade Mage. Guess the Cabal doesn't have the same standards as the Argument."

Ouchie ouch.

"Daisy," Tate said. There was an edge to his voice that silenced her, though she continued glaring at me. The Supreme Enchanter said, "It's not a competition. And it's certainly not our place to evaluate the performance of our allies."

"Even when they operate in our territory?" Christian asked, voice even. "I understand your stance, Supreme Enchanter. But this was a... disaster."

"And you're convinced it's all Wyatt's fault?" Supreme Shaman Sams said, joining the conversation for the first time.

Christian opened his mouth to speak, then shut it again, a

thoughtful look on his face. "No, Supreme Shaman. I'm not saying that."

"Yet many at this table seem to be," Sams said, eyes moving about the table.

That produced a nice, awkward silence.

I glanced over at Eilidh, who wouldn't meet my gaze. She'd not spoken a word to me since the battle. I guessed we were back to that. Having her sitting there while I was being belittled only made it worse. If this were the Cabal's own Archcouncil, I would have lost my shit already. I was trying to keep my cool since we were visitors.

But... Well, as Axel had told me not so long ago, I had a new energy about me. I was done eating everyone else's shit.

So, I opened my big, fat mouth. "Fine. It's all my fault. Fantastic. I'm sure Archie will let me know what a failure I am later. In the meantime, why don't we focus on bigger questions, like, how the hell did an army of dark wizards infiltrate a public event without being spotted? And how did they know I would be there?"

"I am curious about that as well," a new voice said.

I glanced over my shoulder and saw Mothman approaching. I hadn't even heard him open the door. He'd slipped in unannounced, quiet as death. Dude was sneaky.

When he knew he had everyone's attention, he asked, "How could so many dark wizards have entered our territory without being spotted? How could so many gather around a public place without us identifying a single one of them? That, I would suggest, is the biggest failure."

"You were our eyes in the sky," Christian said.

"Indeed," Mothman said. "It would seem Wyatt cannot take all the blame, though he graciously offered to. I shall take some as well. Would anyone else care to share? Or is the burden of blame only for Wyatt and me?"

That caused an even more uncomfortable silence. Among the Argument, Mothman was revered. A member of their council. Someone whose voice they trusted above most others. And he'd stepped up to have my back.

Master Castillo, Daisy, and Big-nose, the bitchy witchy, had nothing to say. No challenge to that. Christian seemed thoughtful. Tate and Whitaker both wore sly smiles.

Mothman turned to the Archmage. "Magnus Holmes, I have long found your council wise, yet you have remained silent throughout this conversation."

Wait. How long had Mothman been in the room? The entire time? Was that why I'd never heard the door open? If he had been, where had he been hiding?

The Archmage put on a disarming smile. "These events were tragic. There are many questions which need to be answered. Perhaps this discussion would better serve us after some rest."

"Agreed," Tate said. "I had hoped to call us together to get an understanding of what happened, not to play the blame game. As ranking members of each of our guilds, we should be embarrassed by this display on all sides."

"We lost people," Daisy said, fist smacking the table.

"And acting like children will not bring them back," Tate said, giving her a stern look. He turned and looked at me. "Wyatt... You are right. The biggest question is how so many dark wizards could have hidden under our noses. And remained hidden, with our operatives having eyes on the hoedown. To have so many gathered there at once..."

And then it hit me. Really hit me. I mean, it was in the back of my mind all along, but it wasn't like I'd had a lot of time to think about it.

"It was a trap," I heard myself say. "They set us up."

"It sure seems that way," Tate said. "They must have known we'd go after Cowan. But what they hoped to accomplish by ambushing you..."

"They wanted to kill me," I said, meeting his gaze. "Same at the festival. My question is, how did they know I'd be in either place?"

"That seems..." Christian said, biting his lip. "Are you so sure it was all about you?"

"I... No," I said, shrugging. "But I've been targeted twice since arriving. Strange, isn't it? That my former team would be here, and that they'd pounce on me twice?"

"No," Archie said.

All eyes turned toward him.

"The simplest explanation is usually the correct one," he said. "You were a target of opportunity, Wyatt. We've been made to understand this Cowan character is often involved with nefarious works. So, the obvious conclusion is that this faction of dark wizards had some kind of business deal with him. Likely a profitable one for him to risk coming out in the open. Our biggest mistake, perhaps, was sending you in at point. We assumed you would go unrecognized. But with your old team on site, they spotted you. Likely assumed you were on to them and moved in to attack. Simple."

Tate and Whitaker both shared a looked. Supreme Shaman Sams looked away. Everyone else either continued looking pissed off or thoughtful about what Archie said.

"Perhaps," Mothman said. "Sure seemed like a trap."

"I'm sure it did," the Archmage replied. "However, the most logical answer is usually the correct one. There was no way they could have known Wyatt would be at the event. So, for the moment, we must assume it is as I said. Perhaps we'll discover more when Cowan wakes up. In the meantime, can someone could tell us about Wampus Cat and the Apple Devil?"

Tate gave Archie an impatient look. "You know about them, old friend."

"So I thought as well," the Archmage replied. "Yet I don't recall ever hearing of them working together, nor for, or with, a larger group. But that is precisely what we saw today. Have any thoughts on the matter?"

Maybe it was just me, but the folks from the Argument all seemed very uncomfortable with the question.

Tate sighed. "You're right, Magnus. It's peculiar, and is as concerning to me as the fact so many dark wizards could've been hiding in plain sight. And for either to have teamed up with those dark wizards…"

"Well," I heard myself say. I hadn't planned on saying anything, but since my treacherous lips had parted, I rolled with it. "At least we don't have to worry about Apple Devil any longer."

Daisy rolled her eyes. Christian looked away. Whitaker gave me a sympathetic smile.

Tate made it all make sense. "That wasn't the only Apple Devil. There're more."

"Oh," I said, feeling a fool. "There are more half-squatches to worry about?"

"Perhaps," Tate said. "As your Archmage alluded to, they aren't known for playing nice with others. They run in their own packs. There aren't a great many of them out there, and most simply want to exist without being bothered. But like any group, there are always a few assholes. Those are the troublemakers. That you saw only one hopefully means there are no more aligned with whatever...this is."

"It is Wampus Cat who concerns me the most," Archie said. "She doesn't play nice with others. That she has aligned with this other faction..."

"Right," Tate said, sighing. "Look, we've got a lot to think about. A lot to figure out. Let's drop it for now. We all need rest."

And with that, the meeting was over.

36

I rejoined my team.

They were waiting to find out what happened at the debrief. And there I'd hoped they'd all gone off to bed. Most looked like they'd had showers, at least. Even Parker, who hadn't really fought. Maybe the outside air made him feel dirty.

Anyway, I was the only one still wearing dirty clothes and dried blood.

Alyita was there, too, arms crossed and scowling. Clearly she wasn't happy about having been left out of all the fun. She'd get over it.

"What's the word?" Parker asked. He didn't exactly scowl at me, but his tone was cold.

"They, were, uh…"

I wasn't sure what to say.

A part of me thought I should soften it. Make it out that we'd done all right. That our own leadership was pleased with us. Or at least shake the narrative a little to make it seem like things weren't so bleak. Maybe that was what a good leader would've done. Maybe a good leader would've focused on the positive, what little there was.

Just then, though, I remembered something my dad had told me a long time ago.

Minimize bullshit one level up and one level down.

Well, I was staring into the faces of one level down, even though I didn't really see them that way. I didn't see myself as some corporate middle manager. Maybe I should have. But I didn't see myself as the "boss." They were my peers, the guys who bled alongside me. Maybe Anthony was an ass. Fred, too. But even with those two, I would've felt like a fraud pretending like I had some right to lord over them.

No, I thought. Better to treat them like peers. To treat them with respect.

Minimize bullshit...

I shrugged. "It didn't go great. Leadership from all parties felt like the op was a shitshow, and about the only thing they could agree on was that it was all my fault."

"Bullshit," Axel said, crossing his arms. "The nerve! Am I right, guys?"

No one replied.

Anthony and Fred made a point of looking away. Barrett just looked angry. And Parker maintained a professional, if not disdainful, blank face.

"They aren't entirely wrong, Axel," I said. "I made some mistakes."

"Yeah. For one, you didn't chop off your former teammates' heads."

"Beyond that," I said, motioning toward Parker. "Grimm tried to touch base with me when everything was going to hell. Mothman cut him off in my head, but I should have gotten back to him. If I had responded to Parker, he might have been able to get allies to us sooner."

Parker's eyes widened, surprised by my admission. He gave me a little nod.

"And you," I said, glaring at Axel. "You went into the hoedown when you were supposed to be waiting outside."

"And good thing I did," he said, echoing my earlier defense. "Otherwise, your fat head would have been removed. Plus, waiting on the sidelines is boring."

"Sometimes we have to follow orders," Parker said, fixing Axel with a meaningful glare.

"Not when they're stupid orders," Axel replied. "Besides, I blended in flawlessly."

"Stop," I said, putting up my hands before Parker could reply. "You're both right. Axel, in order for this team thing to work, sometimes you're going to have to be bored. But the real lesson here is I should have known better than to think you'd stay on the sidelines. I should have insisted you join me."

"Damn right," he said.

"Only because he should have known you wouldn't play by anyone else's rules," Parker said, rolling his eyes. "You're a liability, Axel. I don't know how you two have survived as long as you have."

"Because we're futzing awesome," Axel said, glaring at him. Then he turned back in my direction and sighed. "I'll try to play along, moving forward."

I ignored him and turned my attention to Barrett. "When Apple Devil was charging us, I should have called on you to stop him. I'm not used to having someone with your abilities around. That's no excuse, though. I should have called on you. That screw-up nearly got us all killed."

Barrett didn't reply, only stared at me.

"And?" Parker said, crossing his arms.

"And?" I asked.

Parker glanced at Anthony, who made a point of looking in the other direction.

What had he told him?

Oh...

My gaze re-fixed on Barrett. "And you fucked up, too."

He stared at me for several moments, then, surprisingly, spoke up. "I know."

I gave him a nod, then addressed the others. "Look, we didn't plan on this trip turning into a combat cruise, but twice now, we've been in the shit. We've got to figure out how to work better together. And quickly. Otherwise, we'll end up dead."

"Wait," Parker said, holding up a hand. His gaze moved from me to Barrett and back again. "That's it?"

"Yeah," I said. "That's it."

He was referring to Barrett. I guessed he expected I would embarrass the big guy further. But I saw the pain in his eyes. He knew his mistake.

Parker scowled. "If someone on my team disregarded my direction and nearly got the rest of my squad killed—"

"It's not your team," I said, meeting Parker's gaze. Then I turned to Barrett. "Will it happen again?"

"No," he said.

"Good enough," I replied. I let my scowl drift over everyone until I finally landed on Parker again. "I have to trust you guys. Period. I don't know how shit is done on normal Cabal teams, and frankly, I don't care. It's like this: when we fuck up, we own it. And then we make damned sure we don't do it again. That work for everyone?"

No one responded.

"That wasn't rhetorical," I said, feeling my temper slip. It had been a long night and I wanted to get this thing rounded up.

"Hells yeah," Axel said. "And, uh, guys, I would go ahead and agree. He has that look on his face. The one where he's done taking shit from security supervisors and pops them in the jaw."

"Huh?" Fred said, sitting up straight. "Uh, yeah, I understand."

Anthony snorted. "Yeah, I get it, boss man."

"Understood," Parker said.

Barrett nodded.

Axel elbowed Alyita. "What say you?"

"I'm not on the team," she said, scowling. "I got left behind. Bunch of bullshit."

"Really?" I said. "You think the Cabal normally lets teenagers join dangerous ops?"

"You just said you don't care how the Cabal does things," she said, crossing her arms. "I want on the team for real."

"And you know that won't happen until you finish school," I said. "Come on, Alyita. This isn't an argument you're really going to make, is it?"

"Whatever," she said, then stormed off, right out of the room.

"Huh," Anthony said, chuckling. "At least someone wants to be on this team."

I glared at him.

"What are you talking about, meathead?" Axel asked. "Squirrel Nuts Squad is the tits, you ungrateful mouth-breather."

"The hell did you just say to me?" Anthony said, bowing up. "This little squad is on a crash course. Won't be long before we all end up dead. You're the only idiot who'd volunteer for it."

"I want to be here," Barrett said, turning slowly to stare at Anthony. "No team I'd rather be on."

The former shamus threw up his hands and rose to his feet. "You're all out of your damned minds. Come on, Fred. I heard there's a bar around here. Let's see if we can find some ladies."

"Hell yeah," Fred said, rising to join Anthony. "Good chat, y'all."

As the two of them left, Parker turned and looked like he had something to say. Then he just shook his head and stomped off as well.

Barrett turned and looked at me. "I meant what I said. Won't happen again."

"I know, Barrett. I know."

37

"Wyatt, where are you?"

My fork was halfway to my mouth when Master Serrano's voice spoke into my mind. First bite. I was very much looking forward to my eggs. Now, though...

I sighed.

"Breakfast," I replied. *"What's up?"*

"So, you haven't heard?"

I glanced up, looking at my breakfast mates. So far, it was just Parker and Axel. No one else had made it to the cafe yet. Speaking quickly, I asked, "What haven't I heard yet?"

"Huh?" Parker replied.

"Probably lots of things," Axel said with a mouth full of food. "And plenty more you just didn't listen to."

"Seriously," I said. "No time for games. Master Serrano just reached out through mind-speak. Has something happened that either of you are aware of that I haven't been told?"

Parker shook his head.

Axel tapped his fork against the side of his. "Let me think. Umm... No."

"I guess not," I replied to Master Serrano. *"What's going on?"*

He sighed in my skull. *"You'd better get down here."*

I wasn't sure where "here" was, but within five minutes, Axel, Parker, and I had been escorted to the Argument's brig. At least, that's what they called it. A dungeon in the giant dwarven city. It looked more like a county jail, though, and only had a few holding cells.

This wasn't a place for serious magical offenders. More like a temporary place to hold captives. The Cabal did the same. There were other facilities for holding more dangerous supernatural criminals. Much like the cell where I'd once visited Axel.

None of that mattered, though. What did matter was figuring out why the hell Master Serrano had summoned us to the jail. And what the hurry was over.

Axel, Parker, and I all shared a look. Whatever this was, it couldn't be anything good.

Our escort led us through a few locked and warded doors to where the cells were.

Master Serrano was waiting for us.

And I had no idea why.

Until I saw the cell he stood in front of.

Every other cage was empty. Just the one had any inhabitants.

It wasn't Cowan. Wherever they'd stashed him was somewhere even more secure.

No, this cell had two inmates. Two very familiar inmates.

Anthony and Fred.

They both looked rough.

Anthony had a black eye. Fred had a broken nose and a bandaged hand. They were still in the clothes they'd been wearing the night before, but now they were stretched and torn. And they were both clearly hung over.

It didn't take a genius to piece it together. They'd gotten drunk. And they'd gotten into a fight. Then they'd been detained by our hosts. The only remaining questions were...

Who had they gotten into a fight with? Was anyone seriously hurt? And most importantly...

How much trouble were we ALL in?

I stared at them, unsure what to think. Unsure what to say.

This can't be happening. Not with everything else. It just can't.

I turned to Master Serrano, a sinking feeling in my gut. "What happened?"

"Well," Master Serrano said, taking a deep breath. His usual good humor was gone. Even when he'd nearly been killed by the vaklif, he'd seemed in better spirits than he was just then. This wasn't good. It wasn't good at all. "It would seem two members of your team had a few too many drinks last night."

Anthony snorted. "The drinks weren't the problem."

Master Serrano pounced before I could. His massive frame whirled toward the cell. "Do. Not. Speak."

Anthony gulped and took an interest in what his shoes were doing.

Master Serrano turned and faced me again. There was a fury in his eyes that nearly made me take a step back.

He took a calming breath and said, "These two got drunk and got into a brawl."

"With who?"

"The moon-eyed people."

"Fuck," I said.

It was worth noting Master Serrano said nothing about my foul language. On the contrary, he said, "Precisely."

Again, I wasn't sure what to say. What to think. What to do. This was a nightmare.

I glanced over at Parker and Axel.

One looked very disappointed. The other was struggling to hold back a laugh.

I turned back to Master Serrano. "How much trouble are they in? How much trouble are *we* in?"

He motioned for me to follow him.

Uh oh.

I started after him.

"Hey, Wyatt," Anthony said.

I glanced back at him.

"I'm, uh, really—"

"Shut up," I said. "You heard Master Serrano."

He hung his head again.

I followed Master Serrano to where we could have a private conversation.

Parker and Axel wisely hung back.

Once we were alone, Master Serrano let out another sigh. "This isn't good."

"I know," I said, shaking my head. "I can't believe those idiots. Did any of the moon-eyed people get hurt?"

"No. And that's a relief."

Also a surprise, but I didn't say that out loud. Those little guys barely came up to my waist. I was worried Anthony had punted one through a wall. Instead...

"Wait." I put up my hand and tried to hide my smile. "Are you telling me Anthony and Fred got their asses kicked by garden gnomes?"

The master librarian's eyes narrowed. "This isn't funny."

"Eh, it's a little funny."

"Wyatt..."

"Listen, Master Serrano. You're ninety-eight percent right. This is a huge embarrassment for the Cabal. For the Archmage. For the council. Even more so for you and me. And it further damages our reputation with the Argument, especially after the botched op last night. But come on... At least they were beaten up by little people. There's some gallows humor in that, isn't there?"

Master Serrano stared at me. I met his gaze. It was a standoff.

I won.

The first sign of victory was the twinkle in his eyes. Then he couldn't help but to smile.

"Okay, fine," he said with a huff. "I'll admit it is a *little* funny they got thrashed by the small folk."

"Serves them right for getting into a fight in the first place. What the hell were they thinking?"

"They both swear up and down the moon-eyed people started it."

"Yet, the Argument didn't see fit to throw them in a jail cell."

"Yeah, about that..." Serrano said. "It happened late. Once both parties were separated, Argument leadership was informed. Supreme Enchanter Tate woke the Archmage up and informed him."

"Oh, no."

"Oh, yes. It was our very own Archmage who suggested your team-mates should spend the night in a jail cell."

"Fuck bubbles."

"Fornication bubbles indeed. He touched base with me first thing this morning."

"And how pissed was he?"

"You've met the Archmage. What do you think?"

I sighed. "I think he was overly polite."

"Far too polite."

"He's livid."

"Just so."

"Oh, boy," I said, shaking my head. "This is a disaster. Does he want us to head home?"

"He didn't say so. He only said that two members of the team I was responsible for were arrested in the night, that they were sitting in the Argument's brig, and that I, as a master, should see to the matter straight away."

"Ugh..."

"If I'm honest, I half-expected to find you and Axel sitting here."

"Really?" I raised an eyebrow at him.

He shrugged.

Eh... That was probably fair, actually. I let it go.

"All right," I said, sighing. "So, what do we do?"

"I don't know that there's much to do at this point. They're free to be released. I waited for you. It is your team, after all."

"That you're responsible for," I said, hanging my head. "I'm sorry, Santiago. Really."

"I know this isn't your fault. But please, get your team under control. We can't afford any more...excitement. Not just the op, but also Axel pounding on everyone's doors in the middle of the night. I fear our reputation has suffered enough."

"I understand, and I take full responsibility. Should I speak to the Archmage?"

"God, no," he said. "Leave that to me. I'll let him know you're on top of the situation."

"Doubt that will fill him with confidence."

"It's better than having him think I'm babysitting. Trust me."

"Oh, I do," I assured him. "And in case I haven't made it clear, I'm grateful he chose you to be our handler. I know it puts you in a tough spot, but there's no other master I'd rather report to. I'm sorry I've made a mess of things."

"It could be worse," he said with another sigh. "So, what do you want to do with Anthony and Fred?"

I considered.

It didn't take me long to make a decision.

We walked back to their cells, where Axel was roasting both of them. He had loads of colorful commentary about the two jailbirds. Neither of them argued back, which wore the fun out for Axel pretty quickly.

They only looked up when Serrano and I returned.

I glared at both of them.

"Boss?" Anthony asked, hopeful.

"I have one question," I said.

Both men nodded at me.

"Whose fault was this?"

"Those short little fuckers," Anthony said. "I'm telling you—"

"They started it," Fred said, jumping in. "Honest."

"Provoked you, did they?" I asked.

"Yeah," Anthony said. "That's it exactly. They just kept running their mouths. We talked a little shit back, and one of those little pricks shoved me. And then..."

"And then?"

"Well, you know what happened," Anthony said, looking away.

"I know you got your ass kicked by garden gnomes."

"What?" Anthony said. "No! I wouldn't say that."

"Yeah," Fred said. "We gave as good as we got."

"Oh, well, in that case, I'm *super* proud of you guys."

They shared a look and then glanced back at me. Fred was dense enough to ask, "Really?"

"No, you idiots. I figured getting your asses handed to you by tiny folk was punishment enough, but you failed your test."

"Test?" Anthony asked.

"Yeah, the one question test I just gave you."

"But it wasn't our fault!" Fred said, rising to his feet. "You have to believe us!"

"You're still missing the point," I said, shaking my head. "You know, the Argument said they'll release you into my custody."

"Really?" Anthony asked, eyes hopeful. Fred seemed relieved as well.

"Oh, yeah," I replied. "But I told them I didn't want you."

"What?" both men asked.

"Good news for you. They don't want your stupid asses, either. But they've reluctantly agreed to keep you for the time being."

"You're leaving us in here?" Fred asked. "Come on, man. I'm starving. And Anthony needs a shower."

"Fuck you, Fred," Anthony said. "You stink worse than I do."

"You both stink," I said. "And you're going to sit there until you figure out the right answer to my question."

Anthony started to speak, but I held up a hand.

"Think about what we discussed last night. I'll come by later to try again."

"Fuck you, Wyatt," Anthony said, scowling at me. "You're just doing this to be a prick."

"No, stupid. I'm doing to this to get my point across. Sit there and think about it. And honestly, I'm probably doing you a favor. You're going to have a hard time showing your face once everyone learns you got beat up by garden gnomes."

"You think it'll get around?" Fred asked.

I pointed a thumb at Axel. "What do you think the chances are he's going to keep quiet about this?"

"Zero," Axel said. "I intend to tell every single person I see, whether I know them or not."

"So, there you have it," I said, crossing my arms. "You two idiots can sit there, miserable, hungry, and enjoying each other's stench while we go back and finish our breakfast. Try not to do anything else stupid in the meantime."

38

"Please, take a seat, Wyatt."

Supreme Shaman Sams sat on a carpeted floor. He pointed across from him, his arms long and slender, looking skeletal.

I did as he asked.

We had returned to breakfast when someone from the Argument had come and informed me Sams wished to speak with me. I'd thought it odd, but wasn't going to miss a chance to visit with one of the leaders of the Argument. For one, after the hoedown showdown, I could've used some good PR. And I was curious how their leadership differed from our own. From what I'd seen, the Appalachian Argument seemed less formal.

Of course, if someone visited the Cabal and met Master Serrano, they likely would have thought the same. I hadn't met the Argument's entire council. Or at least, I didn't think I had. It was hard to keep all the names and faces sorted. But I was pretty sure I'd only met a handful of the top dogs.

At any rate, I sat down across from him and studied his face. I didn't dare to guess how old he was. Maybe even in his late seventies. It was hard to say. But there was something about him... I didn't expect he had a lot of time. Probably why this mess with the Cherokee was so important to him.

"How are you faring?" he asked. "After the incident last night?"

"I'm all right," I replied. "No worse for wear. Shame about the folks we lost, though."

"Yes," he said with a brief nod. "It wasn't your fault. You understand that?"

"I do." I paused, considering. I didn't know Sams, but I felt safe being honest. "At least, I understand at some level. I still feel guilty, though. Especially about the witches."

"Of course. They died alongside you. Hard not to blame yourself. Hard not to wonder what you could have done differently. Though I think you've experienced that feeling before."

I stared up at him, remembering faces, many faces I tried not to think about. Faith's was the first to come to mind. I hadn't thought about her in a while. But there were so many. Members of the Memphis Knights, the Pattersons, Voodooists. Willie. Constable Williams. Malik. I'd watched a lot of good people die.

Sams gave me a knowing look. "They stick with you, those ghosts of the past."

I swallowed, unsure what to say. I guessed I wasn't ready for such heaviness right after my first cup of coffee.

"I fear you'll collect more," Sams said, "all your life. There will be many. And you'll always wonder what you could have done differently. Best you don't let it eat you alive."

"I try."

"Good." He gave me a smile. "But I did not ask you here to discuss your ghosts."

"What did you want to talk to me about?" I asked, happy for the change of subject.

He gave me a hint of a shrug. "I wished to get to know you. It's not so often a Blade Mage comes to visit."

"I'm afraid you'll be disappointed. I'm nothing special. Not like your Defender or War Mage. Saw them in action last night. They were impressive."

"You believe you fall short?"

"Well, yeah... Once they showed up, the dark wizards headed for the hills. They were something."

"Don't sell yourself short. They were impressed by you as well."

"Sure didn't seem like it."

"Don't let them fool you. They are young as well. Near your own age."

"And significantly more powerful."

"And yet your enemies escaped when they arrived."

"Yeah, but..." I blinked a few times.

He chuckled. "That didn't come up last night, did it? No one called out that our own Arcane Warriors made mistakes as well. Yet had Christian thought out the situation, he might have surrounded your foes. Instead, he rushed in. I believe he understands the error, though."

"He didn't seem quite so..."

"Brash? No. He is calmer. A strategist. One has to be to be a Defender. He might have seemed frustrated with you, but trust that he will calm, if he hasn't already. He is wise, but has much to learn. Daisy, on the other hand, has a temperamental personality. This, too, comes with the calling. I've never known a War Mage who wasn't a little hot-headed."

"Yeah, she had a lot of colorful things to say."

"Don't take it personally. She was more frustrated with herself. Both were. They had hoped to impress you."

"What? Why? I didn't get that at all."

He chuckled. "They were frustrated that they'd allowed you to end up in that position. Frustrated they weren't there quicker. They blame themselves more than they blame you. Daisy in particular. Trust that she feels shame for her words, though I doubt you'll get her to admit it."

"I...don't know what to say."

"You don't need to say anything. I only wished for you to see beyond what is in front of you. They, too, are flooded with self-doubt, called to a role they felt ill-prepared for. As were we all. It's harder, I think, for you Arcane Paladins. For us Arcane Sages, it's a little easier. Not much. Folks expect us to be wise from the moment our weapons choose us. For you Arcane Warriors, though, they expect you to be battle-hardened champions right out the gate. It is tough for a Shield-bearer and a Hammer to not have a Blade Mage to guide them."

"I'm a Blade Mage and I can barely guide myself. Wait... You're not trying to recruit me, are you?"

"Not at all," he said, shaking his head. "Though I would be happy to have you join the Argument. Believe that. But no, I think you are where you should be. I am, once again, attempting to broaden your horizons. You must forgive me. I am an old man. Often we seek to pass on knowledge. Sometimes it seems that's all we have left."

"I think you have more than that."

"Perhaps," he said, a twinkle in his eyes. "I'd like to think I have one more good bout in me, should the need arise."

"I'm sure you do. And thanks. I appreciate the pep talk. You're right; I hadn't considered any of that. I wouldn't have known... You said their personalities match their calling. What about the Blade Mage?"

"Fierce warriors, courageous souls, and fine leaders."

"Sounds likes you're describing my father."

"I am."

"Not so sure I picked up all those traits. Courageous? More like stubbornly stupid. And few would call me a fierce warrior or a fine leader."

"Oh, I don't know. Did you not lead the Cherokee into battle against our ancient enemy?"

I stared at him.

"Yes, I know about it," he said. "Both Elder Morgan and Elder Thomas filled me in. You saved Alyita."

"I..." I hadn't expected anyone to know about that.

"You don't need to worry. Her secret is safe."

"Thank you."

"Of course. She's a good kid. I know one day she'll be a fierce medicine woman."

"If she chooses that path. Just now, she seems more interested in becoming a wizard."

"And the Coven would like to take her to be a witch."

"Is there anything you don't know, Sams?"

He smiled. "Much, I'm afraid. Including how we might leverage what you accomplished with the Oklahoma Cherokee and your Cabal here in our own area."

"Guessing you know more about that as well?"

"I do," he said, nodding. "Elder Morgan shared the details. Still, don't sell your part short. You were the one who made it happen."

"I'm not sure I can do the same for you here."

"Perhaps not, but I suspect your presence in Appalachia may accomplish more than you can see."

"I hope you're right," I said with a shrug. "I'm happy to help."

"You already are," he said. "Back to your self doubt. You showed great leadership when you settled things between the Cherokee and Cabal. Just as you showed leadership when you saved the Memphis Knights from killing themselves. Just as you did with the voodooists in the swamp."

"That was...a disaster. They both were. So many people..."

"You can't save them all, Wyatt."

"No, but—"

"But you did the best you could, given the circumstances. In both cases, had you not acted... Had you not stepped up as you did, more would have died. You fought devils most folks, even those of us in this world, can only imagine. You led people you barely knew against impossible odds. And you were every bit as stubbornly stupid as anyone could hope. I would say you're living up to your title."

"Thanks," I said, unsure what else to say.

"Now then," he said. "Enough of all that. Let's discuss why I really brought you here."

"I thought it was to get to know me?"

"That was the first reason. It was a test, and you passed."

"Okay?"

"So now, let us discuss the earth and the magic it provides."

39

Supreme Shaman Sams left me in a stupor.

I didn't catch a word of the meetings I had to sit through, too focused on the things he'd said.

It wasn't until lunch that I broke from my stupor, and only then because I saw Eilidh.

Just the distraction I needed.

And...something that needed to be resolved.

I didn't miss the dirty looks from Big-nose and the others. They were past sneers and snobbery. Now they blamed me for the death of two of their sisters, and maybe the ones in Memphis as well. Whatever. Futz 'em.

I stomped directly to their table and stood in front of Eilidh until she looked up at me, a forkful of pasta paused before her mouth. Pretty sure it was fettuccine alfredo. My stomach growled. It could wait.

When I knew I had her attention, I said, "I would like to speak with you."

"Do you not see we're trying to have a nice lunch?" Big-nose asked. "You're ruining the vibe, boy-buck."

I didn't look over at her; I kept my gaze on Eilidh. "Fuck off, Winifred."

Her name wasn't Winifred. Probably. But she kind of reminded me of the lead Sanderson sister, and I'd had enough of her shit to last me a lifetime. Big-nose, that was. Not Winifred. *Hocus Pocus* was great.

"Haven't you caused Eilidh enough grief?" she asked, sneering. "And what could you possibly wish to speak to her about? Every time you're around, more of her sisters die. Haven't you done the Coven enough harm?"

At that, I did turn and look at her. "Listen, you pompous windbag. I'm damned sorry about the witches you lost. Damned sorry. They weigh heavy on my heart, whether you believe it or not. I'll always wonder what more I could have done to save them. Same with the ones in Memphis. But I'm not going to take shit from a self-aggrandizing snob who sat on the sidelines. Easy to blame someone else when you weren't even in the game, isn't it? And yeah, before you say it, I'm sure it doesn't mean much from a dumb fucking man. So, why don't we agree to piss off and leave each other alone? If that doesn't do it for you, then go sit on your wand and spin. Bitch."

There were several gasps from the surrounding witches, and I was sure I was going to hear about this one from Archie. Did not care. Enough was enough.

I turned back to Eilidh, who'd risen from the table.

In a very stilted voice, she said, "I'll be right back."

And then motioned for me to follow her.

We stepped out of Coffee Cave Cafe and walked down the hall, neither speaking.

Finally, I broke the silence. "I really am sorry about your sisters. If—"

"It's not your fault," she said, turning to face me. "I don't blame you, Wyatt. But..."

"But what?"

"I don't think we should speak again."

"Oh."

That was... That wasn't what I'd expected. But I guessed it answered the question.

"Look, it's..." She paused, biting her lip. "It's not what you think."

"You're almost certainly right, 'cause I don't know what I think."

We stared at each other. She was the first to look away.

I sighed. "Look, I'm sorry. I didn't mean to keep bumping into you or causing you any grief with your sisters. I just thought... I guess I thought we were still friends, at least."

"We...are." She still wouldn't look at me. "But we can't be anymore."

"We haven't spoken in..."

"I know."

"I'm, uh..." I scratched my head. "I'm really confused."

"I know." She let out a heavy sigh. "Look, I didn't expect to see you. When I did, I thought it would be best to avoid you. To act professional when we had to run into each other. But I also didn't expect us to end up fighting beside each other again. So..."

I put up my hands. "Eilidh, I get it. Okay. What we had was a brief onetime thing. I just thought we were still...friends or something. It's my bad. I shouldn't have presumed. I, uh, guess I just wanted to clear the air. But I'll stay away, if that's what you want."

"That's the problem, you big dumb idiot."

"Huh?"

She offered me a sad smile. "I don't want you to stay away. But..."

The smile disappeared.

"I need you to."

"I definitely don't understand."

"I know," she said. "And I'm doing a shit job explaining."

"I'm listening," I said, shrugging. "And I'm not going anywhere. Unless you want me to. If you're saying you never want to speak to me again, then that's all you have to say. I'll stay away from you."

"No, I want you to understand. It's like this... You know how the Coven frowns on us having relationships? Particularly with men? Well, it's more than that. I have..." She paused, sighing again. "I'm due to take the vows of a Sacerdotessa."

"I don't know what that is."

"I know you don't. It's... It's a sacred position within the Coven. It's what my mother was. Before..."

"Oh, I see," I said, nodding. I didn't, really. Not completely. But I could figure out where this was going. "And that means..."

"I will be forbidden from having a relationship."

"But that... Does it mean you can't have a male friend?"

"I don't want to be your friend, Wyatt." Her words came out harsh. Cold.

"Oh," I said, feeling like there was a knife twisting in my guts. And then the context hit. What she *really* meant. And I said, "*Oh.*"

"Look, I think you feel a certain way about me. And I was trying to hide the fact I feel a certain sort of way about you. But..."

"It can't be."

"Right."

We stared at each other for several long moments.

"Well, fuck," I said, throwing up my hands. "This is dumb."

"It is."

I looked into her eyes. "But this is what you want? What you really want?"

"Yes." She didn't hesitate.

"Okay," I said, ignoring the crushing weight in my chest. That knife still twisting in my ribs. "Well, I'm glad you told me. And, uh, I hope it works out for you. I will try to keep my space. Sorry. I didn't know. Guess, uh, we should get back."

I turned from her.

She grabbed my arm, pulling me back.

Then...she hugged me.

Face pressed against my chest, she said, "I'm sorry, Wyatt."

"Yeah," I said, unsure what else to say. "Me, too."

40

We didn't walk back to the cafe together.

I took another hall. A longer route.

I wasn't sure what to think. What I felt.

It was weird. All this time, Eilidh had lived rent-free in the back of my mind. I thought about her often. And I guessed I'd convinced myself when next we met, we might have a chance to pick up where we'd left off. It wasn't like I thought there was a real chance we could be together, like, long-term. I never really thought about it, even. But that smitten idiotic part of my brain had just thought...

I didn't know.

I was an idiot.

I guessed it was just... I hadn't been rejected. And without that rejection, I guessed I had clung onto some hope. Which was stupid. I hadn't even realized I'd done it.

Now, though... Now, there was some finality to it.

And that hurt.

More than I'd expected.

I hadn't realized how much I'd cared for her.

I walked through the halls, trying to keep my thoughts from turning more somber. The operation had been disaster enough. Then

Anthony'd and Fred's dumb asses had caused even more embarrassment. And Sams had said some things about connecting with earth magic. He hadn't come out and said it, but it seemed like he knew something about my strange abilities. That had left me in a whirl. And now this? I wished Archie had sent us home. Maybe it wasn't too late.

Anyway, I was feeling a like puppy who'd been caught pissing on the floor when I heard voices just ahead, right around the corner.

Familiar voices.

Masters Serrano and Castillo.

Like Eilidh and me, they'd apparently stepped away for a private conversation.

And they were talking about me. And my team.

Serrano was getting an earful.

"I don't know what the Archmage even thought, bringing those idiots," she said. "They're an embarrassment."

"It's not so bad, Zephyrine," Serrano said, trying to placate her.

She snorted. "Not so bad? If Wyatt's incompetence during the op wasn't enough, now two of his subordinates get into a bar brawl? No offense, Santiago, but the Archmage shouldn't have put you in charge of that mess. It's not fair to you."

"It's fine," he replied.

"No, it isn't. And that's precisely what I mean. You're too easygoing. If they reported to me, I'd have their asses fired. This whole game of giving Wyatt a team. What a joke."

"The Archmage knows what he's doing."

"Of course he does. And he's trying to make a point to our illustrious Blade Mage. Trying to show him he isn't worthy. But Wyatt is too thick to understand. It's one thing to embarrass himself in Cabal territories. But here, he's making a mockery of all of us."

"I don't think that's what the Archmage intended."

"Then why else would he bring them? They're a joke, Serrano. Wyatt is a joke, and Magnus is trying to make him realize it. Trying to make him understand he should end this facade and give up the sword."

"Wyatt has done some great things."

"And he's left a trail of bodies everywhere he goes. You honestly think we wouldn't be better off if the sword was in someone else's hands? You don't think..."

Her voice trailed off as I started back down the hall, back the way I'd come.

I'd heard enough.

And...I wasn't even mad.

I was just...numb.

Too much all at once.

I paused, right where Eilidh and I had spoken. I considered going back to the cafe. That had been my plan. My team was waiting there. The ones who weren't still locked up, that was. I didn't feel much like eating anymore. And I didn't feel much like sitting across the room from her, either.

Instead, I started in a different direction. No plans. Maybe I'd just wander the halls for a while. Take in more of the underground city.

I happened by a bar. Probably the same one Anthony and Fred had gotten into trouble at. I considered getting a drink. Maybe I could get into a fight with the moon-eyed people, too. Get pitched in the cell with them. That'd be a nice coat of frosting for our shit cake.

Snorting at my own depraved sense of humor, I started onward, then paused.

A familiar figure sat alone at the bar.

He glanced up, saw me, and waved me over.

I shrugged. Why the hell not?

"Didn't know you were still here," I said, plopping down on a barstool beside the Tennessee Wildman.

"Yup," he said, taking a sip of his drink.

There was no bartender in sight. That was probably for the best. As much as I wanted a drink, it probably wasn't a good idea.

"Thought you didn't care much for the Argument," I said.

"Don't. But I'm hoping they'll pull their collective fingers outta their big fat asses and go after Wampus Cat. I intend to tag along. Until then, I'm just hanging out in the bar. Hopefully these pricks never ask me to pay my tab."

"You must really hate her."

"That's an understatement."

It didn't seem he was interested in elaborating.

"The others seemed surprised she was working alongside an Apple Devil."

He nodded. "As they should've been. She's been known to stick her nose where it don't belong, but it ain't like her to take up with the, as you put it, half-squatches." He chuckled. "I like that. More surprising to see her working alongside dark wizards."

"What do you reckon it means?"

He shrugged. "Means there's more folks for us to kill. Which is why I'm waiting for these idiots to get their shit together. Even if I could find the ole bitch, I don't relish taking on an army by myself. In my younger days...maybe. But you don't live this long by being an idiot."

"How old are you?"

His reply was a snort. Then he looked right at me. "You seemed to know some of Skank in Boots's new pals. What can you tell me?"

"They're assholes." I shrugged. "Former operatives from the Cabal. Traitors. And...my former teammates."

"Ah," he said, giving me an approving nod. "Then I guess you have a score to settle, too."

"Guess I do."

"Here's to hoping we both get the chance." He held up his glass, then downed the entire thing.

When he was done, he wiped his mouth and rose from his seat. Then, almost as an afterthought, he glanced back at me.

"Course, if I were you, I'd be awfully curious why your own allies let you walk into a trap."

"Not so sure it was a trap. My Archmage suspects my former team and your cat lady friend had some kind of deal with Cowan. Figures they spotted me and took their chance."

He chuckled. "Right. Sure. You're damned lucky to be alive."

"Yeah?"

"Yeah. If you're dense enough to believe some hogwash like that, it's no small wonder you haven't walked into traffic or forgotten how to breathe."

Then he strolled away.

41

I had to hurry to get to my next session on time.

I'd already missed a couple in the morning. Figured Squirrel Nuts Squad had collectively caused enough problems that skipping class shouldn't be added. Plus, I needed something to get my mind off everything else.

I had a feeling the next session wouldn't solve that problem.

It was titled, "De-escalation Tactics: How to resolve conflict without violence."

I felt like someone was trying to tell me something. I damned sure hadn't volunteered for that one, nor had I been invited to be a speaker. I guessed someone figured I needed to sit and listen.

I was just about to step into the conference room when a voice behind me said, "Wyatt."

"Brother Barajas," I said as I turned to find the knight standing there, arms crossed.

The two knights who'd traveled with him each gave me a nod, then made their way into the conference room, leaving Barajas and me in the hall.

He looked pissed. But then, he always looked pissed.

"Heard you got into some shit last night."

"That's the word," I replied.

"Rumor is it didn't go so well."

"I never figured you for the gossipy type."

"You figured right. But I am a little butt hurt you didn't invite us to the party. Sounds more fun than this bullshit."

"Yeah, I also didn't figure you were the type for attending conferences."

"Drew the short straw. Tried to get out of it, but Victor insisted. Said it was good for building character."

I snorted. "Victor said that?"

"He did. But he was smiling. I wasn't."

"That's because you never smile."

"I do too. When I have a reason. Never seem to have one around you, though. Wonder why that is? Anyway, where the hell was my invitation?"

"Wasn't my party."

"Hmm. Well, if you get in any more shit, see that I get an invitation. Need something to get me out of this nonsense."

"You've got it."

With that, the knight headed into the conference room.

I almost followed him, but decided I should grab a water first.

And that was precisely when the Archmage spoke into my mind and informed me I was needed for a different sort of meeting.

I couldn't wait to find out what. I was on a hot streak. No way it was for anything good.

I was right.

It took a few minutes for me to find the room.

When I did, I nearly turned and headed the other way.

Archie was there, along with Serrano. Tate and Whitaker were also present. It wasn't them I was bothered by. It was the other attendees.

In particular, it was one very grumpy-looking Feogh and two of his half-pint hooligans.

Oh, joy. Whatever could this be about?

At least it explained why they had the lights turned down low.

Tate, an annoyed look on his face, motioned for me to take a seat.

Before my ass touched down, Feogh started in. "*This* is who we waited for?"

"Yes, of course," Whitaker said. "The two individuals you had the confrontation with are on his team."

"Ha!" Feogh said, shaking his angry little head.

"I don't think this is the time or place for insults," Tate said. "I'm sure Wyatt is handling the situation."

"Oh?" Feogh asked, glaring at me with his glowing eyes. "What punishment did they receive? What action did you take?"

I didn't hurry to respond. Instead, I tried to seem calm, cool, and collected. Confident, even. Pretty sure I was none of those things. It had been a day already, and I didn't feel like putting up with giant-sized bull-shit from a quarter-sized asshole. But I reminded myself I wasn't there representing myself. I was representing my team: Squirrel Nuts fucking Squad. Goddamned Axel and that stupid name. Anyway, the crew's reputation had been soiled enough. I didn't want to muck it up more.

I let my gaze slowly shift around the room. I didn't expect anyone from the Argument to speak for me. Didn't expect them to help me out of this mess. My own Cabal folks, though? I didn't expect them to help, either, but it sure would've been nice. A great opportunity for Archie to step in and use some of his grandfatherly de-escalation skills. Nope. He was happy to let me sink in the shit. Of course he was.

I tried to put on a friendly smile. Probably came out as a grimace. But I looked Feogh in his glowing sockets and said, "Supreme Enchanter Tate is correct. I'm seeing to the matter."

"What does that mean?" Feogh asked.

"It means I'm handling it. Those involved are receiving disciplinary action."

I wasn't sure, but I thought that sounded like something a leader would say.

"What sort?" Feogh pressed.

"The sort that isn't any of your business," I said, keeping my voice even.

"Excuse me?" he said, leaning forward.

"You're excused," I replied.

He slammed his fist on the table. "We demand—"

"Well, that might be your problem right there," I said, nodding along like I'd just had a clever idea. "You don't get to make demands of me. And I certainly wouldn't expect you to provide me details about how you discipline your own folks. None of my business, is it?"

I might have been pushing my luck, but to hell with it. It wasn't like anyone else was jumping in. I certainly would not eat his shit. Sure, his crew had cared for me when I'd been hurt, but it wasn't like they'd wanted to. Mothman had conned them into it. And it was Tuthid who'd seen to me. The rest had sat on their asses, hoping I would die. So, screw those guys. I didn't owe Feogh a damned thing.

Also, Archie or Master Serrano could have jumped in if they felt I was out of line.

"This is an outrage," Feogh said, glancing toward Tate and Whitaker.

Nope. I wasn't going to let him do that. "Only because you're making it one. Look at me, Feogh. You have a problem with people from my team, not anyone else's. I've already told you I'm seeing to the matter. No, I will not give you any details. So, you can either trust that I'm taking care of it, or you can assume I'm not and continue having a hissy fit. Your choice."

"How dare you? We—"

"How dare *you* speak to me like this?" I replied.

"Your people attacked us! Unprovoked!"

"Unprovoked? Really? Your guys were completely innocent? Didn't do a thing? Didn't shove anyone? Nothing like that?"

He growled at me. Like, actually growled at me.

"Look, Feogh," I said, trying to smile. "Not everyone is telling the same story as you, but I'm not sitting here demanding your folks's heads, am I? Nor have I even asked what you're doing about the individuals from your side who were involved."

"They are being dealt with."

"And I trust that to be true. Reckon you could offer me the same?"

"Wyatt makes a fair point," Tate said, intervening. He motioned toward Archie. "I have it on good authority from the Cabal's Archmage that the situation is being handled."

"I agree, Supreme Enchanter," Whitaker said. "I don't see why both sides shouldn't give each other the benefit of the doubt. Can you truly not take Wyatt at his word?"

Feogh grumbled to himself, then turned his fury on the Argument. "You invited us here claiming friendship. What do we find? Filthy Cherokee. Now this. The Cabal wizards attacked us. Makes us think Argument doesn't want an alliance with moon-eye, after all."

"We do wish to establish a friendship with you," Tate said. "At the same time, we cannot throw away all other alliances for it. You must see that."

"I see much," Feogh said. "Know much. Much that would be valuable to the Argument."

"We're sure you do," Whitaker said, offering him a friendly smile. "And there is much the Argument can offer your people as well. And though they live apart from us, I'm sure the Cabal would like a friendly relationship with your people as well. Let us not create animosity where it is not needed."

"Indeed," Archie said, speaking up for the first time. "Your people are worthy of much respect. I would like to put this incident behind us and instead discuss how we might be of assistance to one another. I'm sure there is much the Cabal could gain from a friendship with you."

Feogh grumbled under his breath, finally turning to me. "Perhaps... we can forgive this. But I want assurance the Cabal won't attack us again. Nor provoke us."

"You have my word," I said, no hesitation. "No one from my team will attack you."

"Hmm," he said, nodding slowly. "Then we will consider it dirt beneath the mud."

And that was that. I hoped.

42

"She said what?"

Axel was beside himself. I knew I shouldn't have told him.

After my lovely meeting with Feogh and company, I'd slipped back to my room to hide for a while. I was done with the world and had time to burn before my next session. Naturally, Axel found me. And, of course, he knew something was bothering me.

At first, I'd tried to pass it off as annoyance with Anthony and Fred. He hadn't bought it.

He'd also called my bluff when I'd said it was about the team. How it seemed like a big mistake. Foolish move on my part. He was Squirrel Nuts Squad's biggest advocate. Said he was going to have a logo made for us. That we needed t-shirts, hats, and stickers.

So, finally, I told him about Eilidh.

And he was beside himself.

I sighed and repeated myself yet again. "She said she's supposed to undertake some sacred vow or something, Axel. I don't know the details."

"Well, you should have asked!" He was pacing, trying to wear out the carpet in my little living room.

"She said it was what she wanted, to follow in her mother's footsteps. It's her decision. But it means she can't have... Well, you know. We have to give her space."

"This is an outrage!" he stormed. "Absolutely ridiculous! I won't stand for it!"

"Do you hear yourself? You sound like a member of Parliament."

"Wyatt, we have to do something!"

"Like what?"

"Convince her it's a stupid idea."

"No."

He stopped pacing and turned to look at me. "No?"

"No," I repeated. "It's what she wants. So, stop. It's over, all right? I know you like Eilidh. And you can still be friends with her. But for me... it's not going to happen. It's over, Axel."

He added pouting to his pacing.

Fortunately, there was a knock on the door, which I hoped would rescue me from his tantrum. You'd have thought he was the one being let down rather than me, upset as he was. We didn't even know Eilidh all that well. At least, that was what I tried to tell myself. One weekend together was not the basis for a relationship. It was all in my head. I'd built her up to something more than she was, and Axel had, too. That was all. No big deal.

I made my way over to the door and found Alyita standing there.

She didn't wait for an invitation but bolted right past me, talking over her shoulder. "You aren't going to believe this shit!"

"What?" I asked, wondering what possibly could have gone wrong now.

She paused, studying Axel. "What's wrong with him?"

"My heart is broken," he said, moping.

"Quit," I said, rolling my eyes. "You're fine."

Alyita glanced between the two of us. "Seriously, is he all right?"

"I'm not!" Axel said, pacing and pouting some more.

"He's fine," I assured her. "What won't I believe?"

"Well, you know your little moon-eyed friends?"

"Yeah, I just came from a meeting with their leader."

"Oh, great," she said, throwing up her hands. "Then this is probably your fault."

"What?"

"So, apparently they have some kind of secret. Something the Argument's big dogs want to know. But they're saying they won't share unless *all* the Cherokee clear out of the compound. That includes me. Bunch of racist little fuck weasels."

"Seriously?" I asked. "For how long?"

"Just a few hours," she said. "At least, that's what Tsali told me. Master Serrano confirmed."

"What the hell?" I said, scratching the back of my head.

What could Feogh know that would make the Argument agree to that? Their big focus was on improving their relationship with the Cherokee. Asking them to leave... Whatever Feogh had was too shiny to ignore.

"So, where are you supposed to go?" I asked, turning back to Alyita.

"I've been invited to join Supreme Shaman Sams for a tour of the Cherokee training grounds. Tsali had already offered to let me visit."

"We'll go with you, then," I said.

"Don't you guys have meetings and stuff?"

"Nope," I replied. "Not now. They just got canceled."

She turned to Axel, who was still sulking.

And that was when he proceeded to tell her all about Eilidh.

Which meant it was time for me to leave.

If we were going on a field trip, then it was probably time to get my idiots out of jail.

43

I used mind-speak to tell Parker and Barrett to meet up in my room.

Then I made my way to the brig.

I ran into an unexpected face along the way, one with a swollen cheek and a black eye.

"Hey, Tuthid," I said, pausing before my former healer and guide.

He looked up at me, surprised. I guessed he hadn't seen me coming. Too lost in his own thoughts.

But when his glowing eyes looked up at me, I saw it was more than that. He seemed upset. Like, *really* upset. Plus, he'd clearly been punched, and more than once.

"You all right?" I asked.

He didn't hesitate, nodding immediately.

"What happened to your face? That wasn't my guys, was it? You weren't in the fight last night?"

He shook his head.

"Then what?"

He shook his head again. "Don't worry about it, Wyatt Man-thing."

"Come on. Who hit you?"

"It doesn't matter."

"I think it does matter."

"Tuthid deserved it. Tuthid questioned when should not."

"Tuthid..." I paused, considering. "Did Feogh do this?"

"Must go. Bye, Wyatt Man-thing."

And with that, he stormed off.

Now I really wanted to hit Feogh. After my guys had gotten into trouble for that very thing, I still wanted to find the pint-sized prick and punt him to the moon.

I couldn't, though. It wasn't my place and it wasn't any of my business.

And I'd just promised none of my Squirrel Nuts would assault the moon-eyed people. That included me, I was pretty sure.

Still...

That was a promise I regretted.

I stomped to the brig.

Anthony and Fred were just how I'd left them. If anything, they looked worse. Absolutely miserable.

Good.

They both sat up as I entered, hopeful looks on their distraught faces.

I stopped in front of the cell.

They stared up at me like two toddlers who'd been in timeout.

"Whose fault was it?" I asked.

"Our fault," Anthony said.

Fred nodded along.

"Explain," I said, then put up a hand. "And I don't want to hear some shit about how you should've known better. I want a genuine answer. And yes, Fred, I know that seems like a lot coming from me after... Well, you know. Still, I want a real answer."

Anthony and Fred shared a look, then Anthony answered.

"It's our fault for letting them provoke us. We should have kept our cool and de-escalated."

"We should've just left," Fred said, hanging his head. "Now that I've had time to dry out, I can't help thinking they provoked us intentionally."

"Right," Anthony said, nodding. "And we fell right into it. Little assholes."

"They are that," I agreed. "You aren't done."

Fred looked surprised, but Anthony understood. "Our mistake didn't just look bad on us. It looked bad on the team and the whole Cabal. Our little squad is already under a microscope. Half-surprised Archie hasn't already shut it down."

"You and me both," I replied.

"Which makes me wonder why he added Fred and me," he said, looking up to meet my gaze. "He knew we wouldn't want to work for you. Did he hope something like this would happen?"

I remembered what the master battle mage had said to Serrano in the hall. The conversation I'd overheard. Maybe she was she right. Maybe... I shook the thought away.

"I don't try to read the Archmage's mind," I replied.

"Right," Anthony said. "Well, I guess I've proven that if your team is the loser squad, then I'm in the right place. Our reputation—yours in particular—already took a hit from that op the other night. The last thing we needed was some boneheaded shit like this. It was a fuck-up." He lifted his head and met my gaze again. "We've never gotten along, Wyatt. That's no secret. But, for what it's worth, I'm sorry. I see how my actions screwed over Parker and the others. Serrano, too. And I feel bad for that."

"Me, too," Fred said.

And that was exactly the sort of honesty I was looking for. Neither of those assholes felt bad about the trouble it had caused me. But they *did* feel bad about the impact on Parker, Barrett, and maybe even Axel. Certainly Master Serrano, who everyone respected.

"Good enough," I said. "I'll get the guards to let you out. You have ten minutes to get to your rooms, shower, and meet up with the rest of the team in my suite. Got it?"

"That's it?" Fred asked, glancing from me to Anthony and back again.

I had already started toward the door, but I turned around again. "What'd I say last night?"

Fred squinted at me, the hamster in his skull spinning.

Anthony answered. "When we fuck up, we own it and move on. Something like that."

"Close enough," I said.

"Even... Even for something like this?" Fred asked.

Anthony stared daggers at him. I'd just given them a "get out of jail free" card, and the former security supervisor wanted to ask dumb questions. What was it with this guy?

"That's how I see it," I replied. "Do I have to worry about you doing something this stupid again?"

"No," Fred said.

"Look, guys," I said, walking back over to the cell. "You both need to decide if you're really a part of this team. I know you don't like me, but the Archmage put you with me for a reason, and I doubt it was to see us fail. Maybe it just amused him. Or maybe, just maybe, he thought it would be good for all of us. Perhaps I'm thinking crazy, but what if he thought it would help us all grow to have to work together? What if this was meant as a genuine opportunity and not just a punishment or cruel joke? If it is, then we'd be damned fools not to make the most of it."

Anthony looked up at me. "You think it could really be something like that?"

"Could be," I said, shrugging. "The point is, we've all got to decide if we're committed to this team. If we're all in."

"Are you?" Anthony asked. "Are you all in, Wyatt? Even with me and Fred here on your squad? And what about Parker, huh? You've never gotten along with him, either. Barrett doesn't say shit and Gunner is on another damned planet. So, tell me, is this really the team you want?"

After everything else that day, I might've snapped. Might have ripped his head off. Metaphorically, of course. Instead, I looked him in the eye and said, "Ten minutes. Clock is ticking."

With that, I turned and walked away.

44

I was halfway back to my room when Master Serrano contacted me through mind-speak.

A few minutes later, I was in a conference room with Christian.

I couldn't imagine what he wanted, but Master Serrano insisted I meet with him. No big deal. We still had a little time before Alyita was due for her field trip. I had every intention of Squirrel Nuts Squad joining her. At least until Christian told me what he wanted.

"We have another op," he said, studying me.

I raised an eyebrow. "Didn't think I'd be invited to another of those."

He gave me a sheepish smile. "We might have been...a little quick to point our fingers after the last. It wasn't all your fault, Wyatt. And, uh, I'm sorry if I made it seem that way."

"No worries," I replied, crossing my arms. "But I'm still surprised I've gotten an invitation."

"Yeah," he said, seeming uncomfortable. "Leadership insisted."

There it was. Christian didn't want my involvement. But his leadership did? Odd.

He met my gaze. "I believe... I am to understand your Archmage was rather insistent."

That was even more surprising. I'd figured Archie would've wanted to keep me as far from trouble as possible. Surely he thought we'd done enough damage.

"What's the op?"

"Guard detail. We're supposed to watch over Cowan."

I raised an eyebrow. "Where is he? Noticed he wasn't in the brig."

"He's in a hidden location. Offsite."

That didn't surprise me. It was the same thing the Cabal had done with Axel when he was accused of murder.

"Why?" I asked. "I imagine you already have guards covering him. Why would they want a Defender and a Blade Mage on it? This supposed to be a bonding exercise?"

"No," he said with a chuckle. "Daisy is coming, too, along with multiple Argument teams. And your own."

"That's a lot of wizards."

"It is." He gave me a serious look. "We have reason to believe his allies are going to attempt a jailbreak."

That also surprised me. The hits just kept on coming.

"Did he tell you that?" I asked.

Christian shook his head. "No, he hasn't said a word since we captured him. Playing the silent game. No, the intel came from the moon-eyed people."

And that surprised me, too.

He continued, "Once you settled your dispute with Feogh, he hinted to our leadership he knew a grave secret regarding our enemies, one he would only share if we agreed to send the Cherokee away."

"So that's why they agreed. I have a mind to go with the Cherokee."

He raised an eyebrow. "You'd rather do that than the op?"

"I'm responsible for Alyita. She's the Cherokee exchange student your folks are so interested in."

"I see. Anyway, once our leadership agreed to Feogh's demands, he shared that he'd been approached by the dark wizards from the other night. Claimed they knew the moon-eyes were disenchanted with the Argument. Offered an alliance. They wanted Feogh to help free Cowan. Said they planned to break him out. Said they need him for some kind of deal."

"And you believed him?"

He shrugged. "Over my pay grade. But I can't see what he has to gain by lying to us. At any rate, he said they plan to attack this afternoon."

"How would they know where you're holding Cowan?"

"Don't know," he said, sighing.

"Sounds like you have a rat."

"Sounds like it."

"Don't feel bad. From what I've seen, there're rats in every organization these days."

He nodded. "From the stories I've heard, that appears to be the case. Seems the entire world has gone mad. Makes it hard to know who to trust."

"Guess that's why we have magical weapons that chose us."

"There is that. I don't know about you, Blade Mage, but I struggle to trust anyone who wasn't chosen by an arcane weapon."

"Your Supreme Enchanter doesn't carry an arcane artifact."

"True," he said, but offered no more.

That was interesting. Was he implying he didn't trust Supreme Enchanter Tate?

"Listen," I said, shaking my head. "Our magical weapons look great on a resume, but they aren't a fair measuring stick. I mean, I might think the same if it weren't for some of the folks I've met, the ones I've fought beside. There are a few here, even. Ones I'd trust with my life."

"I've heard about your friend Axel. Rumor has it you aren't that close with the rest of your team."

"I wasn't thinking about my team. I was thinking about other visitors at your conference. Eilidh, for one."

He nodded. "It didn't slip my notice that you seemed to know her."

"We survived a pretty rough situation in Memphis together."

"The ordeal with the Memphis Knights?"

"Guess you heard about it."

"Who hasn't?"

"Don't know. But I know she's trustworthy. And you have knights here. Brother Barajas likes to keep to himself, but..."

"That's putting it nicely. He looks at everyone like he wants to stick one of his daggers in their neck."

"True. But I've fought beside him twice now, and I'd trust him with my life, no question. Hell, recently he saved me from being crushed by a big-ass monster. Damned creature was nearly indestructible and immune to magic. Barajas attacked it with those two daggers. Didn't even hesitate. Saved my neck."

"The Memphis Knights are good people. Didn't know that about Barajas, though. Guess it explains why he's so high-ranked. I thought it was odd that someone so confrontational could've reached the senior ranks of the holy rollers."

"There's more to him than battle prowess. He's a good guy. I've met a lot of good people out in the shit, most of which aren't Arcane Guardians. You ever heard of Shain Stone?"

"Of course. He's one of the Argument's most wanted."

"Same for the Cabal, but I'd trust him to have my back anytime."

"Truly?"

"Absolutely. No offense, but despite your arcane spear, I'd trust Shain Stone to have my back before you. I'd trust that maniac with just about anything. And Elder Morgan of the Oklahoma Cherokee. A few others from that group, too. There's even a sasquatch I've come to trust."

"I hear you." Then he looked up at me, studying my face. "You know, Wyatt, you might be wiser than I gave you credit for."

"Thanks. I think."

"Anyway," he said, straightening, "we're due to leave within in the hour. You coming with us to get some payback? Or going to babysit?"

I studied him for a second. "I'll get back with you on that."

45

"I'm afraid the Archmage insists."

I glared at Master Serrano. "I don't care what the Archmage insists. I promised to keep an eye on Alyita. I don't feel good about her going off with a bunch of strangers. She's a teenager, Santiago."

"I know," he said, putting up his hands. "But she's also going to be in the company of Supreme Shaman Sams, who is a powerful sorcerer."

"He's also not in the best health. I don't doubt his experience, nor his wisdom, but if they were attacked, can he protect her?"

"I'm sure he can," Master Serrano said. "Besides, why would they be attacked?"

"Because there're a bunch of assholes running rampant in Appalachia."

"The Cherokee are powerful, too. You know this."

"I don't care. And why does Archie want us to play guard duty, anyway?"

"Archie?" he asked, an amused expression on his face.

Oops.

"The Archmage," I said, moving right along. "I figured he wouldn't want me anywhere near an Argument op after the last disaster."

"It surprised me as well," Serrano said. "But he insists. Said to consider it an order."

"Oh, really?" I said, temper rising.

"And he said if you got upset to remind you that was the term of your agreement. That while you would have some independence to operate, you would also take on assignments that he, Master Washington, Master Jackson, or I asked you to. He also said to tell you that he would hold me personally responsible if you refused."

"Bastard," I said, shaking my head.

Checkmate. He knew how to move me like a chess piece. That only pissed me off more.

"I'm kind of surprised," Master Serrano said, studying me. "I thought you would have jumped at a chance to take down your former team. Especially after they've attacked you twice."

"Oh, I *do* want to take them down. It's not that... Shit, Serrano, maybe I'm growing up a little."

That made him raise an eyebrow.

"I didn't like the way Alyita's handler was treating her, so I told him to piss off and took responsibility for her for the rest of the trip. I don't feel right letting her go without us."

"She has an escort."

"But not *our* escort. You're not going along with her, are you?"

"No, I have meetings."

"Of course," I said, rolling my eyes. "Where the hell is the Archmage? I would like to speak with him."

"He thought you might." Serrano let out his biggest sigh yet. "He told me to tell you he was too busy for one of your temper tantrums and to refer back to the previous thing I said."

"That mother—"

"He also suggested I remind you that he bought the wand you carry and paid for the new staff you're having made."

"Which I wouldn't have needed him to do if he hadn't hidden my inheritance. That insufferable ass!"

Master Serrano sighed yet again. "He also thought you might say that, to which he said—"

"I don't want to hear it," I said, stopping him.

"Hmm," Serrano said. "That's actually, uh, precisely what he said as well. Or what I was supposed to tell you he said."

"Of course he did." I shook my head. "So, I have no choice, then."

"That's the spirit," Master Serrano said, grinning at me.

I turned and stomped away. I had to go assemble my team. The team who was gathered in my room thinking they were going on a Cherokee field trip. Instead, we were headed back out into the shit. *Wonderful.*

I'd only made it a few steps down the hall when a voice spoke into my mind.

"Hello, Wyatt. I hope you're well."

"Hello, Mothman. I'm fine. How are you?"

"Quite well, thank you. Listen, your Archmage reached out to me."

I paused in my tracks.

"Yeah?"

"He seemed to think you would have concerns about your young friend joining the entourage to the Cherokee grounds."

"That's right."

"Well, I wanted to assure you I will keep an eye on her for you."

"You're going, too?"

"Yes. It is my tour, after all."

"Your tour?"

"Yes. That's not so commonly known, mind you. I visit the Cherokee regularly. This aligns with my next meeting with them. Which, I believe, is why the Argument's leadership agreed with it in the first place. They can save face with the Cherokee while also appeasing the moon-eyed people."

"I see," I said, nodding along. *"That makes a lot more sense now."*

"Indeed. So, worry not about your young friend. She will be as safe as I am, I assure you."

"All right," I said. That did make me feel better. If there was trouble, Mothman would be better suited to protect her than I ever could be. And Supreme Shaman Sams, who'd made the case that he might have "one" left in him. Plus all the Cherokee medicine men and women. *"Thank you, Mothman. I really appreciate it."*

"Of course. You be careful out there. I fear you'll be in far greater danger than us."

"Right. Thank you."

He was right. Here I was worried about Alyita on a harmless field trip while we were being asked to plan for an inevitable attack.

Priorities, Wyatt. Priorities.

Time to get my team ready to roll.

Time to get a little payback.

46

My team was assembled.

Around my couches.

It wasn't really an Avengers Assemble type of moment. They looked bored, irritable, and annoyed it had taken me so long. Especially Anthony and Fred, who I'd only given ten minutes to prepare, then had taken considerably longer to get back to them. *Ah, well. Futz 'em. Damned troublemakers.*

"So, field trip?" Parker asked, looking annoyed. He wasn't hungover like Anthony and Fred. He just enjoyed the boring-ass sessions and building his network.

"No," I said, glancing at Alyita. "Change of plan. We've been directed to go on another op."

"What?" pretty much everyone said at once.

Everyone except Axel, who said, "Sweet! Clench your butts and grab your nuts! We've got work to do, Squirrel Nuts Squad!"

Parker got right down to business. "What's the job?"

I wasn't sure if I should say in front of Alyita, but I could already tell by her expression she wasn't happy.

"The Argument has reason to believe our friends from the other night are going to attempt a jailbreak on Cowan. We've been asked to tag along to stop them."

That surprised everyone.

"We've been *asked* to participate?" Parker said.

"I'm as surprised as you," I said. "And no, we weren't so much asked as told, by the Archmage himself. He insisted."

Parker's eyebrows rose.

"That's because he knows Squirrel Nuts Squad has the biggest nuts," Axel said, tone serious. "Archie is proud of deez nuts."

Everyone ignored him.

"Any word on how the Argument feels about this?" Parker asked.

"I can't say for sure," I replied. "I've only spoken to Christian. My guess is they're reluctant, based on the hoedown showdown. But this *is* an opportunity for us."

"How do you figure?" Anthony asked.

"Well, for one—" I said, pacing the carpet like a general. At least, that was how I liked to think I looked. "—we have a chance to show the Argument we aren't completely screw-ups."

There were some snorts at this.

I paused and looked directly at Barrett. "And we have an opportunity to get some payback on our former teammates."

The big man responded with a slow nod.

"But, um..." Fred said, putting up his hand like this was a classroom. I really appreciated his newfound humbleness. Gone was the cocky security supervisor. In his place was a scared little man with a stupid mustache. I rather preferred him this way. He gave Barrett a nervous glance, then turned back to me. "Is that a, uh, good idea? I mean..."

He trailed off.

"We've already discussed this," I said. "We fuck up. We own it. We move on. Barrett will keep his cool."

Barrett nodded.

"We all will," I said, glaring at everyone in turn. "We're going to be calm, collected, and professional. Right?"

Everyone nodded.

Except Alyita, who had her arms crossed and was trying to scowl the reality she wanted into existence. "So, I'm on my own?"

"Not completely." I forced a smile. "In fact, I'm a little jealous."

"Oh, yeah?"

"Yeah. You get to hang out with a mythical urban legend. And no one is going to try to kill you."

She didn't seem convinced.

"Just the same," I said, "take your knife and your wand. Keep your eyes open."

"I'll take my tomahawk, too."

"Good idea," I replied. "Everyone else, gear up. Let's get ready to swan-dive into the shit again."

47

We caught a ride in Christian's convoy.

It was a bouncy journey along old country roads, most of which weren't marked. I had the impression they were Argument roads, left without names so folks would assume they were private drives. Just a hunch. The Cabal had similar roads leading to and from the Castle. The sort of roads that if someone happened down them by chance, they'd quickly turn around and head back the way they'd come.

Anyway, it was a half-hour drive that led to a little glade out in the middle of the forest.

The only thing man-made was an old broken-down shack.

Might have seemed odd. And I wouldn't deny that, for at least a moment, I wondered whether we were on the receiving end of a cruel joke. But again, these were the types of things the Cabal set up, too. Places that looked like nothing. Old broken-down shacks and creepy, uninviting structures that held great secrets. In fact, there were likely wards to enhance the creepy vibe. Magic to inspire fear in any Norman who might've happened upon the place. I wasn't rude enough to test their wards to confirm. And the Argument crew disabled them for us to pass through, anyway.

As soon as we were out of our vehicles, one of the squads made a wide perimeter around us, weapons at the ready, looking for any sign of trouble. They were professionals. The Cabal had similar operators. And we were professionals, too, I tried to remind myself. That was a hard sale with Axel talking up a storm, like a kid cracked out on gummy worms.

That might've sounded specific. It was. Even as he blathered on, Axel was jamming gummy worms into his pie hole. While everyone else acted like magical G.I. Joes, Axel stomped along eating candy and asking lots of questions.

Whatever. Fuck it. He could have his fun. I knew he'd be ready when the time came, and I didn't care much what anyone else thought of him. Besides, among the supernatural community, he'd built some renown for being... Well, Axel. So, it wasn't like his wonky behavior would tarnish our reputation any worse than it already was. Least, that was what I told myself.

As we followed the Argument's finest toward the shack, Christian moved alongside me. I hadn't failed to notice how much reverence the Argument's operators had for the Defender. That was different for sure. I mean, at least for me. My father had been respected, of course, as well as our Archmage, Grand Enchanter, Grand Curator, and Grand Shaman. And in the south, Byron Walker held that same sort of respect. They were all older than me, though. Christian was near my age. Maybe even younger. Yet he commanded respect among his order.

He was dressed in his combat gear and struck an imposing figure. All that chain-mail and tactical gear. He certainly looked like a professional monster-punting badass. I wore jeans and t-shirt. Maybe I needed some cool Blade Mage gear. Of course, if I did that, Axel would get *way* too into it and we'd ended up with a house full of Halloween costumes. Maybe I'd just stick with the jeans and t-shirts.

I glance over at Christian. "Where's your partner in crime?"

"Daisy? She's already on site. We're infiltration team three."

"Three?" I asked, glancing around at the many hardened wizard warriors around us. "There're more?"

He gave me a wicked grin. "We don't intend to get caught with our pants down this time. We're bringing an army. There'll be two more teams this size coming behind us."

"Will we have room for everyone?" I asked, motioning toward the shack.

He returned my smile. "Access tunnel."

"I figured."

Just then, the first of them opened the door. They moved some junk around, clearing the floor. The old shack just had rotted lumber and dusty boxes scattered about. Stuff any Norman would've thought was trash. Beneath that, there was a dirt floor. The wizard there raised his wand and a large square of dirt rose from the ground, hovering. Beneath the false earth was a set of stairs leading down.

As we waited our turn to descend, Christian said, "The facility we're housing Cowan in isn't a repurposed facility."

I knew what he meant. Lots of Cabal hidey-holes had been taken over and remade to what we needed.

"It was purpose-built," he continued. "There are three access points: one at the site and two outside of it. We're taking this one, so if our foes have eyes on the front entrance, they won't see us arrive."

"Sneaky," I replied.

Behind me, Axel caught his first sight of the stairs. "Hell yes! I love spelunking!"

"That right, Gunner?" Anthony said. "Figures you would like dark holes."

"I sure do, Burns," Axel replied. "Just ask your mom. I'm her number one spelunker."

There were a few chuckles at that, even from the Argument's folks.

Christian gave me a look, like, *Seriously?*

I shrugged.

No reason we couldn't be professional and still have fun. Especially at Anthony's expense.

Christian continued his description of the underground prison. "So anyway, we have a nice long walk down the tunnel. Cowan's cell is in the center room. Only one way in. We have a larger room for defending it. That's where we'll have most everyone staged. It was built for this type of scenario."

"Sounds good to me," I said. "We'll follow your lead and post up wherever you want us."

"We're hoping to surprise our intruders." He turned and made a point of studying Axel.

"What?" Axel replied with a gummy worm hanging out of his lips. "I'm super sneaky. Just ask Burns's mom. We've kept our relationship secret for years."

"Shut up, Gunner," Anthony said from behind him. "Idiot."

"That is no way to speak to your future stepfather." Axel waggled a gummy worm at him. "Now you aren't getting that new bike you wanted."

Christian gave me a very skeptical look.

"He *is* rather sneaky," I replied, shrugging. "But we might want to put him someplace quiet."

"Like in a cell?" Christian asked. "Maybe gagged?"

"Kinky," Axel replied. "Guess I should've expected a strait-laced Defender to be into weird shit. Not really my thing, though."

More chuckles from the group.

Christian's cheeks reddened. I didn't think the super serious super sorcerer was used to dealing with someone like Axel. It was good for character building.

Still, I threw him a dinghy. Leaning in close, I said, "Best just to ignore him."

"Right," he said. His tone implied something else. Like, if Axel was on his team, he'd know better.

He was wrong. He just didn't know it. Axel was going to Axel and didn't give a damn what anyone thought about it.

"Remember that conversation we had earlier?" I asked.

Christian nodded.

"It applies here."

"I can hardly see how."

"And hopefully you won't have to find out."

We descended into darkness.

48

I had imagined a wizard prison like the one I'd visited Axel in. A smallish underground bunker.

It was nothing like that. Well, it was an underground bunker, but it was massive. More like an underground warehouse.

The tunnel led us to a set of massive steel doors, which guards on the other side had to open for us. They led into a large open room. There were three other massive doors there, two other entry points and one that led toward the holding cell.

It didn't take a genius to figure out which door led to the cell.

There were concrete and steel barriers everywhere, all facing the door we'd come through and two others. Clearly it was designed so a small army could take up defensive positions with their backs to the door leading to the holding cell. It didn't matter which entryway our enemies came through, our side would have all the cover, and they'd have to march through a killing field to get past us.

The entire facility was pulsing with magical energy. No surprise there. The walls, ceiling, and floor were covered in glyphs. This place was warded for warfare. There was no telling what sort of defenses they had lined up. I couldn't believe my former teammates and their new friends intended to break in. They would've had better luck going after Fort

Knox. Of course, rumor had it the Feds had some pretty nasty wizards on retainer themselves, so maybe not. Either way, I'd only seen a little of the facility so far and I couldn't imagine trying to plan a jailbreak.

Christian stopped beside me, a sly smile on his face. "What do you think?"

"This is brilliant," I said, nodding approvingly.

"Does the Cabal have anything like it?"

I paused, unsure how to answer. It had just occurred to me I didn't know much about the Cabal's prison systems. I mean... When I'd worked on a strike team, we'd dumped off plenty of assholes at smaller holding facilities. But since I'd become the Blade Mage, I hadn't really taken many prisoners. I didn't know a damned thing about the Cabal's maximum security facilities. I knew we had them. Just didn't know shit about them. And I definitely should have.

So, instead of answering his question, I just kind of looked at him, like I was too cool to answer a question like that. Christian didn't seem to care.

There were plenty of guards, many stationed behind barriers. Others were milling about.

Daisy saw us and started over, looking none too happy.

"What's he doing here?" she asked Christian, not bothering to look at me.

"The Cabal was gracious enough to loan us Wyatt's team again," he said, voice even. He didn't give away how he felt about the matter.

Daisy wasn't so shy or professional. She scowled. "This is just what we need."

Christian held up a hand and she stopped. In fact, she looked away, a hint of embarrassment on her face.

"Come on," Christian said, glancing over at me. "Let me show you the rest of the facility."

I walked alongside him. The rest of Squirrel Nuts Squad followed. Axel was still chatting and chewing on candy. He was out of gummy worms, though, and had switched to a bag of Skittles. The constant rattle made me want to slap him.

Christian led us past all the barriers to the door which obviously led to the cell. The doors weren't electronic. That would've been too easily wrecked by magic. The amount of wards they had active might've zapped them. Instead, they used old-school bank vault doors, the kind that had a wheel to spin instead of a doorknob.

Through the doors, we found ourselves in another hallway.

There were plenty of sigils and glyphs there as well. More barriers and guards, too.

It was a long, straight tunnel that wrapped around to the right.

Once we made that first right turn, we found ourselves in another long tunnel, similarly barricaded and guarded. In fact, it could have been the exact same hall because it also ended in a right turn.

On we went. And...

Another matching hall with another right turn at the end, only this one was shorter.

I glanced over at Christian, who gave me another sly smile.

The next hall was shorter still, but again, turned to the right, leading to yet another hall, and then another, and so on.

The halls wrapped around the holding room, which meant no one would have a quick entry. Not only would they have to get past the army waiting in the larger room, but then they'd have to work their way through hall after hall filled with guards, barricades, and more wards. I bet they had a few other tricks hidden in there as well. No telling what kinds of booby traps they'd set.

It seemed impossible.

What could possibly have made our enemies think this little prison was worth breaking into?

The halls continued around, shrinking in width and getting shorter, until at last we reached another vault door.

Another set of guards opened it for us.

I did some quick math in my head. My squishy brain had never been a big fan of numbers, but at a guess, we'd already passed well over a hundred guards and operators. Christian said more were still on the way. And there was plenty of cover for them to hide behind.

As the guards spun the wheel, I glanced over at Christian. "Has Cowan said anything yet?"

"Not a word," he replied. "Hasn't said a damned thing to anyone. Not a peep."

The door swung open and Christian marched inside. We followed.

This room looked more like the one where Axel had been held. It was a large square with barricades in each corner. Two guards were in place behind each, all decked out in full battle armor, their faces hidden behind helms.

The cell sat in the center of the floor, the bars also covered in glyphs.

As we approached, Cowan's head lifted, and he looked right at me.

A grin split his lips.

"The Blade Mage," he said, rising to his feet. "What an honor."

49

Cowan had nothing more to say.

It was rather awkward.

He just kind of ignored us, but kept that grin plastered on his cheeks.

Christian asked him several questions. He ignored them all.

I tried. He ignored me, too.

Finally, we left.

Once the door was slammed shut behind us, Christian turned and studied me.

"I don't know." I shrugged. It was obvious what he wanted to know. "No idea why he said hello to me."

"He has outright refused to speak to anyone else. We've had our best people on it. Even Tate and Whitaker have both come by. Not a peep. You show up and he talks."

I shrugged again. "He didn't say much."

"Still more than he's said to anyone else. It's infuriating."

"Maybe that's why he did it. He has a past with the Argument. Maybe he's just trying to get under your skin."

"Maybe," Christian agreed, rubbing his chin. "At any rate, we can't afford to let him be taken."

"I don't know how anyone would dream of breaking in here."

"Me neither. But that's our intel. Best I can figure, they don't know how secure this facility really is."

"How many people would know the location of this facility but not know how well defended it is?"

"Not many. At least...I wouldn't think many."

"Maybe our enemies only got the location, but don't know what to expect. Perhaps they think it's just a little hidden facility."

"Maybe," he agreed, shaking his head.

"Just for the record, though, I don't trust Feogh. He could have made the entire thing up just to get his way."

Christian sighed. "Worst case, we'll be bored for a few hours. Come on. Let's figure out where to post your team."

We started down the hall again.

We'd only made it a few turns when Axel declared, "This is good."

Both Christian and I stopped, turning to face him.

"Really?" I asked. "Why here?"

"Tired of walking," he said, then dumped some Sour Patch Kids into his mouth. Still chomping, he said, "Let's just stay here."

Was that a third type of candy? How much had he brought? Studying his pockets, I saw they were bulging. Had he just loaded up on candy? And wait... When had he bought all of it?

"This will work," Christian said, giving me a nod. "I was considering putting you guys in one of the halls anyway."

"Oh," I replied. I had really wanted to be in the front room. Wanted to see the look on my bitch of an ex-girlfriend's face when she strolled in and found an army waiting for her. But I also knew Christian was reluctant to have us here. Daisy was downright irritated about it. I wasn't sure about the rest of their folks. Maybe it was best if we stayed out of the way.

Christian seemed to read my expression. "Daisy is staying up in the front room. I planned on staying here in the hall closer to Cowan, just in case he tries to pull something. Maybe it makes sense to have you in the middle."

"Sure," I said, trying to hide my disappointment.

If Tanya and her evil asshole pep squad somehow made it through the army waiting for them in the big room, I wasn't sure what Squirrel Nuts Squad could do to stop them. So, basically, Christian had followed orders by bringing us along, but he had planned to plant us in a location where we could do the least amount of harm. We wouldn't be seeing any action, nor would we be stationed with the prisoner.

I forced a smile. "We're happy to go wherever you think we'll be the most useful."

"I'm not," Axel said.

Much to my surprise, Anthony elbowed him in the ribs. He yelped, then simmered down.

"This will work," Christian said.

And with that, he gave us a stiff nod and headed back toward Cowan's cell.

As a team, we all stared at one another, then took places behind barricades.

They didn't seem any happier than I felt. Well, Axel did, but that wouldn't last. He'd grow restless soon enough. Anthony and Fred already looked bored. Barrett seemed irritated, which I could only assume was because we were being sidelined. Parker alone kept his professional mask.

I sighed. Nothing for it but to wait.

50

We waited.

And waited.

Did some more waiting.

And a little more after that.

And...

Nothing.

Axel chomped on candy until he spiked a sugar rush. He was like an over-caffeinated monkey. No small blessing he didn't start flinging poo. Just about the time that everyone, myself included, was ready to commit murder to shut him up, he finally crashed. And oh, did he crash. He passed out on the cement floor surrounded by empty wrappers.

Anthony dug in Axel's pockets and retrieved a pack of Twizzlers, which he promptly tore open, took a few strands for himself, and then passed around.

I didn't figure Burns for a candy guy. Parker either. It didn't matter. We were all bored out of our freaking minds. Everyone took part in eating Axel's candy. It was a team-building exercise.

When the pack was empty, Anthony tossed the empty wrapper on Axel's snoring chest and then checked to see what else he had.

Time crawled on...

Then Christian came by.

He glanced down at the sleeping form of Axel—surrounded by trash—shook his head, and walked over to me.

"Wyatt," he said with a nod.

"Christian," I replied. "You reckon our enemies gave up?"

"Perhaps. Better safe than sorry, though. Can you come with me? I have an idea."

I rose to my feet and made to follow him.

To tell the truth, I felt bad. A little. I had a temporary distraction while the rest of the team remained bored. Whatever. It was good for their character building. Not that we didn't have enough character on our roster.

Christian led me back to Cowan's cell. He didn't say anything until we were nearly there.

"I've been trying to engage Cowan in conversation," he said, not bothering to look at me. "He still won't speak."

"Okay," I replied.

"So…" He hesitated, like he wasn't sure about what he was going to say. "What if you tried to speak to him?"

"Me?" I was surprised. I hadn't expected this.

He turned to face me. "I've tried everything I can think of to get him talking. Even had the guards clear out to see if he would speak to me alone. Nope. I offered him things. Food. Coffee. Water. Nothing. You're the only person he's uttered a word to. Thought maybe it was worth having you try to talk to him again, but this time alone."

"Huh," I said, shrugging. "Worth a shot. Good thinking."

"It was Daisy's idea, actually."

"Daisy?" I replied, again surprised.

He gave me a curt nod. "She may seem brash, but she's also quite clever."

"Never doubted it. The hammer chose her for a reason, right?" Then a new thought occurred to me. "You're okay with me speaking to your prisoner alone?"

"That sword chose you for a reason, right?"

The way he said it made me think he had questions about the

sword's judgment. That was fine. I often questioned its judgment myself.

"All right," I said. "I'm game."

We continued on, then waited while the guards opened the vault door.

Christian stepped in first and summoned all the other guards out.

Then he glanced at me. "I suppose it goes without saying, but don't touch the cell. Don't give him anything. Don't let him give you anything."

He had said it went without saying, but I had a suspicion he'd just said that to be diplomatic. He seemed very concerned about letting me into the cell room alone.

Couldn't say I blamed him. If I were in his shoes, I probably wouldn't have liked it much, either. I didn't feel great about it myself. What if this was part of the plan? What if getting me alone with Cowan somehow played into our enemies' game? I couldn't see how. But if something went wrong, I'd certainly be blamed.

I shuffled on inside.

The door locked shut behind me.

Cowan raised an eyebrow.

I started toward the cell. "Hello, Cowan. I don't think we've been properly introduced. Wyatt Draven, Blade Mage of the Ozark Mountain Cabal."

He wore an amused expression. "The Defender couldn't get what he wanted, so he sent you to give it a try? He really think that would get me talking?"

"Seems to be working."

He snorted. "Not sure what they want with me, anyway. Awful lot of effort for a nobody."

"A nobody? Don't talk down on yourself, pal. You're clearly very popular."

"That's the funny part. The Argument wanted me, but I don't know a damned thing. I'm no one special. Not this time."

"You must be pretty special. Word is your friends are going to attempt a jailbreak."

His eyebrow shot up. "I don't know where y'all are getting your info, but you might want to consider an alternative source, cuz that's bullshit."

"That right?"

He studied me, a suspicious look on his face. Then he started laughing. "Y'all really think that? Y'all really think someone is gonna try to break me out?"

I shrugged. "From what I've heard, you're a major player. Always have your nose in bad business."

"Not like this business," he said, shaking his head. "Hell, I'd rather be in here than out there with them."

"With who?"

He met my gaze. "You don't even know, do you?"

"I know some of the assholes you're running with. Tanya and her crew."

"Aw, of course. The sniper chick. She's cute. Don't really know her. Sure would like to."

It was my turn to study him. He spoke as if he barely knew her. But that didn't make sense. Right after I'd spotted him was when the others had made their move.

"You're probably wondering about that," he said, eyes still locked on mine. "Wondering how I knew who you were, if I wasn't buddied up with your lady pal."

He didn't say more, only chuckled.

I waited. I'd had a lot of practice being bored for the past few hours.

He finally shrugged. "Look, I don't know that crew. I was just asked to play my part. To show up at the hoedown and be seen. That's what I got paid for. They did tell me to keep an eye out for you. Called you a high-value target. I knew as soon as I saw you everything was about to go to hell."

"So, you tried to take me down yourself?"

"I had backup and you were on your own. Figured I might get a bonus if I brought you down. Someone wants you dead real bad, Blade Mage."

"Wait..." I said, studying him. "You said they told you to keep an eye out for me. That means I wasn't the target. Not the primary target, anyway. It wasn't a trap for me..."

"Don't feel bad. Like I said, someone wants to kill you real bad."

"I'm aware. They've tried twice since I've been in Appalachia. But what you're saying doesn't make sense. If the trap wasn't for me, then who was it for?"

He grinned at me.

That was no help.

I considered what he'd said, and I remembered Gabby had said much the same in the previous encounter. I looked up at him. "So, I was just a target of opportunity?"

"Well, aren't you as sharp as the sword you carry," he said, tittering.

This scumbag was annoying, but I was getting somewhere. Even if I didn't get all the answers, just the fact he'd spoken to me would help the team's rep, or so I hoped.

"So, your pals were after someone—or something—else, but when I showed up, you guys tried to kill me instead."

"More or less," he said, flashing me another wolfish grin. "Your sniper gal pal said you were dangerous. How'd she put it? Oh yeah, she said if you showed up, we needed to take you down quick. Said you weren't much in a scrap, but had a legendary ability to fuck everything up. Seems you proved her right."

"On more than one occasion," I said with a heartfelt smile. "So, then, who or what was the actual target?"

He didn't reply.

"Don't go quiet on me now. The way I figure it, you're pretty well screwed no matter what you do. Your best bet is for the Argument to show you some leniency. And they just might. The way I hear it, they weren't looking for your head. Just for your capture. Playing nice will be your best bet. Unless you think your friends can really break you out of this fortress?"

He chuckled again and shook his head. "No one is coming for me. I'm nobody. And I'm happy to sit right here in the safety of this cell. Trust me, I'm safer with the Argument than I am with the psychos who hired me."

"Who?"

"Shit." That time he fell into a full-on chortle. "I just told you I'm scared shitless of them, and you think I'm going to give you a name?

Maybe you're not as bright as I thought. Look, I'm done talking. Said too much already. But for what's it worth, I hope you do get those bastards, because I'd not like to run into them again. No thanks."

"Then why would they spout off about coming to break you out?"

"Why indeed?" he asked, sitting on the floor and resting his back against the bed. "Sure makes you wonder."

And that was it. He would say no more. Not a peep.

And yeah, it *did* make me wonder...

51

"Well, what happened?" Christian asked.

I'd just exited through the vault door. He waited until it clicked shut to ask.

"I think..." I paused, staring at him. "I think we may have been bamboozled. Come on."

I started back toward my team. I intended to kick Axel awake and tell them about my conversation. Get their brains on it. I certainly couldn't unwind it all myself.

As he kept pace beside me, I could tell Christian wanted more information. He wanted to know what had been said. But he also didn't press. I probably would have been less patient, so points for him.

I might've thrown him a bone, but I wasn't sure where to start. I was still trying to put the pieces together myself.

My team was sitting behind their barricades, eating more stolen candy from Axel. He was still napping, of course, but had taken his shirt off to use as a pillow.

I kicked his leg.

"No," he said, swiping at me. "Sleepy time."

I kicked him again.

"Just take him," Axel said, eyes still closed. "I don't care. Nappy nap."

"Axel, get your stupid ass up," I said.

He sat upright, glancing around, candy wrappers still stuck to his chest. His eyes were droopy, but came to life when he saw Anthony had a half-eaten Snickers in his mouth. "Hey! That's mine!"

"You want it back?" Anthony asked, opening his mouth to reveal the dismantled Snickers.

"Guys," I said through gritted teeth. "Fucking focus."

That made everyone sit up straight. Axel even put his shirt back on.

"I spoke with Cowan," I said.

If I didn't have their attention before, I definitely did then.

"Something... Something isn't right," I said, glancing from them back to Christian. "He claims they wouldn't come to rescue him. Also said I wasn't their target the other night."

That made a lot of eyebrows raise, including Christian's.

The Defender shrugged. "He may have just said that first part to trick us into leaving. I told you, he's slippery. Can't trust a word he says."

"I hear you," I said. "But for some reason, I think he was telling the truth. He's terrified of whoever he was working for."

I explained our conversation.

Everyone wore thoughtful expressions.

When no one jumped in, I asked, "So, if I wasn't the target, who, or what, was?"

No one had an answer.

"He may have just been messing with you," Christian said. "I'm sure he's bored."

"I'm sure I'm bored," Axel said. "Can we pick a new spot?"

"No," I said, scowling at him. "This was the spot you wanted."

"Yeah, 'wanted.' That's past tense. In the present tense, I want a new spot. I'm *bored*. And these assholes ate half of my candy."

"You don't need any more candy," I said. "You'll just get another sugar rush and crash again."

"And diabetes," Fred said.

"Seriously, guys," I said, trying not to lose my patience. "Can we focus? I feel like we're missing something vital here. Why would the moon-eyed folk tell us the dark wizards were coming to rescue Cowan if that was a lie?"

Again, there were no answers.

"I've got a bad feeling," I said, shaking my head. "Something isn't right."

"I'll check in with Daisy," Christian said. "Make sure everything is good up front. If it'll make you feel better, we can walk up there."

"Sure," I said, "but it's not that. I can't help feeling like I'm being played."

"You're focused on this business about the target," Parker said.

"Of course he is," Axel replied. "He's all hot and bothered. You can tell. He gets all moody."

"Axel."

"Wyatt."

I shook my head. They were no help. Not sure why I thought they would be.

"Look," Parker said, shrugging, "I think Christian has the right idea."

"Yeah," Anthony said, taking another bite from his stolen Snickers. "Dude was just messing with you."

"No," I shook my head. "He seemed genuinely scared. We know Tanya and her treacherous band of back-biters. We met the Wampus Cat. Met the Apple Devils, too. All tough customers, but none scary enough to make him prefer a jail cell to their company."

I started pacing.

"Daisy says everything is straight up front," Christian said. "No signs of trouble."

"Nor will there be," I said. "Check in with your leadership. Make sure everything is all right at home."

"No one would attack us there," Christian said. "That's better protected than—"

"Just do it," I snarled.

The Defender seemed taken aback.

"Oh," Axel said, eyes widening. He straightened his shirt and stood.

"He's in one of *those* kinds of moods. Everyone straighten up, pay attention, and prepare for imminent violence."

I ignored him. The others, though, they all got their game faces on. That it took Axel to convince them did not sit well with me. *Whatever.* I needed to focus.

Once everyone was quiet, I started mumbling to myself while I paced. It helped.

"Cowan wouldn't be super terrified of Tanya and company. Wouldn't be that afraid of Wampus Cat. Or Apple Devils. So, what does that mean? Everyone was surprised Wampus Cat and an Apple Devil had joined up. What does that tell us? It tells us that whoever is pulling their puppet strings..." I paused, realizing exactly what it meant. "Is super scary."

I looked up at the others, but they were just staring at me. Except for Christian. He had his eyes closed, a thoughtful look on his face. Hopefully, that meant he was calling home like I'd asked. Er, demanded.

I got back to think-walking.

"And if I wasn't the target, then who, or what, was? He had said Tanya had warned them that if I appeared, they needed to take me out because I had a tendency to screw things up. That was why they switched focus to me. Before that, though, what could connect both locations? Other than me. Who, or what, might they have found at both places?"

I realized everyone was staring at me, but I ignored them and continued talking to myself.

"Wait. That's not the right question. He also said he'd been paid to stand out there in the open. He was bait. A lure. But not for me. I wouldn't have given a shit about him. That means, whatever they were after, they were convinced having him out in the open would draw it out. So that means..."

And then it hit me.

Other than my presence, there was really only one connection between the two events.

I turned and stared at the others, jaw hanging open.

"They weren't after me at all," I said, shaking my head. "He was telling the truth... Oh, fuck."

"What, then?" Parker asked. "Or who?"

I blinked, considering. And I knew I was right.

"Fuck. Oh, fuck." I looked up at the others. "They were after Mothman."

Before anyone could reply, Christian whipped his head toward me, a very serious look on his face. "We have to get back. Now."

52

"Alyita has been taken."

For a moment, I didn't realize who'd said it. Turned out, it was me.

The others stared at me. The Archmage, Master Serrano, and Master Castillo. Christian, Daisy, Tate, and Whitaker. For once, none of them had anything to say. They just stared at me.

We were in a conference room back at the Argument's dwarven city. By that point, I was pretty sure I'd seen more of the Argument's conference rooms than I had of our own at the Castle. Which was a stupid thought just then. An invading thought.

Daisy was the first to find her voice. She scowled at me. "I think we have bigger problems than one missing teenager."

Rage bubbled, about ready to boil.

Master Serrano put a calming hand on my shoulder. It didn't help.

Archie spoke up before I blurted out something idiotic. "I think we can agree that *all* the missing people are a priority." He offered Daisy a grandfatherly smile. "You must understand, Wyatt has a close relationship with both Alyita and her grandfather."

"Yeah, and Sams is a member of our council," Daisy said. "And Mothman... Mothman is... He's like our fucking mascot."

"Enough, Daisy," Tate said. "That's enough. There's little use arguing over who's the most important. I'm sure anyone from the Cherokee would argue Tsali and the others are the greatest loss. We need to get them *all* back."

An awkward silence stretched across the room. I could hardly believe it. Could hardly believe this was real. Mothman, Supreme Shaman Sams, the Cherokee leaders, and Alyita... All taken. All kidnapped. That didn't even seem possible.

"I can't believe those little pricks!" Daisy said with a growl.

"We don't know for sure the moon-eyed people set this up," Whitaker said. Daisy whirled on her and Whitaker held up her hands. "Though it certainly seems likely."

"Still no sign of them?" Christian asked.

Tate shook his head. "They disappeared not long after you guys left. No one has seen them, and we've had no luck tracking them."

"Fuckers," Daisy mumbled to herself. At least, I assumed she meant it for herself, but the rest of us could hear.

"Back to our missing folks," the Archmage said, his gaze directed at Tate. "Any ideas where they might have been taken?"

"We don't even know *how* they were taken," Tate said with a weary sigh. "To have captured Mothman and Sams..."

"Required some serious magical power," I said, glancing around the room. "When Cowan spoke to me, he seemed afraid of whoever he was working for. Said he'd prefer to stay locked up in your cell than to be freed. I think he was telling the truth. About all of it. They were never going to try to break him free. They just wanted us to look the other way."

"And that's precisely what we did," Christian said, meeting my gaze.

I nodded, then gave Archie a meaningful look, then Tate, then Whitaker. "They've been after Mothman the entire time. Did you know? Did you guys know that?"

Archie raised an eyebrow at me.

Whitaker shook her head.

Tate, though, he hesitated.

Finally, the Supreme Enchanter shook his head. "No, Wyatt. We did not know they were after Mothman."

The way he said it... There was something there. Something he was hinting at.

The Archmage spoke up. "We're at the Argument's disposal. Let us know how the Cabal can assist."

Tate gave the Archmage a long look, then glanced at me, only for the briefest of moments. He turned his attention back to Archie. "I think you've done enough, old friend."

There was an edge to his tone.

I was missing something. Something important.

"As you wish," the Archmage replied, still maintaining a friendly smile. "Do let us know if you change your mind."

"Wait," I said, holding up a hand. I glanced between the two big dogs. "Just hold on a second..."

Everyone stared at me again.

I met Daisy's angry glare with one of my own. "I understand how important Sams, Mothman, and the Cherokee leaders are to you. I really do. But I was supposed to be watching out for Alyita. I took responsibility for her safety."

"And you failed," Daisy said, shrugging. "Not our problem."

Archie held up a hand to stop me. Tate, Whitaker, and Christian all glared daggers at Daisy.

"I won't tell you again, Daisy," Tate said. Gone was the friendly, laid-back country boy. His demeanor had shifted to something else. Something harder. The real man behind the southernly gentleman facade. He turned his attention back to me. "I'm sorry about your young friend, Wyatt. Truly. The Argument will do everything in our power to bring her back safely. But this is our territory. Our responsibility. I'll not have any more... We're done with outside help for the time being. Please trust us to get her back."

I stared at him, dumbfounded. I didn't know what to say.

If they thought I was going to sit on the sidelines...

Master Serrano's grip tightened on my shoulder. A warning.

I turned to Archie. He fixed me with that same stupid smile.

My gaze shifted back to Tate and the others.

There was a time to run my mouth and a time to be quiet. Judging by Serrano's grip, Archie's smile, and the stern faces of the Argument, this was one of those times. But...

I made a decision.

"What are you not telling me?"

Christian seemed surprised by my accusation. Daisy, too. Even Serrano and Castillo seemed caught off-guard. The others, though... The three big bosses... They just looked at me. Studied me like a cut of meat.

Tate held my gaze, then turned and looked at Archie. For a moment, his face was a blank slate. Then he looked... Well, downright pissed-off. "Ask your Archmage."

Archie still only smiled.

53

The meeting was over. Adjourned.

Our part was done. The Cabal had no authority here.

I couldn't use my title to kick down doors.

I couldn't do a damned thing.

No... There was one thing I could do.

The members of the Argument remained behind once we were excused.

In the hall, Archie had his back to me, speaking quietly with Master Serrano and Master Castillo. They were marching on, walking down the hallway as if they'd already forgotten about me.

"Archmage," I said, realizing my tone was anything but respectful. Screw it. "What was that about?"

He turned to face me, that stupid smile still on his face. "Nothing of particular importance, considering the circumstances. Perhaps we can discuss it later."

"Or now," I said, crossing my arms. "I think we can discuss it now."

"Who do you think you are?" Master Battle Mage Castillo said. "How dare you speak to the Archmage that way?"

"Fuck off, Master Castillo," I said, not even looking at her. My eyes were glued on Archie. "What haven't you told me? And why did Tate seem so annoyed about it?"

"Wyatt," Master Serrano said, trying to calm me. "I'm sure there's nothing to be upset about."

"I'm not so sure," I said, still locked on Archie. "I think the Archmage is hiding something from me."

Archie chuckled. "You're clever, Wyatt. Why don't you tell me?"

I stared at him, wheels turning. What the hell could it have been? How did it relate to the capture?

The answer to the latter was simple... It didn't.

If whatever Tate was referring to had anything to do with this current craziness, he'd have broken it open in the middle of the room. They were old pals, sure, but if it had something to do with finding the others, he would have put it on the table. Even if I was wrong about that, Christian and Daisy had both been surprised, too. So, it was something they didn't know, which was further confirmation it had nothing to do with the missing people.

What, then?

I glanced at Serrano and Castillo. They'd seemed caught off guard as well. So it wasn't something Archie had shared with them, either. Something only he and Tate knew. Likely Whitaker, too. She hadn't seemed surprised. Of course, they were both senior leaders of the Argument, so I doubted much caught them off guard.

The look on Tate's face... It hadn't just been anger. That sigh at the end. It had seemed like he was...hurt. Like he was disgusted with the Archmage. What did that tell me?

And then it hit me.

Archie must have seen something on my face because he raised his eyebrow, as if impressed.

"You knew," I said, sure I was right. "You knew before we even came, didn't you?"

"Wyatt?" Master Serrano said, glancing from me to Archie. He looked to Castillo, but she only shrugged.

"That's why you invited me," I said, still staring at the Archmage. "That's why you put Barrett on my team. You fucking knew..."

Still, the Archmage didn't reply.

"Knew what?" Master Serrano asked. "Wyatt, what's going on?"

I trembled with rage. Fought with everything I had to keep it buried down. To keep myself from losing control.

I forced myself to turn to Master Serrano. "He knew my old team was here in Appalachia. He knew. Got the intel from Tate ahead of time. That's why he brought us. Not because he saw value in us taking part in some lame-duck conference. Not to help with the Cherokee negotiations. Not to meet our peers in the Argument. That was *all* bullshit. He knew if he put me out in the open, Tanya would come after me. He used me as fucking bait."

Master Serrano's eyes widened. "Surely, not. Archmage..."

His voice trailed off as he stared at his boss's boss's face.

"It's true, isn't it?" I asked, focused on Archie again. "You set me up to draw out my former team."

"I also ensured you had fewer vacancies on your roster, didn't I?" the Archmage said. "Ensured you'd have support."

"You asshole," I said.

"Your little team experiment was proving a disaster," Archie said, calm as ever. "I was about to shut it down when Supreme Enchanter Tate reached out. A few of the Cabal's most wanted had been spotted in Appalachia. They'd had no luck tracking Tanya down, though. With the conference coming up, I saw an opportunity. You are right, Wyatt. I knew if we put you out in the open, Tanya and your former teammates wouldn't be able to resist. It worked. Twice, in fact. Shame you didn't do your part, though, isn't it?"

"Maybe if I had known," I said through gritted teeth. "Maybe if you had told me they were here."

"Where's the fun in that?" Archie asked, that damned smile still intact.

I was about to blow a gasket.

"Boss," Master Serrano said, shaking his head.

"Oh, relax, Santiago," Archie said. "I'm joking, of course. Wyatt, I didn't tell you because I didn't trust you to behave. I feared if you knew about Tanya and the others, you'd ignore my orders and go hunting. That wouldn't do. I wanted them hunting you."

"You asshole," I said again, shaking my head. "It's one thing to put my life on the line, but the others... You stitched up Axel, too. And Parker. Anthony. Fred. Barrett. Even Alyita."

"I didn't tell you to send Alyita's babysitter packing, did I? You did that on your own."

"But the others," I said, scarcely able to speak. "You put them in danger, and for what?"

"So we could capture dark wizards. Traitors to the Cabal. Why else? You seem to forget, my job requires me to put people in danger every day. It's the job."

"You could have warned me."

"I couldn't trust you."

"Fuck that," I said, shaking my head. "What the hell is wrong with you?"

"I've told you before, and though I hate to embarrass you in front of Masters Serrano and Castillo, I'll tell you again. I am not your Gandalf. I am not your Dumbledore. I am not your Obi Wan Kenobi. I am not your mentor and I am not here to guide you. I am the Archmage of the Ozark Mountain Cabal, and it is my job to do what's best for our organization. To make the hard decisions. I did not tell you because I do not trust you, and you've done little to earn my trust or my respect."

"Then why bother giving me a team?"

"Because we need a Blade Mage. For your father's sake, and for the fact the sword chose you, I would prefer it was you. That's why I bought you your father's wand. Why I offered to pay for a new staff. But I don't have time to coddle you. Yes, I knowingly put you and your team in danger, because that's what I thought was best."

"And if I died, no big deal, right?" I glanced over at Master Castillo. "Then maybe you could get a better Blade Mage."

"Perhaps so," he replied, shrugging.

"Holy hell," Master Castillo said, staring at the Archmage like she'd never seen him before.

"That's cold, boss," Master Serrano said, shaking his head. "Even for you."

The Archmage smiled at them. "That *is* my job."

I didn't even know what to say. I wanted to hit him. Wanted to pop him right in the jaw. But I wouldn't have landed a punch. He'd turn me into a toad first.

I also wanted to quit. Wanted to storm out. Wanted to tell him to eat shit and die, and never look back. But I couldn't do that, either. If I left again, this time it would be for real. And something told me...

He wouldn't let me.

Something told me he'd make sure Dyrnwyn stayed with the Cabal. I didn't know how, but that was my instinct. I was in the middle of a very dangerous game.

"Well, then," he said, still smiling. "Are we done with the tantrum? I have other business to attend to."

I stared at him, speechless. Couldn't trust myself to speak.

"Very good," he said. "Run along now, Wyatt. And do please try to keep your team out of trouble."

"That's it?" I heard myself say.

"Not sure there's much else to say."

"I meant," I spoke through gritted teeth, barely able to rasp out the words, "about getting Alyita back."

"You heard the Argument. They do not require our assistance. So, yes. That's it. Go join your team. Keep them out of trouble and keep their mouths shut. We are done in Appalachia. The conference has ended prematurely and the Argument wants us to stay out of the way. So, in the morning, we'll head home. Try to get some rest in the meantime."

I stared at him for several long seconds. Then finally, I couldn't help myself. It just came out. "Fuck you."

And I turned and walked away.

54

If there was ever a time I'd felt more beaten down, I couldn't remember it.

I'd made my team out to be a joke.

The Appalachian Argument didn't want our help.

We'd been an embarrassment to the Cabal from the moment we'd arrived.

The Archmage *had* intended to fire my team after all.

And he'd only brought us along to see if he could get me killed. Or to see if I could get lucky enough to solve another problem for him.

Axel, Parker, Anthony, Fred, and Barrett's lives had all been put on the line because the Archmage still didn't trust me. To be used as bait? That's what I was worth to him. Nothing but a worm on a hook.

Even Eilidh wanted nothing to do with me anymore.

And Alyita...

My biggest failure.

If we had just gone with her...

No. I couldn't take on that guilt. If our enemies had taken down Mothman, Sams, and the Cherokee medicine folk, then no doubt we'd have been taken down, too. We'd have just been caught or killed, too. And...

I didn't want to admit it, even to myself, but in all likelihood...

She was dead.

She had no real value to our enemies. They'd wanted Mothman. He was the real prize. Supreme Shaman Sams, too, maybe. And the Cherokee leadership. What use would she be, though? At best, if they knew her connection to me, they might use her as bait, just as Archie had done. And I would take the bait, too. Tanya would know that. Or maybe there was some hope they might keep her alive long enough to try to recruit her. Otherwise... Otherwise she'd be better off dead.

The thought of her a prisoner... Held against her will...

Was there a chance there was any decency left in my old teammates? I would never have thought Zeke would have harmed a teenager. But then, I'd never thought he would have stabbed Barrett in the back. Their betrayal had seemed so sudden, but how long had it been in the making?

But the main problem... The real problem...

I couldn't do a damned thing about any of it.

Even if I wanted to fly off half-cocked and go rogue, I didn't know where to find them. Even if I had the Argument's blessing, I didn't know where to go looking.

"Wyatt?"

The voice broke through my reverie, startling me. I had been so focused as I stomped along, I hadn't even realized anyone else was around.

I looked up.

Eilidh.

Of all the people I didn't want to see just then, she was at the top of the list.

Her witch sisters were with her, including Big-nose. But she must've seen something on my face she because she kept on walking, ignoring me. The others followed.

Except Eilidh.

"Are you all right?" she asked. I noted the concerned look on her face.

Made me wonder what mine looked like.

"I'm fine," I said, and started forward again.

"Wyatt," she said, drawing my attention back to her. "I heard about

Mothman and the others. Is that what you're upset about? I didn't know you were close to any of them."

I spun on her, anger overflowing, but...I checked myself. She didn't know. Of course she didn't know. As Daisy had pointed out, Alyita didn't matter to anyone. Not to anyone but me. Her name had probably never been mentioned as the rumors ran rampant.

I took a calming breath. "Alyita was with them."

Eilidh's eyes widened. "She's been...taken?"

I nodded and looked away, feeling a stinging sensation near my eyes. It was too much. I was nearing a breaking point. Probably past it, truth be told.

"Oh, no," she said, placing a hand on my arm. "Oh, god. What are you going to do?"

I shook my head.

"You don't know?"

I took another breath. "I'm supposed to go home in the morning. Archmage's orders. Argument doesn't want us here. Doesn't want me involved."

"Do they have any leads? A plan?"

I just stared at her.

"So, then... What are you going to do?"

"I just told you."

"No, you told me what you're *supposed* to do. Not what you're *going* to do." She gave me a sly smile. "I know you better than that. What's your plan?"

"I don't have one, Eilidh," I said, feeling that stinging sensation around my eyes again.

I was either squinting really hard or on the verge of tears.

Eilidh stared back at me, studying me. "This isn't like you."

"What isn't?"

"Giving up."

I glared at her. I thought about saying she didn't know me that well, but that felt petty. And it wouldn't have been true. She knew me well enough, in all the ways that mattered. We'd been through hell together. I also considered pointing out that I was just following orders, but that would've been bullshit, too.

As I pondered, she went on. "You know, I hear stories about you from time to time. Rumors about your exploits make it to the northern states, too."

I merely shrugged.

"Yeah." She gave me a smile. "Sometimes I just roll my eyes, especially when you aren't painted in the best light. And you know why? Because I know it's bullshit. I've seen what you can do. I know what you're about. To hell with what your Archmage says. The rest of your council, too. And the Argument and even the Coven. They don't know you, Wyatt. But I do. And you know what else?"

"What?"

"If I were kidnapped by dark wizards, regardless of how powerful they were, there's no one else I would rather have come to the rescue. I'd be hoping it'd be you. Because I'd know you'd get the job done. Always do. Somehow, some way. And I bet that's what Alyita is thinking right now. I bet she's sitting there terrified, but hopeful, thinking you're on the way to save her."

I tried to find words to reply, but none came. I could scarcely breathe.

"So, figure out a way to save her. Mothman, too. He seemed pretty cool. Save them all. You really give a shit what your boss or the Argument told you? Wyatt Draven sitting on the sidelines? Fuck that. And fuck them."

Still, I could think of nothing to say. I just stared at her.

"Come on, Wyatt. You know you'll think of something."

"How?" I asked, feeling a bitter chuckle escape my lips. "I don't know the area. Don't have any connections. No leads. I wouldn't have the first clue what to do. Hell, I was guided here through the forest. I don't even know where 'here' is."

"They say the moon-eyed people betrayed the Argument," she said. "Any chance you remember your way back to their camp? That could be a starting point."

I shook my head. "No chance in hell. We walked through the forest, and at night. Besides, I doubt they'd risk going back there, anyway. Look, just stop, all right? Whatever inspiration you think you're going to conjure up, it's not happening. I'm beaten this time."

She stared at me, biting her lip. "I'm sorry. Just trying to help. I thought maybe you would have learned something from the moon-eyed people. Or where they hid."

"Well, I didn't, okay?" I shrugged. "I don't know shit. I don't have any way to..."

I blinked.

"Wyatt?"

Sometimes I really hated my brain.

There was something there. Some little thing. I hated it when this happened. Something useful was trying to birth itself in my prefrontal cortex. Or maybe not. I didn't really know much about the brain or which part did what. But something was on my mind. Something she'd said had triggered something and now it was wriggling around in there like a worm, trying to break free.

I looked up at her, noticing she wore an amused expression. She knew I was onto something.

This was going to be super disappointing if I didn't figure out what it was.

And then it hit me.

Maybe I *did* know something useful.

But who to ask? Who could tell me? If I went to someone from the Argument, they'd use it. And if I was right, they'd send an army. But... Was that the best idea? Did I trust them to save Alyita? Or was Eilidh right? Did I go do it my damned self?"

I shook my head. First things first. I needed to know if my intel was worth a damn.

"I, uh, I've got to go," I said.

She smiled at me. "Go do your thing."

I turned and stomped down the hall.

I knew one person who might be able to answer my question. And I knew where to find him.

55

The Tennessee Wildman was at the bar.

He glanced up as I approached. "Ain't looking for company."

The little bar had a few folks about, but not many. Mostly just people in for the conference. The mood was quiet and somber. I doubted anyone from the Argument was looking for libations. Not with the proverbial shit hitting the metaphorical fan.

"How convenient," I said. "I'm not, either. I'm looking for answers."

"And you think I'd have them?" he asked with a snort. "Look around you, kid. You've got the whole damned Appalachian Argument to ask, and you come to a half-drunken ape man?"

"I'm guessing you know these mountains as well as anyone."

"On that, you'd be right. Damned right."

"So you know where Bipple is?"

His glass paused halfway to his lips. He gave me a sideways glance and raised his eyebrow. "Now, where would you have heard of a place like that?"

I shrugged.

"And what's your interest in it?" he asked. "Ain't much there."

"Tell me something, Wildman," I said, sitting down on the barstool beside him. "Has the Argument found Wampus Cat for you yet?"

"Hell no," he said, still eyeing me. "You telling me you have?"

The barman came around just then and I asked for two shots of Wild Turkey. I had a suspicion I couldn't trust the barkeep. I mean, this was the Argument's bar. Surely they had him spy on customers. That was what the Cabal would have done.

He poured our shots and moved on.

I held mine up.

The Tennessee Wildman raised his as well. "Cheers."

We clinked 'em and knocked 'em back.

It felt good, that burning sensation running down my throat, setting my chest aflame.

I looked over at him. "I've got a hunch. Thinking I might go check it out. Probably nothing. How do I get there?"

He gave me another long, slow stare. "You'll get there by me taking you, if you're telling me Puss in Tight Pants is there."

"It's a hunch. Not quite a lead. No promises. You in?"

"Ain't got no better prospects. Just you and me?"

"I've got one other for sure," I said, knowing Axel was always down to do something stupid. "Not sure about the rest of my team. Actually... There might be a few other crazy folks around who'll join us."

"Hmm," he said, considering. "If you're right about this, then we'll be up against mighty stout odds, assuming all their friends are there."

"Probably worse than you think, even. That bother you?"

"Not even a little." He cracked a grin. "And we'll probably get into trouble with the Argument."

"Does that bother you?"

"Nope. Makes me want to do it even more."

"The real question is how we'll slip out of here unnoticed."

He chuckled. "Leave that to me. I know where all the side doors are."

"I figured they watched every door."

"They do, but some less so than others. I can get you and whatever crew you assemble out. And I can get you to the place you want to go. I just have one question."

"Shoot."

"If your hunch is good, are we just going to run this time? Or are we going to stay and fight?"

"If I'm right, then it's a rescue mission."

"That snobby-ass Mothman and old Sams?" He shook his head. "What do you care about them for? If we're going to do this, it should be to take out Wampus and those assholes who wanted to kill you."

"Normally, I would agree. I would very much like some payback."

"But?"

"But a friend of mine was also taken. A teenage girl."

"Ah, hell," he said, nodding. "And there I was spoiling for a fight to the death. Fine. Rescue mission first."

"If my hunch is good, then I'm sure there'll be plenty of assholes for you to kill along the way."

"Works for me. Just let me finish my drink first, will you?"

"Take your time. I've got to round up our helpers."

I eased myself from the bar. I was probably supposed to pay, but I figured I'd follow Wildman's example and see if they ever asked. It was time for some rebellious shit. Figured I'd start with the drink and finish by getting myself killed.

I started away, but paused for a moment to use mind-speak. *"Axel, where are you?"*

"Uh, I don't know, actually."

"Of course you don't. Listen, I need you to do me a favor."

"Sure."

"Round up the team. Tell them to meet in my room in five minutes. Everyone except for Parker."

"Uh..."

"What?"

"Sounds like you're up to something naughty."

"Yup."

"Sweet. I'm in. Is it going to be dangerous?"

"You know it."

"Even better."

"Can you do one more thing for me?"

"Sure."

"See if you can find Brother Barajas."
"Oh, shit. It's that kind of thing?"
"Yup."
"Hells yeah."

56

The team was assembled in my room. Including...

Parker Grimm.

I shot Axel a glare and he shrugged in reply. "I told Grimmy he wasn't invited."

"Might have worked better if you didn't tell him at all," I said, shaking my head.

"Well, I had to." Axel threw up his hands. "Anthony and Fred were with him."

"You didn't consider using mind-speak?"

He blinked at me. "No. I. Did. Not."

"Doesn't matter now," Parker said, arms crossed. "I'm here. And I'm very curious why you wanted a team meeting with everyone except for me."

I flashed him a grin. "Would you believe we're planning a surprise party for your birthday?"

"Do you even know when my birthday is?"

"No, I do not."

"Then what's this about?" Parker asked.

"Wyatt wants to do something naughty," Axel said. His cheery tone did nothing to dispel the creepiness of his statement.

"Uh," Anthony said, glancing back and forth between all of us. "I'm uh, like...not into dudes."

"Me neither," Fred said, shaking his mustache.

"Axel," I said, glaring at him. "Please, shut up."

"Only because you asked nicely," he replied. "Now, hurry and tell us what trouble you're getting us into."

Again, I glared at him. I had a whole plan about how to approach this. Okay, that was a lie. I didn't have a plan. I just didn't want it thrown into the middle of the room like a grenade.

"Must be pretty naughty if you didn't want me to know," Parker said.

I held up my hand. "Can we all agree to stop using the word 'naughty?'"

"No," Axel said, bouncing in his seat. "Can you get on with it already? I'm dying to know."

"As am I," Parker said.

"Me, too," Anthony added. "You know... As long as it isn't some weird sex thing."

"It's not a weird sex thing," I said, sighing. Then I got mad again. "Everyone, shut the fuck up."

They did.

"Thank you," I said, pacing the floor while I considered how to broach the subject. Finally, I turned and faced Parker. "Don't take it personal. I didn't want you involved because I know you like to play by the rules. And I knew you'd tattle."

He crossed his arms. "That feels a little personal."

"He's got a point though, boss, er, Parker," Anthony said with a chuckle. "You are sort of a choirboy."

Parker glared at him. "I am not a choirboy. Get on with it, Wyatt. What trouble are you brewing?"

"I may know where Alyita and the others were taken. It's a hunch. Not much of one. But I could be right."

Everyone seemed surprised, but Parker was the first to pounce. "And have you shared this with the Argument?"

"No."

"Why?"

"Because the Argument doesn't want us involved."

"What about the Archmage?" he asked. "Have you told him?"

"No. Archie's orders are for us to get a good night's rest and prepare to head home in the morning."

Parker made to speak again, no doubt to inform us that we should do precisely what the Archmage had directed us to do, but Anthony beat him to the punch. He was shaking his head. "Fucking choirboy."

"I'm not a choirboy," Parker repeated, but with a little more frustration than the first time. He turned his attention back to me. "And you think what, Wyatt? That our little squad has a chance against all of them? And what will happen if we disregard a direct order? The Archmage won't be happy."

"Fuck the Archmage," I said.

That *really* got everyone's attention.

"And I'm not saying that just to be rebellious," I said, holding up my hands. "Do you know why he brought us here? Do you know why he *really* wanted our team to come on this trip?"

Axel raised his hand and waved it around, hoping I would call on him. Everyone else just stared at me.

I met Barrett's gaze. "He knew Tanya and the others were here. He knew if he dangled me out like a carrot, she'd come for me. That's why he brought us. That's why he put Barrett on the team. Anthony and Fred, too. Look, being used like that pisses me off enough as it is. Had he told me, I would have volunteered. But that's the difference, see? We would have had a choice. I don't know how things are done on other teams, and as I said before, I don't really care. I also know I'm not the best leader, but God damn it, putting your lives in danger with no kind of warning is unacceptable. So, I don't really give a shit what the Archmage thinks."

There was a moment of silence. They were stunned. Even Axel.

Parker looked from me to the others and back again. "He admitted that? It doesn't sound like something the Archmage would do."

"Bullshit," Axel said, rolling his eyes. "It sounds exactly like something Archie would do. Or my dickhead dad. Stop being such a fucking choirboy."

"I am not..." Parker trailed off, shaking his head. Looking at me again, he said, "Fine, Wyatt. But you can't really think our little team can take on all those dark wizards and that creepy cat lady."

"It's worse than that," I said. "Someone even more dangerous has to be in involved. I think Cowan told the truth about that. For them to have taken down Mothman and Sams, there has to be someone very powerful in this game. We're talking master level, or better."

"Why do I get the impression you have a suspicion of who that might be?" Parker asked.

"Just a hunch," I said. "Do you remember who Tanya's crew was aligned with back in Memphis? The grays."

"The demon summoners," Parker said.

"That's right. When I saw the replay of Uriah's dad being tortured and murdered, there were three robed figures: one gray, one red, and one black. The black one seemed to be in charge. After that, when I glimpsed their secret cool kid club meeting, those three were there. That jackass in Memphis was just another pawn. A tool to break the knights. We never faced their true leader."

"So, you think it's one of them?" Parker asked.

"I do," I replied. "Could be more than one. Could be someone else altogether. Could be that revenant asshole. I don't know for sure, but if I had to guess, it's the gray one. That's who Tanya and company were working for previously. Makes sense they would be still. The question is what they want with Mothman."

"No," Parker said, shaking his head. "The question is how the heck you think we're going to take down your old team, Wampus Cat, possibly some Apple Devils, a barrel of dark wizards, and now possibly demons and a super-powered sorcerer."

"Grimmy," Axel said, "you can do anything if you set your mind to it."

The sincerity with which he spoke stunned everyone.

"You could even stop being such a choirboy," Axel said, grinning at him. Then he turned to me. "So, when do we leave?"

Ignoring him, Parker asked, "Remind me again, why we aren't telling the Archmage? Or the Argument? Or at least Master Serrano?"

"Because Serrano will tell the Archmage, and he's ordered us to stay out of it. Because the Argument doesn't want us involved. But more than anything...Because they took Alyita. She was *our* responsibility. She *is* our responsibility. And yeah, I know you guys didn't sign up for babysitting a teenager, but I did. And that means something."

I paced again.

"Look," I said, thinking it over. "Maybe it doesn't mean anything to you. Maybe you guys don't care. Maybe she was just an annoying teen you were stuck with. But her safety was our responsibility. And *we* let her down. That kid... That young woman has been through a lot. More than any of you can appreciate. And right now, if she's even still alive, her only hope is that we're coming for her."

"I wouldn't want to bet my life on a team called Squirrel Nuts Squad," Anthony said with a chortle.

No one met his laugh. Not even Fred.

"See, that's the thing right there, Anthony," I said, pointing at him. "You don't take this team seriously. None of you... None of *us* do. Sure, Axel picked a goofy name. And sure, Anthony, Fred, and even Parker, none of you guys want to be here. Maybe you see it as punishment. Maybe you thought Archie was having a laugh at our expense. Well, you know what?"

No one replied.

"Maybe he was," I said, shrugging. "Fuck him. Who cares? Maybe instead of moping it's time to consider that we have an opportunity to prove them all wrong. Anthony, you made a comment about how you deserved to be on the loser squad. Fuck that, too. We're *not* the losers."

"Hells no," Axel said. "We're tits legit."

"Damn right," I said. "And it's time we proved it. If you don't want to go on this suicide mission, I understand. Good chance none of us will make it back. But I'm tired of worrying about what everyone else thinks. And I'm tired of us, all of us—except Axel—being half-ass committed to this team. It's time to whole-ass."

"That, uh, was that supposed to be inspirational?" Parker asked.

I glared at him.

"Relax," he said, putting up his hands. "My attempt at a joke."

"Read the room, choirboy," Axel said, and chucked a couch pillow at him.

"My point," I said, "is we all have to decide if we're all in on this team or not. If you're not, I understand, but just tell me. Because I am. I believe in this crew. I know what each of you is capable of on your own. Together—truly working together—we'd be a nightmare. But that's a problem for later. Right now, you just have to decide if you want to go on this suicide run with me. And I don't blame you if you don't." I looked at Parker. "I won't even blame you if you tell on me. Just...give me time to get out the door."

"You know I'm in," Axel said, shrugging. "Why waltz when you can rock 'n' roll, right?"

"Damn straight," I said.

"And I'm also all in on the team thing," Axel said.

"Of course you are," Anthony said, rolling his eyes. "You picked our dumbass name."

"It's not a dumb name! It's a powerful name." He stood up, waving his arms about. Then he started pacing like I was. "You bunch of soft-served yogurt brains haven't thought about it, have you?"

Everyone just stared at him. Then they stared at me, like I had a freaking clue what he meant.

He groaned and pinched the bridge of his nose. "Ugh, you guys are so dense. Think about it! Our enemies will underestimate a team with that name, but imagine how much more embarrassed they'll be when they're beaten by us. Imagine if Emperor Palpatine was our ultimate enemy, and one of his grand admirals came up and had to admit they were defeated by Squirrel Nuts Squad. Palpatine would straight electrify their punk-asses. It isn't a stupid name. It's an insurance policy. Every enemy will be embarrassed to be beaten by us. Even the other Cabal teams will be embarrassed when we outperform them."

We all stared at him again. This time, though, at least for me, I sort of saw the weird brilliance. He wasn't wrong. I couldn't imagine Tanya having to explain to her evil overlord that her team had been thwarted by *The* Squirrel Nuts Squad. No way that would end well.

"And don't forget, dingleberries," Axel said, "Alyita's safety *is* our responsibility. She's alive; I know it. And she's waiting for us to come save her. It *has* to be us. Squirrel Nuts Squad, assemble!"

That last part didn't go over the way he'd hoped. I stepped in before he could be too disheartened.

"What do you guys say?" I asked. "Are you in?"

"I'm in," Barrett said, rising from the couch. He looked me square in the face. "I won't lose my cool this time. We'll get the job done."

He held his fist up to me. I bumped it.

"Anyone else?" I asked.

The remaining three members stared at me like I was a potato. That was fair. Truth was... I'd thought I had a chance of winning Barrett over. The others...not so much. I knew Parker wouldn't play ball. I had little hope for Fred or Anthony, but thought I would at least give it a shot.

One of them surprised me.

"Axel is right," Fred said, a thoughtful look on his face.

"About the stupid team name?" Anthony said.

"Well, yeah, maybe that, too," Fred said, shrugging. "I meant about how it has to be us." He looked up at me. "If what Wyatt said is true, then I can only imagine that poor young lady has suffered enough trauma. If we don't show up for her..."

And then Fred stood up.

He glanced back at Anthony. "And... It might not have been the team we wanted, but it's the one we've got. In a way, it's a better opportunity than being on any other. As Castle security, I never really got a chance to do anything special. Nothing great. It's not like anyone is stupid enough to actually try to attack the place. I signed up to help people, not to sit on the sidelines. And now there's a young woman who needs help. That's something, at least."

"Thanks, Fred," I said.

He nodded at me. "I'm all in, Wyatt. Ride or die, right?"

"Yeah," I said.

All eyes turned back toward Anthony.

"Well, fuck," he said, rising to his feet. "I knew you idiots were going to get me killed either way. Might as well do it in style. Besides, Alyita is like our mascot or something. She's kind of grown on me. And it's probably worth getting killed to save the young lady. Screw it."

"That's the spirit, Burns," Axel said. "And like I told you before, we almost never die."

All eyes shifted toward Parker, who seemed very uncomfortable. That was an unusual disposition for him. I approved.

"Just wait until we get out the door," I said. "That's all I ask. Then you can tell them. And tell them where to find us, too. Hopefully the cavalry will ride in if everything goes tits to tailbones."

"Better leave them a note, then," he said, scowling.

I raised my eyebrow.

"I'm coming, too," he said, shrugging. Then he gave us all a menacing glare. "And I am not a fucking choirboy."

That... Wow.

"Hells yeah," Axel said, grinning. "I knew you had it in you, Grimmy."

"Just one more question," Parker said. "This it? Or do we have any other backup?"

No sooner had the question left his mouth than there was a knock at the door.

Fred was the closest, so he opened it.

Brother Barajas and the two knights strolled in.

He gave my team a once-over and then turned his gaze to me. "Axel said you needed us. Said you were about to do something naughty."

"Hells yeah," Axel said.

Barajas fixed his perma-scowl on me. "He meant we were going to go kill some motherfuckers, right? It wasn't like a, uh, weird sex thing?"

I glared at Axel, who giggled. "Barajas, if you're coming with us, you can kill or fuck at your own discretion."

The knight shrugged. "Good enough for me."

57

Everyone headed to their rooms to gear up. Everyone except the knights. They'd shown up ready.

Barajas even had his sword strapped to his back.

That had made me raise an eyebrow. He usually just carried his dagger.

He noticed my gaze and said, "Victor insisted I bring it. Said I should wear it around so people would know who I was. Like the leathers don't do the job."

"Haven't seen you wearing it since you've been here," I said.

"Don't care for lugging it around."

"And now?"

"Now we're headed to a fight. If there're any demons around, we'll probably want more than two of them."

"Right," I said, nodding. "I have a suspicion we might need it."

Five minutes later, everyone was ready.

Shortly after that, there was another knock at the door.

I was scared to answer, fearing it would be Master Serrano, or even the Archmage himself. If they figured out what we were doing...

But I'd also told our guide to meet us there.

It was him. The Tennessee Wildman strolled in and took in the crowd. "More than I expected."

"That a problem?" I asked.

He shook his head. "Hell no. If you're right, we're going to need them."

And with that, we packed up and headed out the door.

One more surprise awaited us in the hall.

Eilidh was leaning against the wall, dressed in her battle garb.

"Weren't planning on leaving without me, were you?" she asked, flashing me a grin.

"How...?" I said, trailing off.

"Read it on your face," she replied, pulling herself from the wall. "Maybe I know you better than you think, Blade Mage."

"And you're coming with us?" I asked, still stunned.

"Of course," she said, walking over to give Axel a fist bump. "Let's go get our girl back."

"Hells yeah," Axel said, grinning from ear to ear.

"All right." I nodded, then gave everyone a passing glance. "Final check, just to be sure. You all understand that if I'm right, we're walking into a death trap? And even if we somehow survive, we're all going to be in a shitload of trouble?"

"We almost never die," Axel said.

"And you're going to be the one in most of the trouble," Anthony said, snickering.

Everyone else nodded.

It was a bigger group than I'd planned for. Certainly more than I could have hoped for.

It was a reminder, too.

A reminder that I wasn't the screw-up other people made me out to be. My team might not have believed in me, but they believed in the mission. Eilidh and the knights, though? They were coming because of *me*. To support *me*. And maybe that was what being the Blade Mage was really about. Maybe it was about bringing people together. Maybe, just maybe, Eilidh was right. Maybe I was a little better at my job than most people wanted to give me credit for. But the people who'd bled beside me... They had a different opinion. They were willing to bleed beside me again. And that was worth more than anything.

The Tennessee Wildman led the way.

Axel moved along beside me. In a low voice, he said, "You must have been pretty pissed when Archie said all of that. About using you as bait."

"This isn't really the time," I said, giving him a side-eye.

"I have a point," he said, giving the side-eye right back.

"Fine." I really didn't want everyone to hear about my conversation with the Archmage. That was why I'd sought to shut him down, but every once in a while, Axel had a bit of wisdom worth listening to.

"So," Axel said, seeming nervous about what he wanted to say. "Well, look, you know I don't want to give Archie too much credit. Jerk keeps muting me. Anyway, I guess what I'm trying to get around to is... Well, like, what if..."

"What?" I asked, glancing over at him.

"What if he told you all of that just to get this response out of you?"

"Huh?"

"I mean... What if he told you that shit and forbade you from getting involved just to rile you up, so you'd put a team together and go rescue Alyita?"

I paused. Eilidh, who was just behind me, nearly walked into me. I apologized and got my feet moving again.

"No," I said, glancing at Axel. "Surely not."

He shrugged. "Just a thought."

"He could have just told me to do this."

"No, he couldn't," he replied. "Look, if Master Serrano went against the Argument's orders, that'd be a whole thing. It'd do real damage to the Cabal's reputation. And if Archie ordered him to do that... Shit in a shoe basket. We'd end up enemies of the Argument. See what I'm saying?"

"I'd rather not. But yes."

"So, he couldn't have ordered you to do this. But... You have a reputation for playing by your own rules. He can honestly say he told you not to."

I sighed. It was entirely possible. I couldn't help but to think back to my earlier conversation with Master Serrano, where Archie had given him an answer to every argument I might make. Was the bastard playing me again?

It didn't matter.

The only thing that mattered was saving Alyita.

And Mothman. And Sams. And the Cherokee.

From somewhere behind me, Parker said, "Hey, Wyatt. You left that note, didn't you?"

I didn't even turn back to face him. "That's something you'll just have to wonder about, Grimmy."

He snorted. "No worries. I left one myself."

"Good," I replied. "I'm sure they'll go looking through your room."

Axel chortled. "Man, you two are going to be in *so* much trouble."

"Can't wait," Parker said. "Guess that's one benefit of this being a suicide mission. Are you sure we shouldn't tell someone before we leave? Like Master Serrano?"

Before I could respond, Brother Barajas spoke up. With a chuckle, he asked, "Who invited this fucking choirboy?"

And we all laughed.

At least, everyone on my team.

Parker asked no further questions.

58

Slipping out of the dwarven city was easier than I'd expected.

Wildman made good on his promise. He led us out of the main thoroughfare and into some tunnels, which seemed like they should have been marked "staff only." We didn't pass anyone. Didn't even see another person.

There was one thing I hadn't considered, though...

In the tunnels, I glanced back at Parker. "You've got keys to one of the SUVs right?"

He rolled his eyes. "You're just now thinking about this?"

"I am not a clever man," I replied. "And this is precisely why we need you, Parker."

He huffed. "Of course I have the keys."

I turned my attention back to Brother Barajas. "Guessing you guys have your bikes?"

He chuckled. Answer enough. Of course they did.

It was going to be a tight fit squeezing my entire team along with Eilidh and the Wildman into one SUV, but we'd make do. One thing was for certain: Axel wasn't sitting on my lap.

The Tennessee Wildman continued leading us along until we came out in a parking garage. It was the first time I'd even seen it. It was also the first parking garage I'd ever seen that looked like it had been built inside a cave. Kind of cool, actually.

Which brought up an entirely new concern I hadn't thought about until just then.

"Uh, guys," I said, pausing. "Forgive my ignorance, but I didn't roll in with you. Are there security guards on the way out?"

Parker rolled his eyes again. "Of course."

"Well, darn," I said, hands on my hips. "Didn't even think about that."

"It'll be all right," Wildman said, shrugging. "Doubt they'll try to stop us."

"You think?" I asked.

"How the hell should I know?" he replied. "But we're pretty committed."

He was right, of course.

The knights broke off to grab their bikes.

And Parker led us toward our big ole SUV.

It was definitely going to be a tight fit.

Wildman offered to lie down in the back behind the lift gate. He said it would be better if the security guards didn't see him in the vehicle. Everyone in the Argument knew who he was. If he was spotted, they'd know something was up.

Barrett drove; Parker took shotgun.

That left almost enough seats for the rest of us, except...

Axel had to sit on my lap. In fairness, he was half on Eilidh's lap, too.

There were loads of comments. Far too many comments.

Anyway, we finally got on the road and made it to the security gate. Parker gave them a friendly wave and they let us through.

And that... That was the easy part.

An abandoned coal mine.

At least it wasn't a dank cave or a dusty warehouse.

Made me second-guess my intel, though. But it was just a hunch, after all.

We parked a safe distance away. Wildman assured us he knew a way in on foot.

If the baddies were actually hiding out there, there was no telling what kind of security they'd have. Maybe none. Maybe tons. We could be up against wards and guards both. So, while I didn't fancy another dark stroll through the forest, it made sense. We certainly couldn't just roll up in the party bus.

Wildman led us through the forest. For a big guy, he was incredibly quiet. He never so much as snapped a twig.

For the rest of us, keeping up was a challenge, and we weren't nearly so quiet. As dark as it was, we couldn't see our own feet. Probably sounded like a herd of cattle stampeding through the brush. I worried someone would get lost.

I also worried about stepping on a copperhead. I knew it would happen one of these days. That I'd be on the way to face some evil asshole and I'd end up getting bitten by a snake first.

Anyway, Wildman led us deep into the forest. We walked for what felt like forever before he finally stopped. We gathered around him.

It was hard to make out everyone's faces in the dim light, but I was pretty sure everyone was present. We hadn't lost anyone in the forest.

"We're getting close," Wildman said. "If they're here, we'll run into guards or protections soon."

"Anyone sense any wards?" I asked, reaching out with my own senses.

Nothing.

No one else sensed anything, either.

"I can get closer on my own and have a look," Wildman said. "Or we can move further up the hill. Might be a spot where we can get a better view."

I considered. He could certainly move more quickly and quietly than the rest of us. Axel might've argued, but the Tennessee Wildman had a better chance of getting close without being seen. I didn't like the idea of our guide leaving us, though. The rest of us didn't know our way around. We'd be lucky to find the mine on our own. Hell, we'd be lucky to find our way back to our rides. If we climbed up the hill, though, would we actually be able to see across the grounds?

I glanced up, studying the moon. It was bright. The only reason it was so dark in the forest was because of the trees. I doubted the old mining grounds were completely tree-covered. If we found a spot high enough up, maybe we could get a peek.

"Let's take the hill," I said.

Without another word, Wildman started off again, the rest of us following.

He led us upward, moving more slowly than before. I suspected he was trying to keep us from making too much noise. Smart.

Using my wand, I continued checking for any signs of magical energy, any hint that we might be approaching wards. Axel, Parker, Eilidh, or one of the others would likely sense something before I would. It was also possible they wouldn't. It was possible none of us would. If a super powerful mage had thrown down wards, they could hide them from us. It was hardly worth worrying about. If there was a wizard that powerful nearby, they'd easily kill us anyway. See, I was an optimist. The glass was half-dead.

Anyway, we didn't get murdered and I didn't step on any copperheads. Things were going pretty well. And the Tennessee Wildman found us a spot where we could look down into the mine.

We all stood there, silently staring at the vacant camp.

Unfortunately, by that point, we had a little cloud cover, which made it harder to see. I could tell there were a handful of old cabins. No lights on, though. Bits of rusted machinery, too. An ancient rail system they used to haul coal on.

No signs of people, though. No sign anyone was there, or had been there, in quite some time.

Much to my annoyance, Axel, Eilidh, Parker, Barrett, Fred, Barajas, and the other two knights had all been smart enough to bring binoculars. I had not been. Anthony Burns hadn't either, though, so that made me feel mildly better.

"Anything?" I asked, standing next to Axel.

He lowered his binoculars to scowl at me.

Yeah, yeah, I should've brought my own. Fortunately, since there wasn't anything to see, he quickly grew bored and lent me his.

There was nothing. Just decrepit buildings and forgotten machinery. Old rails.

"Damn," I said, finally breaking the silence.

"Looks like it's a bust," Wildman said.

I ignored his comment and turned to look at Parker. "Glad you didn't tell on me yet? That would have been embarrassing."

"Still will be," Parker said. "By now, someone has surely noticed we left."

I shrugged. I was past the point of worrying about getting into trouble. I just needed to find Alyita.

"What do you think?" Eilidh asked. "Should we go down there? Have a look around, at least?"

I met her gaze, noting the concern in her expression. She was still willing to play along, probably just to make me feel better. But we hadn't seen a damned thing. If the baddies were here, we would've seen something. A light, at least. Anything. Even if they were hiding in the actual mine, there would have at least been vehicles. Or tracks. Something.

There just wasn't.

They weren't here.

I had been wrong.

"I'd rather head back to the bar," the Wildman said.

"Same," Anthony replied.

"Really?" Parker asked, shaking his head. "After what happened last time?"

"Burns doesn't learn from his mistakes," Axel said. "You should know that, having been his boss and all."

I ignored their conversation. It was snowballing toward another Axel and Anthony bickering session. Instead, I took another look through the binoculars.

Still nothing.

Just a little ghost camp.

"What do you think?" Eilidh asked again.

I hadn't realized she'd moved right beside me.

I sighed. "Guess we ought to head back."

No one seemed disappointed. In fact, they quickly turned and started back through the forest.

I started after them, but...

My sword pulsed.

Dyrnwyn vibrated against my back, trying to tell me something.

"Hold up," I said, trying to raise my voice just enough for everyone to hear without shouting.

They all turned back to face me. I waved them back and motioned for everyone to stay quiet.

While they gathered around, I raised the binoculars again. Still didn't see anything.

"What is it?" Axel asked.

"Dyrnwyn."

He nodded. That was answer enough for him. The others needed a little more. Problem was, I didn't know how to explain. Not really.

"I think... I think my sword sensed something," I said.

That raised a few eyebrows.

"What do you mean?" Eilidh asked.

"I mean, it doesn't think we should leave."

There was something about thinking my thoughts at an inanimate object that made me feel a bit loony, but that was my lot in life. So, I thought, *Pulse again if the enemy is here.*

Much to my surprise, it did.

"What?" Axel asked, seeing the look on my face. "What is it?"

"My sword thinks they're here."

"Okay, well," Wildman said, "not that I have a problem taking advice from a chunk of steel, but can it tell us where, exactly? Because I don't see a damned thing down there."

"Trust the sword," Parker said, raising his binoculars again.

I still had Axel's noc-nocs, so I did the same.

Still nothing. Just an abandoned camp, silent as death.

I lowered the binoculars and considered while enjoying the breeze as it washed over me. It was that late part of summer where the days were still hot enough to be miserable, but the nights cooled. After our trek through the forest, the breeze was delightful. It was...

Oh, fuck.

I raised the binoculars again.

Still as death.

That was how I'd thought of the camp.

And it was.

It was *too* still.

Looking through the lenses again, I didn't study the buildings. Instead, I focused on the trees. All around us, the limbs were moving, leaves rustling. But down there in the camp, they didn't so much as shudder.

"Look at the leaves," I said, chuckling. "Look at the tree limbs."

"Huh?" Parker replied.

"Son of a bitch," Barajas said. He dropped his binoculars and gave me a rare grin.

Eilidh was the next to catch on. She turned my way. "An illusion?"

"Has to be, right?"

"What the hell are you all on about?" Wildman asked.

I finally explained.

Axel demanded his binoculars back immediately. That was fine. Even without them, I could see the difference. In fact, it was a better view. More useful. From the distance, and in the dark, I couldn't make out many details. The trees, with their shadowed branches, melded together. But as I stood there watching, I saw a pattern: where the limbs swayed and where they didn't. It was a bubble. Some kind of big-ass magical bubble. We were being fed an illusion.

"So, what do we do?" Parker asked. "I don't fancy going down there blind."

"I take back my offer to go alone," Wildman said with a snort. "Whatever, or whoever, can summon that type of magic, I ain't keen on tackling alone."

"Should I call it in?" Parker asked, giving me a knowing look. "Should we report it?"

I bit my lip, considering. Truth be told, I was kind of surprised he was asking. I'd figured Parker had betrayed us before we'd even left. In fact, I was surprised we'd made a clean getaway.

"Not yet," I replied. "I want to see what's down there."

"Let's go," Axel said. "Wildman and I will lead the way. The rest of you buffoons make too much noise."

"Wait," I said, before he started off. "Slow down. If that is a giant illusion bubble, then you can be damned sure they'll have some nasty wards, too. We trip them and there's no telling what might be waiting for us."

"I'm ready for them," Axel replied. "After sitting in that damned prison all day, I'm ready to fight anything. Literally anything."

"I know," I said, holding up my hand to quiet him. "But we need to think. Need some kind of plan."

"Well, unless you have some way to burst that bubble..." Anthony said, shrugging.

"He's right," Axel said. "Damn it, I hate it when Burns is right. You don't have a way to burst the bubble, do you? I'd much prefer we find a way to make Burns wrong."

"I don't have a way to burst the bubble, Axel," I said, trying not roll my eyes.

"Damn it," he said, sighing.

"Actually..." Eilidh said, "I think you might."

I met her gaze. No idea what she meant.

"Dyrnwyn," she said.

Oh.

Oh, right.

Magic sword.

I nodded at her and drew it from my back.

Hey, sword, you think you can burst that bubble?

It pulsed.

All righty, then.

I thought about how to approach this problem and only saw one solution.

Hey, sword, do you think you can hack the bubble without the enemy knowing?

It pulsed, but, like, in a weird way. In my mind, I imagined the sword shrugging at me, which was weird, since it didn't have shoulders. I took that to mean it wasn't sure.

Glancing at the others, I said, "Be ready. Not sure how this is going to go. There's a chance Dyrnwyn can hack their spell without them knowing. Also a good chance they're going to know we're here. Assume it's the second one."

Without waiting for a reply, I raised my arm and threw Dyrnwyn with all my might. It took the Dyrnerang form and set sail. And since I wasn't strong enough to throw it all the way to the camp, I raised my wand and fired a pumpkin blast at its backside. Had it been a real boomerang, it probably wouldn't have worked. Since it was an ancient magic sword, it fired off like a rocket, right at the bubble.

There was no rippling effect. No explosion. Nothing like that at all.

One second it was the same vacant camp we'd been staring at. And the next...

"Oh, wow," Axel said. "That's a lot of assholes."

59

A whole new scene was laid out before us.

It was the same old camp, rundown and decrepit, the fossils of a long-abandoned operation. Forgotten equipment. The old rail systems they'd used to cart coal out. All the same as it was before, except now, it was teeming with life. And the lights were on.

They were making use of the old buildings. Nearly all of them had lights on. And there were people milling about.

I couldn't make out details from the distance, and Axel had reclaimed his noc-nocs. It was clear they weren't running about raising an alarm, though. So maybe they hadn't noticed that Dyrnwyn had dropped their big-ass illusion spell. Still, though...

"To have summoned an illusion like that..." Eilidh said, echoing my own thoughts.

"And to sustain it," Parker said. "This is high-level magic."

I reached out with my mind, feeling for my sword. It was still within range where I could summon it back. I hesitated, though. No one had noticed it flying in. There was a chance they'd see it if I summoned it back. There was also a chance it had landed somewhere that someone would see it. So leaving it posed a risk as well. I decided to roll with it for the moment. I could still call it back to me, and I was pretty sure it would burn the shit out of anyone who tried to scoop it up.

"Uh..." Axel said.

"What?" I asked.

"That can't be good," he said.

"What?" I repeated.

Not having my own binoculars was really annoying.

"Are you guys seeing this?" Axel asked, completely ignoring me.

"Yeah," Eilidh said. I didn't miss the concern in her voice. I didn't like it, either. "That must be some kind of working."

"But for what?" Parker asked.

"Some kind of big, scary juju," Axel said. "Big scary. I don't like this, Wyatt. Don't like it one bit."

If something scared Axel...

"Let me see the binoculars, Axel."

He still ignored me.

Eilidh rolled her eyes. I wasn't sure if it was at Axel, or me, or both of us. Either way, she handed me hers and I finally got to see what the *uh oh* was about.

I agreed.

Big uh oh.

Near the center of the grounds was a tall metal structure. A tower of some sort. I had no idea what it would have been for, and they'd clearly modified it for their purpose. And they'd re-purposed other old equipment to connect the tower to the old rail system. That was an awful lot of steel touching. If they had been running an electrical current through it, it might've made sense. I suspected they were planning to channel something else.

The bigger concern was at the base of the tower.

And who was imprisoned there.

Mothman.

He was bound to the structure. Metal bands and chains held him in place. All around him were green, glowing symbols. Magic to contain him, and likely to prevent him from using his own. Possibly to stop anyone from trying to free him. There was no telling.

His wings were spread apart and pinned against the tower as well. I couldn't tell for sure, but it looked as if they'd hammered spikes through them, like a butterfly pinned to a cork-board. Some elementary school science project.

"What the hell are they doing to him?" Eilidh asked.

I didn't have an answer. Parker did, though.

"Nothing good," he said, glancing over at me.

He was right. Clearly they intended to use him for some kind of working. Something powerful. Something gnarly. I felt a twisting in my guts. Reminded me of the time Eilidh and I had worked through the blood magic puzzle. This wasn't right. Whatever it was, it was dark and...beyond us.

"We can't leave the old boy like that," Wildman said.

I glanced over at him. "I didn't think you cared for him."

"Don't," he replied. "Never been drinking buddies, but..."

"But we can't leave him like that," I said, finishing for him.

He nodded. "He wouldn't leave me if he found me like that. I know that much. Plus, I'd bet my left nut the pussy cat is down there somewhere."

"You can't seriously want to attack," Anthony asked. "We're out of our depth."

He wasn't wrong.

Before I could reply, Fred said, "You're right, Burns. But so is the Wildman. We can't leave him like that."

"Oh, we're totally going to make a daring rescue," Axel said. "You can count on it."

Anthony groaned.

Parker gave me a long look. "Ready for those reinforcements?"

"Probably a safe time to tattle on me," I said, biting my lip. "As much as I want to rush in and help Mothman, we still need to locate the other captives. And Anthony is right; we'll get smashed if we try to walk in there. There's magic at work here..."

I didn't finish. Didn't need to. They all understood. We were so far out of our league. Like a peewee team lining up against an NFL team.

On the other hand, whatever they were doing to Mothman, we couldn't know how long it would take. And whatever it was, we surely needed to stop it before it finished. To charge in was to invite certain death. But could we afford to wait for reinforcements? And when they showed up, would they cockblock us from helping? Did that matter? Saving Mothman, Alyita, and the others was what mattered. Not doing the damned thing myself.

Perhaps we needed to wait.

I handed Eilidh back her binoculars while I considered the situation.

"Axel, can you..." I didn't need to finish my sentence. I turned and saw he had a drumstick in his ear.

He turned and shook his head at me. "Too far. Can't hear shit."

"Wyatt," Barrett hissed.

I jumped. The big man hadn't spoken a word since we'd set out. The sound of his voice startled me.

"Look," he said, binoculars up to his eyes. He pointed. "Big building on the right. Look now."

I snatched Axel's binoculars and tried to see where he was guiding me. First, though, I noticed three of the moon-eyed people lingering outside one of the old cabins. Little bastards. I'd been right. They'd sold us out. Betrayed us for whatever promises the dark wizards had offered.

Then I shifted the binoculars, searching for whatever Barrett wanted me to see.

"Oh, shit," Eilidh said. Clearly she'd spotted it before me.

I was about to ask when I saw it.

"Oh, no," I said.

It was Alyita. She'd gotten free somehow.

She was on the back side of a building, tucked behind a barrel, her back to us.

"What the hell is she doing?" Eilidh asked. "Can you mind-speak with her?"

I couldn't.

But...

I lowered the binoculars and glanced at Axel. "Did you set up a mind-speak connection with Alyita?"

"Of course," he said, shaking his head at me like it should've been obvious. "I keep trying to tell you, set up the connection with people. It isn't that hard. And Alyita is too afraid to ask you."

"Afraid?" I asked. "Why?"

"Because she looks up to you, dingus. You're her fucking hero. How many times do I have to tell you?"

Well... That made me feel like a real piece of shit. No time for it, though.

"Axel, I need you to contact her now. She's broken free."

"What?"

"Look," I said, handing him the binoculars. "Building on the right, just like Barrett said."

"Oh, shit," he replied almost instantly.

I was annoyed at how quickly he'd spotted her. Finding things through binoculars was always more challenging for me.

"What do you want me to tell her?" he asked.

"Tell her we're here. Tell her we're up here on the hill behind her."

"Got it."

I took the binoculars back and looked down, noticing Alyita's head turning to look our way.

"Okay," Axel said. "I let her know."

"Good. Tell her to sneak up toward us. We need to get her out of there."

"Uh..." he replied.

"What?"

"She said no."

"What?"

"She doesn't want to leave Sams and the others. Said they helped her break free, but she was the only one."

"Tell her we're going to free all of them, but to get her ass up here," I said. "This isn't a game."

"Yeah, uh, I already told her all that, dingbat. She's refusing. Says we should come down there."

"Fucking teenagers," Eilidh said, shaking her head. "This is why I never want to have kids."

"Tell me about it," Anthony Burns said.

"Axel," I said, struggling to keep my patience. "Use that charm you always claim you have to convince her to head this way."

"Uh, Wyatt," Eilidh said. "I think... I think it's too late."

"Huh?" I asked.

"Oh, futz," Axel said. "Futz, fucking, futz. She's surrounded."

I glanced through the binoculars again. There were three hooded figures just ahead of her. Another was on the other side of the building from her. If she moved, she'd be seen. And if any of them moved in her direction, she'd be seen.

Mothman was the target. He'd been the target all along. Shaman Sams was a valuable hostage, as were the senior members of the Cherokee. Everyone else they'd captured? Doubtful. If she was seen, they'd likely kill her on the spot. Or worse.

"What do we do?" Eilidh asked.

I sighed.

Axel grinned. "Time for some heroic shit."

I glanced over at Parker. "You tattletale yet?"

He nodded.

"Then Axel is right. Time for some heroic shit."

60

Axel and I started down the hill.

We had a plan.

Sort of.

Well…

We didn't have much of a plan at all.

That was why it was just the two of us. If we were lucky, we could sneak into the edge of the camp, grab Alyita, and then hightail it back to the others. We would need to be very lucky indeed. And since we didn't expect to have that kind of luck…

We didn't bring the entire crew with us.

I had made a case they shouldn't come down no matter what.

Eilidh had reminded me they'd all signed up for a suicide mission, and sitting on the hillside while Axel and I went off to die wasn't why they'd come along. Parker hadn't agreed. Everyone else had, though. So, we made a contingency plan, just in case.

Also, Axel left one of his drumsticks with Eilidh. My sword was still lying somewhere down in the camp. I considered summoning it, but thought better of it again. Wherever it was, it could get back to me in a hurry. I couldn't risk my flying sword garnering unwanted attention.

Plus, if we got captured and they didn't straight up murder us, I didn't want it locked away. Or worse, lost for good.

So, both of us had a single wand and I had my concealed revolver holstered in my pants. We eased our way through the forest, carefully descending the hillside in the dark.

It wasn't easy going.

The moon's light did little to penetrate the trees and we couldn't afford to summon our own. That would have given us away pretty quickly.

The hill was steep in places, but fortunately the tree cover was dense and gave us things to hold on to. It wasn't just tumbling that posed a risk, but also the potential for noise. If we accidentally kicked over a rock, or snapped a big branch, or took a tumble, we'd surely get the attention of the folks below.

I was just thinking it was taking too damned long when a voice behind me said, "You really are an idiot, you know that?"

It wasn't Axel's voice. Far too snooty to be Axel's voice.

I sighed and turned around.

He was leaning against one of the trees, face hidden in the shadows. Not that it mattered. It never held a singular form for long. Moonlight glinted off his coin as he tossed it up in the air and caught it.

"Who the hell are you?" Axel asked.

"You don't remember me, Mr. Gunner?"

Axel turned to me. "Is he real? Or am I imagining things?"

"It's the Valravn," I said, glaring at the shadowy figure.

"Oh," Axel said, nodding. "Neat. Guess this is the part where he shows up uninvited to tell you what a bonehead you are?"

"Yup," I replied.

"Don't waste your bird breath," Axel said, waving at the Valravn like he could shoo it away. "I've been telling him he's a dummy for years. He has never listened to me, and I'm his best friend. No chance he's going to listen to a weird-ass shadow, bird, critter, thing... What the hell are you, anyway?"

"It's of little importance," he said, ignoring Axel to give me his attention. "I don't suppose I can talk you out of this?"

"I don't suppose you're willing to help?" I replied.

"Of course not." His coin continued flipping, annoying me. "But as usual, I thought I might try. I am looking out for your best interests, after all."

"Bullshit," I said, then glanced at Axel. "The fact he's here means there's even more trouble down there than we thought."

"Considerably more," the Valravn assured us.

Axel shrugged. "We almost never die."

"This time you will," the Valravn said. "Everyone's luck runs out, eventually."

Axel shrugged again. "I'm not worried about it. I'm super sneaky. And not to be rude, but we're kind of in a hurry here."

We both turned away from him and started down the hill again.

He followed.

"Wyatt," he said from behind me. "There are powers at work down there you can't understand or comprehend."

"So, pretty much the norm," I replied without turning to face him.

"No, not the norm," he said. "Worse than normal. There is a sorcerer down there who could kill the both of you, and your friends on the hill, without breaking a sweat."

"Wonderful," I said, and continued forward.

After a moment, though, I paused and turned to face him again.

"Wait a minute..."

"What?" he asked.

I glanced at Axel, who only shrugged. I turned back to the Valravn. "You aren't trying very hard."

"Excuse me?"

"Usually, you try way harder. This time, though... Your heart isn't in it."

"My heart?"

"If you have one," I said. "You aren't really trying to stop me, nor are you offering to help. Which makes me think... You want me to go down there."

He was silent for a moment, just flipping his stupid coin. Finally, he asked, "Do you have any idea what they intend to accomplish with that spell?"

"I don't," I replied. "Enlighten me."

Again a pause.

"No," he said. "That's above your pay grade."

I rolled my eyes. Axel, though, he groaned. "Is this dude always like this?"

"Pretty much." I turned my attention back to the Valravn. "So, you won't say what it is, but I get the impression you don't want it to happen."

"Indeed. But then, neither do you, Wyatt, I assure you. Likely it will fail either way. But just the same, I'm weighing your ability to screw everything up against the odds stacked against you. To go down there is almost certain death. Yet I also know you have a penchant for ruining others' plans, so... It's kind of a wash for me, really. Besides, if you die, so long as the sword isn't lost, we might get a more competent Blade Mage. Surely one who isn't so foolish. Everyone wins, I'd say."

"I'd say you're an asshole," I replied.

"And I'd say you're seriously underestimating our ability to fuck shit up," Axel said. "Now, tell us what the spell is for or get the flock out of here."

"Hey, that's my line," I said.

The Valravn groaned. "Talking to Wyatt is bad enough. Why did I think it was a good idea to talk to both of you at the same time?"

"Probably because you knew I was the wise one," Axel said. "And the prettier one. And sneakier. Better wizard. Better with the ladies. Better at, like, general life stuff."

I turned and glared at him. "Really?"

"Yeah, dude." He nodded happily.

"You're both idiots," the Valravn said, then turned his attention back to me. "I've had a change of heart."

"Oh?" I asked. "So, you're going to help us?"

"Absolutely not. My new hope is that you manage to stop the spell and also get yourself killed. That's the best outcome."

"Great." I rolled my eyes. "You do know I'm not the only Blade Mage in the world, right? Why don't you go harass Byron?"

"Byron Walker is a very respected and capable Blade Mage. He does not need my guidance."

"Is that what this is?" I asked, staring at him, blank-faced. "You call this giving me guidance?"

"Of course. What else? Have I not been helping you all along?"

"Uh, pretty sure you tried to kill us once. Or twice," Axel said. "In the church and then in the cave. Was there another time? Doesn't matter. You definitely tried to kill us."

"We had conflicting interests," he said, then paused. "Actually, no. It wasn't so simple as that, was it? You muppets were helping our bloody enemies, weren't you? Should've gone ahead and killed you then. Would have saved me a tremendous amount of future frustration."

"Uh, as I recall," Axel said, tapping his chin, "pretty sure we kicked your ass."

"Is that right?" the Valravn asked, a hint of venom in his tone. "Is that what you would call it?"

"We don't have time for this," I said, starting forward again. "Our friend is in trouble."

"Your lady friend is of little consequence," the Valravn replied, still following.

"But then, neither are we, apparently," I replied. "You just said you wanted me to die."

"Yes, well, that would be beneficial," he said. "You are too stubborn to listen to my advice."

"Again, I don't think you're quite the guide you think you are," I replied. "Maybe don't sign up to coach a T-ball league."

"I hate children." Clearly, bird brain missed the joke. "They are noisy and smelly and terrible at following directions. Much like you, come to think of it."

"Well, this has been a lot of fun," I said. "Very informative. I mean, really. What would I have done all this time without your wisdom to guide me?"

"Sarcasm doesn't suit you, Wyatt," he said.

"Yeah, Wyatt," Axel said, hands on his hips. "Leave it to the professionals."

"Okay, that's it," I said. "I'm officially ignoring both of you and going to save Alyita. Oh, and bird man, your whole, 'I don't want to get involved because I don't want to piss off the big baddy' is pretty stupid. Obviously, whoever—or whatever—you've been *so* effectively warning me about already knows you're on the other team. You might as well just commit. Dipshit."

And with that, I stomped down the hill.

61

We made it to the bottom of the hill without incident. The Valravn was gone.

The undergrowth was thick around the abandoned mining camp, offering us plenty of cover. We ducked behind a fat tree surrounded by tall bushes. Then we studied the scene ahead.

There wasn't much to see.

Directly in front of us was an old bunkhouse. Assuming she hadn't moved, Alyita was ducked down somewhere on the other side of it. We couldn't see her from where we were hidden, though.

We could see a robed figure loitering just a short way ahead of us. It was a humorous sight. He, or she, was smoking, as if on break. Like some costumed spook house worker, taking a cigarette break after scaring spoiled children.

I might have laughed if I hadn't recognized the robes.

My fears were made true.

Gray. Their robes were gray.

A demon summoner.

A chill ran down my spine, remembering the creepy critters they'd summoned in Memphis. I had hoped to be wrong.

I glanced over at Axel and whispered, "You seeing this?"

He nodded.

I used mind-speak to reach out to Parker. *"Is Alyita still all right?"*

"She hasn't moved."

"Good. I'll have Axel let her know we're close."

"Okay, but we should minimize mind-speak activity."

"Uh... Why?"

"You want our enemies to know we're here?"

"No, not particularly." I blinked a few times. *"Wait, are you saying they can sense mind-speak?"*

"Possibly. It is magic, Wyatt. You know that, don't you? That Normans can't communicate telepathically?"

I bit back an angry retort. I deserved the snobby response. Should have known. If our enemies had wards set up to sense magic, it was very possible they could sense our communications. We couldn't avoid it, given the circumstances, but we could minimize our use.

As if reading my thoughts, Parker said, *"Once you guys enter the camp, we should go radio silent."*

"Got it," I said, annoyed. More with myself than him. I hated his snobby demeanor, but appreciated his experience. I wasn't going to tell him that, though.

"We'll start moving into position," he said, then added, *"If you think it's time."*

At least he'd caught himself trying to be the boss that time.

"Do it," I said.

"All right. Speak soon."

"Wait, Grimm. There's one more thing. Those hooded figures..."

"Yeah?"

"Gray robes."

"Ah, I see. Lovely. Guess you called it."

"Glad we brought the knights with us."

"Right. I'll get everyone up to speed and we'll move. Grimm out."

I glanced over at Axel. "Let Alyita know we're close."

"Already did."

"She all right?"

"She's annoyed we haven't rescued her yet."

"Well, tell her we're on the way."

"Already did. I've been talking to her, like, the entire time."

I stared at him. "You have?"

"Oh, yeah. She's super jealous she didn't get to meet the Valravn. In Cherokee lore, he's called a raven mocker."

"Wait... You told her about him?"

"Uh, yeah," he said, raising an eyebrow. "Was I not supposed to?"

"No, Axel, you were not. You were not supposed to tell *anyone* about the super-powered, evil prick monster bird who thinks he's helping us."

"Oh."

"What do you think would happen if that got back to the council?"

"Um... I guess they'd want to take him down. Wait... Why don't you want to take him down? He tried to kill us, remember?"

I sighed. "Because as much of an asshole as he is, I *do* think he's trying to help in some creepy bird-man sort of way. And he's the only person who seems to understand what's really going on most of the time. Not that he's forthcoming."

"Right. He's very cryptic and dramatic."

"Reminds me of someone else I know."

"Who?" Axel asked.

I stared at him for a moment, then shook my head. "I'm hopeful the Valravn will explain... Well, something at some point."

"All right, well, I told Alyita not to say anything."

"You're still mind-speaking with her?"

"Yeah. I already told you, I've been chatting with her, like, the entire time. Obviously I had to tell her I got in trouble for telling her about the Valravn. Duh."

I glared at him. "Parker said we should stop using mind-speak. Said our enemies might sense the magical energy."

"Fuck Grimmy. But... Yeah, he's probably right. Why didn't you think of that?"

"Me? Why didn't you?"

"Because I'm not important. You're the Blade Mage."

"That's not what you told Archie."

"Huh?" He seemed genuinely confused. "I didn't tell Archie you weren't the Blade Mage."

"No, dingus. You told him you should be in charge."

"Oh, right. Yeah. I Totes McGotes should be in charge. *But*... He didn't put me in charge, did he? That's still you. So... Do better."

I just glared at him.

After a moment, though, he said, "Wyatt..."

That tone in his voice always concerned me. "Yes?"

"Do you ever..." He paused, biting his lip. "Do you ever wonder if we're cut out for this?"

I wasn't sure which surprised me more: the question itself, or his earnest tone. This wasn't like Axel.

"Sometimes," I admitted with a shrug. "You?"

"Hell no. Grow up, Wyatt. There's no time for self-doubt. We've got to save Alyita. Sheesh."

"But you said..." I stared at him, blinking.

"There's no time for self-doubt when you're busy being this awesome. Be mature, Wyatt. Be professional. We're in some serious shit. Now, watch me sneak up and bop this gray-robed bitch on the back of the head."

I glanced up and saw the gray-robed wizard had just tossed cigarette their butt on the ground. They didn't seem in a hurry, though, and were lollygagging back toward the door.

Axel crept out of the tree-line like a cartoon criminal. Or like a kid pretending to be a dinosaur. I raised my wand in case things went south.

They didn't.

Axel slid up right behind his prey and raised a rock, which I hadn't even noticed him pick up.

He swung.

There was a sickening crack as the stone connected with the summoner's skull.

The hooded figure crumpled, but Axel caught them and began dragging them back toward our hiding spot in the brush. I kept my wand at the ready in case anyone else stepped out of the cabin or came around the side of the building.

Axel dumped his captive behind a bush.

I drew back their hood, revealing a man's face near enough to our age. Not anyone I knew, though. And I wondered about that. Not that I'd expected to know him. We were a long way from home, but...

I wondered who he was.

How he'd come to be here.

Where he'd learned his wicked magic, assuming we had correctly identified him as a summoner.

And I wondered how the summoners recruited members. Was it like in certain sports where they drafted up from the minors? Like that group in Treat. They hadn't been high-level sorcerers. Clearly they weren't in the upper leagues. Did the gray-robes pull from less experienced teams and then teach them how to summon demons? Was there a demon-summoning school tucked away somewhere?

I mean... There were plenty of nomad mages around. It was feasible they could have pulled from anywhere, but the idea that someone was recruiting and training them, all under the noses of the guilds... It just didn't seem possible.

And while I was wasting time wondering all these things, where had their demons come from? The biblical Hell? Another hell from another belief system? Or did all the religions have it wrong? Were they from somewhere else entirely?

I had so many question and not a damned one of them mattered just then.

Rummaging through his robe, I found a wand, which I confiscated and tossed off into the forest. I doubted he'd wake up any time soon, and even if he did, I doubted he'd be in shape to fight. That rock to the back of the head? He'd be lucky if he woke up at all.

Beneath his robes he wore tactical fatigues. Lots of pockets. I searched them all, hoping to find a wallet with an ID inside. Every time we'd faced goons associated with the big nasty—whoever or whatever that was—we'd never been able to take one alive or identify who they were.

If it wasn't for the fact we needed to rescue Alyita, I would have been very tempted to drag that asshole back up the mountain.

No luck on the wallet. His pockets were empty save for a pack of smokes and his lighter, both of which Axel wanted for some reason.

I raised an eyebrow as he opened the pack. "You planning on taking up smoking?"

"No," he said as he pulled out all the remaining cigarettes. "I just know there's a good chance we'll die tonight."

"Thought you said we never die?"

"I said we 'almost' never die. And just in case we do, I want an insurance policy. I want to make sure we were as big of a pain in the ass as possible. I want this jerkface to have the worst night imaginable."

"You don't think cracking his skull did the trick?"

Axel didn't reply. He was busy tearing up each of the guy's remaining cigarettes. He started by crushing them, but that only ruined a few, so then he started tearing at them, letting the ruined paper and tobacco crumbs fall onto the sleeping wizard's chest.

It took me a moment to catch on. Axel was always devious, but this was just cruel. If the dude woke up, he was going to be in a ton of pain. A smoke would probably be the first thing he sought. Now they were ruined.

"Damn, Axel," I said with a chuckle. "That's cold."

He grinned. "Now he can have a cracked skull, a concussion, and a nicotine headache."

I nodded my approval. "All right, let's get this show on the road."

We ensured there was no one else around and both stepped out into the open.

I led the way, moving up alongside the building. Slowly, very slowly, I peeked my head around the side.

There was Alyita, ducked down between stacks of boxes, just as we'd seen her before.

Out the other end of the alley, though, were three more gray-robed wizards. Three I could see, anyway. I had to fight the urge to jump back into cover. With their hoods pulled over the heads, I couldn't see which way they were looking. Two of them could have been looking right at me and I wouldn't have known. Jerking my head back would have been more likely to give me away. And clearly they hadn't noticed me yet, or they probably would have reacted.

I eased my head back out of sight and bit my lip, pondering. I couldn't ponder for long. Any moment now another asshole might pop out of the door beside us, or come around the other side of the bunkhouse. We needed to make a move.

If I tried to move up alongside Alyita, there was a good chance I'd be seen. Plus, then we'd have to backtrack, giving them a second opportunity to spot us with twice as much real estate to spot. No, it made more sense to have Alyita come back to us.

Glancing at Axel, I said, "Tell Alyita when she's confident the hooded assholes aren't looking at her to make a move. Come back down the alley toward us."

Without waiting for him to reply, I peeked around the corner again. The hooded figures still didn't look up at me. The low light around camp certainly helped. They didn't seem alarmed. In fact, it looked like they were just chit-chatting. I imagined them talking about the latest sports ball game, or arguing over which Hogwarts house they belonged in. Spoiler alert: I doubted any of them were Hufflepuff. Unless they had some, like, super adorable demons they could summon. Then maybe. I had a flashback of the baby-faced wolf-scorpions. They didn't fit the bill.

Anyway...

After a moment, Alyita's head turned my way. Our eyes met.

She was scared. Terrified, even. But her jaw was set.

Her attention returned to the sorcerers, and after a few moments, she went for it. Alyita eased out of her cover and slowly made her way toward us, sticking close to the walls and the shadows.

As soon as she rounded the corner, she lunged at me.

For a split second, I thought I'd been bamboozled. Thought I was being attacked. Instead...

She hugged me.

I stared down at her, dumbfounded. I had known she was scared, of course. Who wouldn't have been? Kidnapped by sorcerers and taken to an abandoned mining camp? No thanks. Thing was, though, sometimes it was easy to forget she was just a teenager. Alyita was tough as nails. And confident. She'd been through some real shit. Worse shit than most grown-ass adults would ever face. But... She was still young.

So, I awkwardly patted her on the back.

When she pulled away, tears streaming down her cheeks, she

scowled. Then punched me in the shoulder. Hard. Whispering, she said, "Took you assholes long enough."

Axel and I glanced at one another, then he hooked a thumb at me. "Would've been here sooner, but one of us isn't as sneaky as the other."

"We need to move," I said, ignoring his insult in favor of getting us back on task. "We aren't safe."

"I'm not leaving Sams," Alyita said. "Or the others."

I'd known that was what she'd say and was prepared for it. "What was your plan before you knew we were here?"

"To go get help."

"Why?" I asked.

She blinked. Then stared at me like I was a potato. "Well, I certainly couldn't rescue them all on my own."

"And you think the three of us can? If we get caught, do you really think between Axel, you, and me that we can take on all these assholes?"

She looked away.

"Hey," I said, drawing her eyes back to me. "We aren't leaving them. That's not what I'm saying. We're just making a strategic retreat until the cavalry arrives."

She glanced over at Axel, but he only shrugged in reply.

"Okay," she said, looking down. "I don't like it, but you're right."

That was a relief.

I was worried she'd argue further. After Lost City, it felt like she had an over-exaggerated idea of what we were capable of. Now, we could slip back up the hill without having to do something really stupid.

We would exit the same way Axel and I had arrived. I again considered dragging our captive back up the hill. It would be tough, maybe impossible, but I really wanted a prisoner.

I also needed to give the others a heads-up. They were currently spreading out and getting into position to come to our aid. Instead, we could all head right back up to the top of the hill and keep an eye on things while we waited for the Appalachian Argument to bring their army.

"There's just one thing..." Alyita said, crushing my hopes and dreams.

"What?"

"Shaman Sams, he..." She trailed off again, biting her lip.

"What?" I repeated.

"Well, he told me to get away. Said to go for help."

"And?"

"Well, before that, he and Tsali were talking. I don't think they knew I was listening. Sams said he thought... He thought they intended to sacrifice us."

It was my turn to stare at her, blank-faced.

She continued. "He seemed to think that whatever this working was, whatever they're doing with Mothman, the only reason they kept us all alive, is because...they planned to sacrifice us. And...I don't know how long before that happens."

I sighed.

"Well, shit."

62

We couldn't wait. Couldn't slink off and hide.

Once Alyita explained what she'd overheard, there was no choice and no time to debate. We had to free the others, and fast.

I also understood something else.

Before, when she'd refused to leave, it hadn't been teenage stubbornness. She'd known the others were on borrowed time. I just wished she had shared that from the start. Hell, maybe she had and dinky-do Axel hadn't told me. Either way, had I known, we'd have implemented a different strategy.

I didn't know much about sacrificial magic.

I *did* know it violated the Solemn Covenant.

In the Cabal magic school, it was made clear that sacrificing a living being to power our magic was a big no-no. They didn't cover the mechanics, just the no-no parts.

It had been covered in more detail when I was training to join a strike team. They also hadn't given us much in the way of mechanics. Just how to watch for it. How to identify it. But mostly, our training had covered: sacrifice bad. Hulk smash.

My mind drifted back to when the grays had killed the Colonial Coven witches in Memphis. I couldn't remember if it had occurred to me then, but I wondered whether their deaths had been used to charge the nasty-ass summoning spells they'd used. Had the head-chopping party been more than just a show? Was that how they'd called all those demons into the ballroom?

And what was the purpose of the working they were performing on Mothman now?

I cursed the Valravn for not just telling me. *Asshole.*

According to Alyita, they'd been ambushed along a walking trail that led to the hidden Cherokee camp. It had happened so fast no one had had time to react. None save Mothman. Everyone else, including Supreme Shaman Sams, had been hit with a spell and frozen in place. Mothman alone could move, but he'd been hit with a series of glowing magical nets, shocking him and pinning him in place.

The enemy had been so well-prepared that no one could fight back.

I didn't know much about the Cherokee in Appalachia, but catching the Oklahoma Cherokee with their pants down would've been no easy feat. I imagined the Eastern Cherokee were much the same.

What surprised me more, and scared the pee out of me, was that they'd subdued a powerhouse like Mothman and an Arcane Guardian like Sams. Sure, Sams was old, his health failing, but he was still wielded the Arcane Ankh. For him to have been taken so easily...

Well, it wouldn't have been easy. That was the thing. It would have required an immense amount of power, an insane series of spells, and perfect execution.

Our enemies were terrifying. I couldn't imagine what they were capable of.

Anyway, Alyita and the others had been hauled to the camp and locked up in one of the bunkhouses, their hands and feet bound with enchanted bindings. Their weapons had been taken, including Alyita's tomahawk and Sams's ankh. But no one had bothered to check the teenage girl for a hidden knife. They didn't know our Alyita. Once they were locked up and alone, she'd slipped out her knife and tried to cut through her bindings. Unfortunately, the magic had prevented them from being severed.

Shaman Sams and Tsali had worked some magic of their own, forcing enough energy into her bindings to break the spell over them.

That would have been tricky. Damned tricky. Without a wand or staff, they'd had to channel their energy directly into the magically infused chord. If I had tried that, I probably would have blown her wrists to shreds.

It wasn't a trick they could manage a second time. Apparently, they'd tried several others. Best guess, the bad guys hadn't planned on taking so many prisoners. Probably weren't ready to enchant so many bindings. Since Alyita was surely seen as the least threatening of the bunch, they'd probably half-assed hers. She was *just* a teenager, after all.

Once she was free, Sams and the others had managed to break the ward over a window. Sams had told her to go for help and sent her on her way.

And since we didn't have enough to worry about...

Alyita said by the time she left, Sams was all but passed out from fatigue. Tsali and a few of the other Cherokee were worn down, too. I could believe it. They'd popped enchanted bindings and taken down a ward, all without a wand or staff. Nothing simple about either. I wouldn't have even known where to start. But they were big bosses for a reason, right?

And they'd put all their hope in her. She was glad to transfer that hope to Axel and me.

The goal was simple: don't let them down.

Accomplishing that goal, however... Not easy.

We needed her to lead us to the bunkhouse without being seen. Then we needed to figure out how to get past the guards, again, without being seen. Break the wards around the building. Break inside. Free all the captives from their enchanted bindings. Get them all on their feet. Hope they were feeling up to a daring escape after their badass magical efforts. Slip the entire gang outside, once again, without being seen. Sneak everyone back across the mining camp without being seen. And finally, get them all up the mountain without being seen.

Wait, was I forgetting something?

Ah, yes, of course. We also needed to figure out how to save Mothman, who was currently being used in some wicked-ass ritual right in the center of camp. You know, right where loads of assholes were keeping their eyes on him?

So, that was the... Well, it wasn't a plan. Not even close. Just a series of objectives.

But... Easy peasy, right?

Wrong.

As I followed Alyita through the camp, I considered how the hell to pull it off. The answer was simple.

We couldn't.

We hadn't made it terribly far when a voice behind me said, "Hello, Wyatt."

Gabby's voice.

I spun, preparing to defend myself, and regretting not summoning my sword back earlier.

Only when I turned, there was no one there.

I turned back in the original direction I had been facing and found her right in front of me, knife raised at my throat.

"Hold!" a man's voice commanded.

I blinked.

The dagger was at the edge of my neck, Gabby's eyes locked onto my own.

From my peripherals, I caught sight of Zeke and Sophie as they stepped around the side of a building. From the other side, I caught a flurry of gray robes. Footsteps behind me.

We were surrounded.

"Hold," the man repeated. I couldn't see him.

Gabby's eyes flicked from mine to the side. "Why?"

"The master said to take them alive." The speaker came into view. A gray robe, hood pulled low, hiding his features. "He can use them."

"Not this one," Gabby said, knife still at my throat. "He dies now."

"No," the hooded figure said. "The master has spoken."

Gabby growled and turned to face him. Her blade was so close that even moving her head caused the knife to nick my skin. Kind of like a bee's sting. I could feel the blood running down my neck, but dared not move my head.

"You don't understand," Gabby said. "If we let him live—"

"The master has spoken," the man repeated. "We are to put them with the others."

"This is a mistake," Gabby said, reluctantly lowering her knife.

I appreciated her vote of confidence. And I took her desire to kill me as a compliment. If the fake Baron Samedi had heeded her advice back in the swamp, I would have been dead and that prick would have still been alive. Probably. And here we were again.

So, yeah, I took it as the highest compliment. That my backstabbing, treacherous b-word of a former teammate wanted me dead was... Well, it made me feel pretty good about how epically I'd futzed up her plans in the past.

And she was right.

They should've just killed me, because I totally aimed to fuck up their whole party. I just...

Wasn't sure how I was going to do it.

"You would question the master's orders?" the man asked.

"Only when it comes to this one," Gabby replied, pointing at me with her knife. "He'll find a way to cause us trouble. Trust me."

The hooded man chuckled. "I don't see how that's possible. But if you're so worried about him, you and your team can keep an eye on the bunkhouse."

"Count on it," Gabby said, her voice little more than a growl. She turned toward me. "Tanya is on her way."

"Ah," I said, nodding. "Must be posted up somewhere. Guess she saw us."

"Only you two would be stupid enough to break into this camp alone," she said, sneering at me, knife still at the ready. "Idiots."

"Why thank you, madam," Axel said, taking a bow. "We take great pride in our foolishness."

She growled at him.

The hooded man had already wandered off. I could see she was considering it. Thinking about slitting my throat anyway. How much trouble would she really get in?

"Gabriella," Zeke said, tone cautious as he approached. "We have to do what he said."

She turned to Zeke, trembling with rage.

Poor Gabby. She had wanted to kill me so many times now, and no one ever let her have her way. Also, she was probably still pretty pissed about the snake thing.

"You know, Gabby," I said, grinning at her, "I'm sorry about the danger noodle. Truly. I mean... It *was* kind of your own fault, though."

"True," Axel agreed, nodding along. "You really shouldn't blame Wyatt for that. He was just being generous. Let you play with his big ole snake. He couldn't have known it would want to give you kisses."

A tremor ran through her body. Her eyes narrowed.

"I *do* feel bad for you, though," I said, shrugging. "Honestly. You keep pointing out that I should just be killed, and no one listens. God, that must be frustrating."

The knife point moved back up to my throat.

"Gabriella," Zeke said again, his voice a little firmer. "Come on. Don't be foolish."

"Shut up, Zeke," she said, lowering the knife. She pointed a wand in my face instead. "Give me your weapons."

I moved slowly, holding out my father's wand to her.

"Never knew you to use a wand," she said, studying it. "Nice one, too. Now the sword."

"Uh..." I said, scrunching my face. "This is awkward, but, uh... I don't have it."

"Bullshit," she spat, pointing her wand closer to my nose. It trembled in her fingers. I had a feeling Gabby wasn't completely in control. Not like she used to be. She was on edge. Ready to blow my head off.

"Going to the dark side really hasn't been good for your demeanor," I said, holding her gaze. "Do you guys have, like, dark wizard councilors or anything? You should really talk to someone."

"The sword," she repeated through gritted teeth.

"Wyatt," Zeke said, giving me a long look. "Do what she says."

"I don't have the sword," I replied. "Tell them, Axel."

"Oh, yeah," Axel said. "He's totally telling the truth. Archie took it from him."

"Archie?" Zeke asked.

"The Archmage," Axel said, nodding like he was coming up with a pristine lie. I was already terrified of where he was going with this. "Said Wyatt was being irresponsible with it. He was doing tricks and stuff for the kids. I thought it was pretty cool, personally. Not ole Archie, though. He got all bent out of shape and took the sword away. Told Wyatt he was in timeout."

Holy crepes.

Worst. Lie. Ever.

There was no chance they'd believe that.

Zeke and Gabby shared a look. It wasn't one of disbelief. In fact, it was more like...

Yeah, that sounds like the Wyatt we know. *Assholes.*

"Check his back," Gabby said.

Zeke moved around behind me and began patting me down.

He didn't find a sword. He *did* find the revolver holstered in my waistband.

"This is new," Zeke said as he pulled it free. "When did you start carrying a gun?"

"Just trying to emulate my hero," I said, nodding at the giant revolver on Gabby's hip. "I always looked up to you, you know?"

She turned away and relieved Axel of his wand as well. I noted she tucked both into the back pocket of her tactical pants. Something told me she would not dump our weapons with all the others.

She claimed Alyita's knife as well, which she also slid into a pocket.

Then we were ushered along, Gabby leading us.

Zeke walked just beside me. Sophie and the other hooded mages fell in around Axel and Alyita.

"So, Zeke," I said, as we strolled. "How have things been?"

He started to reply, but Gabby whirled, glaring at me. "Shut up. Just shut the fuck up."

"Wow, sheesh, Gabby," I said. "Don't be jelly. I was going to ask you, too. I've just seen you more recently than Zeke."

And then I saw stars.

And then she punched me right in the jaw.

Wait... Those might have happened in a different order. It was hard to tell.

Hurt like hell, though. That was plain enough to keep straight.

The taste of copper filled my mouth as I struggled to keep my feet.

The inside of my lip was on fire, having been crushed against my teeth. At least none of them were loose, so far as I could tell.

"Well, that was unnecessary," I said, rubbing my jaw. "And here I thought we were all old friends."

"Say another fucking word and I'll break your goddamned nose," Gabby said.

"Listen to her, Wyatt," Zeke said with a concerned expression. "She'll do it. You know she will."

I spat out a glob of blood and fought down the urge to ask her what the hell had happened to her. What had driven her to this? But Zeke was right. Back when we'd all still been friends, Gabby hadn't made threats lightly. Now that she seemed on the verge of a breakdown, I doubted much had changed.

She waited a moment longer to see if I would push my luck. When I didn't, she turned and started forward again. We marched along in silence.

63

"We'll be waiting right out here," Gabby said, glaring at me. "Whenever you try whatever stupid thing you're planning, we'll be ready."

With that, she slammed the door in my face.

Maybe she had *too* much faith in me. I didn't have a plan.

Well...I had something brewing.

And she was right. I was almost certainly going to do something stupid. Probably wise for her and the others to hang around outside the bunkhouse. Would've been smarter to come inside and watch us directly. Of course, the way I figured it, Gabby was probably hoping I'd orchestrate a breakout so she could go ahead and kill me. And if what she'd said was true, my ex-girlfriend would be along shortly as well. Lucky me. Not every day you get sacrificed in a magical ritual in front of your ex.

I turned around, taking in the bunkhouse.

Alyita's fellow captives stared up at me, surprised to see newcomers. Axel and I both offered them a friendly wave. And then I noticed another familiar face, one who wouldn't have been captured with the others. I might have noticed him first if his eyes had been opened. Closed, his short stature hid him in the darkness.

Tuthid Pugh, my moon-eyed caretaker. He didn't appear to be

conscious. As I studied his face, I saw he was more bruised and battered than the last time I'd seen him. My blood boiled. Feogh. The little chieftain and his cronies, no doubt. That was a problem for later, though. I had other things to focus on just then.

Shaman Sams sat off to one side, also with his eyes closed. Tsali sat next to him. The medicine man gave Sams a little nudge and his eyes opened, blinking as he took us in.

"Wyatt," he said, voice horse. He sat up straighter, though. "This a rescue? Doesn't look like it's gone too well."

"Not a rescue," I assured him. "This is an assault. All part of the plan. I've got our enemies right where I want them."

He coughed out a chuckle. "I see. Well, do let us know how we can assist."

I glanced around the room. "What's everyone's status?"

Alyita tapped me on the arm and motioned for me to lower my voice. She leaned in closer and pointed at a door on the opposite end of the room. "There are guards posted in the office back there. That's where they have all our weapons and stuff."

That didn't seem too bright.

Again I wondered at the wisdom of leaving the prisoners unsupervised. Arrogance. That was the only explanation. The baddies figured they were safe from their prisoners. What could we possibly do? My former team had a better sense of worry. Glancing out the window, I saw they were still out there, still lingering around the door.

I turned my attention back to Alyita. "Any idea how many guards are in the office?"

She shrugged. "There were three gray robes when we came in. That door leads to a hallway. On one side is the office; on the other are the old restrooms. There's an exterior door on the end. That's where they brought us in. When we passed, the office door was open, and they had our weapons laid out on a table."

"Okay," I said. "Thank you. That's useful."

"You have a plan?" she asked, hopeful.

"More like an idea," I said, offering her my most confident smile. "Wouldn't want to disappoint my old pal Gabby by not doing something stupid."

I moved over and crouched beside Sams.

"You all right?"

He groaned. "A little old for field work."

"Is that what this is?" I asked, forcing another smile. "I thought you guys were camping."

"Not much for camping these days. Prefer the comfort of my own home."

I gave him a long look, then studied Tsali. Both men were staring back at me. I leaned in closer and whispered. "Alyita overhead you talking about this working they're using Mothman for. Said you thought they intended to sacrifice you."

"And you, now," Sams said. "You're with us, are you not?"

I shook my head. "Nope. Remember. All part of the plan."

"You make strange plans, Blade Mage," Tsali said, crossing his arms. "Looks like you're trapped in here with us."

"That's where you're mistaken," I said, again feigning confidence. "All those dark wizards out there, they're the ones stuck with me. They just don't know it yet."

Shaman Sams chuckled again, then met my gaze. "I don't know the intent of the spell, but you can see the tower from the window. I believe they're attempting to channel Mothman's powers, though I can scarcely guess why. Whatever they're trying to accomplish, it's big. Guessing they figure some sacrifices will help it along."

I considered. "What sort of powers does Mothman have?"

"Many," Sams said. "More than I can remember, and many more I don't understand."

"What is he?" I asked.

"Who can say?" Sams said. "He is a member of our council. Many look to him for inspiration and wisdom. And he is indeed as wise as he is powerful. But where he comes from? What his true powers are? He keeps that to himself."

"And you suspect they'll use you, er, us, to power the spell?"

"Why else bring us here? Why else keep us alive? Their spell may not require sacrifice, but adding our deaths into the mix will only make it more likely to succeed. Or perhaps more powerful. Or maybe it'll simply speed up the process. Whatever the case, they surely don't think to bargain with our lives. No; we are to be sacrificed. I'm sure of it. What-ever this is, it must be stopped."

"That's why I'm here," I replied, again forcing a smile I didn't feel. Probably didn't look so good with my bloody teeth, either. But... *Futz it.*

Tsali snorted at me. "If you're planning on freeing us, you could start with these. I'm rather tied of wearing them."

I glanced down at the magical bindings around his hands and feet.

"Not just yet. We've got to work up to that phase of the plan."

"What plan?" Tsali asked, eyes narrowing. "Who do you think you're fooling, Blade Mage? You don't have a plan."

"You're right," I said, shrugging. "But I do have an idea. Probably a dumb one. But sometimes...that's enough. Don't lose hope yet."

Sams chuckled again, then glanced over at Tsali. "Rest easy, my friend. I trust Wyatt."

That...

Well, damn.

I hadn't expected that. Now I felt like I *had* to live up to it. And my idea wasn't much of one. If it failed... No, Axel had been right. There was no time for self-doubt when you were busy being this awesome.

And then the door opened behind me.

My ex stood there, arms crossed, glaring at me.

"Hello, Tanya," I said, rising to my feet. "How have you been?"

"Ugh," Axel said, rolling his eyes. "You have got to be my least favorite of Wyatt's exes."

"The feeling is mutual," she said, glaring at Axel. "I never could stand you."

Axel glanced over at me. "That should have been your first clue to break up with this one."

Before I could reply, Tanya glanced at the gray robes behind her. "Bind them."

Tanya stepped further into the room to make way. Zeke and Gabby also stepped in and spread apart, ready for shenanigans. Several of the gray robes came in as well.

They started toward us.

"Wyatt first," Tanya said. "Then the man-child."

I didn't resist. There wasn't much point.

They tied cords around my feet first, then my hands, and then the friendly bastards pushed me over. There wasn't anything I could do to stop my fall. I hit hard, landing on my tailbone. Pain seared up my spine.

Then one of them leaned over me with a staff and pointed it at my bindings. He uttered a few words and the cords began to glow. They repeated this on my feet.

It was Axel's turn next.

I smiled up at Tanya. "You never answered my question. How have you been?"

"Fuck off, Wyatt," she said, ignoring me.

"Think you guys could at least crack a window?" I asked, glancing at the other occupants, all of whom were sweating. "It's pretty stuffy in here. Would be a shame if someone died of heat stroke before your master gets to sacrifice us."

Everyone paused, surprised that I knew their intention.

I smiled. "By the way, what are your pals doing to Mothman, anyway?"

No one replied, but much to my surprise, Zeke moved over and used his staff to smash out an old window.

Tanya and Gabby both scowled at him. He shrugged in reply. "We'll be able to hear them better. I don't want to sit in this hot-ass room babysitting."

Tanya shook her head but didn't reply.

The gray robes had finished with Axel and moved to Alyita next. The lead one paused, his hood moving up and down, studying her. After a moment, he said, "Maybe we'll take this one with us for a while."

The tone in his voice...

I nearly launched my escape plan on the spot.

"She's a teenager, you sicko," Axel said, rolling to a sitting position. "Don't you fucking touch her."

"Like you can stop me," the man said, then turned his hooded gaze back on Alyita. "I don't mind 'em young. Kind of prefer them that way."

He took a single step forward and stopped, Gabby's knife at his throat.

"What do you think you're doing?" he asked, glaring at her.

"Bind her feet and hands," Gabby said. "Nothing else."

"I don't take orders from you."

"Touch her in any other way and I'll cut your fucking throat," Gabby said.

"And don't think you can help him," Zeke said to the other gray robe beside him. "There are limits to what we will abide. And that... That crosses the line."

There was a long moment of silence.

The lead gray robe turned his head slowly, looking at Tanya. Maybe he thought she would call off Gabby.

Instead, my ex sneered at him. "What are you waiting for? An invitation? You heard her. Do the bindings and then get back outside."

"You fools," the gray robe said, shaking his head. "You think you have a say? If I want to take this girl—"

"Then you die," Gabby said.

"Enough talking," Tanya said. "Bind her. *Now.*"

Gabby moved the knife and the gray robe did as he was told, grumbling all the while.

When he was done, he shoved Alyita over, just as he'd done to us. As his partner enchanted her bindings, he continued staring down at her. "I'll be seeing you soon, sweet cheeks. Count on it." Then he turned back to Tanya. "After the master hears about the hired help getting in my way, of course."

Tanya smirked. "Let me know how that goes for you."

The gray robes started outside. My former teammates lingered a moment longer.

I looked up at Zeke, and when he met my eyes, I gave him a little nod. A small thanks, for Alyita's sake. I didn't know if he understood my meaning or not, but he gave me a nod back. Just the slightest hint.

And then they were out the door.

64

I rolled back up to a seated position and glanced at Alyita. "You all right?"

She nodded. "If I figure out which gray robe that was, I'll kill him."

"Not if I kill him first," Axel said. "I'm going to fry his ass."

"But how will we know which?" Alyita asked.

"Oh, easy," I said, grinning at her. "We'll just kill them all."

They both nodded their approval.

Tsali, though, rolled his eyes. "So, when are you going to launch this plan of yours?"

"Soon," I said, grinning at him.

"That's what you said before," he said, then nodded toward my restraints. "But now you're as stuck as we are."

"Just an illusion," I said, grinning. "Remember, I'm not stuck. Those assholes are stuck with me. All part of the plan."

"Right." He shook his head.

"Did you ever meet Ahuli from Oklahoma?"

Tsali nodded, eyes narrowing. "Yes. Why?"

"You kind of remind me of him."

"I'm not sure if that's a compliment," Tsali said.

"Me neither," I replied, then I ignored him and began scooting my butt across the floor.

It *was* nearing time to put my *oh so* brilliant plan into play, but the more time I wasted, the better. I mean, I didn't want to wait until they sacrificed us all, but a few more minutes would be ideal.

So, I eased my way over to Tuthid, worm crawling by the strength of my butt cheeks.

The little moon-eyed man had woken with all the previous commotion, but he'd yet to speak. He was just staring at me.

I eased up alongside him, and keeping my voice low, said, "Guessing things haven't gone well with Feogh?"

He didn't reply.

"Listen," I said, offering him a smile. I didn't care if the others heard me. In fact, it was better if they did. The poor little guy must have been terrified to be locked up alongside the Cherokee, and not just because of the old feud, but because he knew his people were the ones who'd set them up. I wanted them to hear what I had to say. "I think I know what happened, Tuthid, but you tell me if I'm mistaken. Guessing Feogh planned to betray the Argument and the Cherokee. Guessing these dark wizard assholes promised him vengeance against the Cherokee. And I'm willing to bet you didn't like the idea. In fact, I'm sure of it. And I bet you challenged Feogh. Is that how you ended up here?"

He didn't reply.

"Come on, Tuthid. There's no shame in it. I know you tried to do the right thing."

Finally, he nodded. "You got most of it right. Most."

"What'd I miss?" I asked.

"Feogh didn't do it alone," he said, shaking his head. "The others helped, too."

"They ganged up on you?"

He nodded. "Tuthid challenged Feogh. Declared him unfit. Challenged him to become the leader. Was supposed be a fair fight."

"But the others jumped in?"

He nodded again, then grinned at me with a split lip. "But not before Tuthid popped him good."

"Nice. Fucker Feogh deserves it."

"But now Tuthid will die." He sighed. "Feogh will go back to our people. He will say Tuthid challenged him and lost fair. Feogh is a great warrior. They will believe him."

"Hmm," I said, considering. "What would have happened if he fought fair?"

Tuthid shrugged. "Doesn't matter."

"It does. Would the others have followed you if you'd won?"

He nodded.

"Would they still follow you if you beat him?"

"How can I beat him? Tuthid stuck here with you."

"Humor me."

"What does that mean?"

"It means..." I glanced up and saw that all the Cherokee were watching. Good. "Let's pretend we break out of here. If you beat Feogh, would the others follow you?"

He considered. "Yes."

"Tuthid," I said, weighing my words. "Do you want peace with the Cherokee? Do you want to put your old feud aside?"

"Yes," he said, not looking up at the faces who'd been betrayed by his people.

I put my attention on Tsali. "Tsali, do the Cherokee harbor any grudge toward the moon-eyed people?"

He began to speak, but paused when I winked at him. I could only hope he got the hint. I wasn't referring to the new feud, born out of this betrayal, but the older one. If Tsali could look past Feogh's actions, there was a chance for them to build an alliance.

And sure, I probably should have been focused on other things just then. Like my escape plan. But this was important, too.

Tsali took a deep breath and said, "Yes, the Cherokee would like to establish a friendship with the moon-eyed people."

Tuthid looked up, surprised. "Even after..."

Damn it, Tuthid.

But Tsali didn't bat an eye. "If it is as the Blade Mage said, the betrayal was orchestrated by your leader, who is without honor. You, it seems, are not the same. I can only hope that is true of the rest of your people."

"It is," Tuthid assured him, a glimmer of hope on his small face.

"Well, that settles it then," I said, grinning. "You have to kill Feogh."

Tuthid paused, staring at me. "But the others..."

"We'll take care of them, won't we, Tsali?"

The medicine man chuckled. "Sure, Blade Mage. Just as soon as you get us out of here."

"Speaking of which," Axel said, interrupting the conversation. He rolled on his side so that he was facing me. "Is it time to get out of here yet? I'm bored."

I considered.

"Yeah, it's probably about that time."

65

I really did have a plan.

Sort of.

I just didn't know how certain elements would play out.

And there were about a million things that could go wrong.

Especially the first step. That wasn't ideal. I preferred the unpredictable parts to come later, after the parts I could control were already in motion. Not knowing how the first step was going to go, I couldn't say for certain how the rest would work. That was the main reason I was being coy. That and the fact I didn't know if our enemies were listening.

I had bought enough time, though, and couldn't justify wasting any more. It was go time.

This first part was a concern because it required faith in something I didn't fully understand.

My sword.

I called to it.

But...not quite like I normally did.

In the past, I'd always just tugged on the connection. Summoned it right to me. This time, though, as I called to it, I thought about the need for stealth. I thought about the guards outside and how they would react if they saw a flying sword. And I thought about the window Zeke had opened for us. That was what made the first part of my plan unpredictable. I didn't know if my sword would understand.

It clearly had some level of sentience. It seemed to respond when I thought things at it. But those were typically simplistic things. This time, I was feeding it complexity, and from further away. Could it understand? If not, then things were going to get interesting a lot faster than I would have liked.

If the sword flew straight through all our enemies and hammered through the front door, then I would not have much time. I'd probably be under attack before I could even remove my bindings.

That was another potential problem. Could Dyrnwyn remove my bindings?

Nothing to do but wait and find out.

And wait some more.

And some more.

Fortunately, there were some crickets chirping somewhere in the old bunkhouse, which really added to the ambiance.

Seriously, what was taking my sword so long?

I felt a tinge of panic as time continued ticking by.

Had the first part of my plan failed completely? Was my sword stuck somewhere? Had they found it?

"So, uh..." Axel said, cutting through my thoughts. "About this plan of yours..."

I turned and glared at him. He was still lying on his side in the fetal position.

"Don't give me that look," he said. "This is *super* boring."

I ignored him.

But it was a challenge to ignore everyone else.

All eyes were on me.

Everyone was expecting me to come through. Or at least hoping I might. They were all watching me, waiting to see what I would do. Everyone except for Sams, who had leaned back and closed his eyes, resting. He'd spoken his confidence in me. The others, though... I could see a mixture of hope, doubt, and dread. And I was beginning to wonder if my confidence had been misplaced after all.

If my sword didn't come...

I leaned back and closed my eyes, trying to keep calm.

If my sword didn't come, then I'd have to rely on a later phase of my plan. That was all. We weren't out of hope yet. We still had allies outside, ready to come to our aid. I ignored dark thoughts about what kind of chance they had against so many dark wizards. Eilidh would figure something out. Or Parker. They were clever.

Finally, I sighed, giving up on my sword.

It wasn't coming.

No sooner had I had the thought than I heard a gasp.

Opening my eyes, I saw the hilt of my sword peeking over the windowsill. It rose very slowly, as if coming out of hiding. But much like a puppy, it sped up as soon as it saw me and came barreling right at me. For a moment, I thought it would run me through. That would have made for the most awkward rescue attempt of all time. It stopped just before me instead, hovering right in front of my face, as if it were studying me.

Dyrnwyn changed into a dagger and I raised my wrists, holding them out.

And for phase two of my plan...

It sliced right through the enchanted cords. There was a static hiss as the magic was dispelled and that was that.

I grabbed the floating knife and cut through bindings around my legs.

Then I took a moment to glance out the windows. Fortunately, we were all seated below them. They didn't offer the best view, and none of our adversaries were watching us. That was no small blessing. I wanted discretion a little longer.

I moved to the nearest person, a Cherokee I didn't know, and sliced through her bindings, then moved on to the next.

As I worked on freeing people, I thought at my sword, *"Were you slow because you were being stealthy?"*

It pulsed in my hand.

"Hell yeah. You are the best sword in the world."

It vibrated happily.

I continued moving about the room, trying to stay quiet as I freed everyone. Once I cut Tsali loose, he moved toward the door while making hand gestures at several of the others. For a moment, I thought he intended to go outside, which would bring this escape attempt to a quick end. Instead, took up position on one side of the door and another of the Cherokee took the other. Two more moved to the back of the bunkhouse and took up position on either side of the other door. If anyone came charging in, they'd be ready to jump them.

I continued on, freeing Sams, then Tuthid, Alyita, and a few others. Axel glared at me the entire time.

I freed him last.

Time wasn't on my side then. If anyone barged in, the folks guarding the doors might get lucky, but otherwise, it would be me and my sword versus the world. That meant the next objective was to get everyone's weapons back before we were found out. Still, another idea occurred to me, and it was worth sparing a few seconds for.

The old bunkhouse had plenty of junk lying around: old storage crates, ancient bedframes, and other junk. It was the old bedframes which held my attention. Everyone else, it seemed, wanted me to get the show on the road. Freed of their bindings, they wanted me to charge out the bunkhouse and start hacking down enemies. Bad news for them: I expected them all to help.

I held Dyrndagger up against an old metal frame and tried to cut through. No surprise, Dyrnwyn cut through it like a slab of bacon. I moved to the other end of the frame and cut it again, this time at a sharp angle. I tapped my finger against the tip. It was hot—fresh off the frying pan hot—but more importantly, the tip was sharp.

I'd made a prison shank. Er, a prison shank spear. A... Hmm... I had an even better name for it, actually.

I glanced over at Axel and held it up.

He raised an eyebrow and in a whisper asked, "Really? A spear?"

"Sorry," I replied. "All out of drumsticks. Figured you'd want one after the cool name I came up with."

He crossed his arms, waiting.

"I call it...William Shankspear."

His eyes lit up and he took it from me, giving it a loving pat. Sometimes you just have to make the ordinary extraordinary.

I made quick work of cutting another, and another, and so on until half of our fellow prisoners were armed with Shankspears, or just shanks. I didn't bother kitting everyone. That would have been a waste of time. If it came to a pitched battle, cool name or no, shanks wouldn't get us far against staves and wands. We needed to get their proper weapons back.

I motioned for Axel, Alyita, Tuthid, and Tsali to gather around me. Tsali motioned for someone else to take his place at the door and then stepped in close with the others.

Keeping my voice low, I said, "We need to get your weapons back. Next step is to take the office area Alyita told me about. Not sure how many we'll be up against, but if we can get to the door without being seen, I have a plan."

They all nodded, so I continued.

"Axel, Alyita, and Tuthid will come with me. Assuming we don't get caught going down the hall, we'll stack up behind the door. Tuthid, at that point I want you in front of me. We'll rush in and try to surprise them. You attack low, I attack high. Axel will charge right. Alyita comes in last and goes left. If we're quick and don't trip over our own feet, we can take them by surprise."

"And if you get spotted in the hall?" Tsali asked.

"Then all bets are off." I shrugged. "We fight our way through."

Tsali nodded, considering. "I'll have a few follow you to help carry our gear back."

I nodded.

"All right," I said, forcing a confident smile. "Let's do this."

66

I opened the door and peered down the dark hallway.

There was no one in sight.

Moving slow and staying low, I eased along. The old plank floor creaked and groaned no matter how slowly I moved. I could only hope the assholes in the office couldn't hear us.

The hall was exactly as Alyita had described. A door on the left was said to lead to the old restroom. The door on the right was our destination. Straight down the hall, though, was another door she'd said led outside. If anyone came waltzing through, we would be screwed. If that happened, I'd chuck my sword at them and charge the office.

That didn't happen, though, and we got posted up in front of the office door. Tuthid stood just in front of me, his weapon ready. I'd made him a shorter spear, which I had aptly named Bill Shankspear.

With everyone in position, there was too much risk in asking if they were ready. So instead, I put my hand on the doorknob, took a breath, and swung it open.

For never having practiced a breach together, we did all right.

Tuthid shot forward, and I was right on his heels. Axel came in behind me and slid to the right. Alyita brought up the rear and went left. And...

We stood there, awkwardly surveying the scene.

We had expected a fight. Had expected guards.

There was no fight to be had.

And the guards, well...

I would have been less surprised if the room had been empty.

It wasn't.

The guards were there, but they were dead. All three of them. They were splayed out on the floor, blank eyes looking up at us.

They weren't alone. There was another creature in the room, one that was very much alive.

It was coiled up on a chair, also staring up at us.

A yellow python.

"The fuck?" I said, blinking to ensure what I was seeing was real.

Like a puppy, my familiar wagged its yellow tail.

"Weekend at Burmese?" I asked, staring at the snake. I blinked a few more times, just to be sure. It was her all right. "How the...?"

I glanced over at Axel, who was wide-eyed, and seemed every bit as confused as me.

How the hell had she gotten here? How the hell had she taken out the guards? How had she found us? How...anything? How was any of this possible? What. In. All. The. Fucks?

She raised her head, slitted eyes studying Tuthid. I wasn't sure if she was big enough to eat him, but she damn sure looked like she wanted to try.

I stepped between the moon-eyed man and my yellow python. "Tuthid is our friend."

I had no way to know if she understood me, and I was aware snakes didn't have shoulders, but I couldn't help feeling like Weekend at Burmese shrugged at me.

"Dude," Axel said, shaking his head. "I have *got* to get a familiar."

"I thought you said I was your familiar," I said.

"Dude," Axel repeated. "I have *got* to get a useful familiar."

"How is she here?" I asked. "How is this happening?"

"I don't know," he replied, "but it's like I always say: never look a gift snake in the mouth."

Alyita shoved past us and moved to the little corner table where all the weapons were piled. She scooped up her tomahawk and gave it a loving look. Then a long knife. Then a shorter knife. And another. And another. Then finally, her wand.

I raised an eyebrow. "Those all yours?"

She glanced over and gave me a sheepish look. "Figured I ought to be prepared."

Tuthid also made his way over and recovered a long knife, which to him was like a short sword. He strapped the belt and sheathe about his waist, but kept the knife in his hand. He carried Bill Shankspear in the other, which made me happy. Good to know my temporary weapons weren't going to waste.

Studying the table, though, I didn't see Sams's Arcane Ankh. Of course not. The bastards wouldn't have dumped an arcane artifact on the table with the regular gadgets. They'd probably tucked it away somewhere, hidden it under lock and key. Recovering it could prove challenging.

I stepped from the room, giving the others space to collect the stolen weapons while I watched the outside door.

Weekend at Burmese followed, coiling up just behind my feet. She was a good guard...snake.

So far, my plan had gone better than I could have hoped.

My sword had understood its assignment and snuck in, then made short work of our magical restraints. It had also allowed me to make weapons, something I hadn't thought of until that moment.

Speaking of things I couldn't have thought of...

I glanced down at the serpent coiled at my feet. She was staring up at me, and when I looked at her, she wagged her tail again. I didn't think that was normal behavior for snakes. Then again, neither was traveling eight hundred miles without a car. Or maybe she did have a car. Maybe she drove a big ole school bus. Or a bright yellow corvette. How the hell should I know?

Until that moment, I'd still been convinced Axel had hidden her in his luggage. Now, though?

She had somehow stalked us to an abandoned mine, slipped in unseen, and killed three guards in a tiny office. The same three guards I'd just been planning to take out. And she had done it without stirring up a commotion. I shuddered, considering. We hadn't heard a peep from that office. No screams. No cries. No bodies hitting the floor. How the hell had she done it? How the hell had she done *any* of it?

There was a strangeness in play that was beyond me. Maybe I'd figure it all out if I didn't get myself killed in the meantime, but I suspected this wasn't normal behavior for a familiar, either.

No time to worry about it just then. I was just happy she was on our side. She'd have made for a terrifying enemy.

Once all the weapons were secure, it was time for the next part of my plan.

The stupid part.

67

We charged.

Straight out the front door.

I led the way, bearing down on the nearest enemy.

We'd considered sneaking out the back door, but through the office windows, we saw there were guards posted there as well. Just not as many. Which might've made it seem like a better idea, but we'd only get one chance to surprise them. If we jumped the handful in the back, the small army in the front would come around. So, screw it... I wanted to charge the horde. I wanted to surprise them and bring the chaos. Plus, my wand was in the back of Gabby's pants. As was Axel's. And... Well, who am I kidding? I wanted to see the look on my former teammates' faces when I did exactly what they feared.

Just before I kicked open the door, it occurred to me how awkward and morbidly funny it would be if the others didn't charge out behind me.

Chortling to myself, I swung open the door and went for it.

The nearest asshole was a gray robe who had his back to me. I swung Dyrnwyn without pausing my stride, slicing him from hip to nip as I bolted past.

Tanya and Gabby stood just ahead.

I might've gone for my ex. She was certainly the ringleader of this merry band of butthole backstabbers. And she was, in many ways, the most dangerous.

And...

She *was* my ex.

But she didn't have my wand jammed in her back pocket. And while I had never bumped uglies with Gabby, her fall to the dark side hurt more than Tanya's did. My ex had broken my heart, sure. But that was long before they had betrayed everything they were supposed to stand for. By the time they'd revealed themselves as traitors, I already hadn't trusted her. I'd had years to get over her. And I had.

Gabby and Zeke, though? Their betrayal hurt more than anything. They'd been my friends, more so than some of the others. Malik, our boss, had always kept me at arm's length, never treating me as one of the team. Back then, I hadn't known it was because he was slapping sweat with Tanya. I'd just thought he didn't like me. Sanchez had always been an asshole. Sophie had been reserved and kept to herself. Barrett, Zeke, and Gabby, though? They'd been the ones I'd looked up to. Wizards I'd aspired to be like. People I'd admired.

And Gabby... Gabby had tried to kill me more times than the rest of them.

But mostly...I just wanted my damn wand back.

Gabby had turned at the commotion, probably just in time to see the gray robe fall in two slices. Her eyes widened, surprised. Shock quickly gave way to anger. Probably annoyance, too, since she had totally called it. She had warned them. But had they listened? Nope.

She leaped backward, going for her dagger and wand. My goal was to keep her from using either, so I plodded forward.

I might have had her, but somewhere from the left, someone cast something at me. My sword jerked in that direction, pulling me along with it. That was also new. Clearly it understood I was without my wand and it had to protect me. It worked. Sort of. My sword soaked up most of the blast, but it still staggered me.

I caught Gabby's grin as she raised her wand. "Not as sneaky as you'd like to think, Wyatt."

"That's because he's not the sneaky one," Axel said from just behind me. "I am. Watch."

Light erupted from Gabby's backside, lifting her right off the ground. Blueish bolts danced across her flesh as she began to tremor and convulse.

It only took me a moment to realize what he'd done.

The devious shithead had set up some kind of booby trap on his wand, one he could activate remotely somehow. That was a trick I definitely wanted to learn. It'd have to remain a mystery for the time being, however, because Tanya raised her staff and pointed it at me.

I threw my sword at her.

She'd been prepared for that and dodged. I hoped she'd raise her staff again and my sword would get her on the return. No luck. She spun, watching it come back. She rolled clear again, then turned to point her staff at me. I threw immediately.

This was a dangerous game. Throwing Dyrnwyn had become my go-to. When I'd dueled Chambers, he'd made it clear all the baddies knew that trick. They trained to avoid it.

I could still keep Tanya moving, but without my wand, anytime my sword wasn't in my hand, I was defenseless. If any of the other assholes took a potshot at me, I was toast.

None did, though. They all had their hands full.

Most of the Cherokee were spread out, calling on their medicine and flanking with their weapons.

Tuthid was in the middle of the fray as well. I glanced his way just in time to see him ram a gray robe right in the butt cheek with Bill Shankspear. That made me happy.

Tsali was engaged with a gray robe as well, with Sams just a few steps behind him. Two more Cherokee surrounded the Supreme Shaman, protecting him. That was good. Until we found his Arcane Ankh, someone needed to keep an eye on him. I wished I had a spare wand for him, but as it was, I didn't have one for myself. But if the old guy had any gas left in the tank, he was easily the most powerful magic-slinger on the field.

Meanwhile, Axel knelt over Gabby, rummaging through her pockets.

That accounted for everyone except...

Alyita darted at Tanya, tomahawk swinging. Tanya took a step back, avoiding the strike. In her excitement, Alyita had overswung. Tanya stepped back in and kneed her in the ribs. As Alyita doubled over, Tanya raised her staff, as if she intended to bludgeon her over the head.

I threw, trusting Dyrnwyn not to hurt Alyita.

And I ran toward them.

Eyes always watching for flying swords, Tanya shoved Alyita toward my oncoming sword and dove to the side.

Dyrnwyn did as I'd hoped and adjusted its flight to avoid striking Alyita.

And as Tanya rolled back to her feet, I was there. I lowered my shoulder and slammed into her, knocking her on her ass. I tried to land on top of her, but unfortunately, my momentum carried me right over and I went down on my face in the dirt.

I called Dyrnwyn back to me before I ever made it back to my feet.

I was a hair too slow, anyway. A second before my sword was in my hand, I caught sight of an incoming blur of red. It slammed into my shoulder, tearing right through my shirt and the flesh beneath it. Pain seared my shoulder, but I didn't have time to focus on it.

Dyrnwyn was back in my hand, and I chucked it at Tanya again before she could hit me with another spell.

Despite the fury, I rolled my shoulder, checking that it still worked. It did, so I ignored the pain and smell of burned bacon and called my sword back again.

Zeke stepped in front of Tanya to protect her with his mighty magical shield. I didn't know for sure whether Dyrnwyn could break his super shield, but intended to find out. At least until I heard Alyita yelp behind me.

I spun, seeing that one of the grays had crept up behind her. He had a hand around her throat and his wand up to her head.

"Told you I'd be back for you, sweet cheeks," he said, just before a sword appeared in the center of his forehead. My sword.

I dove as soon as I threw, knowing Tanya would try to hit me in the back with something. I was right and avoided another red blast.

Calling Dyrnwyn back to me, I moved alongside Alyita, ensuring she was all right. She appeared to be, but I knew I wasn't, not after hearing that creepy bastard's voice. Not after knowing what he'd intended. Some dudes needed a sword spiked through their wicked heads. I was happy to oblige.

I didn't have time to worry over her, though, because I noticed Axel was in trouble.

Gabby had come back to life and kicked his legs out from under him.

I ran to assist, but Gabby saw me coming. She summoned her stupid ninja cloud thing, blinding me. I probably should have stopped running then, but I feared she intended to stab Axel in the dark, so I kept on trucking.

Axel did not get stabbed.

He *did* get kicked, however.

By me.

I ran straight into him, slamming my foot into his side and tripping.

I landed on my face again, spitting out dirt. Fortunately, no one could see me through the fog, or else someone would have shot me in the back.

As the smoke dissipated, I caught sight of Axel, groaning and holding his ribs.

When he noticed me, he winced and said, "Did you happen to see a horse go by?"

"A horse?"

"Yeah. Pretty sure I just got kicked by a horse."

"Huh," I replied. "Well, uh, I don't see any horses. Must have gone invisible."

"Stupid invisible horses. When I find that fucker..."

I rolled to my feet and reach out a hand to help him. "If I see any invisible horses, I will let you know."

"Good. You can help me turn it into a glue stick." He glanced around suspiciously. "I don't see any invisible horses, either. But something kicked the shit out of me. It's just the two of us here, though..."

"Weird," I replied. "Guess it'll have to remain a mystery. We better get back into the shit."

"Oh, here," he said, holding up my wand.

I took it from him, delighted to have it back. "Thanks."

"No problem," he said, still wincing. I feared he might have a broken rib or two. "Couldn't get your revolver. Was trying to recover it when she kicked my legs out from under me, called me a pervert, and tried to kill me. Guess that's fair. I was rummaging around in her pants."

"Excuse me?"

He rolled his eyes. "That's where your revolver is. I wasn't doing anything weird."

"It's fine. We'll collect it off her corpse."

"Assuming she doesn't kill us first."

"That almost never happens," I reminded him.

"Right. Now, let's go find that damned horse."

I still didn't see any invisible horses.

I *did* see a lot more assholes headed our way. There were gray robes racing in from every direction. We were about to be severely outnumbered and overrun. I really needed the last piece of my plan to kick off. Unfortunately, it was outside of my control. I could only wait. And in the meantime, fight to the death.

Studying the battlefield, I decided to make my way back to Alyita. She was the one I felt the most responsible for. And she *was* the teenager caught in the middle of this grown-ass adult murder party.

Maybe it was wrong of me. Maybe it wasn't fair for me to worry about her more than the others. Maybe I should have treated her more like an adult. But...

Futz that.

If there was one person I wanted to walk away from all of this, it was her.

I started forward, but didn't make it a single step before a new problem appeared.

Wampus Cat dropped from the sky, landing a short distance ahead. She must have been watching the scuffle from atop the roof.

At nearly the same time, an Apple Devil charged around the side of a building. That had me confused, because I was pretty sure we'd killed that prick. Then two more rounded the corner behind him and I remembered that someone had said there was more than one half-squatch. *Great.* Just what we needed.

My former teammates, gray-robed summoners, Apple Devils, and Puss in Stilettos.

"Hi, lover," she said, purring at me.

"Hello, there," I said, doing the Obi Wan thing.

"I was so disappointed when you slipped away last time." She ran one pair of her hands down her body in what I assumed was supposed to be a seductive gesture. "Like what you see?"

"I'm allergic to cats," Axel said from beside me.

I chuckled. "That's what I said last time."

She shot Axel a glare. "I wasn't talking to you."

"I am also allergic," I said. "Remember?"

"A shame," she replied, showing off her fangs. "I thought we might ditch this shindig and go National Geographic on one another. Guess I'll just have to kill you instead."

"Bummer," I replied.

"Not really. I want to know how you taste."

And that was when the final phase of my plan finally fired off.

68

The Tennessee Wildman raced around the side of a bunkhouse and slammed into Wampus Cat, tackling her. She screeched like he'd grabbed her by the tail. The two rolled.

Eilidh charged in from around the other side of the building, the three knights on her heels.

She pointed her staff at a gray robe and blasted him off his feet. Another of the assholes looked down to see his buddy drop, then looked up just in time to catch an ice scythe in the throat.

A third gray robe also turned and raised his staff, but never had a chance to cast because Brother Barajas leaped on him, burying two daggers in his chest.

From the opposite direction, Parker appeared around another abandoned building and summoned a glowing white ethereal fist, which he promptly used to uppercut an Apple Devil out of his way.

Barrett was just behind him and barreled over a gray robe, smashing him from his feet with his enhanced close-range magic.

Anthony and Fred were with them, slinging spells as well.

And that... That concluded my plan.

Nope, it didn't get us out of the mess, rescue Mothman, or put an end to whatever wicked spell they had brewing, but I couldn't plan for everything.

Now...

The fight was on.

We'd have to wing it the rest of the way.

For a moment, the tables had been turned in our favor. We outnumbered our foes, and our backup had surprised them. Felt like we had a chance.

I saw Tanya moving toward Alyita. *Hell no.*

I ran toward them, raising my wand. Eilidh got there first.

She cast some kind of neon green, sparkly, magical thing, which hammered Tanya's defenses, staggering her.

Tanya replied with a red blast, likely the same one she'd tagged me with. The same one that had seared the shit out of my shoulder, which I was still trying very hard to ignore. Didn't have time for boring old pain.

As the two women clashed, Tanya cackled and jeered. "Ah, the witch! Of course! Tell me, how were my sloppy seconds?"

"Hey!" I shouted, which was dumb because I might've gotten the jump on her. I took exception to her insult, though. I wasn't sloppy.

Eilidh, though, took the jab in stride. "Pretty damned good, actually. Nothing better than finding something good some idiot threw away, you brain-dead bimbo."

"Ha!" Tanya laughed, casting another attack. "Wyatt was a bigger disappointment in the bedroom than he is in life."

Eilidh blocked the attack and raised an eyebrow. "He's become a Blade Mage, has loads of interesting friends, and I hear he's rich now, too. Seems like he's doing all right. And as far as the bedroom goes, not that I'm one to kiss and tell, but maybe you were the problem, bitch. I had no complaints."

In another setting, this conversation might have been hot. As it was...

Oh, who was I kidding? Eilidh standing up for me *was* hot. Hot as hell!

I cast a pumpkin blast at Tanya and looked for an opportunity to chuck my sword at her. I didn't have a clean shot.

Seeing that we were ganging up on his leading lady, Zeke moved in, raising his shield. The old dude was a beast at shielding. One of the best I'd known. Back then, nothing had broken through his defenses. I doubted he had lost a step. Probably had grown stronger.

Tanya knelt beside him, raising her staff to her shoulder. This was their classic move. His shield would protect her while she lined up one of her devastating snipey mc'snipey spells. Left to do their thing, they'd pick my allies apart one by one.

There was one thing I was pretty sure Zeke's shield wouldn't stop.

I threw my sword.

I'd been right before. Zeke wasn't as agile as Tanya or Gabby. Still, he managed to dive clear, narrowly avoiding the Dyrnerang.

I cast a pumpkin blast as soon as I'd thrown, hoping to catch him unprepared. No dice. Zeke was so good at shielding, he didn't need his full concentration to keep up his defenses.

Tanya rolled clear as well. They'd both done their homework. Both turned around, watching my sword come back toward them. Both dove clear again.

Straight up bullshit! No fun at all!

All around us, chaos flowed, but with few casualties so far. I didn't think we'd lost anyone yet, but I didn't have time to take a full account.

Well, I *did* know I'd lost my snake again. Weekend at Burmese had slunk off. I had no idea where she was and couldn't afford to worry about her.

I also didn't know where Gabby had slipped away to, and that was a greater concern, especially while I was engaged with Tanya and Zeke. I expected her to pop out behind me at any moment. Or behind Eilidh or Axel. That scared the hell out of me.

Sophie had disappeared as well. No real surprise there.

Maybe the two of them had slunk off together. Maybe we'd scared them.

Ha! More likely they were gathering reinforcements.

Speaking of reinforcements, I spied several small figures racing to join the fray.

The moon-eyed people.

Feogh led the way, a long knife in one hand. Basically a sword for him. In the other hand, he had a gnarled branch, which I assumed was some sort of casting rod. In my hand, it would have looked like a fat wand. In his, it was too big to be called a wand. Too short to be a staff. A casting rod, then.

I expected the moon-eyes to go straight after Tuthid, to seek and kill the one who'd dared challenged Feogh's leadership.

Instead, they ran toward Anthony and Fred. Apparently they wanted to finish their business with those two. *Uh oh.*

Using mind-speak, I warned Anthony. *"Heads up. The garden gnomes have arrived, and they're headed your way."*

"Oh, hell," he replied. *"Not these little assholes again. Fuck this. I'm out."*

I looked up and saw Anthony had his gaze on the little guys, a look of terror on his face. Were the little dudes really that scary?

Size wasn't everything, I supposed. Anthony was an ass, but he wasn't a coward. If he was afraid of the moon-eyed people, he had a good reason to be. I made a snap decision.

"Axel," I said, glancing over at him. "Help Eilidh. I've got to do something."

He didn't argue. My best friend was a goofball, but a reliable goofball. Made me feel kind of bad about the invisible horse thing. Almost.

I reached out to Anthony again. *"I have a plan. Come to me. Bring Fred."*

Then I raced toward Tuthid.

"Wait," Anthony replied. *"Why are you running toward one of those little bastards? Hell no!"*

I cursed. There wasn't time to argue. There wasn't time for him to be an ass.

I considered screaming at him. Considered barking that it was an order. But I'd never much cared for working for people like that. Besides, ass or no, he'd volunteered for this mission. So instead, I said, *"This one is on our side. If you hurry, I think he can solve your problem. Trust me. Or stay there and get murdered by garden gnomes. Your choice."*

"Damn it," he replied with a groan. *"On the way."*

Tuthid had a problem of his own: an Apple Devil had its sights on him. Probably assumed the little guy would be an easy target. He'd been mistaken. Despite his wee little legs, Tuthid was quick. Every time the half-squatch pounced, Tuthid darted clear, but not before tagging the Apple Devil with his knife-sword or Bill Shankspear. Problem was, neither did much damage.

I'd have to save him. Or so I thought.

Tuthid dodged another attack, but this time, instead of stabbing or slashing at the half-squatch, he tucked his weapons under one arm and clapped his hands.

A second Tuthid appeared beside the first.

The Apple Devil came up short, staring at the two tiny figures.

Tuthid clapped his hands again.

A third appeared. Then a fourth. And a fifth. Each was an identical representation of the last, with weapons and everything.

An illusion spell?

Maybe. The half-squatch wasn't taking any chances. As the five Tuthids charged, the Apple Devil fled.

I made it over to the Tuthids, all of whom were laughing at their retreating foe.

"Not to ruin your fun," I said, pointing with my wand, "but we've got trouble headed this way."

All the Tuthids turned as one, seeing the other moon-eyes moving in. Their expressions turned sour. They tucked their weapons under their arms and clapped once again. Only one Tuthid remained. He looked up at me. "Tuthid...afraid."

I nodded, understanding. "You aren't alone. Not this time."

He turned away.

Anthony and Fred caught up to us then.

"They're still behind us," Fred said, glancing over his shoulder. "Fuck, fuck, fuck."

"It's fine," I said. "We want them to come this way."

"I don't think you understand," Fred said, turning to face me. "Those little guys are terrifying." His gaze moved to Tuthid. "No offense."

"Guys," I said, motioning toward Tuthid. "This is Tuthid Pugh, my friend."

The little guy looked up at me, eyes wide. "Truly? Your friend?"

I nodded, then turned my attention back to Anthony and Fred. "He needs to kill Feogh one on one. We need to make sure the others don't intervene. Once he wins, the remaining moon-eyes will be on our side. Got it? Good, because we don't have time for questions."

Feogh and the others closed in.

I stepped to the side, ensuring he had a clear line of sight on Tuthid.

That brought him up short.

I grinned at Feogh, the little fucker. "A challenge was made, but has gone unanswered."

"It was answered," Feogh spat.

"No," I replied. "Tuthid does not lie. Your friends ganged up on him. Tell me, do all the moon-eyed people lack honor, or just you, Feogh?"

Feogh only scowled, but the others seemed uneasy. Good. That meant they weren't comfortable with what they'd done. Exactly as I'd hoped.

"We are not afraid of you, wizard," Feogh said, raising his gnarled rod.

"You should be," I replied, doing my best to look menacing. "You're going to answer Tuthid's challenge, and this time, your friends aren't going to jump in, or you'll have to fight us all. And this time, Feogh, I'll cut you down my damned self."

I thought it was a pretty good threat. Feogh seemed unimpressed. His lackeys, though, they were nervous.

I decided to press my luck. "No matter how this ends, the moon-eyed people will know of your treachery. They will know that Feogh, and those who followed him, betrayed one of their own. That you are all without honor."

Feogh snorted, studying the bruised and battered Tuthid. The same Tuthid he'd bullied countless times. The same one who was already exhausted from battle.

He liked his odds. I could see it on his evil little face.

"Fine," He said, shrugging. "Come and die, Tuthid."

I glanced down at Tuthid, who was staring up at me.

"Friend?" he asked again.

"Friend," I repeated.

He nodded, then raised Bill Shankspear and thumped it against his chest. "Friend."

Then he stepped forward to face his boss.

Yeah, ole Fucker Feogh liked what he'd seen when he looked at Tuthid. Thing was... I did, too. But where Feogh saw a soft target, I saw someone who had nothing to lose.

Feogh wanted to live. Wanted to rule over his people. He craved power. Dominance.

And poor Tuthid Pugh, he thought himself already dead. All he had was this one chance, one opportunity to make things right. He figured he was dead either way. And that...

That made him a dangerous little man.

They charged each other, weapons clashing. Their movements were little more than a blur, hard to follow even for my experienced eyes.

Neither used magic. I reckoned that was against their rules, which was kind of disappointing because after healing me and seeing Tuthid's doppelgangers, I was curious what else they could do.

Anthony leaned in close, whispering. "So, uh, what do we do if your little pal loses?"

"Fight and die," I replied, grinning. "Quit stressing, Burns. Enjoy the break while you can."

Anthony snorted, but that was the truth of it.

All around us, our allies were fighting for their lives while we watched a duel. It was a bit of luck that none of our other enemies charged in to attack us. Maybe they assumed we were outnumbered by moon-eyed people and didn't need to get involved. Whatever the case, they left us to it, and I wasn't going to complain. Always nice to catch my breath.

And still the two warriors clashed, their weapons meeting time and again.

Feogh had expected an easy fight. He'd been a fool. Tuthid stuck with him, trading blows in equal measure.

I took my eyes from their fight and again assessed the greater battle at hand.

Sadly, we had lost a few of the Cherokee, but there were far more gray-robed bodies on the dirt than there were of our allies.

Eilidh and Axel were still trading spells with Tanya and Zeke. Barrett had joined them. No surprise there. It was good, though, because his presence alone kept Tanya from kneeling to do one of her snipey snipe spells. She knew how quick he was. Couldn't risk taking a knee when the big guy could maul her like a grizzly bear.

Parker had Alyita near him, as well as a few of the Cherokee. I trusted him to watch out for her. Grimmy might have been a choirboy, but he was also a damned nasty battle mage.

Tsali and the other Cherokee were still circling around Sams, protecting him while he... I blinked. The Supreme Shaman sat on the ground, legs crossed, hands in his lap. Was he...meditating? In the middle of a battle? *Whatever.* I was sure he knew what he was doing.

Back to the trouble directly in front of me, Feogh drew first blood.

Tuthid staggered back, a deep cut on his shoulder.

Feogh grinned with all the arrogance of a pint-sized asshole.

Tuthid didn't react. Didn't reply at all. Just charged right back in.

Fucker Feogh wasn't prepared for that. He wasn't prepared for the pint-sized fury that was Tuthid Pugh. He backed toward his allies, but his foot caught and he tumbled backward, landing on his butt.

The leader of the moon-eyed people stared up at Tuthid, his eyes wide with fear. Once, he had tormented Tuthid; now, Tuthid was the tormentor. The fear in Feogh's eyes was palpable.

He raised his gnarled rod and a blast of energy smashed into Tuthid, knocking him back end over end.

Gasps tore from the other moon-eyed folk, but none spoke. None intervened.

Tuthid landed in a crumpled pile of himself, not moving. I couldn't tell whether he was breathing. Whether he was alive.

Feogh glanced up at the shocked faces of his people staring down at him.

"What are you waiting for?" he asked, motioning toward us. "Kill!"

The moon-eyes didn't move. Not at first. They stared from their treacherous boss, then at us, and looked back again, like a hobbit's tale.

I wasn't sure why they were surprised by Feogh's treachery. He'd shown his ass more than once. They'd helped him, even. In fact, it surprised me that it surprised them. Feogh had shown us all who he was.

As the moon-eyes slowly raised their weapons, Anthony said, "Boss?"

"Looks like our break is over," I said, raising my weapons and still trying to look mean.

It didn't help.

A blast of energy walloped my shield, staggering me.

Anthony cast a blue blast of energy, knocking the caster back. The rest raised their weapons.

Much to my surprise, Fred stepped in front of me, raising his shield to protect me. A nice sentiment, but his shield was crushed a moment later and he flew back into me, knocking us both over.

Anthony stayed on his feet an entire second longer than us, then he, too, was knocked on his ass.

Okay, so maybe he was right to be worried about the little tyrants. They were nasty.

One of them raised their own wand, which looked like a twig he'd picked up along the way. The little dude pointed it at Anthony, but Fred got his wand up first and blasted the moon-eye with an orange blast. It knocked him back into his buddies and they tumbled like bowling pins.

I rolled up to my knees, ready to throw my sword. I didn't want to, though. Didn't want to kill any of them. Sure, they'd been bastards, but that was all because of Feogh, who was currently hiding behind his buddies. If he were out of the way, the rest might help us.

A blur shot past me.

Tuthid.

Roaring, he shoved the nearest moon-eye out of his way. The rest darted clear of his fury.

He only had eyes for Feogh.

The leader had barely made it to his feet when Tuthid pounced. It didn't matter.

I was reminded of that old Jim Croce song, "You Don't Mess Around with Jim."

Tuthid slashed with his knife-sword and jabbed with Bill Shanks-pear, his movements a blur. By the time he was done, Feogh was cut in more than a hundred places, but was somehow still on his feet.

His eyes were wide and glossed over. Maybe he didn't believe what was happening.

Roaring, Tuthid, slammed Bill Shankspear right through Feogh's heart.

The leader of the moon-eyed people blinked. He might have fallen, but Tuthid still had hold of the spear. He raised a foot and planted it on Feogh's chest, then ripped his weapon clear. Fucker Feogh fell.

Dead.

The other moon-eyes stared at Tuthid with something between awe and terror.

Covered in his enemy's blood, and much of his own, Tuthid thumped Bill Shankspear against his chest and raised it to the sky. "I am Tuthid Pugh. I defeated Feogh." He spat on Feogh's corpse, then fixed his gaze on the others. "I am chief now. You follow?"

The other moon-eyes glanced between one another. A few stared down at Feogh. One by one they all nodded.

"Good," Tuthid said, then pointed Bill Shankspear at me. "The Blade Mage made this mighty weapon for Tuthid Pugh. A great weapon. It slayed Fucker Feogh. It is called Bill Shankspear."

He raised it again.

The others moved closer, their glowing eyes studying the weapon in awe. The same damned weapon I'd cut from an ancient bedframe. *Meh*. Who was I to judge?

"The Blade Mage is our friend," Tuthid said. "We stand with him. Always."

The others nodded, looking at me anew. Gone was their animosity. In its place was something akin to respect.

Anthony leaned in close. "What the hell is happening?"

"Honestly?" I shrugged. "I have no idea."

"We fight!" Tuthid said, pumping his spear. "We fight for the Blade Mage! Friends! Always!"

The others raised their weapons in agreement.

And then Tuthid led a pint-sized charge into our enemies.

69

Things were going reasonably well.

We'd won over the moon-eyes and were still on our feet. All my former teammates had fled the field while I had watched Tuthid's duel. Wampus Cat and the Tennessee Wildman's royal rumble had led them off-screen. The Apple Devils had followed. That just left a few gray robes, who'd backed off, taking potshots from a distance. I wanted to help Wildman, but we'd have to find him first. Otherwise... Yeah, things were going reasonably well.

Maybe, for once, things would go our way.

Ha! I knew better than that.

No sooner had that slimy worm of a thought wriggled through my skull...

Something howled.

I sighed.

Probably should've been scared. Probably should've pissed myself.

I knew that sound. It hadn't come from the mouth of a human, nor any animal.

Fucking demons.

So annoying.

I'd wondered why there weren't more assholes attacking us. There was my answer.

Instead of engaging in a magical fisticuff, the other grays had been busy summoning their pets.

Scanning the battlefield, I spotted Brother Barajas. The two other knights were alongside him. For the magical battle, they'd been a little out of their element. Now, they were about to become the stars of the show.

As soon as I approached, Barajas said, "I heard 'em."

"Glad you brought your sword?" I asked.

He snorted.

"Well, I am. With Dyrnwyn, that makes four of us who can slay the fuckers."

"Four ain't so many," he said, rubbing his chin. "How do you want to play it?"

I turned, surveying the field. We were still in front of the bunkhouse. There was another across from it, turned longways. That meant there were two thoroughfares to reach us. Except there was another bunkhouse in the middle of one of those lanes, which split it into two smaller paths. They would come at us from one or more of three lanes.

Three paths to guard.

Three knights.

We would be stretched thin.

If I'd had the time, I might've lamented being left in charge of this shindig. I certainly hadn't asked to be, but so far, it seemed everyone was happy taking my lead. I would have expected Sams to take charge. This was his territory, and he *was* the Supreme Shaman of the Appalachian Argument. His eyes were still closed, though, lost in his trance.

I also might've expected Tsali to take charge. I wasn't sure of his rank in the Cherokee. Didn't remember it being mentioned when we first met. Obviously he was an elder. Could've been a peace chief, too. Or even a war chief. Whatever his role, clearly the others took their queues from him.

And there was Parker, who had a habit of acting like he was in charge. This time, I might not have minded. He had experience leading teams in the field. He'd been a senior shamus, after all. For once, it seemed like he was going to let me run the show. Lucky me.

Even Brother Barajas, the quiet and surly knight, was the turcopolier and Sergeant at Arms of the Memphis Knights, third in command behind Victor and Uriah. He had more experience leading than me, too.

I was reminded of what Mary Beth had said.

The best leaders are those who step up when no one else is willing. Who take charge when it's needed.

And I... I needed to make a decision. Quickly.

The three knights were still gathered around me, waiting. Just three of them. With an unknown number of demons on the way.

I knew what to do.

No, that wasn't quite true.

I didn't know what to do. Not really. I just knew what was coming and had an idea that might get us through.

"Three teams," I said. "One of you standing with each. I'll be the flex, since I can throw my sword. Barajas, you're with my Squirrel Nuts. Take the big lane."

He nodded.

I pointed at the next knight. "You're with the Cherokee." Glancing at the final knight, I said, "You're with the moon-eyed people."

They didn't argue or ask questions; they split off to go do their jobs. Had to love the practicality of the Memphis Knights.

Racing toward Tsali, I used mind-speak to relay my plan to Parker and asked him to gather our team. Then I reached Tsali and quickly explained it to him. Then I ran to Tuthid and did the same.

The teams began forming up, standing shoulder to shoulder across the lanes, their knights in the center.

Everyone got in place just before the first of the demons appeared around the bend.

A wolf-scorpion-baby.

Nasty little fuckers.

I'd met them before, back in Memphis. It had the body of a wolf, the stinger of a scorpion, but the adorable little face of a human infant. Sort of. Its face was pale white, and translucent, allowing a view of the meat and black ichor squishing about within. It *did* have those cutesy wootsy chubby cheeks, though.

The monster just stood there, staring at us with its creepy little face. All innocence and menace.

Another came around the corner a few moments later. One of those centipede-spider-sucky-face-dudes. The ones that had the centipede bottom half, the human male torso, and the weird spider legs coming from its back. I would never forget the weird sucking sounds it made with its butthole mouth. I never had figured out whether they were trying to kill me or kiss me.

And, of course, the next was one of the spindly ones, the big skinny pricks with the weird joints that moved in strange directions. I hadn't forgotten how quick they were.

More and more packed in, including new varieties I'd not yet had the pleasure of meeting.

One was a big-ass translucent snake. I could see right through its scales to its spine and all of its internal organs. It, too, had the head of a human baby. Why wouldn't it?

Another had the body of a gorilla, but with a super long ostrich neck and beak.

More and more arrived, piling in, all different shapes and sizes.

I sensed a shift around me: uneasy confidence replaced with fear. Only a few of us had faced these little nightmares before. Not that having met the scary fuckers previously made them any less terrifying. Everyone, it seemed, was on edge. Growing more terrified by the moment.

They came from all three lanes, surrounding us on all sides. No doubt they planned to hit all three groups at once. But they hadn't attacked yet. Their mere presence was sucking the fight out of my fellow defenders.

I had to do something. Had to boost morale. Somehow.

There was only one thing I could think of.

I started laughing.

It wasn't forced. Wasn't fake. It was a genuine laugh, bellowing from the pit of my gut, from that dark place where you chose to either laugh or cry.

People gave me sideways glances.

Parker raised an eyebrow and so did Barrett. Fred looked at me like he'd never seen me before. Eilidh gave me a real look of concern, as did Alyita. Even Axel glanced over and said, "Dude."

"Don't you get it?" I asked, turning in a slow circle, ensuring everyone was paying attention. "Don't you know what this means?" When no reply came, I continued, "It means we're winning. Means we've scared the shit out of the grays. Wimpy-ass warlock wannabes. They couldn't take us in a straight fight, so they slunk away, tails tucked, and called out their pets. And you know what else?"

Still moving in a slow circle, I laughed again.

"I've faced these scary little bastards before, and frankly, they aren't that fucking tough!"

I hurled Dyrnwyn at the mass.

The dark wizards might've been training to avoid my throws, but their pets weren't. I couldn't say how many that first throw slew. Too many to count. Dyrnerang hacked through demons like they were made of butter. They melted in steaming piles of black goo.

Actually, I'd forgotten about the stinky ichor puddles. Shit was gross.

The rest howled their fury.

"Oh, shut up, you whiners!" I called back at them. "You'll get your turn to die like your friends!"

As soon as Dyrnwyn returned to my hand, I raced to the next lane and threw again, carving up another pile of beasties.

The demons charged.

If there were spells to kill them, we didn't know them, so our magic-slingers used force spells to push the monsters back, forcing them to collide and trip over one another. Whenever one got close, the assigned knight would dart in to kill it.

One knight per lane wasn't enough to kill them all. Wasn't even enough to keep up with the charge, but the others kept the buggers at bay via magic and melee.

My original plan was to run to whichever side needed help and hack down demons as well. Chucking Dyrnerang at them was loads more fun. Also, charging in and hacking wouldn't have done a damned bit of good. There were too damned many, and they were too damned quick.

I raced from one lane to another, throwing my sword and heading on to the next before I even called it back. Turned out, throwing my sword was a much more effective tactic. For once, I was the most effective killer on the battlefield. Wished I'd known the Dyrnerang trick in Memphis.

But then... That felt like a lifetime ago.

And it felt like I was a different person.

Maybe it was just my exhausted, adrenaline-fueled brain, but I wasn't sure the "me" from Memphis would've been able to get this far. Likely I would have been dead a few times over. Certainly this rag-tag band of warriors wouldn't have been so inclined to follow me. I'd grown a lot since then. Sometimes, it didn't seem like it, but it was true. I had.

It wasn't just my abilities, the new wand, or my growing connection with my sword.

It was me. I was changing. Growing into my role.

Weird.

I wasn't so sure that former version of myself could've pieced together this location, convinced the team to join me, broken everyone out of their magical binds, escaped the bunkhouse, rallied the troops to fight, enacted a plan to win over the moon-eyed people in the middle of a battle, and killed swaths of demons, all while being the de facto leader. I wasn't so sure that former version of myself could have even faked the confidence needed to make others want to follow my lead.

It *was* interesting to consider how much I'd changed.

It *would* be interesting to see how far I might still go.

Shame I was about to die and would never find out.

Racing from lane to lane and chucking my sword over and over was a lot of work. I wasn't sure how long I could keep it up. And I wasn't fast enough. Each time I made the circle, more demons were pressing in. Dyrnwyn was incredibly effective, but I needed three blade mages to make this work. Maybe six, so we could take breaks. Or all the Memphis Knights.

The beasts pressed closer and closer, piling in around the defenders.

There was nothing for it but to keep moving. I'd run and throw until my legs gave out or my arm fell off.

As I ran to the Squirrel Nuts side, one of the gorilla-ostrich demons nearly broke through. Barrett hammered the monster, launching it back into its friends. But as he did, it spat out a long, toad-like tongue, which coiled around his arm. It tugged, pulling the big guy toward the horde.

I was beside him then, swinging my sword through the tongue and cutting him free.

I was too slow, though. His momentum was already carrying him forward, toward certain death.

Axel grabbed onto his belt and leaned back. A good effort, but Barrett was too big for him to anchor.

Anthony stepped in and also grabbed the back of Barrett's belt. Together, they yanked the big guy back across the fighting line. But all three tumbled backward, falling on their asses.

A gap was created.

The demons howled and darted forward, an opportunity presented.

I jumped in, swinging Dyrnwyn from side to side, hacking through tails, faces, torsos, and necks. More specifically, I sliced through a wolf-scorpion-baby's stinger, an ostrich neck, a skinny torso, and a precious baby face.

Then I threw my sword and took off again, letting the others refill the gap.

We'd saved Barrett, but it had cost me time. Precious time. Already, the other two lanes were being pressed on.

The Cherokee crew were being pushed back, losing ground.

The moon-eyed people hadn't yet lost ground, but weren't faring any better. I glanced their way in time to see a monkey-like six-armed critter jump over the defenders and land in their midst. The demon spun, lashing out with a big tail, knocking down several of Tuthid's crew, including their assigned knight.

The demons pounced.

I threw my sword right over the fallen knight's head, hammering through the demons tearing at him.

My throw saved him, but I'd made a mistake. In a rush to save the knight, I'd thrown in a straight line rather than my normal Dyrnerang curve, so I didn't carve up so many. Not nearly enough.

I called my sword back and threw it again while Tuthid helped the fallen knight to his feet.

And again, I'd lost more precious time.

The Cherokee were faltering, but so were the Squirrel Nuts, which I had just left. Both lines would snap at any moment.

There was nothing I could do.

I just wasn't quick enough.

Even as I had the thought, one of the skinny ones slipped through a gap in the Cherokee line. It bowled over two of the defenders, knocking them from their feet. Their assigned knight charged, hacking down the monster, but that opened his back to a wolf-scorpion-baby.

A Cherokee woman—I didn't know her name—leaped in front of the knight, taking the stinger to protect him. It was among the bravest acts I'd ever witnessed. She didn't know the knight. Likely didn't even know his name. But she understood that if he fell, then her friends and allies would fall. She gave her life to save the others. And she didn't hesitate.

There was a time when I would have blamed myself. Would have cursed myself for being too slow. But that was something else I'd learned along the way. There were many things I could take blame for. Many mistakes I'd made. But I couldn't be everywhere and do everything. And also, perhaps more importantly, to have laid that blame on myself would have diminished the sacrifice she made. No. It wasn't mine to take. I couldn't claim that guilt, but I could damn sure remember her sacrifice.

And her screams.

I'd like to say she died quietly, Stoic, even.

That would be a lie.

She died screaming, a sound I would never forget.

But the demon died screaming, too, my sword tearing its torso from its ass.

The gap was open now. More demons pounced, pushing through.

No. No. No.

This was it. We were screwed.

My only option was to jump in and start hacking them down,

which meant I wouldn't make it back to the other lanes in time to help them. I was staring at a tsunami, helpless to stop the waves from crashing down.

I charged in, sword swinging, cutting down demon after demon.

It wasn't enough. They swarmed around me, breaking the line.

Risking a glance over my shoulder, I saw the Squirrel Nuts line was broken as well. And the moon-eye.

I couldn't stop it.

I couldn't save everyone.

I couldn't save any of them.

A blur shot past my head and a raspy voice shouted, "Enough!"

Supreme Shaman Sams's voice.

I spun, seeing the blur which had shot past my head was an ankh.

His ankh. An Arcane Ankh.

Just like my sword, it was the ankh which had chosen him. Apparently, whatever magic the dark wizards had used to keep it from him weren't strong enough to hold it forever.

He pointed it to the sky.

A blast of white light shot from the staff, spreading like a mushroom cloud, washing over us.

Something wonderful happened.

Something magical.

Demons went flying. They were hurled backward, smacked by the white blast, but the rest of us remained untouched. While the demons tumbled over each other, battered around like bowling pins, the humans and moon-eyes were left standing where we were.

The demons howled their displeasure. Poor things.

As soon as they were on their feet, they charged again. Another blast sent them reeling once more.

And our lines re-formed.

I wasn't sure what kind of magic Sams was brewing up, but I was damned glad he'd finally joined the party.

He turned his attention toward the Squirrel Nuts lane and summoned forth a giant blob of light, which shot down in the center of the demons. Those weren't merely knocked down. Instead, white lightning arched through the horde and they all...exploded.

Every demon facing my team erupted into piles of goo.

Wow.

A pained look crossed Sams's features, and I suspected that spell, whatever it was, had taken a toll on him.

His voice spoke into my mind. *"Wyatt, take your team and go save Mothman."*

"What about you?" I asked, moving toward my team, who were all staring at the goo pond at their feet.

"We'll mop up the demons and come find you."

"You make it sound easy."

"Maybe not so easy. Not sure I can manage another blast like that, but I can certainly push them back and let the knights tear them apart. Might take a bit, but we'll join you as soon as we can."

"Your power and experience might be better suited for saving Mothman."

"If I were twenty years younger, no doubt. Gods, how I miss my seventies. So much more energy back then."

That brought me up short. Shaman Sams was in his nineties? No wonder he'd needed a few breaks along the way.

"Can you handle them?" I asked. *"Truly? I won't leave you all here to die."*

"I have a little life left in me yet. Don't fuss over my old bones."

"All right," I said, then paused again. *"I don't know how to stop the working."*

"You'll figure it out, Wyatt. I believe in you."

"Thank you," I replied, and meant it. *"Guess you had one left in you after all."*

"Guess so. One more thing…"

"Yeah?"

"Should the worst come to pass and one of us falls, I want you to know it has been an honor to fight alongside you. I'm glad you came to Appalachia. You remind me so much of your father. Godspeed, Blade Mage."

70

We raced toward the tower.

It was just Squirrel Nuts Squad with our temporary additions of Eilidh and Alyita. It would have to do.

I'd considered leaving Alyita with Sams, but had cast the idea aside. I doubted she'd be any safer with them. Maybe less so. And I knew she'd just sneak off and come looking for us anyway. I think, maybe, sometimes, part of being a leader is knowing when you can't force your will on others and instead figure out how to work around their stubbornness. Or maybe I didn't have a damned clue. Either way, I brought her with us.

There was one final bunkhouse between us and the tower. We piled up along the back wall, scouring for enemies.

Easing to the edge, I peeked around the corner.

I had a clear view of the tower, where Mothman was still bound, still suffering, and still in need of saving. Symbols glowed all around him, all around the tower, and even on the ground at his feet. It seemed the base of the tower was in the middle of one particularly large glyph.

What concerned me the most, though...

Mothman was alone.

No guards. No hooded figures roaming about. Not even a demon.

Just a few tall trees nearby. That was it.

Leaning over my shoulder so he could also see, Axel said, "So, that's a big fat trap."

"Yup," I replied, and ducked back around the wall, thinking.

The others each took a turn peering around the corner, taking in the vacant patch of ground.

Finally, Parker asked, "So, what do you want to do?"

"Anything in the Cabal's SOP for walking straight into a trap?" I asked.

He shook his head. "Nothing you've ever done has been covered in the handbook, Wyatt."

"Wait, there's a handbook?" Axel asked, eyes widening. "That would have been useful to know, like, years ago. Would have kept me out of so much trouble."

"You know," Anthony said, rubbing his chin, "sometimes I can't tell when you're making a joke or just being stupid."

"Anthony," Axel said, tone reproachful. "That is no way to speak to your future step-father."

I held up my hand before the two fell into another insult-fest.

"Okay," I said, gathering my thoughts. "Obviously it's a trap. Best guess, they'll wait until we get out into the open and rain hell on us. If my former teammates are there—and we have to assume they are—then Tanya will be posted up. Everyone should understand how her snipey snipe spell works. It's a two-phase working."

"A what?" Fred asked, raising an eyebrow.

"Do you know how anti-tank missiles work?" I asked, glancing around. I got a few nods, including one from Alyita, which surprised me. "They have an initial charge that strikes first, breaking through the tank's armor. Then a secondary charge slides through and wrecks shit. That's basically how her snipey snipe spell works. It has two blasts. The first will rend your shield. The second will smoke your ass. Got it?"

Everyone nodded.

"And expect Gabby to attack from behind. I think we've all seen that at this point. So keep one eye on your butt. If you hear so much as a whisper behind you, turn and fire. No hesitation."

"Understood," Parker said. The impatience in his tone suggested he wanted me to get on to the plan portion of my plan.

I ignored him.

"Zeke is a master at shielding. Don't bother trying to break his defenses. Sophie, well, I don't know what the hell she is anymore. Used to be our intel person. Never worked in the field, but I know she's got some attack spells now. Can't say what all the gray robes can do. And if we run into any demons, I'll take them down with Dyrnwyn."

"So, what's the plan?" Parker asked.

"We don't know how to stop the working," Eilidh said. "That's our biggest problem."

"And it's probably booby-trapped," Axel added. "That's what I would've done. I would have booby-trapped the shit out the area around the tower, just to blast your punk-asses."

"And," Anthony added, "if they're posted up like you say, then there's a good chance they saw us playing peek-a-boo just now. Probably know we're here."

"So...we're screwed," Fred said.

"That's the spirit," Alyita said, rolling her eyes.

"So, what's the plan?" Parker asked for the umpteenth time.

"Oh, Blade Mage!" a voice purred from afar. "Come out and play, lover!"

I was instantly reminded of that old movie, *The Warriors*. Except Wampus Cat wasn't clinking glass bottles, and referring to me as "lover" lost some of the luster. *Icky*.

Peeking around the corner again, I spotted her.

She stood near the tower beneath a tall tree. She wasn't alone.

The Tennessee Wildman was on his knees before her, beaten and bloodied. An Apple Devil stood on either side of him.

Seeing my head poked out, she offered me a little wave.

I waved back. No sense in being rude.

Then I ducked around the corner again and frowned at Anthony. "Guess that answers your question. They know we're here."

And something else became apparent as well.

"They're using Wildman as bait. Which means my old pals are out there. Wampus Cat doesn't know me well enough to think I'd try to rescue him against impossible odds. Tanya may think poorly of me, but Zeke and Gabby? They know I won't leave an ally behind. So, as Axel put it, this is definitely one big fat trap."

Axel wore a smug smile. "I'm right about the booby-traps, too. Wait and see."

"Yeah, well, that's a problem we'll have to figure out when we get there," I said, studying their faces.

They were all watching me, waiting for me to make a call. Waiting for me to lay out a plan. Problem was...I didn't have one.

But I noticed Parker was about to speak, and before he could repeat his monotonous question again, I started thinking aloud.

"I'll take point. But I'll need two volunteers to roll into this trap with me."

"Oh, you know I'm down to clown," Axel said, grinning. Of course he'd be eager to walk right into a trap. And of course I was taking him.

Eilidh seemed about to volunteer, but I looked up at Parker. "And you, Grimmy."

"Thought you were looking for volunteers?" he said, frowning.

"Changed my mind," I said, shrugging. "Operational efficiency. Surely *that's* in the Cabal handbook. Keep up."

He snorted.

"I need someone with a beastly shield," I said, expression serious. "No telling what we're walking into, and don't forget what I said about Tanya. They may not know Eilidh and Alyita are with us, so let's use that to our advantage."

Parker nodded, which was good. I wanted his buy-in. Needed to know my idea wasn't completely asinine.

I continued. "They may attack the moment we step out into the open. Or they may let us get closer. I want the rest of you to wait here until the fun pops off. If Tanya fires, maybe you can see where she's hitting us from and force her into cover. But more importantly, I want you watching our asses in case Gabby pops out behind one of us."

"Eilidh should do that," Alyita said, her expression serious.

I blinked, trying to piece together her logic. She barely knew the witch. Certainly didn't know what she was capable of. Eilidh seemed as confused by the suggestion as I was. Finally, I just asked. "Why?"

Alyita grinned. "Because she likes staring at your ass."

Eilidh's face reddened and she looked away. I'm sure my face looked the same. The others, though, they found it amusing. Except for Parker, who scowled at our immaturity.

I continued explaining the plan. "It's up to you when you make your move, but I would like Eilidh, Alyita, and Barrett to stick together and come around this side, flanking wide."

The three of them nodded.

That just left two. "Anthony and Fred, you guys go the other way. Same thing. Swing wide."

"Got it," Anthony said, nodding.

"Understood," Fred added. "But, uh, what if the demons show up?"

"Then close in on me," I said, shrugging. "Dyrnwyn will handle them."

"But what if you go down?" Anthony asked, scowling at the looks he got from the others. "What? It's a fair question."

"If I go down, then one of you had better scoop up my sword and see if it'll let you use it."

"Don't worry, gang," Axel said, expression serious. "I'm positive Dyrnwyn will choose me as Wyatt's successor. And I'll take those demons to pound town."

We all stared at him.

"What?" he asked.

"Axel," I said, "I don't think that means what you think it means."

"Eh, whatever," he said, yawning. "Can we go already? I'm bored."

"One more thing," I said, glancing around to ensure I still had everyone's attention. "Eilidh was right. We don't know how to deactivate the spell. So, unless anyone has another idea..."

I paused, waiting to see if anyone had a suggestion. They didn't.

"Then the plan is to fight our way there and figure it out."

"And don't forget about the booby-traps," Axel said.

"Right," I replied. "Let's do this."

"Uh, just one thing," Fred said, putting his hand up.

"Yeah?" I asked.

"Um, I just wanted to say..." He shuffled his feet nervously. "Well, I know you guys are used to this stuff. Some of you, anyway. But, like, this is the first time I've been in the shit. The *real* shit, you know? And..."

"Don't worry, Fred," Axel said, slapping him on the back. "It's like I said. We almost never die."

"Right," Fred replied. "It's just... I know it's only been a short time, and I know we don't all see eye to eye, but... Well, this the coolest damned team I've ever been a part of. So... Thanks."

I met his gaze and nodded at him.

Then I looked at the others, noting the grim determination on their faces.

My heart swelled with pride.

Fred was right. This was a kick-ass team. A damned fine group to die with.

"Let's do this," I said.

And stepped around the corner.

71

The moment I stepped out in the open, I expected to get blasted in the gut or rammed in the butt.

Neither happened, thankfully.

I strolled along with Dyrnwyn casually slung over one shoulder.

Axel walked on one side of me, humming "Take Me Home, Country Roads" while twirling a drumstick.

Parker was on the other side, all stone-faced and professional-like. He wasn't humming anything.

All we were missing was some badass entry music. You know, something better than Axel humming John Denver. And no, that's not a mark against John Denver or his lovely song. That is an insult aimed at Axel's humming. And Axel as a person.

I wondered if this was how Wyatt Earp felt on his way to the O.K. Corral. All nervous energy, expecting to get rammed in the butt. Probably helped having his brothers and Doc Holliday alongside him. I sure as hell felt better having Axel Gunner and Parker Grimm on either side of me.

"You might as well call out the others," Wampus called. "I can smell them, you know."

"It's rude to go around sniffing people," Axel said.

I didn't bother to reply, just kept onward, marching toward her.

Parker leaned in closer. "You know, Wyatt, your plan didn't include anything about what we're supposed to do if they don't attack."

"I thought that was obvious."

"Oh?"

"*We* attack."

"All right. That your entire plan?"

"Nope. We're also going to kick their asses."

"And free Mothman," Axel whispered, also stepping closer.

"Damn right," I said, eyes forward. "And nothing is going to stop us."

"Well," Parker said, shrugging. "Easy enough, I suppose."

"It's simple, Parker," Axel said, grinning like an idiot. "Damn sure won't be easy."

Wampus said something else, but I ignored her. My eyes were locked on Wildman's, as his were locked on mine. There was a message there, I could tell. I just wasn't sure what it was. But I had a sense he was trying to tell me something.

Might have been trying to warn me of the trap I knew was coming.

May have wanted me to know he wasn't too beat up to get back in the mix.

Or he might have been thinking about his favorite cookie recipe.

Whatever the case, it didn't really matter. I had a plan of my own, and I wanted to spring my trap before they sprung theirs.

I thought my thoughts at my sword.

"Hey, you understand the guy on his knees is on our team, right?"

It vibrated. A good sign.

"Perfect."

I threw.

Not a Dyrnerang throw, but a quick, straight pitch, right over top of Wildman's head, aimed at Wampus Cat's midriff.

She dove clear, exactly as I expected. Catching her off guard wasn't the point. Freeing her captive was.

I guessed I read his message correctly, because the moment my sword passed over his head, he lunged to his feet and sucker punched an Apple Devil, laying it on its ass.

He spun around just as the other Apple Devil came to its senses. Wildman lowered his shoulder and spear tackled it to the ground.

I called Dyrnwyn back and it vibrated the moment it hit my hand.

"Move!" I shouted and dove forward.

A blast of energy struck down behind me.

As I came up, I glanced over my shoulder, seeing the blast had struck where Axel had just stood. He'd dodged it, thankfully.

But that answered that question. Tanya had realized my sword could warn me. Now, she was trying to take out my friends.

She had tried to kill Axel.

That... That was unforgivable.

Gabby appeared behind Parker, raising her knife. There was no way I could warn him in time.

I didn't need to.

Parker spun. An oversized, ethereal, white, glowing fist formed on the end of his wand just before he upper cut her right in the chest. She launched off the ground like her feet were made of rockets.

All right.

My team was ready for the fight.

I turned and raced toward Mothman.

That was our goal. Our target. Free Mothman.

I had no idea how to take down the spell, but hoped Dyrnwyn might help. And maybe, just maybe, I would have a few seconds to figure it out while my teammates held everyone's attention.

Just had to get there first.

I sped on, racing right toward him.

I was nearly there.

And...

The ground beneath my feet began to glow, my only warning. It didn't come quickly enough.

Pink lightning arched up toward me.

There was a loud pop.

I had time for two thoughts.

The first was that I was flying.

The second was... *God damn it.* Axel had been right.

There were booby-traps, all right. And I'd stepped right onto one. He was going to be so smug.

And then the lights went out.

72

"Take me Home, Country Roads" was stuck in my head, playing on a loop. *Thank you, Axel.*

Otherwise, the only sound I could hear was a hollow ringing.

That was all right, because I wasn't sure where, who, or what I was.

My brain was groggy soup. Mashed potatoes covered in gravy. *Mmm, gravy.*

In a way, the John Denver tune was the only thing anchoring me to reality, though I wasn't sure what reality was.

At some point, I became aware I was me. And if I knew that, it was a good sign I was still alive. Also, I was pretty sure the afterlife—be it nothing or a path to some heaven or hell—did not have John Denver as a soundtrack. Though, I certainly could've been mistaken about that.

I forced open my eyes. The world was blurry and out of focus.

No, that wasn't entirely true.

One thing came into focus.

A butt.

A very shapely butt, hugged tightly by combat pants.

I blinked, thinking I was imagining things. Maybe my brain really was fried.

Nope, I was definitely looking up at a lovely female butt.

I liked it.

Had to be the nicest backside I'd ever had the privilege of admiring.

Wait... Was I supposed to be admiring it? Would it have been floating there, above my face, if I wasn't supposed to be admiring it? Surely not. I thought I might just lie there for a while, enjoying my view.

Where was I, though? And who owned that lovely rump roast?

The figure turned, moving her rear out of view.

I opened my mouth to protest, but no words came out.

The face of an angel looked down at me.

Well, damn. Maybe I *was* dead. Sort of made sense. Only an angel would have such exquisite junk in her trunk. Wait, was I going to get in trouble for admiring an angelic ass? *Uh oh.*

The angel's mouth moved, saying something, but I couldn't hear.

She looked familiar, this angel, but I couldn't place her. No surprise. I still wasn't totally sure who I was.

She *did* look an awful lot like...

Eilidh!

Of course it was Eilidh. I should have known the moment I saw... Well, those parts of her I had intimate knowledge of.

She was still trying to say something to me.

I couldn't hear her over the ringing in my ears or the tune of John Denver.

I tried to reply. Tried to tell her I couldn't hear, but still, my mouth didn't seem to work. Or at least, if it did work, I couldn't hear myself.

Another form came into view. It had the precious face of a baby, but...wasn't quite right. It was all pale and translucent. And it had...a scorpion stinger? Were babies supposed to have stingers? That didn't seem right, but I didn't know shit about kids, so...

Where was my brain when I needed it? Oh, right, it had been turned into melted jello.

The baby with the scorpion stinger leaped at Eilidh.

She spun, summoning an ice shard onto the end of her staff, and hammered into the monster's precious little face.

I tried to yell for her to stop. I was pretty sure you weren't supposed to hit babies with ice scythes, but... Well, she *was* the angel, so she probably knew the rules. Certainly better than me.

Wait... No. I was missing something. The filing cabinet in my brain was short a few folders.

The baby with the stinger hit the ground, rolled, and bounded back up on its four feet.

Four feet... Babies didn't have four feet. Again, I didn't know shit about babies, but... I was pretty sure they were supposed to have three at most.

I decided, right then and there, I didn't trust that baby with its four legs. I didn't care how precious its chubby wittle cheeks were. It was being tricksy, I was sure of it.

Eilidh twirled her staff and cast some kind of glowy orb that slammed into the baby and sent it rolling out of view.

Ha! Served it right. Sneaky brat.

A ball of blue energy slammed into Eilidh's back, crackling against her magical shield. The impact staggered her and she turned, nearly falling.

Yay! Her butt came into view again. All was right with the world once more.

Wait, no...

Another burst of magic crackled against her shield, but she stood upright, back straight, staff held out before her.

Oh, shit.

It finally clicked.

She was protecting me.

The thought hit me like an arrow through the heart.

Whatever the hell was going on, Eilidh was standing guard over my dumb ass. And I was just lying there staring at her butt. Not my finest moment.

It all came back to me then.

Who I was, what I was, and where I was. My vision cleared, too. And my hearing.

And I remembered what had happened.

I had stepped on a trap. The same traps Axel had warned me to watch out for.

I was lucky I wasn't dead.

Probably...

I still wasn't sure how bad a shape I was in, but judging by my strange thoughts—and the new sensations of pain racing through my flesh—it hadn't given me a back rub or a body massage.

I tried to move and found I had control of some of those systems. I made it onto my side. That was a start.

Taking in a wider view, I realized we were in the middle of absolute chaos.

The team was spread out, mostly fending for themselves.

Gray robes and demons were running amuck. My former teammates were in the mix as well.

We were in trouble. *Real* trouble.

I realized something else as well.

"Take Me Home, County Roads" was still humming through my skull, but it wasn't John Denver's voice I heard. And what probably should have been my first clue was there were no instruments. Just lyrics. It wasn't just a manifestation of my messed-up imagination, either.

Someone was mind-singing to me.

"Axel?"

"Finally," he replied, exasperated. *"Stop staring at Eilidh's butt and get your lazy ass off the dirt before you get her murdered."*

"Huh?"

"She's been protecting you, dummy. Standing there fawning over you while you napped."

"Really?"

"This is not the time for you to go all doe-eyed, dipshit. Get your dumb ass up, summon your Super Saiyan Blade Mage sorcery, and do some work. Sheesh."

I tried to rise, but stumbled, nearly falling. I would have, but Eilidh caught me.

"Come on, Wyatt," she said, one arm wrapped around me. The other held her staff out to defend us. "Please get up."

There was something in her voice...

Desperation.

That fired me to life. She needed me. They all needed me.

Problem was...

The world was still spinning. And I felt like throwing up.

Not good.

From the corner of my eye, I saw the wolf-scorpion-baby charging in again, right toward Eilidh's back.

I didn't know where my sword or wand had landed, but one would answer my call.

I pushed free of Eilidh's grasp and lunged toward the oncoming demon, calling my sword as I did.

Dyrnwyn leaped into my hand just as the wolf-scorpion-baby pounced. The dumb critter skewered itself on the end of my sword, which was great, except its stinger was in striking range and aimed at my face.

I stared up at the sharp end as it came barreling toward my eyes.

Warm demon gunk splattered my face instead.

It had turned to goo at the last possible moment. Instead of getting stung, I got slimed like a celebrity guest on a Nickelodeon game show.

If that wasn't foul enough, my momentum carried me forward and I splashed down, face-first, in the stinky, warm puddle of demon gunk.

I wrenched my head up, trying to breathe through the rotting death stench.

Wiping my eyes clean, I looked up and...

Locked eyes with Mothman.

His glowing red eyes were as menacing as ever. But there was something else in that gaze now.

Pain.

He was suffering. Whatever they were doing to him, he was in pain. Incredible pain.

His voice spoke into my mind, barely a whisper. I guessed that was all he could manage.

"*Kill...me.*"

"*No,*" I replied, unsure whether he could hear me. I didn't have my wand and I wasn't sure I could communicate back so far without a focus. It didn't matter. Killing him was off the table.

I struggled to find my feet again.

Eilidh still stood over me, protecting me. My guardian angel.

It was a damned bit of luck Tanya hadn't taken her—or me—out while I was down. Would've been an easy shot.

A moment later, I realized why. It wasn't luck at all. It was Axel Gunner. He held her attention, keeping her from dropping to a knee and using her snipey snipe spell. My guess was he'd been doing that the entire time. That was a dangerous game, but I had to trust him to handle it, at least for the moment.

Glancing up, I saw the exhaustion on Eilidh's face. She'd put everything she'd had into protecting me. They all had.

Where were Sams and the others? They hadn't made it yet. Had they gotten hung up dealing with more demons? Or had they been overrun and murdered?

And where was the Appalachian Argument? They were welcome to bring the cavalry at any moment. Surely they were on the way, after Parker told Master Serrano where we were and what we'd found.

"We've got to free Mothman," I said, my voice hoarse and raspy. "Our only chance."

"No shit," Eilidh replied, staying focused on shielding us. "Welcome back."

Right. We already knew that. But... It was more than that. Something told me we were nearly out of time. I still did not know what the spell was, but I sensed it was bad news. Like, *really* bad news. I could feel it in my bones.

Glancing at the ground, I quickly spotted my wand. That was a relief.

Armed with both my sword and wand again, I gave Eilidh a nod. Together, we started toward Mothman. I didn't run this time. Didn't want to get exploded again.

He was just ahead, but felt so far with a sea of booby-traps between us.

A wolf-scorpion-baby saw me from across the way and charged. It didn't share my reservations about running across the ground in front of the tower.

And...

Boom.

There was a thunderous roar and the little bastard shot into the air, pink bolts arching through its body.

It crashed down in a smoldering pile, smoking and twitching.

Shit.

Was that what had happened to me?

It was a blessing I hadn't pissed my britches. A wonder I was still alive at all. And no surprise I felt like a backpack full of bruised buttholes.

That created an entirely new problem. Or at least one I'd finally come around to appreciating.

Never mind all the assholes trying to kill us, or the fact I didn't know how to dispel the working. I didn't even know how to get to the chap without being murdered via pink stuff.

I paused my march and raised my wand, hoping I might sense the invisible traps.

No dice. Not a whiff.

Again I was reminded there was clearly at least one incredibly powerful sorcerer in play here. Had to be. Likely someone who could have powerbombed our asses into outer space.

But why hadn't they?

The answer was obvious.

Whoever they were, they were focused on the working.

Once we broke their spell, though...

That was a problem for later.

We had ninety problems, but a super wizard wasn't one.

Surely they'd find the time to come kill us later.

Or...

73

"*Wyatt, heads up,*" Axel's voice said into my mind.

His warning was not necessary.

I felt the presence before I saw them. Could feel where they stood, their power broadcasting like a billboard. Like the lights of Vegas.

Standing some distance away was a figure in a gray robe. Looked just like the others. They were not like the others, though.

Wizards could sense one another. We could feel each other's power.

But once a wizard gained *real* power, they learned to conceal it. Learned to hide how powerful they really were. Just then, though, I suspected the gray robe was showing off. Wanted us to know what we were up against.

There was something else to that power, though.

I'd sensed powerful sorcerers before. I'd spent enough time around the masters and Arcane Guardians to get a feel for big boss energy. I mean, they typically hid it, but I'd fought alongside a few of them. It was harder to hide in the middle of battle. And I'd seen some of the things Archie could do.

It wasn't just the sheer magnitude of power. It was...

It didn't feel right.

Like the magical energy around them was...ill. Sickly. Warped. Twisted.

Wrong.

I wasn't the only one who felt it.

The battle came to a screeching halt, all eyes drawn toward that beacon of foul magic. Toward that figure who looked so much like the others.

When he spoke, his voice was distorted, filtered through an evil asshole autotune.

"Enough," he said. "You have fought bravely, but you have become a nuisance."

I agreed.

And I wanted to be an even bigger nuisance.

I threw my sword at him.

It was a bit far, but I trusted Dyrnwyn to do its thing.

My sword hadn't made it halfway when the gray robe casually flicked his wand.

Dyrnwyn turned course and shot off into the night sky like a comet.

I reached for my connection with the sword, trying to call it back to me.

No answer came.

Our connection had been severed. It had traveled too far too fast. I could no longer sense it.

My sword disappeared over the hill. Gone.

Dread washed over me.

Was it just the distance? Or had the bastard somehow cut my connection? Was this permanent?

That empty feeling swept in, much as it had when I'd faced the vaklif. Same as when I'd woken up in care of the moon-eyes. It was like losing an arm or leg. A part of me had just been cut away.

And if my sword had been no use against this dark sorcerer...

Oh, fuck.

I glanced over at Eilidh, who stared back at me, the same question in her eyes. What could we do?

The big boss gray robe began waving his wand around.

I readied myself, though I doubted there was much I could do if he blasted me. Maybe he was weakened, most of his focus still on the Mothman working. *Right. Yeah. Sure.* That should have scared me more than it did. The spell he was using Mothman for was big-league shit. Way over my pay grade. And this asshole had the strength and expertise to casually roll out and smite us while he kept it rolling? What kind of super-powered nonsense was this?

The ground before him began to glow, forming a massive glyph big enough to park a tank inside of. Yeah, that's right. This big swinging dick didn't have to bother drawing out his sigils like the rest of us peasants. He just willed the damned things into existence, and again, all while still torturing Mothman with his super spell.

And he still had the capacity to chat while he worked.

"Wyatt Draven, you once said you'd come for us. Do you recall that bold threat? Back in Memphis, it was. Well, here I am. Was it all just bluster?"

I tried to think of something clever to say. Gave it an honest effort, but couldn't think of a damned thing. Wouldn't have mattered, though. I'd have had to swallow the lump in my throat before I could speak, anyway.

The glyph glowed more brightly.

I had a feeling I knew what was coming, and it was nothing good. A lot of nothing goods.

I was wrong.

It was just *one* nothing good. Not an army of them.

Just one.

Singular.

It was the biggest damned demon I'd ever seen.

It stood on cloven hooves with black furry legs that led up to a pale, translucent, humanesque torso, much like a satyr. That humanish torso was super masculine and muscular. Like a pro bodybuilder who'd sold their soul to the Devil. Chiseled by the gods. Well, except for one boob, which was very female. That was...weird.

Maybe not as weird as the rest of the creature.

One arm was large and muscular, almost human-looking, but ended with claws I was sure weren't meant for scooping ice cream.

Its other arm ended with a very human hand, but the rest was... It was thin and impossibly long, like a whip. Or like a tentacle with one of those big foam hands on it.

Its head was shaped like a goat, with long curling horns. The features were not goat-like, however. Its mouth had rows of fangs and its eyes... It had numerous red eyes packed together like a spider.

Oh, and my head was about as tall as the translucent thingy dingy dangling between its legs, which also could clearly be used as a weapon.

Somewhere behind me, I heard Anthony's voice. "What the fuck is that? No, wait. I don't want to know. Screw you guys. Seriously! Why did I sign up for this shit?"

I shared the sentiment.

This monster was among the most terrifying things I'd ever seen, and... I'd just lost the only weapon we had that likely could have hurt it. *Oops.*

The gray-robed wizard, having summoned his big pet, turned and walked away, leaving us alone with this new giant demon. I guessed he figured it was mean enough to do the trick.

I got to work, warning the others through mind-speak, repeating the same message over and over.

"I can't sense Dyrnwyn. Don't know how we'll kill this thing. We have to stop the spell on Mothman and run like hell."

Less of a plan and more of a strategy.

I ignored everyone talking over one another in my skull. A shame, because one of them might've had an idea. But I didn't have time to sort their responses because the *new* big boss was marching toward us. Or maybe it was just a boss rather than a "big" boss. Certainly didn't qualify as a mini-boss. *Whatever.* It was a big, scary-ass monster, and it was marching toward us.

Closing my eyes, I focused on my sword again, trying to feel for it. Still nothing.

It might've been a good time to call for a retreat. We could wish Mothman well while we booked it the heck outta there. Problem was, we were still surrounded by the original assholes, and seeing their big buddy appear, they were feeling pretty good about themselves. They attacked again.

There was no way we could get everyone out. No way to retreat.

And...I wouldn't have, anyway. There was something about the spell which irked me. Something I couldn't understand. Something in my gut that told me we *had* to stop it.

We had to finish the mission. That was all there was to it.

I turned to Eilidh. "See what you can do about Mothman, yeah?"

Without waiting for a reply, I started toward the big demon. Figured I'd head him off at the pass and meet him midfield, away from the others.

No magic sword. No plan. No idea how to even hurt the damned thing.

I only hoped I could keep its attention long enough for someone to figure out how to free Mothman or dispel the working.

Then we'd just have to escape. *Easy peasy.*

Besides, how tough could one big-ass demon actually be?

74

Pretty damned tough, it turned out.

I hadn't made it two steps when the super long whip arm shot out and bitch-slapped me right off my feet.

Seriously. It slapped me. Didn't punch or strike. Just slapped.

I was on my ass, cheek stinging, while the demon threw back its head and laughed. It sounded a lot like a heifer in heat. The jerk probably thought I was embarrassed, but my pride, what little there was, remained intact. Getting slapped down by a demon the size of a tank came with bragging rights, as far as I was concerned.

As soon as I was back on my feet, the hand snaked out again. This time, I was ready. I batted the incoming slap away with a pumpkin blast, which sent it back the way it had come. The demon responded quickly, whipping it back toward me again. I blasted it away a second time.

This was a game I could play. It would certainly keep its attention.

The demon had other ideas.

It swung again, then charged, hooves pounding.

Uh oh.

I had just enough time to fire a pumpkin blast, then dove from its path.

The other arm, the one with the claws, took a swipe at my face, missing by inches.

I turned and fired a pumpkin blast into the back of its kneecap, thinking I could trip it up. No luck.

It turned, swung its arm, and made to charge again.

A lightning bolt shot down, slamming into the demon's head. A crack of thunder followed.

The demon turned and mooed at Axel, who I hadn't even realized had come to join me.

Smoke billowed from the top of the demon's head where the bolt had struck. It seemed otherwise unharmed. Just annoyed.

Then it bitch-slapped Axel off his feet.

I applauded the demon, then summoned another pumpkin blast and fired it between the boss demon's legs. Right into that big ole translucent thingy dingy.

It mooed in rage and charged me again.

A sheet of ice appeared on the ground between us. The demon didn't notice.

Turned out hooves weren't great on ice. Who'd have thunk it?

It fell right on its goat-bug face and continued sliding toward me.

I ran out of the way and looked up to see Eilidh nearby, then turned and ran toward her.

"What about Mothman?" I asked.

"I don't know how to stop the spell, either."

"Okay. Well, I have a dumb idea. Follow me!"

As the demon regained its feet, it studied the field, eyes shifting between the three of us. I wanted it coming toward me again. It didn't. Instead, it chose Axel as its target.

That dingus had switched his focus back to Tanya again and had his back to the tank-sized demon. He should have known better. You never turn your back on a tank-sized demon. That was boss demon 101.

But Axel also knew that Tanya's snipey snipe spell was a nightmare, and she was down on one knee with her staff pointed at him. So, maybe he'd made the right call.

I charged the demon, unsure what the hell else to do.

Tanya fired.

Her snipey snipe spell ripped right through Axel's shield, as I'd expected.

Time slowed.

I knew what came next.

The secondary blast.

The one that would kill him.

But Axel's arm came up and he struck his best Captain America pose as his superhero lightning shield formed in front of him. The secondary blast struck it, sizzled, crackled, and popped.

Axel remained unharmed.

For once, the little asshole had taken my warning seriously. Which annoyed me, since I'd totally forgotten to heed his about the booby-traps. Maybe he would listen to me a second time.

"Axel! Move!"

He spun, eyes widening as the demon bore down on him.

Something I should have expected happened then.

A sheet of ice appeared between Axel and the demon.

Its hooves took to sliding and it went down yet again. Problem was...

I was racing to put myself between Axel and the demon. Racing at a full sprint.

I, too, hit the ice.

As my feet began to slide, I had a split second to consider how funny it would be if I got myself killed by running into Eilidh's spell rather than getting murdered by one of our enemies. That'd be hilarious. *Just* hilarious.

Fortunately, the demon was already sliding by when I slammed into it. I ended up on the thing's back and grabbed hold of one of its horns to keep my grip. Climbing up its back, I slammed my wand right into one set of its many eyes and fired a pumpkin blast.

Little eyeballs blew.

The demon boss mooed.

A hand grabbed hold of the back of my shirt and yanked.

It was the whip hand. The whip hand had gotten me.

I was flying.

Flying was bad.

Though I *did* appreciate the breeze on my face. It was nice. Refreshing, even. Wouldn't last, though. The problem with flying wasn't the flying. That part was pretty all right. Quite fun, actually. It was the landing that was the problem.

I once saw a video of Travis Pastrana when he wrecked a Subaru WRX during a rally race. The car had bounced, flipped, bounced, flipped, bounced, flipped, and so on. That poor Subie had flipped more times than seemed possible. I remembered thinking, *Amazing he survived.*

That was me.

I was the poor Subie.

I bounced, flipped, bounced, flipped, bounced, flipped, and so on, more times than seemed possible.

I was like a skipping stone popping across the top of the water. At least, that was how I imagined myself.

Every bounce struck my body like thunder. Every skip rattled my senses.

Until, at long last, I came to a final thud.

The air was knocked from my lungs. The world spun. I might've thrown up, but couldn't seem to locate my stomach. Every inch ached with a dull thrum, a promise of pain to come. A lot of pain.

I didn't even want to think about what kind of damage I'd taken. Which was convenient, because thinking was a real challenge anyway. Turned out I wasn't doing so well at breathing just then, either.

My eyes opened somehow, taking in a world which refused to hold still. Pain flared behind my eyes. Everything was fuzzy. The world in motion. A ship on a stormy sea.

I needed something to focus on. Something to center myself on.

My eyes locked on two red orbs.

They were...familiar.

Mothman.

Crucified above while I lay at his feet.

Huh. I'd made it to him. How about that?

Which also meant...

I'd landed in the middle of the minefield.

That wasn't important. Not yet. Breathing was my priority. Somehow, I managed to suck in a breath.

"Wyatt..."

Mothman's voice spoke into my mind again.

"Run."

Ha! Glad to see he still had his sense of humor. Like I could run anywhere. There was no telling how many of my parts were broken.

"Leave me," he said. *"Run."*

"Fuck off," I replied. Or tried. Again, I didn't have my wand, so it was probably a one-way conversation.

I didn't have my sword, either.

Didn't even have my little revolver. *Freaking Gabby. Thief.*

I had no way to protect myself, and wasn't sure I could've even if I'd had a weapon.

This was bad.

I tried to move. Forced myself to roll. Pain shot throughout my body, but somehow, I got over on my side. It was a start.

Except...

I saw that one of those weird, sucky-face centipede demons was headed toward me. The ones that wanted to kiss.

No. No. No. Oh, hell no.

I did not want to play sucky face with that thing, and I wasn't sure how I'd stop it.

I didn't have to.

It hit one of the booby-traps, sparked pink, and launched into the air like a rocket, still making suck faces as it flew away.

And that... That gave me an idea. A stupid one. *Perfect.*

75

I rolled again, despite the shooting pains.

I still wasn't sure whether I'd broken anything, but the adrenaline pounding through my skull helped me ignore my agony. Somewhat. Slowly, I made it up to my knees.

Tanya was busy with Parker. Otherwise, I'd have been toast. Anthony and Fred were supporting him, trading spells with Sophie and Zeke. Barrett was keeping the demons off their backs. Alyita was staying between the lot of them, also occasionally casting, but keeping an eye out for trouble. That was good. The Tennessee Wildman was still trying to handle Wampus Cat and her Apple Devil buddies on his own.

As I watched, Gabby made an appearance a short distance from Barrett. If it had been anyone else, she might've tried to sneak up on them, but she knew what the big man could do if she got in his range. Wasn't worth the risk. Instead, she was trying a different tactic.

Taunting him. Hurling insults and trying to get him to charge her. Just like before.

I cringed, fearing what came next. The others needed Barrett. Without my sword, there was little we could do about the demons, and he was the best suited to keep them at bay. If he charged at Gabby, the others would be overrun. My team was about to get mutilated.

Except...

Barrett didn't take the bait.

He ignored her.

Again, I felt a swell of pride. Barrett had put his need for revenge on hold, for the better of the team, just as he'd promised he would.

Gabby's eyes turned, meeting mine, and widened.

I didn't know what I looked like, but I'd already concluded I was in rough shape. So, it could have been that. Maybe I looked like an easy target. Or maybe she was surprised to see I was still alive. Whatever the case, I didn't have time to futz about.

Back to my idea...

Axel and Eilidh were still holding the boss demon's attention. A game of cat and mouse, but with lightning and ice. And simple force blasts to keep the whip hand at bay.

Neither of them could keep up the pace much longer. They were expelling too much energy too quickly.

I waited until one of them glanced my way and waved. It was Eilidh who saw me. She seemed surprised, too.

Geez, how messed up was I?

A moment later, she glanced my way again and I motioned her toward me.

That time she gave me a look that said, *Are you out of your damned mind?*

Quite possibly.

I waved her toward me again, and this time, Axel took note as well.

Both eased my way, still dancing with the giant demon.

As I waited, I noted the coppery taste in my mouth. I either hadn't noticed before or just hadn't paid it any mind. Blood. Where was that coming from? I didn't feel any new cuts in there.

Ah, well, that was a problem for later. Just the like the strange tremors I felt running up and down my spine. Or the wobble in my legs. My shaking hands. Pain with every labored breath.

I forced myself to stand up straight, ignoring all of it.

And...

I must've lost a few moments because one second I was patiently waiting for them to bring the demon over and the next they were halfway to me.

Close enough.

"Hey!" I growled. Or garbled. It didn't really come out right with a mouth full of blood. I spat and tried again. "Hey! Over here, you big ugly duckling!"

From my peripherals, I saw Gabby had edged closer. The others as well. Not good.

She'd realized I was hurt. Probably saw I didn't have my sword or wand, too. I was an easy target. Just needed a few more seconds, though.

"Hey!" I yelled again.

Finally, the boss demon turned, taking me in with what eyes it had left. The ones I hadn't removed. I hoped it remembered it was me who'd done that. Hopefully we all didn't look the same to it.

"Hey, you weak little demon bitch!" I called, pointing toward my eyes. "Having trouble seeing, or what?"

It mooed its outrage.

"That's right. I'm the one who took out your eyes. Care for another round? Or are you too afraid?"

I didn't know whether it understood a word I'd said, but it understood the context. Understood I was taunting it.

It mooed again and charged.

Perfect.

Well... Maybe perfect. I was gambling my life that there was another booby-trap between us. If not, it was going to squash me like a bug. Wouldn't that be funny?

So, how did Wyatt die? He taunted a big-ass demon and then just sort of stood there and let it crush him. Was the weirdest damned way to die, but that Wyatt, he never was too bright.

Unfortunately, there was one thing my addled brain hadn't taken into consideration.

The whip hand.

Still barreling toward me with its bulk, the whip hand shot out. I had no way of defending myself. The big fucker could've cracked my skull. Or could have just thrown me again.

Instead, the hand wrapped around my throat, lifting me off the ground. Clearly this wasn't the first time the big bastard had grabbed a human by the throat, because he applied just enough pressure to cut off my oxygen supply without snapping my neck. How considerate.

And stupid.

It had me. Could've killed me right then. Instead, it wanted to get up close. Wanted to gloat before it ended my life. Goats shouldn't gloat.

As they say, pride cometh before the booby-trap.

The barreling brute stomped right onto one of the traps. Pink light erupted, arching across its flesh.

I had about a quarter of a second to appreciate how clever I was before I noticed the pink lightning racing up the whip arm.

Well, damn.

76

I was aware of noise first.

That was different.

And it wasn't Axel serenading me this time, either. It was the sounds of battle. All the chaos.

The fact I recognized the sound for what it was, and that I remembered who, what, and where I was, had to be a good sign. Maybe the boss demon had soaked up most of the pink punch.

But I'd fallen again, hadn't I? I wondered how much additional damage I'd soaked up. *Ha!* Like I'd be able to distinguish it from the previous damage. I was so messed up there was no telling which injuries came from which stupid thing.

Once again, my first sight was of a butt, though this one was not so pleasant to gaze upon.

Stupid man butt.

Looking up, I saw it belonged to Fred and his handlebar mustache.

Like Eilidh before, he stood over me, protecting me.

Again I felt a swell of pride. Or maybe that was a broken rib. Who could say?

Of all the members of my team, Fred was the last I'd have expected to stick his neck out for me. I had popped him in the jaw, after all.

Embarrassed him multiple times. But we were on the same team now. Brothers in battle, even. He had said he was proud to be a part of this team. And for the first time, I was glad he was there, too. Glad he was one of us.

His mustache, though? It would forever remain an outsider.

But where were the others?

I risked turning my head and saw a smattering of bodies. Friends and enemies alike were all but on top of me, still fighting. Best guess, my former teammates, Gabby in particular, had seen me get zapped again. They wanted to finish me while they had the chance. Squirrel Nuts Squad had moved in to protect their nut. Me.

Turning my head in the other direction, I saw it was no less crowded.

And I saw the boss demon. It was sitting on its butt, disoriented. I knew the feeling. Knew it too well.

I also knew it wouldn't take long for the brute to recover.

"Wyatt..."

Mothman's voice.

"Use it..."

Use what?

I couldn't use anything just then. I was weaponless, busted up, and broken.

"You know..."

Know what? What was he talking about? Was he delirious? Was *I* delirious? Was I just imagining his voice in my head?

"It's inside you..."

Inside me? What was inside me? Other than scrambled organs and broken bones?

"The earth."

The earth?

The...earth was...inside me?

Yup. He was definitely delirious.

I watched as Parker got staggered by a bright yellow burst. Couldn't see who'd cast it. A wolf-scorpion-baby charged in, leaping at his back. Barrett darted into view, slamming his bulk against the creature and hammering it offscreen. Then he hunched over, struggling to breathe.

Beyond, I saw the Tennessee Wildman still taking abuse from Wampus Cat and her pals. Dude was tough as nails. Had to give him that.

I saw Eilidh and Alyita trading spells with Gabby. Behind Gabby, Tanya had dropped to one knee, her staff raised up to her shoulder.

It was pointed at me.

She had me.

I tried to move, tried to roll, but my body would no longer heed my commands. I even tried to summon the earth from inside of me, whatever the hell that meant.

Nothing.

I couldn't do anything.

I was powerless.

Time slowed.

This was it. I'd finally pushed my luck too far.

I was going to die.

My treacherous b-word of an ex was going to kill me.

Icky. Anyone but her. Literally anyone.

I watched as the end of her staff lit up. Saw the blast coming.

A shadow fell over me.

Fred.

I met his gaze. Saw the determination there. And...something I'd not seen there before.

Respect.

And I realized...

He'd stepped in front of me.

He'd put himself between Tanya and me.

I tried to shout. Tried to warn him. Tried to remind him about the secondary blast. I wasn't quick enough. My mouth was a slug, crawling at the same frozen pace as my reality.

The first blast shattered his shield.

The second wrecked his body.

A massive hole appeared in his abdomen.

He blinked, then fell.

Fred landed right beside me, hitting the ground like a brick.

He didn't move.

Didn't stutter.
Only stared at me, his eyes glued on mine.
He didn't speak. He couldn't.
He wasn't breathing.
Security Supervisor Fred was dead.

77

Something broke inside of me.

A voiceless scream. A firestorm, raging through my chest. A fury I could not contain.

My fingers gripped the dirt as I cursed, struggled, and failed to rise.

It was no use. I couldn't get up. Couldn't unleash my righteous fury. Couldn't...

I paused.

That dirt...

The very dirt between my fingers...

It was as if I could feel it. I mean, of course I could feel it. My fingers were pressed into it. It was more like...

I could sense it.

I could *feel* it. Could feel *through* it.

A new platform of awareness had opened in my mind. I could sense through the dirt. I could feel the roots of the grass, just below the surface. Could sense the worms crawling through its carcass. And I went deeper, mapping out the ancient tree roots there, buried deep.

They were listening, those roots.

Open to my suggestions, willing to aid me.

They cried out, sensing the foul magic atop their precious ground, polluting their home. They could feel it on the wind, too, through their leaves. They knew this magic was wrong and they wanted it gone. Wanted it removed.

I paused.

Was I losing my mind?

Almost certainly.

But I rolled with it, because I realized something else through this strange feedback system. There were spots on the ground even more tarnished by the foul magic. Smaller areas, thick with the stuff.

The booby-traps.

Glancing over, I saw Tanya, saw her scowling that she'd missed her target. But through the dirt and those willing roots, I sensed where she stood. I knew which ground was beneath her. And I knew there was a booby-trap just beside her.

I beckoned the roots forward, urged the nearest to strike. To lash out at that dark magic.

For Fred.

A root shot forth, breaking the surface right through the center of the trap. It activated.

Tanya was knocked back, pink lightning arching across her flesh.

Ha!

Pain.

I blinked.

It had hurt. Not me. No. The root. It had been hurt by the magic. Scalded. Burned crispy.

But it was worth it.

The tree was delighted with the result. Willing to accept the pain.

Again, I was probably losing my mind, but continued along for the ride.

I didn't get the impression the plants, or dirt, had a conscious. Not in the way I understood consciousness. More like...base feelings.

Surely I was just out of my mind. Incapable of intelligent thought.

But that wasn't quite right, either.

When I'd opened my senses to the earth, my own sense of awareness had strengthened. The pain in my body had eased, along with my weariness. The pain still waited for me, I knew, but so long as my mind was open to the plants, the weakness of my body was somewhat left behind. Or, like, somewhere else. Back with my body. It made little sense, and I didn't have all night to ponder.

There was work to do.

Looking up, I saw a wolf-scorpion-baby was posted up, waiting for a chance to flank one of my allies. It, too, stood just beside a booby-trap. I popped it.

The demon shot off toward the moon.

I laughed at its misfortune, though no sound came out. The plants shared in my joy.

But popping zits wouldn't save my friends. I needed to go bigger.

My gaze shifted to Mothman and the tower he was bound to.

Yes!

It was as if the plants all cried out at once, delighted by the idea. That was where the foulest of the foul magic was, where it truly polluted their soil. Where it threatened their home.

All right. So, let's free Mothman. We'll push the damned tower over if we have to.

Yes!

I pushed, driving the roots toward the tower.

And...

I pushed my magic along with them. As though the dirt had become my wand. My staff. My focus. I could channel magical energy through it.

Yet...

This energy was different. It wasn't my normal magic. That well was nearly dry, as exhausted as my body was. But this strange energy... The well was vast. Full. A dam ready to burst.

It wasn't entirely foreign to me. I'd felt it before. It was the same magic Elder Morgan and Master Washington had been trying to help me tap into. I didn't know how. Didn't know why. But it was answering my call.

And somehow...Mothman had known. He'd known...

There was no time for questions.

I focused on him. Focused on my roots.

Something else interesting happened. Channeling my strange magic through the plants didn't just drive them toward the tower; it strengthened and enhanced them. The roots were growing longer and stronger with each passing moment, feeding off this strange but somehow natural energy.

The first of them wiggled from the ground—no bigger than an earthworm—at the base of the tower. They climbed slowly at first, wrapping around that ancient metal, easing their way up like a snake up a tree.

More came behind them, fueled by my will. They continued sprouting and growing at a rapid pace until branch-sized roots were climbing alongside the smaller ones.

And I could feel the tower. Could sense what they sensed. Could feel what they felt.

Free him. That was my command. My strongest thought. *Free Mothman.*

Yes!

A smaller vine reached for the nail in Mothman's foot. As I... No, as the plant touched it, my... No, the vine's flesh was seared. Pain. But again...worth it.

I wrapped myself around the nail and began to pull and tug, even as it crisped my flesh. I wasn't strong enough, and the pain was unbearable. I grew stronger still, wrapping more of myself around that nail, pulling harder.

At the same time, I continued climbing higher as well, pushing more and more of myself onward, wrapping myself around more of the spikes which held him in place. Probing at the chains that bound him. Reaching for his wings, to free them.

I was everywhere all at once.

I was the roots. And yet, I was me.

My team was still in trouble, but now I could sense where each stood atop my flesh. The enemies, too. Each time one of my foes stepped too near a trap, I popped it, blasting them.

I could sense the boss demon, too. The plants hated it. They detested its unnatural presence. Their hatred was my own. But there wasn't enough of me, of the roots, to worry about it just then. We had to free Mothman.

But the beast was rising, getting back to its feet, ready to join the fray again. If it did, all would be lost.

I focused all my will on tearing at the spikes in Mothman's flesh.

I was wrapped around them all now, the ones in his feet, his hands, and his wings. I pulled against the chains as well.

My roots were tearing through the ground, the size of tree trunks.

The tower let out a groan.

If I couldn't free him, I would knock it down. Surely that would break the spell. We might all die in the process. Surely Mothman would, but I knew he would understand, as would my team.

But then...

The first spike, the one in his foot, popped clear.

A moment later, another popped out of his wing.

Behind me, the demon boss rose to its full height.

Another spike shot free.

Still, the chain held. I probed every inch of it, hunting for a weak link in the enchanted steel.

And I found what I was looking for.

I wrapped myself around it, calling on more of myself to help me pull.

The demon boss started forward, marching toward my prone body.

I just needed a little longer...

I pulled with everything I had.

The link gave way.

The chains exploded off him.

The remaining spikes could not hold him.

Mothman was free. *The* Mothman was free.

There was a roar like a thunderclap, followed by a great sucking sound as the spell faltered. A wave of energy erupted from the tower, smashing forward like a hurricane gust. Everyone was knocked from their feet. Everyone except the demon boss.

It took a single step forward and I looked up, meeting its cruel gaze. It stood over me, victorious. Ready to crush me.

A black blur passed overhead.

Mothman slammed into the demon, knocking it back across the

clearing and hurling it into one of the old bunkhouses. The entire building crumpled around it, burying it.

That wouldn't stop it for long.

Still... We'd done it. We'd stopped the spell. And Mothman was free. He could go for help. The rest of us, though...

Mothman circled overhead.

The others were back on their feet, the fight on once again. Maybe I could help them. I could do little to help against the demon boss.

But there was something else, too.

My sense of awareness through the ground had spread even further. My detailed awareness wasn't so strong the further out I pressed, but I could sense the trees in the hills, the brush, and grass, too. And, like an antenna, it stretched my awareness further.

I sensed something out there. Something which had been lost.

My sword.

Dyrnwyn was out there, somewhere in the forest, and...

I blinked.

It was...moving.

That couldn't be right.

I pushed my awareness further. It *was* moving. Racing toward me. Coming back to me at speed.

I sensed another presence out there with it. Something familiar, though I couldn't say what.

Was something, or someone, trying to return my sword to me?

I called to it, pulling on that precious connection.

It answered my call.

Dyrnwyn took flight, sailing toward me, along with...that other presence.

Both were flying straight toward me.

I blinked again.

That didn't make sense...

Again, I wondered if I'd lost my mind, but doubted my broken brain could have conjured such a bizarre idea.

My sword came into view, flying through the night sky, but...

It didn't look right.

Something was hanging off the end, waving through the night sky like a streamer.

A big-ass python.

And then it all made sense.

Weekend at Burmese had gone to fetch my sword. She'd brought it close enough that I could sense both of them, and then had hitched a lift, riding my sword across the wind. And why not?

Using my dirt map, I sensed for my wand. It was nearby.

I called on the roots. They shot forward, exploded from the ground, lifting my wand and tossing it to me.

I let go of my connection then and was immediately nauseated, exhausted, and in pain.

But my sword was coming, and so was my wand.

I reached up with one hand, catching my wand.

Dyrnwyn touched down in my other hand, landing gently.

Weekend at Burmese secured herself around my shoulders.

At my feet, a patch of purple and white flowers had grown. I didn't remember having done that, but Fred looked peaceful, lying among them.

And the tower, it was leaning over and broken, covered in roots.

The demon boss let out a roar, climbing from the rubble of the bunkhouse.

"Mothman," I said with my mind. *"Mind giving me a ride?"*

In reply, Mothman circled, swooped, and scooped me right off the ground.

He flew straight toward the demon boss.

It saw us coming and raised its whip hand to strike. I raised my wand, but before I could fire, Weekend and Burmese leaped from my back, latching her jaws onto the incoming hand. She wrapped around the tentacle arm, constricting and wrestling it under her control.

With that out of the way, Mothman threw me at the demon.

I raised my wand and fired a pumpkin blast into its remaining eyes, blinding it.

At the same time, I took my sword in a reverse grip and slammed it into the demon's forehead as I crashed into it.

It fell, dying.

And so did I.

78

Just kidding.

I didn't die, but it damned sure couldn't have hurt any worse if I had.

I splashed down in a goo pond. There was a loud pop in my leg and I was sure something had shattered. That didn't stop me from sliding, though. The demon boss had ruptured, turning into an icky slip and slide.

Once I finally came to a stop, I cried out in pain, then tried to wipe the goo from eyes so I could see.

Hmm. Well, that can't be good.

The front of my foot was pointed toward the back of my knee. I was no orthopedist, but I was pretty sure that wasn't right. I was confident in my original diagnosis. *Not good.*

The urge to vomit attacked my senses again, but I was pretty sure my tummy had abandoned me *way* earlier in the evening. Any parts of me with any sense had surely hightailed it. My ankle, foot, or whatever the hell was twisted backward, could attest.

I struggled to orient myself.

The spell had been broken.

Mothman had been freed.

The big-ass demon had been slain.

I doubted anyone would blame me if I went ahead and passed out. Or went into shock.

But there was still work to do.

My team was still in trouble.

I turned just in time to see Gabby appear behind Alyita.

And like with Fred, there wasn't a damned thing I could do to save her. No spell I could cast, no throw I could make, nor any plants I could call on to save her. There was no time.

But it slowed again, anyway.

Gabby's knife came up.

And a freight train slammed into her. That freight train was name Barrett. He knocked her right off her feet, hurling her to the ground.

Zeke stepped into frame then, blasting Barrett off his feet.

Parker was there, though, hammering back at Zeke with his ethereal punch spell. It shattered against Zeke's shield, but the old dude wasn't able to finish Barrett, and that was what mattered.

Sophie raised a wand to shoot Parker in the back, but Anthony covered him with a shield.

I heard shouts from the other direction and turned my head. More gray robes were gathering round. We were about to be outnumbered again.

And if that super big boss gray robe showed up...

I glared at my stupid broken leg. If I could've made it to my feet, I could've headed them off, chucking Dyrnwyn.

Reaching for the ground, I realized I couldn't sense the earth any longer. The connection had been severed and I was back to where I'd started, not knowing how to call upon it again.

So, I started crawling toward my friends.

The going was slow.

I watched as Mothman swooped down and scooped up an Apple Devil. He carried it up toward the stars and then just dropped it. The half-squatches were tough, but that one landed with a splat. It wouldn't be rejoining the fight. Brutal.

The remaining Apple Devil was focused on Axel. In fact, it was charging right at him.

I thought to call out a warning, but Axel was looking right at it and waiting with all the patience of a rodeo clown. Clearly he had a plan.

As the half-squatch bore down on him, he spun, summoned his Captain America lightning shield, and slammed it into the charging beast. It staggered, falling to its knees. Axel rammed his other drumstick right up the Apple Devil's nose. "How dare you sully the good name of sasquatches by working with the bad guys?" he cried. "Scotty would be ashamed of you!"

And then he summoned a lightning bolt...right inside its skull.

I don't think he expected the result.

The Apple Devil's skull exploded, showering him in gore.

So Axel didn't need my help.

The Tennessee Wildman didn't, either. Despite being beaten to hell for half the evening, the rugged bugger was still on his feet. And despite Wampus's extra arms and bravado, when the last of her half-squatch buddies died, she decided she'd had enough. She turned to flee.

The Tennessee Wildman caught her by the tail.

He jerked her back toward him and slugged her in the back of the head.

She tried to get away again, but he still had her.

Much to my surprise, she raked her claws against her own tail, severing it. Then she bolted out of there, running on all sixes.

I kept on crawling.

Tanya and Eilidh were engaged, up close and personal. My most favorite witch knew not to let my least favorite bitch get out of her reach. But Tanya wasn't bad at close-ranged combat, either.

Eilidh swung her ice scythe at Tanya's head, but Tanya ducked, came in close, and popped Eilidh in the jaw. She staggered back. Tanya used her staff like a sword, pushing Eilidh's own staff outward, opening her front. Tanya reached for the knife on her belt.

Eilidh was quicker.

Her hand shot up, drawing a backup wand. Even as she swung her arm, an ice sickle formed at the end, which she rammed into Tanya's ribs.

My ex let out a breathless cry and staggered back, a shard of ice still embedded in her flesh.

Ha! Suck it, Tanya!

The others raced in to protect their leader.

Zeke caught Tanya, wrapping his arm around her while bolstering his shield.

Gabby leaped on Eilidh's back, riding her to the ground, knife raised.

I still wasn't close enough to help.

Alyita was.

She landed a kick to the back of Gabby's head, knocking her off Eilidh.

And then Sophie charged Alyita from behind, grabbing her by the hair, just like the first time they'd met. She jerked the younger lady's head toward her with one hand and raised her wand with the other. Sophie intended to cast right in Alyita's face.

Hell no.

I hopped, skipped, and managed to pop up to one foot. I dove forward and threw, trusting Dyrnwyn to not hit Alyita.

Sophie glimpsed my sword coming and took a step back to avoid it.

But Dyrnwyn had other ideas.

It changed course, dove, and...

Did something I'd never seen it do before. Something I hadn't known it could do.

It landed...

Right in Alyita's free hand.

Her other still held her tomahawk.

Alyita's eyes widened, every bit as surprised as me. But she wasted no time.

She twirled, ripping her hair free and swinging Dyrnwyn.

Sophie was smart enough to dart back, avoiding the sword strike, but then immediately stepped back in, raising her wand. She probably thought she had an opening. Probably didn't fear the teenage girl. She was older, wiser, and was likely a stronger mage. But she'd never been much of a brawler. Doubted she'd even had much close quarters training.

Alyita, though? Alyita was Cherokee, raised in the old ways. Raised with a tomahawk in her hand.

The same tomahawk she'd swung as she spun.

Sophie never saw it coming.

She cried out as the blade buried deep in her ribs, eyes wide with surprise. She staggered backward, studying the tomahawk buried in her midriff.

Alyita did not hesitate. She darted in, jabbing Dyrnwyn through Sophie's ribs as well. Then she stepped back as the woman fell.

Gabby, back on her feet, rushed in to help.

She met Barrett again along the way.

He slammed into her once more, but this time, he didn't let go. He pulled her in close, even as Gabby raised her knife. To anyone else's eyes, it might have looked like he was hugging her. In fact, he was squeezing. Crushing her.

Even from a distance, I could hear her bones cracking.

Gabby cried out and the knife slipped from her fingers.

Barrett tossed her to the ground.

I was nearly there and raised my wand as her trembling hands went for her big-ass revolver.

Before she could draw it, though, Barrett scooped up her fallen knife and rammed it into her gut.

Gabby gasped, then went limp, falling back to the ground and staring up at him.

Barrett watched her for a moment, then turned away.

The gray robes moved in to assist Zeke as he dragged Tanya to safety. They didn't attack, though. And they didn't sic their demons on us.

They were...retreating.

I blinked.

Wait...

Had we just won?

That didn't seem possible.

I crawled closer to Gabby, seeing her lips tremble as she stared at the knife in her gut.

That was a painful way to go. She might still have tried for her revolver, but she was surrounded then. It wouldn't have been much use.

Her eyes slowly turned to meet mine and she sneered. "Come...to gloat?"

"No," I replied, then got up to my knee and pushed her over on her side.

She cried in pain and protest.

Then I reached into the back of her pants. "Just want my gun back."

I ripped my revolver and holster clear, then let her tumble to her back.

She still glared at me, then looked up at Barrett, who wouldn't meet her gaze.

"You still...wonder why?" she asked, looking at me again.

I shook my head. "Not really."

"No?"

"Nope. You made your bed, Gabby. Go ahead and die in it. I don't care why. Not anymore. I'm going to kill you all just the same."

"Damn right," Barrett said, finally turning to look at her. "You're all ghosts. Just don't know it yet."

"I do know," she said, leaning back. "I do now. I regret..."

"No," I said, cutting her off. "You don't get to do that. You don't get to speak your peace at the end. We're not going to pretend your life had some kind of meaning. Our friend is dead over there because of you and the others. How many more lives have you claimed? Huh? No, you don't get mercy, Gabby. You don't get pity. No forgiveness. No last words. Not from this crew."

"Yeah," Anthony said, crossing his arms. "Fuck you."

Axel threw his arm over Anthony's shoulder. "We agree twice in one night? What's the world coming to?"

Anthony shrugged Axel's arm off and turned to glare at him. His gaze flicked to Fred and back again. "Thought you said we never die."

"I said..." Axel deflated, hanging his head. His reply came out as little more than a whisper. "Almost. We almost never..."

He trailed off.

Parker let out a cough and pulled my attention back to Gabby. "Gut wound. Slow killer. Maybe we can take her back with us. We might not be interested in her regrets, but there're plenty of other questions we might find answers to."

Gabby started to laugh, but it turned into a bloody cough. "You think they'll let me leave here alive? You're fools. All of you. But..."

"But what?" I asked.

She met my gaze. "For what it's worth...I hope you do kill them all, Wyatt. Not the team, but... The rest. And...I think you will."

I stared at her, not sure how to respond.

For a moment her eyes closed and I thought maybe she'd passed out. Then they sprung open again.

"And..." she said, staring up at me again. A tear streamed down her cheek. "I'm... I'm proud of you, Wyatt. Proud to see what you've become."

And with that, she closed her eyes, lay back.

Those... Those were the last words she spoke.

79

We weren't out of the woods yet.

The gray robes had backed off, but they hadn't exactly run away with their tails tucked. They were reforming on the other side of the field. It must have occurred to them that there were still more of them than there were of us. And we were beaten and tired. Surely they knew that.

I had nothing left. My adrenaline was all tapped. Pain and exhaustion were taking its place. Likely I'd be taking a nap in the next few minutes, whether we were in the middle of a battle or not.

My teammates only looked somewhat better. None of their legs were bent in the wrong direction, at least. So they were certainly in better shape than me.

All except...Fred.

Fred was gone.

Dead.

Someone on my team had died. That was...a lot to process. But now wasn't the time for it.

My eyes shifted to Gabby, struggling out her final breaths and ignoring us. I didn't know what her death meant to me. She'd been a vicious enemy. But once, she'd been a friend. That was something else

I'd deal with later. Just then, I needed to figure out how to get my team the hell out of there before the gray robes attacked, or worse, the big boss showed up again.

Mothman landed on the ground beside me.

"The dark wizards are regathering," he said.

"Can you lead the others out of here?" I asked. "Can you get my team to safety?"

"Only if you're coming with us," Eilidh said. "I'll carry you if I have to."

"Might be a better job for Barrett," Axel said.

Barrett snorted his agreement.

"You guys need to hurry," I said, pointing at my foot. "I'll only slow you down."

"Don't be ridiculous," Mothman said. "I can carry you, no problem. But we must hurry."

"We need to find Sams and the others," I said, pointing back in the direction we'd left them. "We can't leave them behind if... If they're still alive."

Even as I spoke, more gray robes gathered around Zeke and the injured Tanya. There were at least twenty of the bastards. Were they breeding them? How could there be so many goddamn dark wizards right under the Appalachian Argument's nose?

The answer was obvious.

The same way they'd hid under the Ozark Mountain Cabal's nose.

The same way they'd hid under the Southern Circle's nose.

"I am a long way from my full strength," Mothman said, "otherwise I could handle this riff-raff on my own. I fear you're right, Wyatt. We must flee. I will carry you."

"Oh, to hell with it," Parker said, surprising me with a sigh. "I'm too tired to run. Let's just fight to the death already."

"That's the team spirit!" Axel said, slapping him on the back.

"Damn, you've lost your mind, too, boss?" Anthony said, rolling his eyes. "It's like you idiots *want* to die or something."

My gaze shifted to Alyita, who was standing to the side, staring down at her tomahawk, which was still buried in Sophie's midriff. It occurred to me then what a weight this was for her. The rest of us...

We'd all killed before. But her... Had she ever killed someone? I knew she'd tried to kill me a few times, but that was...different. And...

Constable Williams.

She had killed Constable Williams, back in Oklahoma.

But even that... She'd been Spearfinger at the time. I didn't know if she even remembered it, or if it was like a cloudy dream. Or maybe she did remember. We'd never talked about it.

This, though? This was Alyita. Not Pathkiller. Not Spearfinger. Alyita.

While the others argued the merits of our impending doom, I crawled toward her. She was only a few steps away.

She noticed me coming and glanced down at me. "Guess you'll be wanting this back?"

She held out my sword.

I took it from her. "You all right?"

She nodded but said nothing.

"You know... It's, uh, never easy, taking a life."

She glanced over at me, then looked away again. "Guess that's why you fought so hard to save me from, you know..."

"Yeah," I said, wincing as I dragged myself into a sitting position. "Something like that. Also, you were a kid and so were the others. You deserved a chance. You deserved to get to choose your own path."

"Guess I chose," she said, still looking away, "and went down the same path anyway. Maybe I should have stuck with Pathkiller after all."

"There's a difference," I said.

"Is there?" she asked, her gaze whirling on me. There was a fury there, though it may have been a little misplaced just then. Her view shifted back to her tomahawk. "When my grandfather gave me that..."

"He never thought you'd actually have to take a life with it."

She nodded.

"Well, he's not here, but I'd know he'd be damned proud of you."

"For being a killer?" her tone was bitter, cold. "For becoming the very thing you both tried to save me from?"

"No, for standing up for something. You shouldn't have been put in this position, but you were. And you fought to protect your friends and allies. You fought to stop a bunch of assholes from doing wicked shit."

"Doesn't feel that way."

"Never does," I replied, sighing.

Then I dragged myself toward Sophie.

She was still breathing.

Her eyes opened, staring into my own.

Alyita let out a gasp and took a step back.

And I saw a solution to Alyita's problem.

Not much of one, but it was something.

I drew my revolver and put it against the side of Sophie's head. Then I blew her brains out.

Alyita jumped. So did the others.

Ignoring the ringing in my ears, I re-holstered my revolver and reached for the tomahawk. I ripped it clear of Sophie's guts and wiped the gore off on my ruined jeans.

Then I turned and held it up to Alyita, who was staring at me wide-eyed. I forced a smile. "There. You didn't kill her. I did. And good fucking riddance."

Alyita's trembling hands reached out and took her tomahawk back from me.

"Wyatt," Parker said, "trouble's coming."

I looked up and saw the gray robes were marching toward us, more of their demon pets surrounding them. There was no sign of Zeke or the injured Tanya. Nor Wampus Cat.

"Hell's bells," Wildman said, picking himself up from where he'd been resting on the ground. "You folks sure like to party."

"I'll do what I can," Mothman said, stepping out in front of us. "Flee."

"So, that's not really how this works, Mothy," Axel said, shaking his head. "Squirrel Nuts Squad does not abandon its own. We keep our nuts together. And right now, you're all nuts in this big happy sack. We all go, or none of us go. Right, team?"

I think he expected a more enthusiastic response, but it was quiet for a few moments.

Finally, Anthony spoke up. "Can't believe I'm going to die beside you, Gunner. Weird little bastard."

"He's right, though," Parker said, his gaze meeting my own. "We're a team. We fight together. We die together."

"Damn right," I said, rising to my one good knee.

I raised my wand and leaned my weight against my sword. Weekend at Burmese slithered in front of me, coiling into a ball, ready to protect me.

Parker moved alongside me. Then Axel. Eilidh was next, along with Barrett. Alyita stood alongside us as well, a determined look on her face, a wand in one hand, her tomahawk in the other.

"Hell, I like these guys," Wildman said, winking at Mothman. Then he limped to move alongside us. "Almost enough to leave Appalachia for the Ozarks. Almost."

Mothman nodded and moved back to join us.

"Hey, Mothy," Axel said as we watched our enemies approach. "I have a question."

"Is it pertinent just now?" Mothman replied. "Or can it wait?"

"Uh, I think I better ask now," Axel said. "On account of the whole dying thing."

"Must be an important question." Mothman nodded at him. "Shoot."

"Do you really like beans and Sprite?"

For a moment, I didn't think Mothman would respond. But finally he said, "I don't care for the beans, if I'm honest. The Sprite, though... Yes. I'm rather fond of fizzy drinks."

"Cool," Axel said, nodding. "Guess I can die happy now."

"Glad I could oblige," Mothman replied.

We all turned our focus to the coming horde.

This was it... Our last stand.

Futz it.

Except...

A short-statured figure with glowing eyes moved alongside me. In his hands was a short spear. One I might even call a Bill Shankspear.

Tuthid had arrived, and around him, the other moon-eyed people gathered up. They were short a few members, though.

Tsali appeared on our other side, the Cherokee in tow. They, too, had lost some people.

"Wyatt, what did I just say to you about having fun and not inviting me?" the voice of Brother Barajas said as he eased through the crowd to stand alongside me. " 'Bout to start taking it personally."

Supreme Shaman Sams spoke from behind. "Sorry it took us so long, Wyatt, but we are here now."

I was about to reply, but noted the line of approaching gray robes had faltered. The numbers no longer favored them. But still... They knew we were exhausted and beaten. They had nothing to fear.

Except...

All at once, their heads jerked, as if they heard something the rest of us couldn't.

Then they turned and....

Fled.

Like, as fast as they could.

Ran for their lives.

We all stared in shocked silence.

Axel was the first to speak, and I felt he really caught the sentiment we all felt.

"The fuck?"

In moments, the gray robes had all abandoned the field, disappearing among the bunkhouses. We were alone, our little army standing quietly in the dark.

From somewhere behind me, another very familiar voice said, "Ah, there you are, Wyatt. Making trouble as usual, I see."

I turned, blinking.

The Archmage.

He strolled calmly toward us, Supreme Enchanter Tate right beside him. They looked like they were out for a pleasant evening stroll.

Supreme Curator Whitaker, Christian, and Daisy were just behind them, along with Master Serrano and Master Castillo.

Behind all those big dogs was an army of wizards, a hundred or more marching toward us.

The Appalachian Argument had finally arrived.

Archie came to stand just before me, an amused expression on his face. "Wyatt."

"Archie."

"You have quite a lot of explaining to do," he said, still seeming far too amused. "For starters, why are your toes pointing in the wrong direction?"

I scowled at him. "I'll explain everything, but you're getting ahead of yourself. You should know the drill by now. First, I pass out."

And that was exactly what I did.

80

I woke up in bed.

And that was fine by me. I thought I might just stay there for the rest of forever. But there was one thing nagging me...

Groggily, I opened my eyes and glanced around. It appeared I was in my bed back at the Argument's dwarven city. Weekend at Burmese was coiled up near my feet. Otherwise, I was alone.

There was a single lamp lit, offering a bit of light. Just enough for what I needed.

Throwing back the sheets took considerably more effort than I expected. Turned out I was sore pretty much everywhere. Everything hurt. It even hurt to breathe, which made me wonder if I'd broken a rib or six.

It didn't help that a fat python was lying on the sheets, either. She looked up at me and flicked out her tongue in a gesture I took to mean she was annoyed with me disrupting her comfort. She'd get over it.

I sighed with relief, staring at my foot. It wasn't in a cast, but was wrapped in medical tape. More importantly, it was pointed in the correct direction.

Thinking about it all twisted, the way it had been... I felt nauseated again, just thinking about it.

And then I realized I was hungry. Starving, even. When was the last time I'd eaten? How long had I been asleep? With no windows, there was no way to know.

I glanced over at Weekend at Burmese. "Don't suppose you could fetch me a burrito?"

I'd never known snakes to have much in the way of facial expressions, but she had one then, and it suggested my request would not happen, and that I could eff right off. She was just surly about me disrupting her nap.

"You know... No one told you that you have to sleep with me."

That time she looked at me like I was a potato.

Great, now I was forced to take shit off a python. As if dealing with Axel and my moody sword weren't bad enough.

Speaking of Axel...

The door opened and he came strolling in, a big grin on his face. More importantly, he held a takeout box in one hand and a carton of chocolate milk in the other.

"About time, you lazy heifer," he said. "Thought you'd never get up."

"What time is it?" I asked.

He shrugged. "Tomorrow. At least from where you're time traveling from."

"How long have I been asleep?"

He shrugged again.

"Can you tell me if it's morning, day, or night, at least?"

"Morning," he replied. "I think. I just had breakfast with the others, so I'm thinking it's morning. Time is a relative construct. Could be Christmas, for all I know."

I nodded. So I hadn't slept for days. Unless it was Christmas, in which case I'd lost quite a lot of time. Didn't think that was likely, though.

I eyed the chocolate milk. "That for me?"

"Oh, this?" he said, holding it up. "Hell no. This is mine. If you want chocky milk, you can get your lazy ass up and go get it yourself."

"You know I was injured, right?"

"Everyone was injured."

"Did anyone else have a broken leg?"

"Did anyone else ignore my advice about booby-traps?"

"I didn't break my leg on the booby-traps, asshat. I broke it dive-bombing that big ole goat demon."

"Hmm," Axel said, rubbing his chin. "I don't appreciate your excuses, but... That was pretty badass. Probably the coolest thing I've ever seen you do, so... Here."

He handed me the chocolate milk and the box.

Curious, I opened it and saw an apple fritter staring back at me. Beside it was a blueberry cake donut, as well as one covered in chocolate. My inner fat kid leaped for joy.

"Thank you," I said, reaching for the fritter. "So, what's the word? Any idea how much trouble I'm in?"

Axel shrugged and plopped down in the love seat on the other side of the room. "No one has said much. At least not to me. Parker and Serrano both seemed pretty worried, but then, they're always worried. The way I figure it, we saved Sams, Mothman, and the others, and stopped the baddies from doing whatever evil jerk-face thing they were up to, so we can't be in too much trouble. In fact, they ought to praise us. Probably will. Bet I'll get a medal. And Archie will certainly promote me to your job."

"That what you think is going to happen?"

"Well, the way I see it, the rest of us were just following orders. You were the one who went rogue."

I snorted and chomped on the fritter. It was heavenly. Magical, even. There were few things better in life than a well-made apple fritter. I chased it with a chug of chocky milk. Also heavenly.

Still chewing, I said, "I thought you were of the mind that Archie intended for me to break the rules."

"I don't recall that," he said, all innocence. "But even if that were true, what I would have said was that he could not publicly support you. And that means he'll have to publicly discipline you."

"Yeah, well, that's not going to happen," I said, tearing into my apple fritter. "We did what we had to do. And if we hadn't..."

"Preaching to the choir there."

"Everyone else all right?"

He opened his mouth, then shut it again. A concerned look crossed his features. "I'm a little worried about Alyita. She hasn't said much."

I nodded. "I'll talk to her."

"Good idea." He popped up from his seat. "You should probably go take a shower. You're going to have a lot of visitors soon."

"Great," I replied, watching him head for the door. "Wait... How the hell am I going to do that with a broken ankle?"

He turned around, ensuring I could see him roll his eyes. "Your ankle isn't broken, dummy. They fixed it with magic and shit. Ever heard of it?"

"How the hell was I supposed to know?"

"Maybe the fact it's facing the right way?"

"That doesn't mean..." I scowled at him. "I can see they turned it the right way. But there's not a cast or anything."

"Which means..."

I threw my empty chocky milk carton at him. "That doesn't mean I can walk on it. What did they say?"

"They said you could walk on it."

"That's it?"

As we argued, Weekend at Burmese raised her head and shook it at both of us.

I scowled at her. "Don't you start. You chose this life for yourself."

Before all I hold dear, I swear to the moon and back, my damned snake sighed at me.

That took us both by surprise.

Finally, Axel said, "They said they fixed you up. The healers straightened out your leg and melded it back together. Said you should be able to walk and stuff, but you need to take it easy, get lots of rest, blah, blah, blah. Fixed your ribs and a few other broken bits and bobs, too. You really beat the hell out of yourself this time."

"Got it," I replied.

"Oh, and they really did use magic. I wasn't lying about that. Turns out magic is real. Who'd have thunk it?"

That time, I chucked a pillow at him.

81

They might have fixed my broken parts, but everything still hurt like hell. Taking a shower was more challenging than I expected. I was sore from tit to tailbone and beyond. From pinky toe to temple and everything in between.

I guessed I shouldn't have been surprised. If the Guinness Book of World Records had a line for who'd had their ass beaten the most times by supernatural assholes, my name would surely have been there. I'd have to talk to Poppy Cash about getting some of her miracle goops and potions to keep on hand. It seemed I was destined to get beaten half to death on the regular. I would've said this time was worse than usual, but there was that time Alyita had cracked my skull. Pretty sure I'd broken my leg then, too.

Whatever.

The water felt nice. Too nice. I sat under the faucet for what felt a lifetime, dozing. Probably wasn't my brightest idea. Then again, and continuing my trend of macabre humor, how funny would it have been if I survived dark wizards and demons just to drown in the shower? *Hilarious.*

At some point, I finally washed up and dragged my sorry butt back out of the shower.

I blinked, surprised to find Weekend at Burmese coiled up on the floor, eyes on the bathroom door. I guessed she was on guard dog duty. It was weird, since she hadn't come in with me, and I hadn't heard her open the door. Also, she didn't have hands, and I couldn't imagine her using her jaws to turn the knob. Maybe she had. She certainly was too fat to squeeze under the door.

Weird ass snake. I wasn't sure I'd ever get used to her.

Getting dressed wasn't any easier than showering, but it was nice to have clean clothes on again.

And that was about all I could manage, so I crawled right back into the bed.

A few minutes later, Axel reached out to me through mind-speak. Apparently, he and Alyita were waiting in the living room.

No surprise she would be my first visitor. I had a suspicion Axel had fetched her and hadn't bothered to tell anyone else I was awake yet. He was smart.

I informed him they both could come in, so long as he brought me another chocky milk. I still had the blueberry and chocolate donuts to eat, after all.

He did not bring in a chocky milk. *Jerk.*

Alyita moved to the love seat, her eyes downcast, not wanting to look at me.

Axel plopped down on the floor, his back to the wall.

"Hey," I said.

"Hey," she replied, still not looking at me. "Axel said you wanted to talk."

"I do. You all right?"

She nodded.

"Are you, though? Because you sure don't seem like it."

"I am," she said, finally looking up at me. "And...I'm sorry. I shouldn't have acted that way in the field last night. I'm sorry if I let you down."

"Let me down?" I glanced at Axel, who shrugged. Turning back to Alyita, I asked, "Why would you think you let me down?"

"Because..." she said, finally looking up at me. "I was... I was being a baby. And we were in the middle of danger, and..."

I held up my hand to stop her.

"I'm not disappointed in you," I said, carefully choosing my words. "You didn't let me down. Quite the opposite. I was damned glad you were with us."

She blinked. "I thought... I thought I was just a burden."

"A burden?" I shook my head at her. "Hell no. You were badass. Brilliant, even. If you were done with school, and were an adult, I'd see about adding you to the team for real. You more than proved yourself."

"But..."

"But you froze up after you thought you'd killed someone?" I asked. "Alyita, you'd be a monster if it didn't bother you."

"But you... You finished the job. She used to be your teammate and you just... You didn't even hesitate."

"I've been at this for a while. Axel, too. And Sophie has been trying to kill us. A lot. Look... It was the same for me the first time. And there for a while, I... I started to think *I* was becoming the monster. I feared I was turning into the very thing we fought against. But that wasn't true. There's a big difference between the monsters and me. You know what it is?"

She shook her head.

"You," I said, motioning toward her. Then I pointed at Axel. "Him, too."

"I don't understand."

"It's friends, Alyita. People I care about. That's the difference. I've killed more people than I'd care to count at this point. And sometimes, I still wonder if I am the monster, but see, that's just it. That's the very thing that separates us from them. Last night, Axel and I didn't walk into that camp hoping to commit murder. We went down there to protect you. I've never killed someone for greed, glory, or power. I don't go looking for trouble. I don't *want* to kill anyone. But I damned sure won't stand by while innocent people die, just so some evil asshole can have their way. That's the difference."

She bit her lip. "I guess so."

"I know so," I replied. "And I also know your grandfather is going to be very proud of you when he hears about this. He also may never speak to me again, but I promise you, Alyita, if he saw how you acted lat night, he'd be damned proud. You stood for something. Stood for what was right. You fought to protect your friends. Your allies. You didn't run or cower. And you didn't have a choice but to strike down Sophie."

"Well, you did," Axel said. "But the other choice would've been pretty damned lame. She would've killed you. And she would've killed the rest of us, if she could. Wyatt is right. Taking a life is never easy, but you have to ground yourself in the reality that you did it for the right reasons. That's all you can do."

She glanced between the two of us and nodded. "I guess... I guess what bothered me... Your former team wanted to kill us, yes, but they'd also defended me from that man... So, I just think... Were they all bad? Was I wrong for killing her?"

I rubbed my chin, considering. "I don't think anyone is all good or bad. But the world isn't just shades of gray, either. There are genuinely good people. Your grandfather and Elder Thomas come to mind. Master Serrano, too. That doesn't mean they haven't done bad things, mind you. Doesn't mean they haven't acted in a way they regret. The reverse is also true. Even evil assholes do decent things from time to time. The world isn't black and white, but it isn't just gray, either. My old teammates chose their side. *They* aligned themselves with darkness."

"At the end... I heard what Gabby said to you," Alyita said, looking up at me. "It seemed like she might have regretted it."

I nodded and sighed. "Maybe she did. I don't know. Hell, I don't even know why they did what they did. Why they turned their backs on the Cabal. Why they became dark wizards. Ultimately, it doesn't matter. Whatever their reason, it can't be justified. They chose. That's the difference, Alyita. That's what makes us different. I would rather die than become whatever it is my former friends have become. But you already know that."

She nodded and looked down. "I guess... I guess I'm just afraid of becoming Spearfinger, again. Or something worse. I came so close to..."

"But you came back," Axel said. "And that's what matters."

"And the very fact you're worried about it is a good thing," I added. "But guilt, shame, and self-deprecation are the quickest roads to hell. So, don't wallow in it. Trust me, I know."

"I *wanted* to hurt her, though," she said, looking up at both of us. "Sophie, that is. I wanted to hurt her."

I nodded, considering my words.

Axel beat me to it. "Yeah, well, I wanted to hurt every goddamn one of them. I wanted to break them. Wanted to make them suffer. The question is, why? It's like Wyatt said. Not for power. Not for glory. Not for greed. I wanted to hurt them because they wanted to hurt my friends. Because they wanted to hurt me. Because they were torturing Mothman. Because they wanted to hurt people who'd never done a damned thing to them. Fuck those guys. They don't deserve your guilt or your pity."

"And that really makes a difference?" she asked. "It really matters?"

"It does," I said. "It's just... What you went through last night.... What we *all* went through. It's not normal. That's not what normal people deal with. It creates trauma, and you have to learn to cope with it or it'll eat you up inside. It's like I said. It wasn't so long ago I questioned who I was. Whether I was becoming the same as the monsters I fought."

"How'd you get over it?" she asked.

"By remembering what I was fighting for," I said, shrugging. "I wish Stone were here."

Axel chuckled. "Yeah, now there's a guy who knows trauma. And one who'd put it in a very blunt perspective. He'd probably look at you and ask why you're beating yourself up for killing assholes."

"And he'd be right," I said. "Stone has been through the worst the darkness has to offer. He's bathed in it. Everyone in our world thinks he's a nut job. Out there day after day, hunting monsters. But truth be told, I think he may have a better handle on his sanity than the rest of us. He doesn't question it. Knows good from evil and doesn't have to second-guess himself."

"Must be nice," Alyita said with a sigh.

"But the rest of us," Axel said, giving her a serious look. "We have to rely on each other. Have to trust each other."

"You always seem so confident, though," she said. "Like everything is just a game."

"No." Axel shook his head. "That's not it at all. Life is not a game,

Alyita. Life is one short ride. All we have. And most people spend too much time on superficial bullshit. Worried about how others view them, worried about their status, justifying their own shitty behavior, or beating themselves to death with guilt. Not me. Fuck that. I'm going to squeeze every bit of juice out of this existence I can."

"But you never seemed bothered by any of this," she replied. "Either of you."

"I'm bothered every day," I said, shrugging. "I'm lucky I'm not a complete headcase. Sometimes at night, I lie there and think over and over about the mistakes I've made. The things I could have done differently. Where I went wrong. Lives that were lost because I made a poor decision. That sort of guilt... I can only learn from it and do better. But my own morales? Questioning whether I'm falling to the dark side? No. I anchor myself in the lives I've saved. The people I've helped. I remind myself why I choose to fight."

"But couldn't you just delude yourself?" she asked. "Couldn't you end up lying to yourself?"

"An unfortunate number of people do just that," Axel said. "And not just for big shit like this. People lie to themselves every damned day. They struggle to see through their own bullshit and refuse to hold themselves accountable. Always justifying their crappy behavior. Like Wyatt said, the fact you're questioning your own motives is a good thing. That's healthy. Letting the scale tip too far, though... That's just as dangerous. You can't lie to yourself and pretend everything you do is righteous or justified. But you also can't lie to yourself and pretend everything you do is wicked and worthless. Neither is healthy. You have to be honest. Especially with yourself."

"He's right," I said. "Look at me. I spent years being bitter at the Cabal. And for what? I've spent so much of my life doubting myself. Spent so much time thinking I wasn't worth anything. Even recently, with this team, I doubted whether I was right to lead it. But that's all bullshit. I've learned to anchor myself in my accomplishments. Not to be cocky or arrogant, but when that negative voice pops up in the back of my mind, I remind it what I *have* accomplished. What odds I've beaten. And that gives me the confidence to move forward. And this... It's much the same. You're worried about turning into Spearfinger again, and you're damned right to be. But you should also anchor yourself in the fact you beat it once. How many people have come back from something like that? Not many."

"Just don't get big-headed," Axel said, "or I'll have to knock you down a few pegs."

"And he *is* good at that." I chuckled. "I never have to worry about getting too big of an ego with Axel around to point out what a dingus I am."

"Seriously," he said, shaking his head. "I warned you about those booby-traps."

I rolled my eyes at Alyita. "See?"

She smiled.

And that... Well, that was a damned good sign.

82

Our chat with Alyita was interrupted by another visitor.

Archie.

Apparently he had a key to my suite, or just magicked the lock. The weird part was that Axel hadn't given anyone else a heads-up that I was awake. It was like he just knew.

On top of that, he arrived right after we'd gotten Alyita cheered up. Like he'd been outside with his ear pressed against the door, waiting for the right time to intrude.

He didn't knock or anything, just let himself right in.

Axel and Alyita abandoned me, which made me take back every nice thing I'd ever said about either of them. I didn't want to be left alone with Archie. I didn't really want to talk to him at all.

Yet there he was, an amused smile on his face.

And he just stared at me like a creepy grandfather, waiting for me to break the silence.

Forget that. I was happy to go back to sleep.

"How are you feeling?" he finally asked.

"Like a bag of bruised buttholes."

"My, what a colorful description."

"Probably the pain meds talking."

"Probably not, since you weren't given any."

"Oh, well," I said, scratching the back of my head. "Pain magic, then?"

He offered me one of his grandfatherly smiles.

"Oh, just get on with it," I said, rolling my eyes. "How much trouble am I in this time?"

"Not as much as you might think. The Argument is rather embarrassed about the whole ordeal. Plus, both Sams and Mothman sang your praise. You made quite an impression with those two."

"Well, that's uh...different."

He smiled again.

"Guessing we didn't take any bad guys alive?"

"Of course not."

"Not even Gabby? She was still breathing when I passed out."

"Died soon after," Archie said. "Regrettable."

"In more ways than one."

"Indeed."

"So, do we have any idea what it was all about? What the point of their spell was? What they were trying to do with Mothman?"

He stared at me for a long while before responding. "There are... theories."

"Care to share them?"

"No."

"Didn't figure. Good plan, boss. Just keep on keeping me in the dark. It's not like I risked my life to stop it or anything."

"Now that you're awake, you should see to your team. Make sure they're all faring well after such a...trying evening."

"Trying? Is that what you would call it?"

"Yes."

I stared at him.

He stared back.

"You manipulated me," I said, finally.

"Is that what you think?"

"Don't do that," I said, shaking my head. "Don't reply with questions. I've had enough of your head games for the moment. You manipulated me into taking brash action. Axel called it, and I think he was right."

"Mr. Gunner is often too clever for his good. Or he thinks he is, at least."

"So, you're admitting it?"

"I admit nothing. Only that I had confidence you would resolve the situation, as you have in the past."

"No," I said, shaking my head. "This time you fucked up."

He raised his eyebrow at me.

"You deceived me to get me here in Appalachia. You could've told me my former team was here and I would have volunteered. Instead, you used me as bait. And then you manipulated me again and riled me up so I'd do something stupid."

"That is quite some theory," he said, crossing his arms. "But if it were true, and I'm certainly not saying it is, then I must have quite a lot of confidence in you. So, then, tell me, where was my mistake?"

"Fred."

"Fred?" he asked, blinking.

"He's dead," I replied.

"Yes. A tragic loss. But he did his job, and he fought bravely. So, where is the mistake? Do you not think I should have put him on your team?"

"You don't get it, do you?" I chuckled. "You've spent so long moving people like chess pieces..."

We stared at each other for a few moments.

Finally, I said, "Manipulating me and putting me in danger, that's one thing. I can tolerate it. But putting my team's lives in danger, and under false pretenses... That's unforgivable. You may be wiser than the rest of us, but you fucked up when you gave me a team. Not because I'm a bad leader. No. You underestimated what it meant to me. What my people would mean to me. Fred is dead, Archie. He died on *my* team. I couldn't save him. And I have to live with that."

"And so do I."

"Damned right you do." I shook my head at him again. "But that's not my point. I won't forget what you did here. I won't forget your part in this. The rest of the Cabal may revere you, but you've lost my trust, and that of my team. Now, is there anything else? Or are we done?"

He nodded, unbothered. "That is all for now. We'll head home tomorrow."

"Great. Now go away and let me get some rest."

I laid my head back on the pillow and ignored him. A few moments later, I heard the door shut behind him.

83

Slowly, the members of Squirrel Nuts Squad all trickled in.

Losing Fred weighed heavily on everyone, but there was also some mirth. We'd survived impossible odds. Got the job done. And Squirrel Nuts Squad had become celebrities. At least with folks around the compound. Axel and Anthony were eating it up. Even Parker seemed to bathe in the praise. Only Barrett remained sullen.

I asked to speak to him alone.

There wasn't much to be said, though.

I thought the deaths of Gabby and Sophie would've impacted him more. I thought he might need to talk about it. Maybe he did, but not with me. Instead, he just thanked me for the opportunity and asked when we were going to finish the job. Tanya and Zeke were still out there somewhere. I doubted an ice shard to the ribs would slow my ex down for long.

Other visitors trickled in. Some were there to congratulate us, others to thank us. And some came to offer condolences for Fred. Most were some combination of all the above. My teammates dragged all the chairs from the living room into my bedroom. And then they began stealing them from other suites, presumably their own. It became quite the little party, with people gathering in my bedroom, coming and going, or just hanging out. I didn't mind.

Master Serrano came by, his worry at peak levels. I wasn't sure whether Archie had filled him in our conversation, or if it was just seeing me laid up that had him concerned. He didn't say. But it was good to see his smiling face either way.

Much to my surprise, Master Battle Mage Castillo also came by, and even hazarded to offer something close to praise. Or at the least, she didn't pick apart my every decision. So, that was something.

Tuthid came and thanked me for helping the moon-eyed folk. With his lead, they'd already made amends with the Appalachian Argument and had formed a new, albeit shaky, alliance with both the Argument and the Eastern Cherokee. Given their treachery, they'd be on rocky ground for a while, but I had confidence Tuthid would see things resolved.

Brother Barajas and the knights also stopped by. They brought me a case of beer and a bottle of Jameson. God bless the Memphis Knights.

Leaders from the Appalachian Argument also came. Archie had told the truth. They didn't have the vitriol that Archmagus Melancon had had for me in the Southern Circle. On the contrary, they were grateful and apologetic. Supreme Enchanter Tate fell over himself apologizing, and said my team was always welcome in the Argument. Supreme Curator Whitaker fussed over my injuries like she was my grandmother and even brought cookies. Christian seemed the most embarrassed. Daisy, though, she surprised me. She gave me a stern nod, said she heard we kicked ass, and wished she would have been there for it.

Then Mothman came.

The others cleared out when he arrived, somehow sensing he wished to speak with me alone.

He stood there, studying me with his glowing red eyes, arms behind his back, in some kind of regal pose.

"How are you faring, Wyatt?" he asked.

"I'm good. How about you?"

"I am well," he said with a curt nod. "I recover quickly."

"Glad to hear it."

"I owe you a great debt of gratitude. Had you not acted as you did—"

"I would say we're square. You saved my life first, remember?"

"Ah, but this was more than saving my life." He began pacing about the room, his arms still clutched behind his back, hidden beneath his folded wings. "That spell..."

"What was it? Do you know?"

He turned, studying me. Not answering.

That was all right. I could come back to it. I had another burning question.

"How did you know about my earth magic?" I asked.

"I could sense it in you from the moment we met."

"That is...something. Do you know how I can call upon it again?"

He shook his head.

"Damn," I said, sighing. "That was only the third time I've used it. Every time has been during a high-stress encounter. I've been studying. Working with Elder Morgan from the Oklahoma Cherokee, and with our own Master Enchanter, Thibault Washington. Neither seem to understand much about it or how to help me call upon it."

"A shame. Sadly, I cannot help you with it, either. It is a faint thing. Hidden to most eyes. But I could see you had a strong connection with the earth. I could feel its magic upon you. Much like..."

"Much like what?"

He shook his head, then smiled at me. "Never mind that. I can only suggest you continue working to unlock it. Clearly you have a gift. But you asked me about the spell."

"I did."

"I do not know for sure what they intended."

"But you have an idea."

He nodded. "Yes, a very concerning one. So much so that I intend to leave the Argument for a time."

"What?" I asked, surprised by this revelation. "Where will you go?"

He paced again, seeming thoughtful, and making a point of not looking at me.

Finally, he said, "I am reluctant to say. I've not shared my destination with the Argument, either. And I do not wish to speculate aloud, for I hope very much that I am mistaken."

I stared at him, not sure what to say. "So...why mention it at all, then?"

Again he studied me, a serious look on his face. "What do you know of the history of magic, Wyatt? What does your Cabal teach you?"

That...caught me off guard. Left me dumbfounded. "I, uh, well, there're lots of theories about our history and stuff. Mostly lore, though. No two accounts match up. Um, I mean, I know the druids have something to do with the Arcane Artifacts. Outside of that, I'm no historian."

He nodded, as if he expected as much. "Don't feel bad. Few are as knowledgeable as they should be, and much is cloudy. It may be a good time to begin your studies anew. To refresh your knowledge of that lore."

"Okay. Any particular part you think I should focus on? Surely you didn't come here just to tell me to study history."

"No," he said, pausing. "I came to warn you. I think there may be greater things in play than anyone realizes."

"Oh, well, good news there." I grinned at him. "I am *very* aware of that. Painfully aware, quite literally. And on several occasions. That knowledge has literally been beaten into me."

"Yes, of course. But... Well, I think the gravity of the situation may be more dire than even you realize. Keep your sword close. I fear it will be needed in the days ahead. I'll say no more on the matter for now. I must take my leave and see what I may uncover for myself. Until then... Be careful. And know that I greatly appreciate what you did for me, as well as for the Argument. I will not forget it."

With that, he turned to leave.

"Uh, hey..." I called at his back.

He glanced over his shoulder.

"You never said what history I should be studying."

He nodded slowly. "The history of the Arcane Artifacts may be a good place to start. And perhaps the Canticles of Gaultier. I'm sure Master Serrano has them in your library. A bit of light reading."

With that, he was gone.

More cryptic shit. *Great.* Why couldn't anyone ever just tell me what the hell was going on?

I sighed. I guessed I'd just have to keep hacking my way through evil douchebags until I carved out the answer myself. And... Yeah, I guessed I could probably do some light reading.

84

Eilidh was the last to visit.

That kind of hurt.

The crew was all piled into my room again when she showed up. Once more, they shuffled out. This time they left the suite completely, Axel saying something about heading to the cafe.

She studied me for a time, then grabbed a chair and pulled it over beside the bed.

"Hey," I said.

"Hey," she replied.

"I, uh, wanted to thank you. If you hadn't given me that little pep talk... And if you hadn't gone with us... Well, I owe you. Big time."

"No, you don't," she said, reaching out to take my hand. "We're friends, Wyatt. Friends look out for each other."

"Friends, huh?" I said, forcing a smile.

She gave me an amused grin. "And...maybe something more. But..."

"But you're still going to go through with your thing," I said, nodding at her while trying to ignore the pain in my gut. "The, uh, sacred, uh, whatever you called it."

"Sacerdotessa." She nodded. "I have to. And...I need you to understand."

"I do," I said, though that wasn't entirely true. "I want what's best for you, Eilidh. I want you to be happy and all that other corny shit. So, if doing that makes the rest happen for you, then I understand. I mean... It's not like we've ever had all that much time together or whatever."

She gave me a serious expression. "But I have enjoyed every moment of it. It meant...a lot to me. I hope the same is true for you."

"It is," I assured her. "It very much is."

She leaned over and kissed me on the forehead.

"I guess this is goodbye, then?" I asked, struggling to keep my voice even.

She nodded, looking away. "We'll be leaving in the morning, same as you, I hear."

"And after running off with my team, it probably wouldn't look good for you to be hanging around us, or me, right? I mean... They're probably already giving you nine kinds of hell over it."

She nodded.

"Well, that sucks," I said, shrugging my sore shoulders. "Would have been nice if... I don't know. If we'd had a little more time."

"Yeah, it would have." She rose slowly to her feet. When she looked at me, I could tell her smile was forced. "You know, before, I just didn't want to cause you undue pain. I think that's kind of stupid now."

"It is," I said, meeting her gaze. "Pain caused by you is...better than nothing at all."

She brushed my hand again. "I feel the same."

"Good," I said, swallowing the lump in my throat.

"You shouldn't be alone," she said, surprising me with the sudden statement.

"Well, I'm not," I said, coughing out a chuckle. "I've got Axel, right?"

She returned my laugh. "Yes, well, that's not what I meant. You're a sweet guy with a lot to offer. Don't spend the rest of your life alone."

"This coming from the witch who's about to swear off relationships?"

"Yes," she said, shrugging. "Find someone. Please. For me. I hate the idea of both of us being alone and miserable. Will you do that?"

"I, uh... Yeah, Eilidh. I'll do that."

She nodded and started for the door.

"Eilidh," I said, staring at her back.

She paused.

"Are you sure you're not making a mistake?" I asked. "Are you sure you're making the right decision?"

She shook her head. "No. Not really."

Then she walked out the door.

And returned half a second later.

Closing the door, she flipped the lock behind her.

When she turned back to face me, I raised an eyebrow.

"Fuck it," she said, shrugging. "I'm already in trouble. What's a little more?"

She stomped toward me with a purpose, pausing only when she reached the side of the bed.

"So, uh..." I said, meeting her gaze. "What's happening?"

"How injured are you?"

"Um, mostly just really sore."

"Good," she said, nodding. "I can work with that. You'll just have to hold *really* still."

Then she took off her clothes.

85

We left early and with little fanfare.

Tate, Whitaker, Christian, and Daisy came to bid us farewell.

I didn't get to say goodbye to Supreme Shaman Sams. He was still resting. Still recovering.

I didn't see the Tennessee Wildman again, either. I checked the bar, but he wasn't there. According to Tate, once we'd returned from the battle, he'd crashed for a few hours and then slipped away. No surprise. He wasn't the type to hang around.

Saying goodbye to Eilidh had been the hardest. So, we'd said nothing. We'd enjoyed each other's company one last time, shared one final kiss, and that was it. She was gone.

Going her own way and plotting her own course.

Out of my life forever.

I'd meant what I said. That I wished nothing but the best for her. And I hoped things worked out just the way she wanted.

Still hurt like hell. I tried to ignore the icky feeling in the pit of my stomach. Tried not to think about the fact I might not see her again, and how, sadly, that might be for the best. If I did see her, it would be as nothing more than passing acquaintances. Once she took her vows, that would be it. No room for relationships. No room for feelings or any of that weak nonsense.

Yeah, I was trying really hard not to think about it.

I still didn't understand what it was she was signing up for, exactly. But it wasn't any of my business, either. She had made her decision. She would have to live with it.

And so would I.

So, since I was trying so hard not to think about it, I could think of little else.

It wasn't as though there was much else to do.

The ride back was a somber one, everyone lost in their own thoughts. Even Axel was unusually subdued. Maybe they were just tired. I knew I was. I crashed in and out the entire damned way.

But I suspected the loss of Fred was taking its toll. That first day, everyone was just happy to be alive. But now it was settling in. We'd lost someone. Our team was one person and one handlebar mustache short. Poor Fred.

That was something else we'd have to worry about when we got back.

In the meantime, I just tried to sleep more.

86

I was getting dressed when the doorbell chimed.

Knowing Axel wouldn't be bothered to answer it, I started toward the living room, expecting Parker, Anthony, Barrett, or Alyita.

Arriving back at the Castle, I'd stayed at my dad's old place again. No sense in going home. Not yet. There was still one last piece of work that needed to be done. Besides, I had figured Archie would want me to give the council a rundown of events in Appalachia. Give them a chance to pick it all apart. For once, he surprised me. I'd received no summons.

Unless the person knocking on the door...

I shook my head. No. It was one of the Squirrel Nuts, just a few minutes early. That was all. Had to be.

Without giving it another thought, I swung the door open.

And blinked.

It was not a member of my team.

Nor was it someone fetching me for the council.

It was Sanchez.

I stared into his cold eyes and he stared into mine.

Beside him, a Rottweiler sat on its haunches and yawned, bored with our silent exchange.

"Sanchez," I said, finally.

"Kid," he replied.

And then we stared at each other some more.

He didn't like me.

I'd never liked him much, either.

The time we'd spent together on the Kingsnakes had not been pleasant. He was a jerk and a bully. I didn't do well with either. If someone had asked me who was likely to betray the team, Sanchez would've been my first pick. I would've been mistaken, of course. When Tanya, Zeke, Gabby, and Sophie had betrayed the team, they'd betrayed him as well. He'd taken a nasty whack over the head, too. Gabby had delivered that blow, if I remembered correctly.

The last time I'd seen him, he'd still been in the hospital recovering. We hadn't spoken since. I hadn't even known he was still around. Had no idea what he'd been doing in the time since. And I wondered if the dog at his feet was the same one I'd given him. Or at least, the one he thought had come from me. It had been Axel's doing, actually.

I could guess why he was there, though.

"You heard?" I asked.

"Is it true?" his eyes narrowed. "Gabby and Sophie are dead."

I nodded. "Two down."

"Two to go," he replied.

He went back to staring at me. Just watching me.

I really didn't have time for this. "Look, Sanchez..."

He held up a hand and proved I was wrong about why he was there after all.

"I want in," he said.

"What?"

"I want in," he repeated, as though it made more sense the second time. "I want to join your team. The Squirrel Nuts, or whatever the fuck you call it. I want in."

It was my turn to stare silently. He was the last person I would have ever expected to volunteer to join my squad. And frankly, he was about the last person I wanted on it.

"I don't know where they are," I said. "Tanya and Zeke. I don't have any leads."

He shrugged. "They'll find you."

"Might take a while."

"I've got time."

"I'll...consider it."

"You need me. When it comes down to Tanya and Zeke, you'll need me."

"We almost got them without you."

"Almost," he replied with a snort. "If I'd have been there..."

"It wouldn't have made a damned difference."

His eyes narrowed and he started to speak, but I held up my hand this time.

"I said I'll consider it. But there's something you ought to know first, Sanchez."

"What's that?"

"I'm not the same kid you used to bully. In the time since we've worked together, I've killed more dark wizards and demons than I can count. I've fought monsters you couldn't imagine. So, if you think you can push me around and start the same old shit, you're going to have a really bad time."

"I know. Barrett told me."

That...surprised me. It wasn't like they'd been super close back in the day. And Barrett barely spoke to anyone.

He continued, "I'm not here for all that. And maybe I'm not as big of an asshole as I used to be."

I raised an eyebrow at him.

He shrugged. "Or maybe I am. Point is, I want to go after Tanya and Zeke. Way I figure it, they're going to come find you eventually. When they do, I want to be there. I can help you take them down, more so than anyone else. In the meantime, you'll get a good little soldier. I'll follow orders. Just don't expect me to call you 'sir.' "

"I don't expect anyone to call me 'sir.' I prefer 'my lord.' "

He snorted. "Good luck with that."

"Like I said, I'll consider it. Now, if you'll excuse me, I have a funeral to get ready for."

With that, I turned and went back inside.

87

We went to the funeral together.

Axel, Parker, Anthony, Barrett, Alyita, and me. Squirrel Nuts Squad.

Alyita wasn't an official member of the team, sure, but we all agreed she'd earned her temporary status. At least until this was done. She'd been through hell with us. Had been there when Fred fell. She *was* part of the team.

We all wore dark suits, except for Alyita. She'd donned a black dress. Axel had helped her with her makeup again. And, much to my surprise, he'd even donned a proper suit rather than a tangerine one. But he was wearing a fake mustache.

A fake handlebar mustache.

I had scolded him, but he'd assured me, in his weird Axel way, that he meant it to pay respect to Fred. I had sighed and decided to roll with it.

The suits had come from Archie. At least, that was my guess. I certainly I didn't own one. Though I had kept my tux from the ball. Hardly appropriate for a funeral. Anyway, the suits had been delivered that morning. And once again, they fit perfectly. It was creepy.

I wasn't sure what kind of turnout to expect for Fred. I doubted he'd had many friends. I mean, I knew when an asshole died we were all supposed to pretend they weren't an asshole in life, but... That was dumb. Fred had been an egotistical jerk when I'd met him. An absolute ghoul.

He'd grown on me in the end, though.

He'd earned my respect.

And I think I'd earned his, too.

But that didn't erase the past. It didn't mean he hadn't been an ass. So, I doubted he'd had many friends.

When we arrived, there were only a few people. About what I'd expected. Probably other Castle guards. The only two I recognized were the blonde and brunette receptionists I'd met the same time I'd met Fred. They'd been a delightful pair.

And then more people showed up.

Plenty more.

Plenty I did not expect.

It was like Constable Williams's funeral all over again.

One larger group started toward us, with two familiar faces at the front of the pack. The first was Elder Morgan. The second was Tsali. That *really* surprised me. Among the group were other Oklahoma Cherokee I knew, but there were also members of the Eastern Cherokee, ones who'd been with us in the battle.

They spotted me and started over.

I greeted Elder Morgan with a handshake. "I didn't, uh, expect to see you here."

He smiled. "Yes, well, as I am to understand it, he was a member of your team, and one who volunteered to help rescue my granddaughter. I would not miss it."

"Nor I," said Tsali. "We fought beside one another. So, we came to pay our respects."

"Thank you," I said, "I would have thought..."

"That we have our own to see off?" he asked.

I nodded.

"Indeed we do," he said. "And we shall. But first, I wished to come and pay my respects to your fallen. If not for you and your team..."

"Thank you, Tsali," I said. "That means a lot."

"We didn't come alone," he said, motioning toward the edge of the cemetery.

Another group had appeared.

This was led by Archie. Beside him was Supreme Enchanter Tate and Supreme Curator Whitaker. Along with the parade was our very own Grand Enchanter Gunner, Master Serrano, and several other members of our council. And Christian and Daisy were both with them, too.

That...surprised me.

No one had told me the Appalachian Argument was sending anyone. I certainly hadn't expected them to show up in force.

"Given recent events," Tsali said, bringing my attention back to him, "the tribe feels it's best if we encourage more interaction with our cousins here. So, I must confess my journey to the Ozarks was not just for the funeral."

I followed his gaze to Elder Morgan, who was now hugging the life out of his granddaughter. Alyita was hugging him back with equal ferocity.

"Good," I said, smiling at Tsali. "You'll both be stronger for it."

"Indeed," he said. "I believe your council and that of the Argument share a similar sentiment."

I nodded. "I should probably go say hello."

He nodded and I moved toward Archie and the others.

Christian saw me coming and stepped out to greet me. He held out his hand.

I took it. "Thank you. I didn't know you guys were coming."

He offered me a hint of a smile. "I think they wanted it to be a surprise."

That caused me to raise an eyebrow.

"I believe your Archmage felt it would boost the morale of your team."

"I see," I said, rubbing my chin. I refrained from smarting off about how it was Archie's games that had landed Fred in the dirt.

"I think..." Christian said, biting his lip. "I think I owe you an apology, Wyatt."

That also surprised me.

"Before we met, I'd heard stories about you, of course. And then, when I met you, I, uh, I think I underestimated you. It seems, though, that there is more merit to those stories than I might have appreciated. You're a good man. I hope I become half the Arcane Guardian you are. And, uh... Daisy feels the same way. Don't let her tell you otherwise."

With that, he turned and rejoined the others, leaving me standing there, speechless.

"Ah, Wyatt," Archie said, motioning me over.

I forced my feet forward, still stunned by Christian's words.

Tate stepped forward and took my hand, and a moment later Whitaker gave me a hug. It was a whirlwind of greetings.

And...it was sort of funny, too.

As the leadership from the Appalachian Argument fawned over me, my own leadership of the Ozark Mountain Cabal watched. Some of the assorted masters seemed surprised. Others seemed annoyed.

That was the funny part. I was more respected by another guild's leadership than my own. How wild was that?

What's more, I didn't feel the same bitter resentment I used to. No. I thought a lot of that was gone. Sure, I was still tired of their shit, and was even tempted to take their precious sword and move east, but I wasn't resentful. Not anymore. They were what they were. And no doubt some of my reputation was my own fault. Maybe it was fair. Maybe it wasn't. Didn't really matter anymore. They would come to respect me or they wouldn't. And for the first time, I realized I truly didn't give a damn.

Once that was settled, I started back toward my team, but Master Washington's big hand gripped my shoulder. Leaning in close, he whispered, "I heard about what you did. With the plants."

I gave him a nod. "Any idea what it means?"

"Not a clue," he said, meeting my gaze. "We should talk. Later."

He let go of my shoulder and I started toward my team again.

"Master Serrano," Archie's voice said.

I paused, glancing over my shoulder to realize the master librarian had been walking along just behind me. He turned back to Archie. "Yes, Archmage?"

"Won't you be joining us?" the Archmage asked, motioning toward our guests.

Master Serrano smiled and said, "I'll catch up after."

"You'll be viewing the ceremony with Wyatt's team, then?" the Archmage asked.

"Yes sir," Master Serrano said. "Fred was in my chain of command. Part of Squirrel Nuts Squad. I should be with them."

The Archmage was silent for a moment, just studying him. Finally, he nodded and turned away.

Master Serrano gave me a pat on the back, and together, we marched back to join the others.

The ceremony wasn't particularly long.

Nor particularly emotional.

But one thing did strike me. Punched me right in the gut, in fact.

From the Cherokee to the people from the Argument, they hadn't known Fred. So, they hadn't come for him on a personal level. They'd come out of respect for the team.

All those people... They'd come because they respected us.

I turned, studying their faces. Axel. Parker. Barrett. Anthony.

An unlikely team, but one that worked. And Fred had been a part of that, too.

And I couldn't stop thinking about his sacrifice. That look on his face as he'd stepped in front of me.

Nor the echo of Axel's words, meant to be a joke.

We almost never die.

Almost.

I sighed.

Fred had not forgotten my warning about Tanya's spell.

No, he had known what was coming. Had chosen it.

Fred had died...to save me.

I stared up at the sky, wondering how many more we might lose in the days to come.

I feared the answer.

Feared the road ahead. Things were getting worse.

I felt eyes on me and looked across the way to see the Archmage staring at me.

His gaze gave nothing away.

But I had a feeling I knew the sentiment. He was thinking the same.

It was getting worse.

The game was getting more dangerous.

The only question was... What fun awaited us next?

Whatever it was, I wouldn't face it alone. I had my team. And I had friends. Damned good friends. We'd be ready.

The End

ACKNOWLEDGMENTS

J.H. Fleming, as always, for editing my work and putting up with my never-ending stream of nonsense. Oh, who am I kidding? I'm an absolute delight all the time and she's lucky to have me. Don't tell her I said any of this!

Victoria, David, and Chris for being early readers and helping find my many mistakes. It's kind of like *Where's Waldo?* but with words. The wrong ones. Special shoutout to David for finding the typo where Barrett stood up from the crouch.

Also a big thank you to everyone who has contributed a rating or review to the series! Even the bad ones! I was blown away and humbled to see *The Blade Mage* reach 500 on Amazon.

And another big thank you to everyone who as signed up for the newsletter and/or followed me on BookBub, Facebook, Amazon, and everywhere else. And for the lovely messages and comments I've received. Means the world to me. It's been wild seeing *The Blade Mage* audience grow and I can't wait to see where we go next!

ABOUT THE AUTHOR

Phillip Drayer Duncan has written over ten novels and is the only author who has ever sponsored a racecar...probably. His work has been published by Blackstone Publishing, Yard Dog Press, Pro Se Productions, Seventh Star Press, and Happy Omega Publishing.

Along with reading and writing, he enjoys kayaking, fishing, video games, and telling bad jokes. Phillip's natural habitats include the rivers and lakes of the Ozarks, but he may also be spotted at a con or concert. During the cold season, he hibernates beneath a pile of books and video games. He is generally an approachable creature; however, it's best to give him snacks to ensure he won't bite. Cookies are best.

His earliest books were acted out with action figures and scribbled into notebooks. Today, he uses a computer like a real grownup, though he refuses to act his age the rest of the time. If it would pay his bills, he'd be playing with G.I. Joes right now.

His greatest dream in life is to become a Jedi, but since that hasn't happened yet, he focuses on writing and eagerly awaits the next season of *Firefly*. He demanded we mention that he is a best smelling author.

PhillipDrayerDuncan.com

GRIMM'S APPLE SPICE DIRTY DUMP CAKE

I can't believe I agreed to contribute to this nonsense. Whatever. Okay, here it is...Grandma Grimm's recipe.

Ingredients:
· 1 box of spice cake mix
· 1 can of apple pie filling
· 1 block of Kerry Gold Irish Butter
· 1 tub of whipped cream

Instructions:
· Pre-heat your oven to 350.
· Dump the apple pie filling into the bottom of your cake pan and spread it out evenly. Grandma Grimm always chopped the chunky apples into smaller pieces.
· Pour out the spice cake mix over the apple pie filling. Spread it out evenly.
· Cut the block of butter into smaller squares. Lots of smaller squares. You're going to spread them all over the top of the dry cake mix. Cover as much ground as possible.
· Bake at 350 for about 45 minutes. Maybe 55.
· Let it cool down.
· Serve with cool whip on top.
· That's it.

Yeah, that's right. I bake this dirty mess of a cake. I'm not a fucking choirboy!

(Note from Axel: *He totally wears a cute little apron over his suit when he bakes. It's adorable!*)

ALSO BY PHILLIP DRAYER DUNCAN

Catalysts – Featuring 2 Blade Mage & 1 Moonshine Wizard Story. FREE & only available by signing up for the Phillip Drayer Duncan Newsletter.

The Blade Mage:

The Blade Mage

Of Song and Shadow

The Memphis Knights

Rebel Medicine

The Southern Circle

Anything but Cozy

The Moonshine Wizard:

Moonshine Wizard

The Distilled Shorts Collection:

First Job

The Ogre & The Primates

A Sword Named Sharp

Hunting one Like Us

The Monster Beneath the Bed

The Hunt for the Dark Wizard

Assassins Incorporated:

Assassins Incorporated

Assassins Incorporated: Rehired

CATALYSTS

"Duncan's cinematic storytelling is perfect for this yarn."
— Kristofer Upjohn, Horror is Art

A BLADE MAGE & MOONSHINE WIZARD COLLECTION
PHILLIP DRAYER DUNCAN

Don't forget to pick up your **FREE** digital copy of...

Catalysts

featuring the ***Blade Mage*** prequel shorts...

The Generic Mage
&
The Last Great Blade Mage

Join Wyatt and Axel as they hunt down a wicked clown goblin and live the experience of Wyatt being chosen as Blade Mage.

Get Catalysts **FREE** by signing up for the Phillip Drayer Duncan Newsletter at...

PhillipDrayerDuncan.com
Happy Reading!

www.ingramcontent.com/pod-product-compliance
Lightning Source LLC
Chambersburg PA
CBHW030743030726
47497CB00001B/103